"Come here, Lenore"

a rich, lazy masculine voice commanded from the shadows. The girl tensed but did not move. "Here, I said." His long sinewy arm reached out and hauled her so close that her soft young breasts were crushed against his hard chest and the buttons of his coat bit into tenderness.

"Why d'ye not obey me?"

"I'll obey no man and certainly not you."

He laughed. Then his lips came down on hers in a compelling kiss. His mouth twisted over hers, forcing it open. Deftly, deliberately he thrust with his tongue so that she tingled when he abruptly let her go.

"A whole month we've been on the run, you and I," he murmured. "Yet still you fight me. Why?"

"I'm not yours," she replied unsteadily.

"Think you not?" He laughed, as if answering a challenge, and seized her again. She fought desperately as his strong hands pushed down her bodice, releasing her blossoming breasts. She struggled, she knew, as much against her own wild nature as against the arms that held her fast. Suddenly she lost her footing and they fell together, like falling leaves, to the soft forest grass. Her senses swayed and tumbled, she felt herself yielding to the power of his desire for her . . . and she was borne up in ecstasy beyond the treetops to some bright world where summer never ended and winter never came.

Also by
Valerie Sherwood

These Golden Pleasures
This Loving Torment

Published by
WARNER BOOKS

This Towering Passion

by Valerie Sherwood

WARNER BOOKS

A Warner Communications Company

WARNER BOOKS EDITION

Copyright © 1978 by Valerie Sherwood

ISBN 0-446-81486-5

Cover art by Jim Dietz

Warner Books, Inc.,
75 Rockefeller Plaza,
New York, N.Y. 10019

A Warner Communications Company

Printed in the United States of America

Not associated with Warner Press, Inc.,
of Anderson, Indiana

First Printing: November, 1978

10 9 8 7 6 5 4 3 2 1

Dedication

To all the cats I've loved—
and to wonderful Fuzzy,
who smiled in adversity,
most of all.

Contents

Prologue...................11

BOOK I: THE LOVERS...................15
Part One: The Handfast Bride...................17
Part Two: The Cavalier...................69

BOOK II: THE MISTRESS...................137
Part One: The Toast of Oxford...................139
Part Two: The Forsaken...................309

BOOK III: THE LONDON WENCH*...................379
Part One: The King's Doxie...................381
Part Two: The Orange Girl...................441

Author's Note

Although the historical background of this novel is as authentic as my research could make it, this is a work of fiction and should be so regarded. The encounters with Nell Gwyn, Charles II, Killigrew, and Lady Castlemaine are, of course, pure invention. It was another two years before Nell appeared on the London stage, another five years before she became the King's mistress. But even allowing for small deviations in the interest of clarity and plot, the spirit of these lusty times is carefully preserved.

Valerie Sherwood

England 1651

PROLOGUE

It was dark in the woods, but moonlight reached down through the branches and illuminated the rapt face of the girl, her violet eyes shadowed under dark lashes. Her shimmering red-gold hair cascaded around her bare shoulders, and the pale tops of her round breasts were silvered by the half-light.

"Come here, Lenore," a rich, lazy masculine voice commanded from the shadows. The girl tensed but did not move. "Here, I said." His long sinewy arm reached out and hauled her so close that her soft young breasts were crushed against his hard chest and the buttons of his coat bit into tenderness. "Why d'ye not obey me?" Lenore, for all that she was held close and thrilling to his touch, gave her head a willful toss. "I'll obey no man, and certainly not you."

He laughed, his eyes deepening as he tilted her chin up to smile down into her reckless face. "Faith, I think you mean that," he murmured. Then his lips came down on hers in a warm, compelling kiss. His dark hair fell forward to mingle with her own shimmering strawberry tresses, and his mouth twisted over hers, forcing it open. Deftly, deliberately he thrust his tongue with his tongue so that she tingled and was panting slightly when he abruptly let her go.

"A whole month we've been on the run, you and I," he murmured. "Yet still you fight me. Why?"

"I'm not yours," she replied unsteadily.

"Think you not?" As brusquely as he had left her he swooped down on her again, and this time there was a small tussle as Lenore's bodice was pushed down so that her blossomed breasts burst free and her skirts were pulled up along her white legs. Desperately she fought him now, her breath coming raggedly as she struggled as much against her own wild nature as against the sinewy arms that held her fast. Suddenly she lost her footing and they fell together, like falling leaves, to the soft forest grass in the shadows of the oak branches.

Twisting and turning in a last effort to escape him, Lenore felt a sweet restless frenzy rushing through her as she was crushed in the arms of her cavalier. Her senses swayed and tumbled as her defenses buckled. His questing hands roving over her body at will moved her to passion, and she felt herself yielding, yielding to the force of his will, the strength of his arm, the power of his desire for her.

The world slid away, forgotten, and the coolness of the night was unfelt as the fever of wanting him raced tumultuously through her blood. A pulse beat in her forehead, and a wave of guilt was quickly overwhelmed by an all-consuming desire that flashed through her.

She clung to him and murmured incoherently as her body quivered and her back arched and she flung herself against him. Then his passion enveloped her like a bright flame and she was borne up in ecstasy to some high bright world beyond the treetops where summer never ended and winter never came.

When at last she floated down and lay quietly beside him, brooding in the dappled moonlight, she remembered the day she'd met him, not so long ago....

BOOK

I

THE LOVERS

PART ONE

THE HANDFAST BRIDE

Worcester, England 1651

CHAPTER 1

All day the battle for England had raged beneath the hot September sun. The girl with the shimmering red-gold hair knew well her danger as she reined in her galloping white horse on the brow of a low hill overlooking the town. In her fine apple-green dress, she looked as carefree as if she were out for a canter in the country. Only her quickened breathing betrayed her excitement as her breasts rose and fell, thrusting against the thin material of her tight bodice. At a sudden boom of guns her horse reared up nervously, pawing the air with his forefeet, and the girl's yellow petticoat billowed, showing a flash of dainty white legs.

"Quiet, *Snowfire*," She patted his tossing mane with an affectionate hand and spoke softly to soothe him. The girl was as jumpy as he, for twice she'd been stopped by Cromwell's men and only her quick wits had got her through at all.

Now she frowned as she pondered the City of Worcester in the valley that stretched out below her. Brilliant sunlight glinted on the spires of ancient Worcester Cathedral rising majestically above the smoke of battle. To the west beside it the River Severn's placid surface glittered like so many golden coins tossed beside the town. Directly below she could see a confusion of armed men rushing about and hear shouts and screams mingling with the neighing of horses and the clash of arms. Death lay between her and the city gates, and even a brave man might hang back from what the girl intended to do. But Lenore Frankford was eighteen and impetuous and headstrong. Jamie—*her* Jamie—was in the town, and she had come to get him and bring him home.

Flame-haired Lenore had ridden in from the Cotswold Hills, and all the way there had been rumors—most persistently that Cromwell had won and young King Charles and the Scots were in flight, but sometimes the other way around. Now her slender shoulders straightened and her delicate jaw set grimly. No matter that she was English and Jamie was a Scot. How the battle went— that was the will of God. But she *must* be there to know the outcome, and if the Scots lost, to find Jamie quickly and spirit him away. Her neighbors in the Cotswolds had discovered that Jamie had gone to join the invading army, and if Cromwell won and Jamie came home, he might well be hanged as a traitor.

Handsome Jamie . . . the night before he left, she'd cried into her pillow and told herself she no longer loved him. But when she'd waked to find him gone, she'd remembered abruptly that he was *hers*. And being hers, neither death nor the Roundhead army could have him. She had not yet relinquished her hold on him. It didn't matter that they'd quarreled over that honey-haired wench with the swinging hips who had so brazenly flaunted herself before him at the smithy. Jamie had flared up at Lenore's taunts and they hadn't spoken since—nor had he crept as usual up the creaking stair to her tiny attic room to while the night away with warm embraces.

His sister Flora had noted cynically that Jamie was sleeping on a pallet downstairs, but when confronted by Lenore's mutinous expression she'd held her tongue—

only looked pointedly at the pallet, Lenore had and turned away. Now her fingers gripped the reins tautly. Lovers they might no longer be, but she was determined to bring Jamie home safe and make him humbly apol- ogize--before she gave a haughty shrug and stalked out of his life. *Forever.*

It was not love but something more complex that had brought fiery Lenore to the brow of this low hill.

She gave that glittering cathedral spire below her a worried look. She *must* reach Worcester. If she could but cross that intervening vale of death and carnage and get into the town, somehow she'd manage to find Jamie and talk some sense into him. All day as she rode, she'd been marshalling her arguments. Scolding wouldn't move him, she knew. She'd point out the bitter truth that Crom- well was Lord Protector of England and King Charles— if he lost—still a fugitive, except perhaps in Scotland. What a fool Jamie would be to throw away his life for a lost cause!

If that argument failed, she'd throw in his sister, tell him vibrantly how lost Flora would be without him (though probably the shoe was on the other foot). As a last resort, she'd even claim she was pregnant and heap recriminations on him that he'd go off to fight for a chancy cause leaving her and his bairn to starve!

Lenore frowned as she studied the field below, hoping for a lull in the battle, and thought of all that Jamie Mac- Iver had told her: Two years ago in Scotland he'd fallen afoul of the kirk when he had rebelled at attending church services every day, indeed four long services on the Sab- bath, and had challenged the dour Covenanter's denial of his right to laugh and dance. Hotfoot, he'd departed for England with his widowed older sister Flora. It was Flora's widow's mite that had purchased the smithy at Twainmere, a tiny crossroads village in the Cotswolds dotted with quaint thatch-roofed houses of honey-colored stone, built in Tudor times.

In Twainmere, at sixteen, wild Lenore was the town flirt. Every man hungered for her. It was murmured al- ready that she wasn't averse to a kiss beneath some grape arbor or spreading meadow tree—although, it was re-gretfully added, that was as far as she went. For now. Ah, the man who got her'd have a hot wench on his hands; he'd need to be sturdy, they chuckled, else those clinging white arms would send him to an early grave! A tease, but waiting for marriage—and already she'd had plenty of offers. Why she'd taken none of them, no one could guess. Perhaps she hesitated to leave her delicate sister Meg, who was married to Tom Pratle, the town drunk, and regularly miscarried (because Tom beat her, it was whispered). Anyway, the orphaned sisters were close, and both could read and write after a fashion, having been brought up next door to the vicarage and the old vicar having been fond of them. Well, Tom Pratle had brought them low, all right!

The little portion their hard-working carpenter father had left them had swiftly gone into the rum pots, and Meg had turned almost overnight from a smiling, light-footed lass into a dejected woman who walked bent over with her eyes fixed vacantly on the dusty road. There'd be no dowry for her little sister Lenore, either—not that she'd need it, for by the time she was twelve Lenore had a challenging look that made men straighten up and look after her thoughtfully. At sixteen she'd acquired a siren's figure and a provocative sidewise glance that set the lads' hearts athump. But poor Meg's health, never good, was failing, and Lenore stayed faithfully with her, taking Meg's part when Tom Pratle staggered home surly and drunk and knocked his bride across the room into a sobbing heap.

Understandably, Lenore was shy of marriage, having before her the terrible example of her battered sister Meg. Unconsciously she had formed a grudge against all men, from watching Tom Pratle's drunken fits of anger and brutality vented toward his wife. Love had been lacking in Lenore's life, for her mother had died early and her father had turned grim and forbidding after that. The only real affection she had known had been Meg's—and she was intensely loyal to Meg.

The loveless girl was making men pay for it.

She had become a shameless flirt and a tease, enjoying her power over men's unruly senses, deliberately inciting them to passion and always skipping away—just in time.

When two years ago the young Scot had arrived and set up his smithy, Lenore's predatory ears had pricked up as rumors of his blond good looks reached her. Promptly she had ridden over to have her horse shod. Her white stallion was named Snowfire. She had inherited him as a colt from her father, who had taken the colt in barter payment for some work just before a falling beam had ended his life. Besides her clothing, Snowfire was Lenore's only possession, and she was passionately fond of him, showering on the horse all the affection she withheld from the hot-eyed swains who pursued her so ardently. Snowfire returned her affection and nuzzled her daintily when she fed him sweets filched from the kitchen.

He was fast as the wind, and when they galloped down the dusty road, the horse's white mane flying, the girl's skirts billowing and her long brilliant hair streaming out behind her, they were indeed a sight to see.

When the pair of them flashed into the smithy that day and Lenore dropped lightly from her prancing mount's saddle to stroll toward the tall young smith, Jamie MacIver had stopped with his tongs in midair and stood staring.

"D'ye always ride like that?" he'd wondered.

"Always."

"Ye should race him at the fairs," he murmured, "Get ye a good lad to ride him and——"

"I'll ride him. He's my horse."

His shrug said a woman couldn't race at the fairs; that was man's work.

Lenore couldn't have cared less about racing Snowfire. She let Jamie go about his business of shoeing the horse, but stood nearby and watched him, letting her dark lashes droop low on her satin-smooth cheeks as she studied the young smith through wicked violet eyes.

That tall blond leather-clad Jamie was aware of her, she had no doubt. His blue eyes had paid Lenore silent

compliments and had traced every line of her slim, delicious figure as she moved restlessly about beneath the
great chestnut tree that shaded his smithy. Noting that,
she picked a time when his eyes were riveted on her and
idly reached up a white arm to touch a bird's nest poised
on a lower branch. That indolent gesture caused her pert
young breasts to soar forward against the thin material of
her bodice, and she was gratified to observe that the
young smith was so distracted he nearly burned himself
by reaching absently, in the wrong direction for his
bellows.

Lenore rode away from the smithy with her heart racing, intrigued by good-looking Jamie and absolutely certain that she had won him. Patiently she had waited at her
brother-in-law's cottage for Jamie to come calling, to
shoulder his way through the other eager youths who
thronged about her, vying for her favors.

It was a rude shock when, two weeks later, basket in
hand, she sauntered to market—and saw Jamie MacIver
strolling across the village green. Looking even more
handsome than usual in his sleeveless brown leather jerkin and square-toed shoes, his fair head was bent over a
plump blushing village maid who skipped along beside
him. He had looked up to see Lenore, who had come to
a halt, her mouth open, regarding him. Seeing her stiffen,
he had nodded affably. Then with a sweet smile he'd forgotten Lenore and had taken the hand of the simpering
girl beside him and lightly stroked her arm so that she
burst into a rapture of giggles.

Her face stained red with anger, Lenore had whirled
about. With her market basket still empty, she had curtly
brushed by two young bucks, ignoring their extravagant
bows, and stalked home to nurse her hurt pride. It was a
terrible setback to her vanity indeed, for already she had
counted Jamie MacIver her own—a new notch to be
scratched into the red heels of her best shoes—and here
he was hovering over somebody else! And after showing
such interest in her that day at the smithy!

She had flung the front door of the cottage open violently and almost collided with her brother-in-law, Tom

Prattle, sober for once, and just going out to rectify that, no doubt. He skipped nimbly out of her way, for all his girth, and yowled, "Ho there, Lenore! Have a look where ye're going!"

Lenore scarcely heard him. She'd rushed past her surprised sister, who was sorting through her mending on a bench by the window, and hurried up the crude stairs to stare into the little sheet of polished metal that served her as a mirror. Why, she had asked her beautiful reflection stormily, had Jamie not chosen her? Everybody else did! She did not ask herself why it should matter so much.

As the weeks passed, Jamie continued to flash his bright smile in Lenore's direction—but always with some other girl dangling happily from his arm. Lenore seethed. In a town where young girls often served their male callers honey-cakes, Jamie sampled all the sweets of the village . . . but not Lenore's. It was becoming painfully clear to her that carefree Jamie was as big a flirt as she was.

Cornering the Scot became Lenore's main ambition. She managed to be near him at church—but that did no good. There, as at the marketplace, Jamie always seemed to be surrounded by sweet young things who smiled coquettishly.

Lenore persevered. She found so many pretexts to bring her horse to the smithy that Flora scowled at the sight of her. But then gaunt Flora scowled at all the pretty girls who chased her handsome younger brother. Sometimes Lenore wondered why.

Time passed, and still fickle Jamie played the field. By now he had tasted not only all the single honey-cakes the village had to offer, but some of the married ones as well, and there were rumblings against the young Scot in some quarters. But his tall sister Flora could stare down anyone with her fierce mien, and so far no one had charged him with adultery or brought a bairn to his door. Incensed that Jamie should prefer others to her, Lenore bided her time.

Meg, frailer than ever, had gotten pregnant again.

Lenore had implored her many times to leave Tom, insisting they could go away together and find work in some far village. Meg was adamant about staying and desperately tried to placate her bully of a husband. One night, while Lenore was sleeping, Tom had come home drunk and, with a bellow, had kicked Meg across the room. She'd hit her head on the doorjamb as she fell. Lenore had waked at the racket and rushed in to find Meg unconscious on the floor and Tom himself, passed out and snoring loudly, sprawled across a bench.

With murder in her heart, Lenore had picked up the poker from the hearth. She might even have brought it down on Tom's head, but at that moment Meg had stirred and moaned and Lenore had flung it aside to kneel beside Meg.

"Are you bad hurt, Meg?" she'd asked anxiously as her sister's eyes fluttered open.

Meg had given her a wan smile which faded as she saw the poker lying on the floor. "Did Tom hit me with that?" she'd wondered in horror, touching the side of her head with her fingertips and wincing.

"No, I was about to use it on him," said Lenore dryly, and Meg had seized her wrist in an anxious grip and whispered, "No, no, you mustn't," and let Lenore help her to bed. The next day, though Lenore urged her to stay in bed, Meg had insisted on getting up and going about her household chores as if nothing had happened. It was washday, and Lenore was inside sorting clothes when she heard Meg scream.

Meg had been drawing water from the well; she had reeled dizzily from her concussion and tumbled over the low stone side into the well. Lenore had managed to pull her out, clinging to the wooden bucket. But Meg had been injured internally against the rough stones in her fall. That afternoon she had miscarried and neither the midwife—nor the doctor, hastily called—had been able to stop the bleeding.

Lenore had watched her sister's life drain away in a red flood, but had been unable to save her.

Tom Pratle was found and sobered up and marched

home. But he was too late to tell his young wife goodbye. He sat there in a daze mumbling to himself and was still so shocked he could only stumble to the churchyard to see her laid to rest among the mossy stones.

Even through her grief, Lenore knew that she should leave. It was no good staying on in the cottage with her brutal, drunken brother-in-law. She should take her pick of the eager swains who haunted the cottage and marry.

She postponed her decision, striking a truce with her brother-in-law, cooking his meals and ignoring his frequent absences and drunken ways. As her mourning for her beloved sister subsided, Lenore once again found her thoughts turning to Jamie.

Then last Midsummer's Eve there'd been dancing around the big bonfire on the low green hill outside the town (dancing was forbidden by the harsh laws of the Lord Protector, but most villagers ignored that; for time out of mind the people of Twainmere had danced round "St. John's fires" at summer solstice). Fiery-haired Lenore, with her lissome waist and swaying walk, had been eagerly sought as a partner. Soon Dick Fall and Stephen Moffat were warring over which would claim her for the next dance. Fired by the memory of her casual kisses in the May-flowering fields both young bucks were the worse for ale and clamoring loudly. It would have been easy for Lenore to choose between them and stop their brawling.

But nearby Jamie was watching. A very handsome Jamie in a white linen collar Flora had laundered to snowy perfection and buff trousers that showed the leanness of his hard thighs. Eager that he should see how *other* men felt about her, Lenore shrugged and let the matter come to blows, saying crisply she'd dance with the winner.

Amid disapproving glances, Dick and Stephen tore off their woolen jerkins and somewhat unsteadily squared off to fight. From the corner of her eye Lenore watched Jamie. He appeared unmoved. Blows were exchanged, and soon the friends of each began to cheer on the contestants. For a time Lenore stood with the group and

27

watched bitterly as the two young men surged back and forth, smashing big country fists into each other's faces. She pouted angrily—both of them were already so bruised and bloody they'd be no fit dancing partners when they finished!

Abruptly she'd turned her head to find Jamie watching her with a narrow concentration. Her heart gave a lurch. She knew that look! It was interest—the interest of a man in a maid. And interest was but a prelude to desire . . . .

On impulse Lenore had eased her way from the cheering crowd and wandered off to the deserted other side of the big bonfire where the bright flames made dancing red and yellow patterns on the dark forest trees. From the corner of her eye she could see the handsome young Scot all the girls wanted follow her with his light catlike step.

When they were entirely out of sight of the others, alone beside the roaring fire, she had whirled to face him. Her white dress was turned to fiery orange-red like her hair by the rippling flames. Jamie, too, had stopped short and stood negligently, measuring her with his narrow glance.

With sparkling eyes they had faced each other there, the flirt and the philanderer. Without a word being spoken, a challenge was flung, a challenge accepted.

Then he had swooped a low bow and taken her hand. And there in the leaping light of the flames of summer solstice they had danced—a skipping country dance—after which he'd whirled her into the shadow of a big oak trunk and clasped her in his sturdy arms and drunk deep of her kisses.

Lenore was shocked by her tingling response to his touch. She was a tease, well accustomed to arousing men's passions without ever satisfying them, always cool, always the absolute mistress of her emotions.

But not tonight!

CHAPTER 2

Tonight Lenore found herself reluctantly being drawn into a leaping shadow world of desire enhanced by the dark forest and the roaring flames, a world whose boundaries she knew but sketchily. Aware that her fiery spirit was aflame with the crackle and excitement of the fire, the Scot had traced his own fiery trail with his hands along her neck and arms and bodice—even as his mouth held her own entrapped. Lenore had felt a wild bursting response to his kisses. Inwardly she scolded herself for that. Naturally Jamie was an accomplished lover—after all, he practiced every chance he got!

Still, her body knew a strange new lethargy and it was difficult for her to get up the strength to push him away. Bosom heaving, she had leaned back against the rough bole of the tree to get her breath and considered him with wide eyes and parted lips. For she was eighteen and her own wild blood was racing. Merciful heaven, she'd been near to losing control! A moment more clasped in those warm, demanding arms and she might have sunk with him to the shadowed summer grasses and let him take her as he'd taken half the village!

Perhaps I love him! she thought dizzily.

Leaning with one arm braced against the rough trunk that rose above her head, Jamie smiled down on her. He stroked her cheek with gentle fingers, let those fingers wander idly down her throat and over her white shoulder, bared from the sudden wrench with which she'd pulled away from him. Lenore trembled, but she held her ground. Always before, she'd been mistress of herself in these encounters—she must get control of herself!

"Lenore." His voice caressed her. "This was no chance meeting—I've sought you out."

Heart thudding, Lenore studied the Scot through shadowed lashes. What lie was this?

"Sought me out?" she murmured—a bit breathlessly, for now he was kissing her eyes, her forehead, the bridge of her nose.

"Aye." He drew back, suddenly serious. " 'Tis plain you're the girl for me, so I've waited till now. For 'tis Midsummer's Eve—and that's a time for handfasting in Scotland."

"Handfasting?" she asked, her voice only a whisper above the crackling of the flames.

"Aye." One of his arms encircled her waist, holding her close while the other lightly caressed her. " 'Tis an old Scottish custom. On Midsummer's Eve, a man and a maid may clasp hands and live together for a year. Should either wish to leave the other within that year, they may do so, with no shame to either. But if they stay together for a year and a day, then they are man and wife." He stepped back and held out his hand and his eyes burned down into hers. His voice was rich and earnest. "I ask that ye take my hand, Lenore, and come live with me till next Midsummer's Eve."

More than the heat of the flames burnished Lenore's silken cheeks. "Live with you?" she faltered.

"Aye. There'll be no shackles of gold to hold you, Lenore. Should you wish to be free of me, you could go at any time and I'd no put up a hand to stop you. Even though my heart would be breaking," he added hastily.

Like a bucket of cool water, rage swept over Lenore.

"Handfasting's not the custom here," she said sweetly, stepping away just out of reach.

"Remember, I'm a Scot," he sighed.

And a liar! she thought grimly. Seeking to bed but not to wed! Ah, but what a handsome seductive liar! Her heart still pounded from the strong hard feel of him against her slim body, and she was still vividly atingle from the gentle brushing of his lips against the tops of her white breasts.

"Besides," he added, "none need know. You could say you'd moved in to help my sister Flora—indeed, she has too much work to do. A kind thing you'd do of your charity, Lenore! And who's to know our sleeping arrangements?"

"Flora," stated Lenore coldly.

He shrugged. "Flora'd not go against me. Not only am I the only brother she has left, but I've always been her favorite. We've naught to fear from Flora."

Lenore took a deep breath. He'd been after her all along—just as he was after every girl! And with a sweet smile he had offered her this. Oh, the gall of him! It shamed her that she was still shaken by the sweetness of his kisses, for in his arms she'd known an awakening passion she had never felt in the arms of the bumbling village bumpkins who stole a kiss a-Maying. It shamed her that her arms should burn to hold this man and make him hers.

For it was a cheap thing he was offering her. Not honest wedlock.

She stood stiffly, like a woman in shock.

Jamie did not seem to notice. He moved closer; he was only a breath away. "Ah, Lenore, to me you're more than a woman," he murmured raptly against her silken hair. "Day after day I've watched you, wanted you. Winning you has been my goal."

His *goal!* Not his love—his goal! That she had felt the

same way about him in no way dampened her fury. To hear him say that—and about *her!*

Glowing with anger, Lenore's violet eyes had narrowed. By heaven, she yearned to take him up on it! To use him and fling him aside—as he doubtless intended with her. Ah, he was begging for a setdown! And she was just the one to give it to him.

"Jamie," she murmured, casting her eyes down so that he should not see their angry light, "you do me too much honor."

He had the grace to catch his breath for a moment. "No more than you deserve," he declared staunchly.

Quivering at that barb, she jumped as a drunken bellow reached them: "Lenore! Where are you? I've won, Lenore! It's my dance!"

Some devil prompted Lenore to stretch her hand gracefully toward Jamie. In as calm a voice as she could command, she said softly, "I take thee, Jamie MacIver, for my handfast bridegroom for a year—as is the old Scottish custom."

"Lenore." Jamie clenched her hand. His voice had deepened. Almost roughly he swept her up in his arms and she lingered there, half-dizzy with his kisses—then abruptly she remembered what she intended and fought free.

"No, Jamie," she declared breathlessly. "It cannot be tonight. Hear them? They are calling me. I will be missed and there'll be talk. No, I must come to you. Later."

"When?" scowled Jamie, reluctantly releasing his grip. Feet planted, he stared down at Lenore doubtfully.

"Soon," she lied in a tremulous voice, for this was one bargain she never intended to keep. Handfast bride, indeed! Let him imagine she was his, let time alone tell him she had tricked him—for it would soon be apparent to him when she went about her business and stayed away from the smithy. He certainly deserved it, philanderer that he was!

"Tomorrow," he insisted, catching her wrist.

"Perhaps," she whispered in a throaty voice. "Ah, Jamie, let me go. My brother-in-law must not hear that

I was gone from the dancing so long—he's got a fierce temper!"

Jamie scowled at her. "I've heard of his temper," he growled. "If he shows his teeth at me, I'll slap them for him. From what I've seen of Tom Prattle, a few bruises wouldna hurt him. Indeed they might improve him."

She gave him a bright, insincere smile, wishing she could bring that about, and pulled free. She could hear Jamie's low call of "Tomorrow" as she ran lightly back toward the fire and around it to the dancers where big Stephen, who had won the bout, held out a bruised hand. Lenore kept a bright, fixed smile on her face as he stumbled about the grass with her in what passed for a dance.

From a distance, beneath lowered brows, Jamie watched them, but he did not attempt to dance with her.

Lenore's color was high. With all her heart she yearned to make the young Scot jealous. To big Stephen's delight, she spent the whole evening with him, smiling enticingly up into his bruised face, where one eye was almost swollen shut. Dick Fall, the loser, sat disconsolately on the grass and watched them.

"I'll walk ye the long way home," Stephen ventured, when Lenore said she must be going.

"Can I trust you?" she murmured archly. "The last time we were alone together—among the berry bushes—you tore my bodice!"

" 'Twas not me that tore it," he insisted. " 'Twas a berry branch."

" 'Twas your big bumbling hand," she said sweetly. "But if you promise to be good . . ." She gave him a provocative look.

"I'll not lay a finger on ye!" he declared intensely. "I swear it, Lenore!"

Off they went together, strolling back toward the village. Lenore could feel the young Scot's smouldering gaze boring into her back as the bonfire and the few who were left dancing around it faded from sight.

Lenore thought it likely Jamie would stake himself out at some likely spot and watch the cottage, checking up on her return. With glinting eyes, she told Stephen she'd like

33

to stop by the churchyard and sit on a gravestone and talk. Stephen was in a mellow mood tonight. His head was aching and his eye hurt and he was sore in every bone, but he'd cornered the prettiest girl in the village and she wanted to sit and talk the night away!

Eagerly he perched on a moss-covered gravestone opposite her, but he was mindful of his promise to be good —only twice did she have to slap his hands away.

He proposed twice.

The last time she rejected him absently, for it was almost dawn and by now Jamie—if he was watching the cottage, and she was wickedly sure he was—would surely suspect the worst. Promising to walk out with him later in the week, Lenore slipped away from Stephen and made her way quickly along the back hedges and kitchen gardens to the back of the cottage.

Tom Prattle had been drinking heavily when she'd left for the bonfire. She presumed he'd now be sleeping it off—with the front door latched. But she'd make it back the same way she'd got out—through the kitchen window. She eased one shapely leg over the low sill and with a plop landed on her feet on the kitchen floor.

It was a bad landing. In the dusky interior she knocked over a pot, and Tom Prattle, who was dozing on a bench against the wall, sat up with a start.

"Back at last!" he bellowed. "I've been waiting for ye! And where's the lad ye've been lying with, tell me that!"

"There's no one!" cried Lenore. "I've been—I've been out looking for herbs in the woods!"

"At sunup? Ye're a liar!" he bawled. "Ye aim to get yourself pregnant by some likely lad that won't marry you and make me take care of the brat!"

Lenore's face whitened. "I'd die first!" she grated. "The reason you've none of your own is because you near beat my sister to death!"

" 'Tis a rotten lie!" he shouted, his face turning purple with wrath. It was so near the truth that he paused and glared evilly at his young sister-in-law. He missed Meg, missed her warm young body, missed her care for his comforts—when, he asked himself, had Lenore ever

34

bothered to prepare his favorite pudding or put a warm stone in his bed? She seemed to think it was enough pay for her keep that she did his laundry and scoured and cleaned the house and gathered herbs and firewood and prepared plain meals! Why, he could hire some likely wench at starveling wages who'd do all that and warm his bed, too—and not with warm stones, either! And now Lenore dared blame him for Meg's death! Why, it was her had put all those ideas in Meg's head about cuttin' down on his drinkin'! If Meg hadn't plagued him about it so, he'd never have struck her so hard that day! She was all right the next day, wasn't she? 'Twas the fall in the well that killed her!

His bloodshot eyes took in the trim figure before him, the rumpled hair, the rebellious stance. Lenore didn't knuckle down to him the way Meg had. She stood with both feet planted as if daring him to do his worst.

Suddenly it seemed to him that this flame-haired vixen was the cause of all his troubles. Without her, he'd still have Meg! By heaven, he'd give her what for! He'd pound her black and blue, and if she gave him any lip, he might even smash a few teeth out of that pretty face!

With a roar he seized a stick and began to belabor her. Lenore tried to strike the stick away and got a weal across her right arm instead. Her arm half numbed by the blow, she darted across the room, but he pursued her into the next room.

With a screech she fell against the front door, clawing frantically at the latch, for well she remembered the beatings Meg had suffered at those big calloused hands. Gasping, she got the door open as Tom lunged toward her. Almost together, the two of them burst through the front door of the cottage and early risers of the village were treated to the sight of Lenore running down the narrow lane sobbing angrily. Behind her puffed her heavy brother-in-law, his face red and contorted. He was flailing at her—though seldom striking her, for agile Lenore soon outdistanced him. But his loud recriminations pursued her, causing cottage shutters to fly open and heads to lean out, agape.

35

All the dusty way to the village smithy he pursued her —howling at the top of his voice. By now they had collected a running crowd of interested villagers following them—mostly lads who'd smarted under Lenore's teasing ways and now laughed and hooted heartlessly to see her "humbled" by her outraged brother-in-law, who was howling she'd been out all night, she was no better than a whore!

At the smithy, Jamie, just starting up his fire, flung down his bellows and leaped up as Lenore ran to him, sobbing. He looked magnificent with his sleeveless leather jerkin opened to reveal a heavy-muscled chest, lightly furred with gold, and mighty arms agleam with sweat in the early morning heat.

"What's this?" roared Jamie, grasping Lenore with a big competent hand and pushing her behind him as Tom Prattle and his upraised stick came to an astonished sliding halt in the smithy yard.

"The girl's my charge and no concern of yours, MacIver," Tom told the young smith sullenly. He kept a wary distance from Jamie's long reach nonetheless. "She's been out all night and up to no good. Stand aside while I give her the beating that's due her."

" 'Tis a lie!" shrieked Lenore from behind Jamie. "I was out early gathering herbs!"

Jamie planted his feet and assumed a belligerent stance. "She's your charge no longer!" he declared.

Lenore's surly brother-in-law blinked. "Next ye'll be telling me ye're taking her to the kirk, MacIver," he said with heavy sarcasm.

"She may not have told you, but I'm taking her into *my* household," a cold new voice said, and Lenore turned to see that Flora had come out from the cottage behind the smithy and was brandishing a broom menacingly. "Away with ye all!" she cried. " 'Tis not right that an unmarried girl of eighteen should live in a house with a drunken widower. For shame that ye'd beat a lass, Tom Prattle!"

Tom, outmatched, glared at them all equally, while

36

behind him the onlookers held their collective breath. Then with an angry gesture he flung his stick on the ground. "I wish ye joy of her," he growled at Flora. "She can go to work for you or to perdition—but she's left my house for good. I'll not have it said any girl in my charge is a common strumpet!"

"None will say it in my hearing," Flora said grimly, advancing on Tom and gesturing Jamie back as he stepped forward flexing his big muscles threateningly. She lifted the broom. "Any man who's not off my property in one minute will get a taste of this—and that goes for you, too, Tom Prattle!"

All present hastily retreated before the dour Scotswoman with her flashing blue eyes and upraised broom. Lenore gave her a grateful look and turned to Jamie. "I had to leave Snowfire back there," she cried tearfully. "He's mine, and I'm afraid that beast of a Tom Prattle might hurt him—will ye get him for me, Jamie?"

Jamie gave the slouching figure of the retreating Prattle an angry look. "That I will!" he cried, leaping on the back of a horse that stood patiently waiting to be shod and pulling Lenore up with him. "And your clothes, too, you shall have, and all your possessions. Any man who tries to stop you will feel the weight of my fist!"

They clip-clopped past Prattle, who stood looking as if he might have apoplexy, and when they rode back again down that dusty lane, it was with Lenore astride Snowfire and Jamie carrying a large tablecloth knotted at the corners which contained her worldly goods.

It had all happened so fast, Lenore could scarcely credit it. Without a word, Jamie handed her over to Flora and returned to his bellows.

"It's very kind of you to take me in," stammered Lenore as she accompanied the older woman into the plain-scoured cottage. "I don't know where I'd have gone once Tom turned me out!"

But Flora brushed aside her thanks. "What I've done, I've done for Jamie," she declared coldly. "He's told me he's asked ye to be his handfast bride and ye've accepted.

I don't hold with handfasting, but if it's what Jamie wants, I'll no stop him. There's enough work for two women here, what with the hens and the hogs and my bit of garden. We'll see if ye can work as well as flirt your skirt!"

Handfasted! Lenore had forgotten her promise—that promise she'd never meant to keep. She felt cornered.

But brisk Flora was sweeping her along.

"You'll sleep up here." Flora led her up a rickety stair to a tiny room Lenore guessed they had used as a storeroom, located above the kitchen. The roof sloped down under the eaves, and there was but one window, but it contained a straw pallet and a small chest. " 'Tis small, but 'twill give you privacy," Flora pointed out. "I sleep in the main room, and Jamie in the kitchen. I'd take you in with me but . . ."

But you'll be handfasting, was obviously what she meant. Lenore's face suffused with color. She wanted to turn and run, but it was too late now. Too late to take her choice of the swains who'd swarmed about, now that her miserable, vicious brother-in-law had branded her a harlot before half the village. Who'd have her now? Big Stephen, perhaps—but she'd no wish to wed an uncouth clod. And Jamie, she admitted reluctantly, *had* leaped to her defense—the only one who had! He'd faced down Tom Prattle and rescued Snowfire and her clothes from the cottage. Flora, too, had stood up for her and had offered her shelter.

Left alone in her small room to "unpack" her few possessions, she picked up her best pair of shoes and studied the notched red heels ruefully. Those notches represented her conquests—every notch was an offer, whether proposal or proposition, from one of the village males. She remembered last night, and how she'd felt when Jamie had taken her in his arms—and abruptly she put the shoes down. Last night, in the wild light of the bonfire, Jamie had made her an offer, but she felt no inclination to dig a notch into those gay red heels to commemorate the event.

Her violet eyes shadowed. Tonight no doubt he'd try to creep into her room. If not tonight, then soon. Living here in the cottage with an ardent rogue like Jamie, there'd be difficulty holding him back.

What worried her and made her cheeks burn as she thought about it was—did she really *want* to hold him back?

Running from her own hot thoughts, she hurried downstairs and spent the whole day in Flora's company, following her about, learning where everything was and how Flora did things.

But night . . . that night she dreaded . . . came all too soon. A glorious gold and orange sunset—and then it was on them.

That first night Lenore stayed in the cottage behind the smithy she had been restless and tense in her strange surroundings. She had to own that the room under the eaves was no smaller than her own back home in her brother-in-law's house, in fact it might even be a mite larger. And it was very neat, as became Flora, who scrubbed and scoured and labored mightily from dawn to dusk on every day but the Sabbath—and even then Lenore was later to find her sometimes surreptitiously dusting or cleaning out cupboards, in defiance of the Puritan strictures.

After a hot day the night was warm but leavened by a cool breeze that had come up in the evening and now fluttered through the open shutters, making them creak protestingly. Lenore, lying on her pallet, lay fanning herself and listening to the night noises. A branch of the great wych elm behind the cottage scraped against the house, and outside there was the cry of an owl, stalking the moonlit fields and forest on fluffy wings. Through the floorboards, which had wide cracks in them, Lenore could hear Jamie move about the kitchen below, and tensed warily every time his footsteps seemed to be approaching the rickety stair which led up to her room. Though she had been bold enough last night at the bonfire—yes, and now she realized her recklessness—she was jumpy and ill at ease tonight, feeling herself no longer mistress of the situation.

Supper had been nerve-wracking. She'd jumped when spoken to, been scarcely able to swallow a bite of Flora's good mutton pie, and awkwardly dropped a trencher when she'd helped Flora clear the table. She'd been painfully conscious of Jamie's amused glance when she'd announced—with a virtuous look at Flora—that she'd best go to bed early for she'd need her sleep if she was to put in a good day's work tomorrow. At this remark Flora's eyebrows might have shot up just a trifle, but she'd looked quickly down at her mending. Thankfully, she'd refrained from comment.

With great ostentation Lenore had climbed the wooden stair, called down a firm good night and made a great to-do of loudly latching the door. Once inside, she'd dragged the heavy chest against it and stood and surveyed it with some trepidation. She was not sure that Jamie's heavy blacksmith's muscles could not move that chest if he'd a mind to, and Flora had mentioned casually at dinner that she slept like a log.

But downstairs the sounds were reassuringly normal, with no hurrying footsteps ascending the stair. Soon she heard Flora bid Jamie good night and retire to the main room. Now was the moment when he'd gallop up those stairs and break down the door to her room! Tensely Lenore lay still, straining to hear.

Jamie apparently finished what he was doing in the kitchen below—Lenore suspected him of enjoying a late snack of ham and brown bread, for he'd a healthy appetite —for the sounds ceased. Then she heard the outer door open and close. That was too much! Was Jamie off to visit some buxom village wench who waited with latch ajar? Outraged, Lenore scrambled up from her pallet to peer out through the open shutters. Through the leaves of the branching wych elm, she could see Jamie standing in the moonlight below, clad only in his breeches. His hemp-colored hair was turned to ghostly white in the pale light and his muscular body was silvered, so that he seemed to her for a breathless moment a man of silver, out to take the air. She ducked back lest he look up and see her watching him and found her heart beating rapidly as she lay back upon her straw pallet.

Ah, what a man he was . . . no wonder the girls in the village all simpered and giggled and flirted their skirts when Jamie passed by! Half the doors in town must have been left unlatched in hopes he'd come calling!

But Lenore had had more time to consider her situation now, and it had come to her that she did not want to be Jamie's handfast bride—or anyone's bride, for that matter. She preferred her freedom. Of course there was too much talk of her in the village right now for anyone to take her in and give her employment—except employment of a nature she'd not care for! Although her heart was filled with the silver sight of him there below in the moonlight, she intended to keep her door firmly latched and her heart as well, and to make sure that Flora was always nearby in the daytime. Let Jamie cast all the slanted looks at her he wanted—*that* should discourage him!

Meanwhile, she'd ask adroit questions at the market and learn if there might not be a position for a likely girl at the next village—for her heart sank at seeking employment here, where she'd lost her reputation. All those who'd wooed her for wife—now they'd be seeking her out and making lewd proposals! It was incredible to her that a man could beat his wife to within an inch of her life and then turn around and accuse her sister of being a harlot. And the townspeople believed *him!* Anyway, the only job available locally that she knew of was as milkmaid to old Dunster—and that would amount to moving in as his mistress, for everyone knew that when Dunster was in his cups he'd break down any maid's door that was convenient.

No, she'd best while away the time here, enjoying Jamie's discomfiture that she did not drop like a ripe peach into his arms, and helping out Flora to pay them back for their kindness in taking her, in when her brother-in-law had driven her out.

41

With this thought firmly in mind, she began to drowse, lulled by the night noises, the cry of a night bird, the scraping of the branches against the house, which had grown sharply louder as the wind came up.

As the wind came up! Lenore sat up sharply. *There was no wind!* Even the little breeze there had been before had died down, leaving her skin damp from the summer heat.

She whirled to look at the open window. A dark shape there blotted out the moon, and Lenore stifled a scream—it was Jamie. Now she knew the reason for the loud scraping. He'd been climbing the big wych elm outside her window. And now as she opened her mouth to protest, he flung a muscular leg over the sill and vaulted into the room.

"Go away!" she hissed angrily.

"And why should I do that?" asked Jamie in an amused voice. "Modesty is one thing, and I could understand your latching the door for Flora's benefit. But you're my handfast bride—promised to me by your own words no later than last night!"

"It wasn't modesty. I lied to you," said Lenore flatly. "It was a promise I did not mean to keep. I am grateful to you for taking me in, and for standing off Tom Prattle, but your handfast bride I've no intention of being."

She could not see his face, for he was still a dark silhouette against the light. He had been advancing toward her, but at her words he checked. "Lied?" he demanded unpleasantly.

"I—I but meant to humble you," muttered Lenore. "For thinking you could have me so easily, when half the village has asked me to the kirk!"

"So 'tis the kirk you want," he said more kindly. "Well, if we stay together for a year and a day, 'tis the kirk you shall have! My word on it!" He moved toward her.

Lenore crept backward on her pallet until she was crouched against the wall. She did not like the firmness with which he was moving toward her. "I take back my promise!" she cried, hastily clutching a sheet over her. "Get you back downstairs, Jamie MacIver!"

"Ah, Lenore," he said easily, "ye'll find promises made

to me are not so easily broken." To her horror, she saw that he was removing his breeches.

"Put them back on at once," she cried, averting her eyes. "And get you gone!"

" 'Tis not my intent to spend this bridal night in my breeks!" he retorted, tossing them from him and standing there before her, a dark silhouette, naked as the day he was born. Lenore, blushing furiously, looked away, and she heard him chuckle. Then the sheet was torn from her clutching grasp and sent flying, and even as she dived to the side trying desperately to elude him, he pounced on her.

Lenore gasped as his sudden heavy weight crushed her down against her pallet.

"I'll scream!" she warned, twisting in his arms.

Jamie laughed. "Screams won't wake Flora. She sleeps like the dead. But ye might alert some traveler on the road to burst in—and then we can explain to him how you promised to live with me for a year!"

"You wouldn't!" gasped Lenore, twisting her head from side to side and with great effort managing to keep his lips from her mouth. And then a startled "Oh!" as she felt her chemise leave her shoulders with a jerk that burst the ribbon drawstring that held it up. "Now see what you've done!" she cried, seizing on this grievance in hopes of diverting him. "You've torn my ribbon and—" Her voice rose in a near shriek as one of his big hands grasped the now loose-hanging material that lay across her bosom. She fought to secure it from him, but with a sudden downward tug the material slithered to her waist, leaving her creamy breasts exposed to his ardent gaze. Clutching at the material with one hand, she struck with the other at his face, seeing the gleam of his smiling eyes in the moonlight.

Lazily he pinioned both her arms in one big hand and slid the other hand beneath her smooth back. Coolly ignoring her comments—for Lenore was reviling him with every angry word she could think of—his lips traveled a burning path over her trembling breasts.

"Lenore, you protest too much to be believed," he

murmured, and his warm lips shut off her angry protests.

Lenore couldn't have told whether she was more alarmed or excited. Having said no, she felt obliged to fight for her virtue. Against Jamie's blacksmith's strength, that was of little avail. Her breath was nearly cut off, and her heart was racing. Held firmly, feeling the heat of his body, the strong ropy muscles of his arms and his hard chest and thighs pressed against her, she found her own defenses faltering. She was young and her body cried out for love, to be held in a man's arms. Jamie, who was used to easy conquests, was fired by Lenore's temptress ways and taunting refusal of him at the last—he felt no qualms at taking her. For was she not his handfast bride, by her own word, and his by right?

Lying there powerless beneath him with the breath sobbing in her throat, Lenore's soft body quivered to passion against her will, for she had meant to fight him bitterly. Jamie's skillful hands caressed her everywhere, until even where it was touched by the cool moonlight, her body was aflame. Once again Jamie had wakened strange wild passions in her, and this time—this time they were sweeping her on to a frenzy of desire that caused her suddenly to stop struggling, to relax her limbs and to wrap her arms about his neck in a fierce embrace.

Jamie scooped her to him as fiercely; she thought he muttered something and her response was breathless, incoherent.

Then it came—a sudden agonizing thrust between her thighs that made her cry out and sink back, weak and almost swooning. But even through the pain as her senses swam, she felt a call from deep inside her as if something chained and savage within her was struggling to be free. Against her will she could feel her body respond to him as passions deep within her fought to surface. It was shattering, this fire that consumed her body, that consumed her mind. And when it was over and she lay damp with perspiration and quivering from her struggle, she said weakly, "I—I did not think it would be like this."

"The next time will be much better," he promised, dragging his fingers lightly over the soft tips of her

44

breasts as she lay on her back. As if he had touched a raw spot, her quivering nerves leaped, and he gave a low laugh at this involuntary response. She tried pettishly to brush away his hand, but he persisted, exciting the pink nipples to hardness between a thumb and forefinger.

Over her weak protests, he took her again, and this time to her surprise she felt almost immediately a deep tingling glow within her. It was not just her outer skin that welcomed him, but all her innermost being. Those chains she had forged over the horror of her brother-in-law's brutal treatment of Meg, chains that had held her emotions bound and gagged all these years, were burst at last, and her savage inner self released. Flames seemed to burst through her loins and with a moan, Lenore flung herself upward against him. For wild primeval moments they clung together, straining violently, trying to meld their very bodies into one. When he had finished and rolled over to consider her, she gave a long gasping breath and looked at him with wonder.

Jamie laughed. "Did I not tell you?" he teased. "Ye've a wild nature, Lenore, and 'tis surprised I am to find ye a virgin!"

She gave him an affronted look and flipped over on her side, presenting the curving line of her back to him.

"Ah, but I'm pleased about it," he murmured, tracing her spine from neck to buttocks with questing fingers that made her squirm. But she wasn't speaking to him after that remark. Surprised she was a virgin, indeed!

Jamie sighed and tucked a great arm under her. Her anger didn't keep her from nestling against his shoulder and soon she heard his rhythmic breathing. She stole a look at him. Her lover had fallen asleep.

Lenore was wakeful. The anguish and splendor of her initiation into being a woman haunted her. Lying there beside Jamie, she looked up at the white moon through the branches outside the window very thoughtfully. She knew she could leave on the morrow. She could take her things and simply depart, trudging to the next village there to try her luck at employment. Failing that, she could try elsewhere—another village and another. Here in Twainmere the villagers might whisper behind their hands and nod wisely, guessing rightly that she'd become the young Scot's mistress, but in some other town none would know how Jamie had used her.

But . . . there was that in his strong body that thrilled her, and she knew in her heart that all the next day she'd be impatient, looking forward to the night when Jamie would clamber again through her window . . . or perhaps the door would be left unlatched. For it was no secret from Flora that Lenore was Jamie's handfast bride.

His handfast bride . . . Lenore's expression softened and she stole another look at the sleeping Jamie, his handsome features illumined by the moonlight and his hemp-pale hair turned a shimmering, snowy halo. The chest that rose and fell beside her with his even breathing was a manly chest, deep and wide . . . the whole naked length of him was manly.

Now that the storm of her passions had abated and she could think more sanely, Lenore asked herself: This wild sweet feeling that possessed her—could this be love? Perhaps she loved Jamie, perhaps that was why she had so flamed up in his arms.

To be a handfast bride—perhaps that was none so bad after all. 'Twas the next best thing to being truly wed at the kirk. She pondered on that and gradually her spirits rose. There was a certain status in being a handfast bride; for Jamie had given her a promise, too, that he'd be hers forever if he stayed by her side for a year and a day.

Tonight, fresh from her lover's arms, Lenore was filled with the reckless confidence of youth. She smiled dreamily as she snuggled against the shoulder of her sleeping Scottish lover. Her James would never leave her, she promised herself. When St. John's fires burned in the Cotswold Hills next June, he'd be hers for life. Then she'd take him to the kirk for all the neighbors to see!

CHAPTER 3

Life with Jamie and Flora had an entirely different flavor from the tug-of-war existence she'd known with Meg and Tom. Their table—no lavish board, but set with the gruel and meat puddings and dark bread Lenore was used to, for Flora was determined to adapt to English ways—rang with political arguments. Both of them disliked the Lord Protector, and Jamie sometimes grumbled that life among the Puritans of England was no better than life among the Covenanters of Scotland. But they both knew and were grateful that Twainmere was an out-of-the-way backwash and had escaped the full fervor of drab Puritan ways and harsh Puritan laws.

"In Scotland you'd be put in the pillory for railing as you do!" scolded Flora.

"Here, too, did the right people but hear me," retorted Jamie gloomily.

Lenore listened and wondered. Everyone knew that young Charles Stuart had crossed from Holland and the Scots had risen to greet him. At Gowrie House on the Tay he'd been crowned King of Scotland even though—ominously—Cromwell's army had occupied Edinburgh on Christmas Eve. In March Charles had entered Edinburgh, and Jamie'd heard a rumor that he was training twenty thousand men to invade England.

" 'Tis nothing to do with us," said Flora firmly. "We're English now, Jamie."

Jamie gave her a steady look, but said nothing, and Flora's expression softened. Lenore had learned to respect Flora. A woman of simple virtues—a barren widow, she called herself, though she was still handsome, tall and blond and blue-eyed like her brother—Flora had at first been standoffish; she had not welcomed the English girl with open arms. "You'll be the death of him," she'd predicted gloomily. "For Jamie's too free with his ways here, just as he was in Scotland—and mark you, 'twill land him in trouble here the same as it did there." She shook her head. "Handfasting—bah! Ye should be proper wed."

Lenore thought so, too, but it hurt her pride to say so. She didn't want to beg for a husband! She wanted Jamie to take her hand and lead her joyously to the kirk.

As the days passed, living so close in the tiny thatched cottage, tending the little kitchen garden together, eating all their meals at the same table, Flora grew fond of Lenore, who was always eager to do her share of the work.

"Are ye with bairn, Lenore?" she asked bluntly one day as they washed clothes.

Lenore blushed fiery red and shook her head in embarrassment. Flora had never before given any indication that she heard the nightly creak as Jamie climbed the wooden stair to Lenore's room.

"He'll never wed ye—ye know that, don't you?"

Lenore didn't know that. She gave Flora a startled look.

"But if ye got pregnant, then I'd make him take ye to the kirk if I had to kick him every step of the way," said Flora in a fierce voice.

"Well, I'm not pregnant," muttered Lenore, disliking the idea that Jamie would have to be booted to the kirk.

48

"I don't hold with handfasting," sighed Flora, casting a gloomy look at Lenore. " 'Tis seldom permanent."

Lenore bit her lip and bent over the clothes she was scrubbing, using perhaps more force than was necessary to get them clean. Jamie loved her, she was sure of it. He was so ardent, so possessive. Why, he didn't even want her to go out! "Let Flora go to market," he'd say, smiling down at her. "You stay home."

By the end of the second week she knew why he wanted her to stay home. On a brilliant sunny day Flora, on her way to the pigsty with a bucket of slops, fell and twisted her ankle, and Lenore went to the market in her stead. To her shocked surprise, she saw Jamie bending over a buxom farm girl who was giggling and looking boldly up into his blue eyes as if daring him to kiss her. When Lenore came up to them, the girl gave her a contemptuous look that made Lenore want to slap her rosy face. It said plainer than words: *You're nothing but his mistress, everybody knows that! But me—I'm looking for a husband, and Jamie's wed to no one—he's fair game!*

The girl flung away, and Jamie looked a little upset. "Where's Flora?" he demanded. "I thought she was going marketing today."

"She fell and hurt her ankle," Lenore said through tight lips. He'd have taken her arm, but she thrust her market basket at him, banging it against his ribs. "I'll need you to help me carry things, there's a lot to buy."

Jamie accompanied her docilely enough, but once out of the corner of her eye she saw him turn and look after the farm girl with a fleeting smile.

"What's her name?" she asked crisply.

"Who?"

"You know very well who! That girl you were talking to!"

"Oh, that one—Lizzie, I think."

"She seemed very friendly with you."

"Ah, that's just her way. Lenore, you're not jealous?" He gave her a wicked look.

Lenore, who was very jealous, snapped "Of course

49

not!" and kept her back as stiff as a poker as she loaded him up with her purchases.

He teased her out of her ill humor as they walked home, but after that, whenever he was gone, she wondered. Flora watched her shrewdly. "Have a child," she recommended.

Lenore gave her an irritable look. That wasn't the answer to everything. Suppose she *did* have a child and Jamie had a wandering eye anyway?

Perhaps, she thought bitterly, she didn't understand Jamie. Perhaps things were different in Scotland. She began to ask him probing questions about Scotland, only to be told in that easy voice that he was English now.

For a time Jamie really had thought himself English, Lenore knew. In June—no matter how many sidelong glances he gave likely maids who walked by his smithy with a swinging gait—he had clasped his fiery young handfast bride in his arms and dreamed the nights away. All through the lovely days of July he seemed to forget the war clouds gathering in the north. But when, on the last day of July, Charles rode south at the head of a largely Scottish army, Jamie again bethought him that he was a Scot.

He was restless and irritable in August. By now Lenore had rightly guessed what ailed her Jamie—he yearned to be out there with the men of the heather, marching to the wild sound of the bagpipes. She tried to make him forget by long, wild, languorous nights when he lay on her breast and the night sounds were muted by the reckless joyous singing in their own ears as they clung together, firing each other's passions, and were swept up toward the stars in ecstasy.

But Jamie's roguish attention continued to wander. When one of the village girls was married and Jamie, riding Snowfire, won the wild race for the bride's garters, Lenore had brooded at him. Irritably she watched his uproarious glee as he outmatched all the wedding guests in drinking the bride-ales—and turned and went home alone, determined to teach him a lesson. That night, when Jamie came upstairs and shut the door behind him, she pretended to be asleep.

"Lenore," he whispered. "Ah, Lenore, ye're awake—I can tell from your breathing!"

Lenore sighed and turned over, the moonlight silvering her rumpled hair and the carefully exposed tops of her white breasts. She opened her violet eyes, gave Jamie a devastating smile, and reached up a playful finger to trace the golden hairs that furred his bare chest. "You woke me," she said reproachfully. "And me with a headache! You'd best sleep alone."

But her sparkling eyes belied her words.

"You've no headache, you minx!" growled Jamie, reaching for her and flipping her back toward him as she would have turned away.

The flat of her palm pressed against his deep chest kept him at a distance. "Do you love me, Jamie?" she asked idly.

"Aye." His voice was thick. "That I do."

She forgot about teaching Jamie a lesson. Instead she sighed gently and opened her arms. Eagerly her Scot swept back the light coverlet and claimed her. Bright shone the moon on their wildly thrashing bodies . . . but when the sun shone again he was gone. Lenore could hear him whistling in the smithy as he worked, pounding nails into horseshoes. His bold gaze followed honey-haired young Mollie Paxton as she sidled by with a basket of eggs for the vicar, and he called after her and swept off his battered hat and bowed. Mollie's laugh tinkled and she swaggered a bit too seductively as she walked on toward the vicarage.

Watching from the cottage window, Lenore simmered. Jamie loved her ripe body . . . at night when his blood was hot. But by day he loved all the girls. Loved them equally, as far as she could see.

She stalked downstairs and Flora, without looking round, said, "Is that you, Lenore? Help me with this hot tallow, will you? I can't seem to get these candles poured right."

51

Flora's voice was strained and reminded Lenore that there was more than Jamie's women to worry about.

" 'Tis no wonder," said Lenore with concern. "Your hand's shaking. Here—let me do it."

"I didn't sleep much," admitted Flora, gratefully handing the candle mold to Lenore. "I don't seem to sleep well any more."

Lenore gave her a compassionate look. Flora was thinner and her eyes were haunted these days. Preoccupied and brooding, she seemed unaware of Lenore's sudden coolness toward Jamie that morning. At sunset Flora looked out across the wine-red hills toward the north—the young King's army was moving down from the north. " 'Twill be a bloody business," she muttered.

That night, as she'd done so often lately, Flora had a nightmare. Lenore, lying curled in the curve of Jamie's arm—though she'd hardly spoken to him all day—heard her scream and leaped up and ran down the stairs to find her shaking in a cold sweat.

"I saw blood," Flora murmured brokenly, her hands covering her eyes as if to shut out the sight. "A red splatter that spread and spread until it covered the whole countryside."

Lenore hushed and calmed her and returned to her bed, but as she lay beside Jamie, who hadn't even waked, she suddenly felt cold. It was said the Scots had The Sight, and Flora was a Scot. Blood . . . she'd seen. Did that mean the countryside would really rise as Scotland had to join the dispossessed young King? If so, England would indeed be awash with blood, for the Lord Protector's armies weren't going to give up their lives so easily. Even the wisest men in the village shook their heads and muttered that Cromwell's grip was firm, that England was held in strong hands—too strong for the young King to wrest free. On her pallet, Lenore shivered, and a prickle went down her spine—as if death had caressed her with light questing fingers.

Flora's dark premonition caused Lenore abruptly to make up with Jamie. The next day he was delighted to find her all smiles and warm caresses, waking him with a kiss and leaning over him so that the tips of her soft breasts dragged lightly, deliciously across his bare chest. His eyes kindled and he pulled her to him. "Ye're a hard wench to understand," he murmured into the flaming cloud of her hair. "But for all your wicked moods, I'd rather have you than all the rest."

It was as near as he ever came to a commitment to her, and Lenore's heart sang.

Had Charles and his Scots won handily, Jamie might have stayed with his arms cozily wrapped around his fiery young handfast bride—even if his eye roved occasionally. But things went badly for the young King, and when word reached Twainmere that the Scots were deserting and fleeing back toward the north, Jamie ground his teeth at this information, while Flora looked more dour than ever.

When a peddler stopped at the smithy to have his horse shod and idly called the Scots cowards and said Old Noll —meaning Cromwell—would send them baying home like dogs, Jamie's face went white. He picked a fight with the peddler and ended up breaking his arm.

That night he didn't come home at all, and the next day there was ale on his breath and honey-haired Mollie Paxton came strolling by, swinging her hips, and stopped to give him a long, slow look. Lenore, on her way to the well for a bucket of water, stopped in her tracks to watch them. They couldn't see her, for she was shielded by a luxuriant moss rosebush that was Flora's pride, but she could see Mollie's arch look and heard her say something about "last night."

The two had a bad fight over that, and Lenore ended up slamming her bedroom door in Jamie's face and latching it. She half expected him to burst through her window and quickly shuttered it, but he did not; instead, he sulked downstairs in the kitchen. The next day even Flora noticed that they weren't speaking.

They might have made it up, but when the King's forces advanced on Worcester, Lenore woke to find Jamie gone. Gone to Worcester, Flora told her grimly. Gone, too, was his big two-edged claymore that he kept hidden.

Lenore and Flora exchanged worried glances. They both knew what that meant.

The neighbors knew, too, for some had seen Jamie ride away to the north, claymore in hand. Now even those who had countenanced Lenore's behavior in moving in with the bonnie Scot turned their heads away bitterly. Some muttered behind their hands to each other, and when she went down into the village with her market basket, more than once she heard the words "hanging tree."

So Lenore determinedly donned her best summer dress —for hadn't her mother told her when she was little that a girl always had a better chance of getting her way if she looked pretty? Her wide white linen collar was plain and caught at the throat, but flared out, exposing a smooth expanse of bosom and the tops of her tantalizing breasts. Uncorseted—indeed, needing none for her naturally slender waist—she smoothed down her apple-green bodice, which outlined her lovely thrusting bustline and plunged into a slight V just below her waist. With great care she tucked up her slit overskirt of apple green around her hips on each side to let her gay yellow petticoat show to best advantage. Three-quarter sleeves flared out into great slashed puffs below her shoulders and ended midway down her slender forearms with wide white linen cuffs. Her thick shining hair was combed up from her forehead and caught up behind in a round braid with a few wavy locks hanging fashionably loose.

She was not richly gowned, but there was not a man for twenty miles who would not turn his head to look at her.

Satisfied at last with her appearance, Lenore had set forth on Snowfire and ridden north for Worcester.

Her intention was simple: she was going to bring Jamie home. Home before the battle was joined, if possible, home while they could still lie about it and say he'd been somewhere else and not at Worcester offering his services to the King! For a great battle was shaping up at Worcester, that was certain, and it was best Jamie not be in it. Jamie might be a fool—indeed, Lenore was beginning to believe it—but this time, at least, she intended to save him from himself!

It was uneasy going. She had found food for her horse at a friendly farmhouse. She had told them a glib story about a lost colt, and the farmer's wife had offered her meat pie and coarse brown bread and had let her stay the night in their loft. Cromwell's men were everywhere, she told Lenore cheerfully. The next morning it proved true.

In the morning mists Lenore found her way blocked several times by people with carts, hurrying away from the coming battle. Twice she had talked her way through outposts of Cromwell's men. She had no papers, but she was so young and so lovely and so obviously un-armed that she brought a smile to the lips of even the most war-hardened soldiers. They'd made lewd remarks, but they'd let the girl with hair of molten gold go on her way and watched her departure wistfully.

Now on the crest of the low hill above Worcester, through the puffs of smoke, she studied the way the battle went. Lenore's vision was excellent. A flash—per-haps of diamonds—caught her eye and she leaned for-ward, squinting into the blinding sun. That man in the buff coat leading the charge with his sword held high and his black curls streaming behind him—it was his breastplate she had seen glittering. Could he be Charles Stuart, whom Jamie proudly called the "King of Scot-land?" As she watched, his horse was shot from under him and a melee of soldiery obscured him from her view. She turned, shaking out her hair in the sticky heat and running her fingers through to comb it—what matter if it were loose or bound? She was like as not to fall to a musket ball, anyway, where she was going! Her resolute gaze swept the field.

Clearly Roundhead troops had been stationed where she now sat astride her white horse—which accounted for its desertion now. They must have pounded down into the valley below and were even now pressing the Royalists back toward the town. Across the Severn was strung a bridge of boats . . . so Cromwell held both

55

sides of the river. Her jaw tightened. Jamie was on the losing side this day.

Even inside the city walls she could see bursts of smoke—so there was fighting there, too, the Roundheads had broken through. No matter, she must get in and find Jamie. As she waited for an opening, her head lifted and she tensed. In the sector just below her that led straight to the city gates, there was a momentary slackening in the battle as the cavalry surged forward in another direction, pushing the foot soldiery back, cutting deep into their ranks. That would be the young King's forces making another charge. But dead ahead there was no hand-to-hand fighting at the moment—though musketry fire came in bursts.

In the momentary lull, Lenore took a deep breath, nudged Snowfire with her knee, cantered down the hill gathering speed, and thundered between the lines at full gallop. A volley of shots erupted nearby, and the white stallion, little deterred by his light burden, took off like the wind, running in long strides like the racer he was.

Men reloading their muskets rubbed smoke-reddened eyes at the sight of the slender girl with her red-gold hair streaming out behind her and the horse's flying white mane gleaming in the sun. Her white legs flashed as the wind whipped her yellow petticoat up around her thighs, and those men ahorse, who could easily have stopped her, paused in their tracks just to view her, while those with guns who could have brought her down from a distance gaped open-mouthed.

About to give the order to fire, one startled young officer, confronted by this incredible vision, shouted hoarsely, "Hold fire!"

"My mother's ill in Worcester—I must reach her!" cried Lenore as she raced by. "My mother—" The wind caught her voice even as it caught her shimmering hair that streamed behind her in a fiery golden shower, a moment before she and Snowfire plunged into a pall of smoke. But she was a woman and beautiful, and there was none in all that battle-scarred crew who wished to bring her down as Snowfire emerged from the smoke at a dead run and skimmed like a gull toward the city.

Just outside the gates she plunged in among a rout of dirty, bleeding troops that staggered back into the shelter of the town, while others desperately covered their retreat. They jostled about her, but they did not deter her.

Indeed, to some she must have seemed an angel come to their aid, this fiery-haired beauty on her white horse with its tossing mane, as clean and shining as they were bloody and battle-grimed. In the sticky heat she was swept forward with the massed men, looking anxiously from side to side for sight of Jamie.

Then she was through the gates and into the town.

She found it a place of wild confusion. As the troops around her dispersed down a narrow side street in an attempt to regroup, some limping, some at a staggering trot, she saw that the dead, the moaning wounded, were heaped carelessly about. Racing down the valley she had had no time to grasp the terrible things she saw, but here she was sickened by sights on every side. The gutters were stained red with blood, and at a cross street ahead she could see Roundhead soldiers charging through, their officers shouting orders. Musketry could be heard on nearby streets and a great puff of smoke rose above the housetops to her left where some building must be afire. Townsfolk ran distractedly back and forth, men and women calling out, asking each other for news or help. The King's men still held the Town Hall, someone shouted. As she wheeled Snowfire sharply about to avoid an overturned baggage wagon and narrowly missed a darting child, Lenore heard a man bawl that the King and a handful of cavaliers were making their stand on the south side of the outer wall at Barbour's Bridge—but the Ironsides would chop them up!

The Ironsides . . . that was what they called Cromwell's Roundheads. Cromwell obviously had the young King on the run. God knew where Jamie was now. But somehow she knew she must find him and get him back before news of the battle's outcome reached the Cotswolds.

Even as she thought it, a number of Roundhead soldiers charged around a corner, scattering some screaming old women carrying a big butter churn. Her white stallion reared up as they dashed by, and she was hard put to keep him from bolting as a boom, which must have been exploding black powder, split the air. Swept along with the tide, with no clear destination, Lenore was impelled forward.

Up ahead she could see officers commandeering horses. She must avoid losing her horse at all costs, for Jamie and she would need to ride fast and far when this rout was over. To her right yawned an open doorway, the oaken door swinging in the breeze; within she could see no one. A deserted house . . . perhaps its owners were among those who lay in their blood in the gutters, being trampled under the horses' hooves. A driverless cart careened wildly past her over the cobbles and turned over just ahead, obscuring those commandeering the horses from her view. On an impulse, Lenore turned Snowfire and rode him right through that open doorway, ducking her head to clear it. In the gloom she quickly dismounted and slammed and barred the door.

Behind her, Snowfire moved uneasily, disturbed by the screams that reached them from a side street and the whinnies of the frightened horses that were still trying to drag the overturned cart. Still blinded by the bright light from outside, Lenore patted his gleaming coat to soothe him.

From a corner behind her came a low laugh, and she stiffened.

"This wine must be better than I thought," came a rich masculine voice. "Now I'm seeing visions—a girl on a white horse riding right into the house!"

Lenore whirled around. As her eyes adjusted to the dim light, she saw sprawled on a low wooden bench with his back against the wall and one long booted leg stretched out along the bench while his other rested on the floor, a tall fellow surveying her. A lounging black-haired cavalier with all the grace and dash of his kind, he regarded her with interest from beneath his broad-brimmed plumed hat. His sword—a bloody one he had not bothered to wipe clean—was tossed on the table before him which supported his muscular forearm from which the sleeve had been ripped off. She noted that his boots were dusty and that a pewter tankard was grasped in one strong hand.

The stranger raised that tankard slightly in salute. "There's wine in yon barrel," he said. "Best we drink it up before it falls to Cromwell's short-hairs!"

"Why are you not fighting?" cried Lenore, afraid for her Jamie if even the King's cavaliers were deserting.

The tall man shrugged. "The battle is long since lost," he said indifferently. "I charged with the King through the Sidbury Gate—'twas a brave charge, but we were too few. Leslie refused to fight, and his men merely watched us cut our way back and forth through Cromwell's lines as if they were spectators at some game. The reinforcements from Wales did not come—if they arrive now, they'll be too late. 'Tis folly to continue. The King is mad to do so. Myself, I'll sit here cozy with my wine and make my way out of town with the dusk. Why came you here?"

"I've a—" she tripped over the word—"a husband in the King's army."

"Your husband's a fool to leave you," he said softly.

"We're—handfasted," she admitted honestly.

"Ah?" His gaze flickered over her softly rising and falling breasts, round and ripe as apples hanging on the boughs. "Handfasting's no marriage. You're a free woman in England. . . ."

Lenore tossed her head. "Why'd you have the window shuttered and the door open?" she demanded.

He shrugged. "That was how I found it. As I passed by I saw food on the table—and fighting makes me hungry." He offered her an oatcake and she shuddered and shook her head, still queasy from the sights in the streets. "And then I saw the wine." He held out his

59

tankard invitingly, but she turned away from him, unbarred the shutters, and leaned out to be sickened again by what she saw.

A screaming woman ran by dragging a young soldier who must have been long since dead. And another, weeping, carrying a little girl slumped in her arms. Horsemen moved impatiently over the cobbles of the narrow street now. Some of the horses' flanks were red with blood and the cavaliers' faces were grim as they streamed by. Lenore hastily pulled the shutters to a slit so that they would not see her mount behind her and perhaps seize him.

"You should help," she said sharply. "Those are your comrades out there."

"The cause is lost," he said, and there was an icy note in his voice that reminded her that he was a tall, broad-shouldered man in his prime with a bloody sword on the table, and she but a girl of eighteen, handfasted or no. "Come dark, ye'll be glad to slip away with me. How do they call you?"

"Lenore Frankford," she said, giving him a black look.

" 'Tis a soft name," he observed. "But ye look none so soft." He chuckled. "Faith, ye look as if ye're eager to join in the battle!"

Lenore, anxiously scanning the street for sight of Jamie, ignored him. She winced as someone ran by outside, howling that the King had fled. She yearned to go looking for Jamie immediately but realized that in the confusion she'd only get trampled or seized and questioned by the soldiers—or worse. Besides, she feared to leave Snowfire here lest she not find him when she returned.

Thinking of Snowfire made her realize he must be hungry. She rummaged around and found a bucket of water and some grain in a crock and gave both to Snowfire. As she patted that lovely arched neck with its tossing mane, he nuzzled her hand softly.

Vaguely comforted, she turned to regard the cavalier with whom she shared this hiding place. He was an easy subject for regard, for there was that about him to stir the blood and set the senses atingle. He had cool dark gray eyes beneath dark brows—eyes that she felt could face up to a cannon or an angry maid with equal aplomb. And a kind of taut watchfulness, for all his debonair manner and easy posture, indicating that he could spring forward in a bound, swinging that bloody sword that lay so carelessly tossed on the table within easy reach of his hand.

"I should think that would worry you—hearing the King has fled," she said contemptuously.

He shrugged. "Charles has his own hide to consider, as I have mine. He's a brave fellow, but you see, there weren't enough of us brave fellows." His mouth twitched in amusement at her angry glance. "Too many of us refused to fight," he explained.

She stared at him. "Like Leslie's horse?"

"Like Leslie's horse," he agreed. "Probably halfway back to Scotland by now. As we should be. Better that we'd never left Holland."

She fetched a sigh. "There is no hope, then?"

"None at all," he told her cheerfully. "Oh, Charles may reach the throne of England some day, given time and circumstance and a bit of luck. But I doubt not Cromwell will be dead when that happens. For he's a clever soldier, for which few give him credit."

She turned away from the dark cavalier, feeling a sudden respect for his view, and continued her anxious survey of the street, where the noise, which had been more distant, was rapidly increasing. Suddenly an avalanche of men poured into her line of vision—Royalists pursued by Roundheads. A volley of shots shattered the leaded panes of the windows across the street.

"Bar the shutters!" cried Geoffrey, springing forward to drag the heavy table against the door—and none too soon, for even as the table reached position there was a splintering sound as a frightened horse's hooves drove nearly through the wood.

Lenore, hastily slamming and barring the shutters, turned to soothe Snowfire, made nervous by the pandemonium outside. She stifled a scream as a ball ripped through the door and Geoffrey leaped across the room to push her to the floor.

"Stay down," he muttered, shielding her with his body. "Ye've a better chance that way."

Half suffocated beneath him, with the hard-packed earthen floor at her back, Lenore gave a screech and clutched him as a pike impaled itself in the wooden shutter with a crunch and was abruptly snatched free. Then with a thunder of hooves the battle surged on up the street to collide with another body of men at the cross street and erupt into neighboring streets and alleys.

Lenore shuddered and pulled away from the arms that held her as the howling madness without subsided into a distant din as the battle took itself elsewhere.

"Faith, tis a grand opportunity missed," murmured her cavalier, dragging his hand impudently across the soft peaks of her breasts as he rose.

Angrily Lenore slapped his hand away, hearing his low chuckle as she scrambled up and unbarred the shutter to peer out cautiously. Two men lay dead in the street, one with his head blown off and one hacked to pieces. A couple of dazed-looking pikemen were dragging away a third who groaned as he was dragged over the rough cobbles. They swore as a shutter, torn loose in the battle, fell down heavily upon the body they were dragging. The groans stopped abruptly. One pulled the shutter off and said stupidly, "He's dead. Jeremy's dead."

With a half-human howl the other set off down the street at a run. "I'll kill the bastards!" he sobbed. The other continued pulling dead Jeremy away. "Come back, Tim!" he called frantically.

Lenore covered her face with her hands and swayed against the shutter.

"How could you *not* help them?" she asked haltingly.

"Have some wine," he said sharply. "It will steady you."

Lenore almost choked as the warm liquid poured down her throat, but it did steady her. She wavered to a bench and sat down.

As if he wanted to talk to someone, he told her of

himself. His name was Geoffrey Wyndham. He was the second son of an old and aristocratic family. He'd broken with his father, who quaked at the very thought of Cromwell, over drinking and wenching, he said negligently. And having no prospects, he'd followed Prince Charles to France. There he'd raised merry hell and been somewhat surprised when the Prince had embarked for Scotland. Of course, he'd gone along, but he'd found it a cold land and dour, full of ranting Covenanters (here Lenore found herself thinking guiltily of Flora). This ride south to take the throne of England he'd considered a wild, unlikely venture, but then he was given to wild, unlikely ventures and who knew, it might have worked out.

Only it hadn't.

So now the King was fled and with the dark he'd flee, too, and with luck they'd both make it to safety. Again he offered her wine and oatcakes. This time she took them absently and ate and drank, for she'd need her strength to get Jamie back to the Cotswolds before news of the outcome reached them—if indeed she could do it at all.

She pulled a bench over by the window the better to watch through the crack in the shutters. It was hot and dim and her clothes stuck to her, and there was a hypnotic sound to the low voice of the man behind her who —although she did not know it—was watching the light from the crack in the shutters play over her hair and thinking she looked like an avenging angel.

Outside she heard someone bawl, "Did ye hear, 'tis said an angel on a white horse galloped down from the sky and into the town."

"Aye, I heard it," answered a coarse voice. "Dashed through the city gates and disappeared, so it goes."

"Think you it is a sign?" asked the other, awed.

"I doubt it," grumbled his friend. What else he said was lost to their hearing. Lenore reddened at a chuckle behind her.

"So that's how you arrived?" murmured her cavalier from his corner. "Faith, it took courage!"

"I'd have come more decorously had I thought they'd let me through," said Lenore sulkily. "I've no pass—I dared not let them stop me."

"Well spoke." He nodded. "It seems we are birds of a feather. You flew into town unannounced—and I am about to fly forth from it in the same manner."

"It would have done you more honor had you stayed to fight beside your King," cried Lenore, irritated by his insolent manner.

"By now my King has fled also," he said cynically. "You heard them say it. The pity is that my King had not the sense to see the battle was lost—as I had."

She turned away from him in a huff and continued to watch out the window.

"Why did you come here?" he asked curiously, after a while. "There must be something that keeps you staring out the window. And surely 'tis more normal for a girl to shun a battle than to seek one."

"I must get Jamie back before the village knows he went to fight for the King," she admitted. "For he's a Scot, and there are those who might kill him for it." ·

"And yourself as well," he murmured. "Since you live with Jamie—even though he's not taken you to the kirk."

Stung at that, she said stiffly, "Handfasting's an old and time-honored custom in Scotland!"

"I don't doubt it." He sounded amused. "And clever it was of your Scottish laddie to think of it! I'll remember that, the next time I'm in Scotland!"

She wanted to throw something at him. Instead, since the dusk had deepened, she said stiffly, "I must go look for Jamie now. Thank you for the oatcakes and wine."

"Look for him at Barbour's Bridge—'twas where the King went at the last," he advised. He gave her directions, and she reached for Snowfire's reins to lead him out. "Nay." His hand closed over her wrist in a grip of steel. "You'll go without the horse, mistress. I need him to make my escape."

Lenore drew a deep breath. Somehow she had known it would come to this. "If you do not let me take him,"

64

she said fiercely, "I will cry out and alert the Roundhead soldiers that there's a cavalier hiding in here."

"And I will say you're my doxie and we'll go to hell together," he countered imperturbably.

Lenore paused. It was dark in here, but she could still see the wolfish gleam of his eyes. He meant what he said, and what good would she be to Jamie dead? "I—I cannot let you take Snowfire," she said shakily. "He's too dear to me."

Something in her voice must have touched the hard man who gripped her wrist. "I'll meet you at the south wall, at Barbour's Bridge," he said in a changed tone. "And you can ride away on Snowfire. You have my word on it."

She hesitated, afraid to trust him, but realized she had no alternative. She shook his hand away and flung out. His low laugh followed her as she eased through the doorway, looked up and down to see if it was safe, and then fled down the dark narrow street hugging close to the house fronts, stifling a scream as some roof tiles, loosened by the musketry, crashed down beside her.

Down dark side streets she passed; she could see lanterns waving as groups of Roundhead soldiers searched the houses, looking for Royalists. She could hear the clash of steel, and shouts, and sometimes musket shots as men were taken and dragged out. Lenore started to turn back to warn the dark cavalier but stayed herself. He'd taken Snowfire and she couldn't be sure she'd ever see him again—let him fend for himself! With a toss of her head she pressed on, and whenever she passed a group of soldiers she cried out frantically, "Jamie, Jamie! Have any of you seen my little brother? He's wandered off! He's about so high." She indicated knee-height and rushed on.

Always, they let her pass.

At the city gates she was stopped, but again the same ruse worked when she asked anxiously if she could but step outside and call her little brother and then come back in again, for she feared the dark outside. A gruff middle-aged officer peered into her face in the lantern light and said, "Let the wench out to look for her brother," when the guard would have stopped her. Reluctantly the guard let her pass. Others, she saw, needed papers to get through. She wondered how her dark cavalier would fare.

Out she went and found her way along the south wall. The going was slippery with gore, and there were sights that made her stop and retch. Townsfolk passed her, mournfully carrying back their dead. And Roundhead soldiers, grimly bearing back their wounded and their dead. She wandered about, peering into the faces of the fallen, looking anxiously into a face here, bending over a body there. But of course, she told her thudding heart, Jamie was fled to those low hills over there. Surely he could not be hiding in the town, for there he was sure to be discovered.

She was a long way from the city gate now and stumbling over the uneven ground. Suddenly in the darkness there was a soft hoof-fall behind her and a low whinny. She turned sharply about, peering into the dark. Snowfire nuzzled at her arm, and almost at her side, so silently had he approached, was her dark cavalier from the town.

But a very altered cavalier. The moon came out for a second from behind its cloud cover and gleamed on that dark determined visage. Nothing else seemed the same. Gone was the plumed hat, the lace boothose, the satins and velvets and froth of Mechlin at the throat. Instead that same dark mocking face looked out at her from under a sober Puritan hat, and his collar was as plain as his clothes were drab and serviceable. Then the moon slipped back behind those low-hanging clouds and Snowfire was only a white shape in the darkness.

"Faith, you're monstrous changed," she observed in a tart voice that belied how glad she was to see him and how thankful she was that Snowfire had been brought safely through the city gates.

"I watched the street for someone my size and cut him down and dragged him in and changed clothes with

66

him," he said easily. "Too bad I had to slash this coat with my blade. It's ugly enough without that."

She shuddered, thinking of that sudden pouncing from the dark, the swift and silent blade . . . the bloody aftermath.

" 'Tis a good disguise," she agreed faintly. "And I thank you for bringing my horse to me."

"It was nice of me, wasn't it?" he agreed. "When I could so easily have ridden away and left you."

Lenore tossed her head. "Snowfire's devoted to me. He'd have broken free and gone home to me at the first opportunity."

"Oh? That's nice to know."

Lenore was hardly listening. She was casting around her helplessly for Jamie, and so overlooked something light and steely in his voice that might have given her warning. "I don't know where Jamie could have gone," she said, her tone forlorn. "Think you he may have fled with the King?

" 'Tis possible but hardly likely. Those who fled with the King will not be newcomers to his cause, but his own friends who were with him in France, I don't doubt."

She looked about her at the dark, low hills. "Then maybe he's out there?" she asked hopefully, trying not to see the horrors over which she stepped as he dismounted and followed her, leading Snowfire. In the brief flashes of moonlight she was shudderingly aware of bodies tumbled about, missing arms and legs, the ground slippery with gore. Suddenly her voice died away. In that brief gleam as the moon had flickered through the clouds again, she had glimpsed a face . . . a face she knew.

"Jamie," she cried in a soft agonized voice, and knelt beside him, and now the treacherous moon that had hidden him from her came out and showed him in sudden vivid light. He lay on his back with arms outflung. His eyes were open and the same clear blue, his hair was just as gold. He might have been resting, his body flung onto the turf on a summer's afternoon after playing at bowls.

Except for the hole in his leather jerkin which was stained dark red with his blood. Except that the blue eyes which gazed up at the scudding moon saw nothing, would see nothing ever again.

"He's dead," observed her cavalier conversationally.

She looked up at him through a blaze of scalding tears. "I'll take his body away," she choked. First her blessed sister taken from her—now her beloved Jamie! "He'll have decent burial in the churchyard!"

"Ah, that you will not," the man beside her said silkily. "For to bear him away is to proclaim you were with him—and that's to hang for treason yourself. And that I've no mind to let you do. We'll away at once, for I hear soldiers coming and there's no time to lose."

"I won't leave without Jamie!" Lenore sprang up, snatching at Snowfire's bridle.

The tall cavalier sighed and his fist clipped her jaw. Not terribly hard, just hard enough that she slumped senseless and he reached out with his other arm and quickly caught her as she fell. Mounting swiftly, he swung Lenore up before him on the big white horse. Snowfire was rested now but nervous and eager to be away from this scene of blood and carnage; when Geoffrey dug his heels into the horse's flanks Snowfire responded violently. Away toward the low hills they thundered with only a shout and a musket ball behind them before the line of trees had swallowed them up.

PART TWO

THE CAVALIER

CHAPTER 4

Lenore came to groggily, with a pain in her jaw and the jolting realization that she was lying flung face down across a saddle, her long hair streaming. She gave a strangled cry, and a voice she seemed to recognize said solicitously, "I hope I didn't hurt you too much, but you needed convincing and I hadn't time to do it more gently."

She choked in fury as memory came flooding back to her. This madman had hit her—and stolen her horse! That he had stolen her as well had not yet occurred to her.

"Let me up," she gasped, and a strong arm obligingly swept her up so that she found herself seated sideways in front of him with his arm supporting her. As she wriggled she realized that it was not only supporting her, but it was wrapped around her waist in a steely grip. Her hip was pressed embarrassingly tight against his hard thigh. She glared up into that dark face that gave her only half attention as his keen gray eyes narrowly watched the track for sign of soldiers. "If you're stealing my horse, at least have the grace to let me off. I'm going back."

"Ah, that you're not, mistress," he murmured. "Must I put you to sleep again to convince you?"

In fury she bent and sank her teeth into a muscular forearm. His other hand came around and jerked her head up by her long hair and he cuffed her lightly—but hard enough to whip her bright head from side to side. For the moment she had his full attention.

"Wild I know you to be," he said in a low voice, every word increasing in coldness. "And foolhardy, too. But staying alive is a habit of mine that I plan to continue. And I'd remind you, mistress, before you decide to scream, that Cromwell's men are all about. D'ye hanker to be dragged back and questioned?"

"I'd tell them nothing," Lenore declared fiercely, her fearless violet eyes meeting his hard gray ones in the moonlight.

Geoffrey gave a low contemptuous laugh. "On the rack? Would you not? Or perchance encouraged by hot irons?"

She fell into silence at that. Even brave men told their secrets when their bodies were broken on the rack.

"I see I have reached you," he remarked dryly. "Don't look so despairing. Don't you know there'll be people in Worcester who sympathized with the King and will give your lover a decent burial?"

At that reminder of Jamie—who in the heat of the moment she'd forgotten—she fell to weeping and swayed precariously.

His sinewy arm tightened about her. "I wonder," he muttered, half to himself, as he bent and pushed her down to avoid a low-hanging branch, "had I fallen, would any have wept for me?"

"Of course not!" she sputtered, dashing the tears angrily from her eyes. "You steal horses and strike down women!"

"Only on rare occasions," he said coolly. "And if you keep your head and manage to stay silent, Mistress Lenore, I'll even take you with me!"

Anger temporarily glazed over her grief. He sounded

as if she should be grateful he'd kidnapped her! "Where are you going?" she demanded haughtily.

"Now, that I'm not certain as yet. Away. Somewhere there are fewer soldiers, if I can find it."

"They'll be on all the roads."

He nodded. "And we'll need to rest this horse if he's to keep a good pace. About now, I should think. This looks to be a good place."

He halted in a small copse and slid from the saddle, taking her with him. She tried to jerk away, but the arm locked about her kept a tight grip.

"No, Mistress Lenore, you'll not be leaping astride and riding away like the wind," he said grimly. Taking a short leathern thong from his pocket with his other hand, he tied her right wrist tightly to his own left wrist, kept the end of the thong in his hand and sat down. Perforce, Lenore sat down with him. "I'm going to sleep for a few minutes," he told her, leaning back against the bole of a tree and stretching out his long legs.

"Sleep?" she cried indignantly. "How can you sleep with soldiers all about, hunting us?"

"Easily," he said, his tone imperturbable. "With luck there'll be no soldiers ride by, and you will wake me with a touch if you hear anything. Agreed?"

She did not answer and he closed his eyes, while Lenore, uncomfortably aware that her thinly clad thigh was pressed close to his lean, hard-muscled leg, tried to wriggle away. Instantly one eye opened and he took hold of her other hand, pulled her half across him, and threw his arm about her. "Hold still," he commanded. "Your life may depend on my being able to stay awake for long hours this night."

Indignantly Lenore remained where she was, annoyed by the implied familiarity of his arm about her, even more upset by the weight of her soft breasts resting against his leather-clad, rhythmically breathing chest. There seemed to be nothing to do about it but fume, so she remained there as stiffly as she could, hating the intimacy he had forced upon her and trying to hold her whirling thoughts on Jamie's tragic death.

73

Around her the woods were quiet and dark. It was hard to believe a bloody battle had been fought not so far from here.

In about twenty minutes her cavalier roused himself. "Ah, a good nap," he said and, untying her wrist from his, stretched mightily.

Lenore, who'd been tensed and waiting for this opportunity, leaped up. She had almost made it onto the white horse's back when a pair of strong hands seized her by the hips and pulled her back. With a violent kick she knocked the cavalier off balance and they landed, rolling, on the soft grass beneath the trees. They came to a halt with his arms locked around her and herself pinned underneath him. His dark face was so close she could feel his warm breath on her cheek. It smelled fresh and heady, like the tang of wine. She told herself that was because he'd been drinking and tried to struggle from beneath him.

But he'd no mind to let her go at this point.

"Ah, it's a soft creature you are, Mistress Lenore," he murmured, one of his arms beneath her moving so that his warm hand traced along her spine and up the back of her neck until his fingers twined into her red-gold hair. "And indeed I'd prefer to enjoy you on the spot, rather than to take you on a wild ride cross country just to escape some soldiers who'd like nothing better than to kill us both, but you see, that's the way it is."

He rolled off her, while keeping his fingers twisted in her hair, and pulled her to her feet none too gently. "I do not like to tie you, mistress, for if they catch us, you might have a chance to escape while I hold them for a bit, but . . . I've need to have my attention elsewhere and not upon your sweet body. Could it be you'd give me your word not to try to escape?"

She made a sound like a spitting cat and twisted her head away from him, even though it hurt her, for her hair was pulled painfully as he kept his grip.

"Well," he said pleasantly, "then I've no choice except to enjoy you right now, have I? Faith, it might gentle you a bit at that!"

74

"I'll scream loud enough to bring all the Ironsides in this part of the country down on you!" Lenore threatened fiercely. But for all her bravado she was frightened, and her breath came faster as she drew quickly away from him.

Geoffrey's eyes gleamed and for answer his mouth suddenly crushed down on hers and he pulled her to him, flattening her soft breasts against his brawny chest. She gasped as his tongue probed wickedly and his hands sought places she had thought inviolate from him. Wildly she told herself that it was only her fury that made each touch pulse and ring through her body in tormenting waves. Now his hands were swiftly undoing her bodice and pushing down her chemise impatiently. With an electric shock she realized that he was impudently caressing her bare breasts. They tingled beneath his touch, and to her rage the soft round peaks of her nipples tensed to hardness. She thought he chuckled at that and was so incensed she nearly wrenched her shoulder out of joint in a desperate bid for freedom.

But her opponent in this battle of wills was tall and broad-shouldered and strong above the average. Easily he held her, and when she was trembling like an aspen in his arms—both from the unwonted exertion and from something else she refused to give a name—he bore her gently to the ground, falling upon his arms so that she landed softly, still writhing in his grip.

Abruptly—and in horror—she was aware that her skirts were riding up around her hips, that a warm hand hand had brushed aside the skirt of her chemise. She started violently as that same hand now parted her thighs and his lean leg came down firmly between her knees. Every touch of him seemed to burn her, and she gave a great lurch as his hard masculinity made a sharp deft thrust within her.

With a moan she made a last savage effort to twist away from him and was aware of a scalding madness that was stealing over her as he held her in that firm unyielding yet somehow caressing grasp. Rhythmically he moved within her, and her pulse beat violently as the

75

blood cascaded through her veins in wild rhythm. Her whole tempestuous body was giving him back its wild answer—and to her shame, it was an answer such as she had never given to Jamie, for all she'd been his handfast bride. A sob caught in her throat at her body's hot betrayal, for now as the flames of his passion mounted, her back arched toward him and she pressed upward fiercely against him in a rhythm that matched his own.

Over to their right came the sound of hooves and a hoarse cry. "See anyone?"

She felt the lean body above her stiffen to rigidity and her heart almost stopped until another voice, frighteningly near, said in a thick West Country accent, "Nay—no one. 'Twas only a deer."

There was a grunt and the first voice called. "Then we'd best be off, for 'tis men, not beasts, we're hunting this night!"

She lay rigid as the hoofbeats faded away, but the pulse in her forehead continued to beat. His mouth left her lips for a moment and she heard him murmur, "Lenore, Lenore. . . ." in her ear, felt his hot breath tickle her ear, and turned her head away with a moan.

Moving triumphantly now, as if he sensed her hot surrender, reveled in it, he deliberately drove her on to peaks of passion, swept her down wild reckless valleys and up tumultuous slopes to reach the very heights of desire—and fulfillment.

When he had finished and she lay silent and panting, he lifted his head and kissed her eyes, which were wet with tears.

"Come," he said softly, "ye've no reason to weep."

She jerked away shakily from his hand, but this time she did not struggle as they mounted Snowfire. She only kept her head turned from him bitterly, so that he could not see the shame and rage etched on her tear-stained face.

Her handfast lover was dead, she had been violated by a stranger, and—damn him, must he hold her so close? Her breasts were resting on his arm, making her remember what it had been like a moment before on the

76

cool grass. She wriggled to be free of that arm, but the motion seemed only to please her captor. It was in that position that they rode on, with Lenore sulking and her dark cavalier airily content with life.

All that night they rode through woodlands, resting occasionally, avoiding the sound of troops. Through most of the next day and the following evening they hid. Though there was a little food in Snowfire's saddlebags, they were still ravenously hungry. When Geoffrey would have touched her, Lenore turned a cold white shoulder toward him, and he desisted.

"I hope you know now not to leave me, mistress," he said on a cold note of warning. "For you might end up romping in the hay with an entire Roundhead regiment."

Lenore shivered, but she kept her back turned to him. She had not spoken to him since he had raped her.

"Come now," he said cajolingly. "I didn't mean to frighten you. We're safe enough for the present." He reached out and patted her arm.

Lenore, whose gloomy thoughts had been on Jamie, jerked it away. "Have you no respect for grief?" she demanded bitterly. "Or do women always fall to you like ripe plums?"

"Not always," he said, moving away from her. And added quietly, "You are not the first woman to have lost a lover to war."

"Don't remind me of it! Had we not quarreled—"

"Ah, so he left you in anger?" he said thoughtfully.

" 'Twas over another woman—a silly quarrel," burst out Lenore, furious at the implication. "Jamie would have left to join the King in any event." She was not entirely sure that was true, but it eased her conscience to believe it. She flashed Geoffrey an angry glance, to find his hard gray eyes looking at her with some sympathy.

"I begin to understand you," he murmured. " 'Tis not your heart but your conscience that pains you."

Had Lenore had something in her hand at that moment, she would have thrown it at that thoughtful saturnine countenance. As it was, she tried desperately to hold her wavering thoughts on Jamie—golden Jamie whose handfast bride she'd been, Jamie her true lover. Not this—this maddening cavalier whose lightest touch made her tremble!

"Perhaps we should declare a truce for a time, you and I," he said in a quiet voice. "Our situation is desperate enough. If we are seen to quarrel it will attract attention, and we must use the same story or be suspect." To her mutinous expression, his gaze took on a steely look. "D'ye yearn for the gibbet, mistress?" he asked softly. "For the Lord Protector's judges would be glad to place you there—after the Lord Protector's troops have had their fill of your charms."

Lenore paled. For a moment she saw them trapped, taken. Saw that long lean body beside her bound and thrown to the ground. Saw the glittering eyes of the troops in the firelight as they gathered around her—men too long without women to care for the niceties. Saw herself, screaming, tossed from man to man . . . all the night long. A vision of hell.

Who was to say the same might not happen to her if she returned to Twainmere? Her only safety lay in the company of this hated cavalier who watched her with a narrow gaze beneath straight black brows.

"I will do or say nothing to endanger us," she said in a low reluctant voice. "And now"—her tone sharpened as she remembered he had raped her—"if you will spare me your comments?"

"It is enough that we understand each other," he said in a stern voice, and turned his aquiline features away from her.

When they mounted he continued to ignore her, hauling her up before him as unfeelingly as if she were a sack of meal. He kept his face turned away from her as if he cared no more for her than she did for him, although her soft breasts still bounced on his lean arm and her hip was pressed tight against his hard thigh. She shook her head as she felt the irritating brush of his shoulder-length hair, which swung occasionally against her cheek as he turned his head alertly to study the terrain.

78

Lenore had been sitting stiffly upright and now she tried to stretch her aching back muscles.

"Are you comfortable, mistress?" he asked suddenly.

Lenore sniffed, straightened up again, and forebore to answer. Angrily she tried to keep her wavering thoughts on Jamie. And Twainmere. And all that she had lost . . .

They reached Stourbridge, their arrival half concealed behind a farmer's big haycart, but checked as they saw the road ahead was blocked by a troop of Cromwellian horse. They were leaving abruptly when Geoffrey's sharp eyes recognized, in a cluster of beggars milling around as if afraid to enter the town, a face he knew.

He reined in. "Hal," he called in a low voice.

Warily a shuffling beggar, bent under a large pack, looked up. Instantly his eyes lit up, and he detached himself from the raffish crew and shuffled forward with a swift glance behind him. "Around yon turn there's a thicket, Geoffrey," he muttered. And loudly, "Alms, for pity!" The rest of the beggars might have joined them, but Geoffrey gave Snowfire a jab with his knee and they were off around a turn in the road they'd just traversed before the lumbering farm cart could move enough to give Cromwell's soldiers a clear view of them.

Into the thicket they plunged, Lenore protesting angrily in her fear for Snowfire's eyes at the thorns, and tearing the skin on her arms as she tried to sweep the reaching branches away from his head. Once inside, they waited.

In a little while the thorn bushes parted and the "beggar" joined them. He bowed deeply to Lenore, who gave him a wan and somewhat puzzled smile. As he straightened she noted the finely drawn lines of his face, the delicate skin of his hands—a gentleman's hands—and was not surprised to learn that this was Lord Harold Trowbridge, late of the King's party, who'd come by this way. She listened as Hal Trowbridge gave Geoffrey a grim picture of the extent of the Royalist defeat: two thousand dead, three thousand taken prisoner. King Charles was in headlong flight—even the royal coach with all his papers and four hundred pounds in money had been left to the Roundheads.

Cromwell's victory was complete.

Geoffrey sighed. " 'Twas an evil day we rode south from Scotland, Hal."

His friend nodded curtly. "An evil day indeed. And now there's an end to it." He too fetched a sigh. "The King was here with some sixty of his officers. 'Twas here I left them and traded my clothes with a beggar. The poor devil thought he'd the better of me in the bargain, but that well-known red velvet coat of mine may get him flung into jail as a Royalist!" He touched Snowfire with some envy. "You're lucky to have such a fine mount, Geoffrey—even though he must carry double. I lost my horse a ways back. She'd been hit by one of Ironsides' balls and was bleeding bad. I couldn't see her suffer, so I finished her off." He looked sad. "She was a good nag and had been with me for a long time. So I left the royal party, for I could not accompany the King on foot."

"Where do you go now, Hal?"

Hal shrugged. "I'm safe enough. I'm making my way to friends nearby who can hide perhaps one man in their priest hole." He looked from Geoffrey to Lenore, anticipating the next question. "But three . . ." He shook his head wearily. "They'd refuse."

"Whither went the King's party, Hal?"

"To a safe house at Boscobel, I heard one say."

Geoffrey was thoughtful. "Can y' give me directions to Boscobel, Hal? Mayhap they'd shelter us, too, if they can care for sixty horse!"

Lenore hardly listened as Hal gave Geoffrey directions. She was light-headed from lack of food and fighting exhaustion. She'd had several days' hard riding, the crushing blow of Jamie's death, and the turbulent emotions that Geoffrey had stirred up within her. Her head drooped as Hal left them, moving stealthily out of the thicket. They waited a while and then followed.

Snowfire was tired, too. He was dragging when, in a driving rain, they reached the estate of Boscobel and swiftly identified themselves.

Aye, the King's party had been here, they were told as they were ushered into the hall out of the wet. They'd fed him buttermilk and eggs and purée of milk and apples. They'd cut his hair with a knife and dressed him as a woodsman. He had hidden out in the woods in a hollow oak in the rain while the house had been searched, and was now gone. In answer to Geoffrey's insistence that he must rejoin the King, they conjectured that the King was perhaps gone to Madeley where a Mr. Wolfe had hidey-holes for priests.

Lenore revived a little as their hostess served them fricassee of eggs and bacon and some of that same purée of milk and apples, which was served, she was told proudly, in the same black earthen cup out of which the King had supped. She listened as all at the table fell warmly to discussing the battle. The conversation was full of "might-have-beens." Had not the earthworks they called the "Royal Fort" fallen, had not the foot soldiers been pushed into the narrow confines of Worcester's streets, had Leslie's horse not defected . . . It made Lenore sad to hear it, and she bent her mind to other things, hot private memories that still seared her, and bitterness that chance should have thrown her afoul of the law so that she must ride in company with this— this rapist!

Suddenly her mind was jerked back to the present, for across the hastily spread boards her gray-bearded host mused, " 'Tis strange how wild rumors spread. 'Tis said at the height of the battle a naked avenging angel with long golden hair came charging down the hill on a white horse and disappeared into the city looking for the King, but he had fled. So the avenging angel disappeared and left the field to Cromwell. Think you there is any truth to the story?"

Lenore choked on her purée, but Geoffrey smiled expansively and nodded toward Lenore. " 'Twas this lady, garbed as you see her now." He then launched into a smooth lie of being swept away from the King's guard and lying thought dead on the battlefield until night when he was "revived by this lady who was looking for her husband among the slain"—again he nodded toward Lenore.

Their hosts were touched by this recital—especially since the reminder of Jamie's death brought tears to Lenore's violet eyes—and gallantly offered them shelter at Boscobel, but Geoffrey was of the opinion that the house might well be searched again and they'd best away from it, lest both they and their hosts suffer.

Lenore roused herself from her grief. "Snowfire is too tired to go on traveling double, even though he's eaten and drunk," she told Geoffrey flatly.

Her host gallantly interceded to press on Lenore a bay horse left by one of the King's cavaliers as too winded to continue, but now with rest and feed quite recovered. Flustered by the welter of lies and half-truths Geoffrey had so skillfully spun about her, Lenore hesitated, but Geoffrey hastily accepted for her. So to her **irritation she** found herself riding away from Boscobel on a smallish bay while beside her Geoffrey bestrode her beloved Snowfire.

"Why did ye hold back at their offer?" Geoffrey exploded testily when they were well out of sight and hearing of the house. "God's truth, ye needed a horse!"

Lenore swung around in the saddle to face him angrily. "'Tis you who need a horse, Geoffrey Wyndham!" she flashed. "I *have* a horse, and I'll thank you to return him to me. Now!"

Geoffrey gave her an astonished look. Then he threw back his head and laughed, a long peal of mirth that lit his dark face and seemed to light the rainswept gloom. "I cannot do that," he explained, "for this white stallion is the faster horse, I've no doubt, and I've no mind to let you go charging off into danger the moment it suits your fancy."

A hot flush covered Lenore's cheeks. He'd already had his way with her—what more danger was she likely to encounter than that? Her scathing expression spoke volumes.

"I know what you're thinking," he said. "And I'll own I'm sorry, Lenore—not for holding your lovely body in

82

my arms, but that I did not wait till ye were ready to welcome me."

She stiffened. "That day will never come," she said in a bitter voice.

"Still," he murmured, "ye did not betray me at Boscobel. Ye could have said ye found me drinking wine with my feet propped up instead of lying sprawled upon the field of battle. Why did ye not charge me with it?" he challenged her.

Lenore's head whirled. Why had she not indeed? It had been a clear opportunity to strike back at him for taking her. "I—" she muttered. "I—they might have killed you had they thought you played the King false. They might have killed us both," she added hastily, for something flickered in his eyes. In another moment he was going to thank her for shielding him! "Snowfire is tired," she said desperately, "and this bay horse is rested. Snowfire's been carrying double, and you are much heavier than I. Geoffrey"— she was pleading now for the white horse she loved—"if you'll let me ride Snowfire, I give you my word I won't try to escape."

Her dark cavalier hesitated. "In women's word I place little reliance," he said grimly.

"You can rely on mine!" she flashed. "Get off—I'm changing horses with you!"

There was the ghost of a smile on his face as he dismounted.

"Perhaps you're giving your word because you like my lovemaking?" he suggested softly.

It was too much. Lenore's open palm cracked across that smiling mouth, and she felt her arm caught in a grip that hurt. His dark face was thrust down close to hers, and there was the devil's own light in his eyes.

"Do that never again, mistress," he warned in a low level tone. "Or I'll turn you across my knee and pull up your skirts and spank your white bottom till it's pink as your cheeks!"

He let go of her arm and suddenly seized her by her slender waist and lifted her from her bay mount to Snowfire's white back. Lenore thought the tired horse brightened, and she patted his neck and ran her fingers lovingly through his thick mane. She was rewarded by a soft whinny.

Geoffrey was watching her. Perhaps it was compassion she read in his face. "We must go softly now," he cautioned as he mounted. "For the countryside is alive with Cromwell's men. They know now the King has slipped through their fingers, and they'll be searching everywhere."

Cromwell's men . . . that was why she could not go back to the Cotswolds. She wondered if anybody had told Flora that Jamie was dead. It made her feel sad.

She roused herself from this reverie. "If I go with you," she said in a strained voice, "you must understand that I am not your doxie. You'll not take me again against my will?"

His expression hardened, and she could not read it.

"Not against your will," he said shortly.

They had little to say to each other that day or the next. They tried for London, but the roads were well guarded and Geoffrey hesitated to try to run that iron gauntlet. Instead they sought the back roads, going nowhere. Geoffrey showed no inclination to talk to her, preferring instead to listen for the sound of hooves that might mean soldiery and to keep his erect hawklike head swinging about for any sign of trouble. Lenore understood that Cromwell's men were beating the countryside for "traitors" and how easily their lives could be forfeit and so followed him doggedly.

But with Snowfire stumbling from fatigue and herself reeling in the saddle, trying to jar herself awake, she began once again to think of Jamie and her life at Twainmere and great tears rolled down her cheeks. As her breath caught in a sob, Geoffrey, who had been riding ahead, suddenly swung around in the saddle and cast a penetrating look at her.

"Why are you crying, Lenore?" he asked.

"I was thinking of Jamie," she answered miserably. "Jamie was not a soldier as you are." Her voice broke.

84

" 'Twas his father's claymore he took with him. He'd have had no chance against experienced troops."

"Every man must fight a first battle," he said, dropping back to walk his horse beside hers. "To survive it, 'tis best to have luck—and your Jamie didn't have that. But look at it this way, Lenore: battle-luck he had not, but woman-luck he had, for while he lived, he had you."

His voice was caressing, but it did not console her. Her tears rained down the harder.

Geoffrey sighed and peered through the trees. "I discern you're hungry and will take a sorry view of things until you've eaten. It would seem there's an inn up ahead and no soldiery in sight. Since we've no money, think you that you could distract the landlord and his lackeys with some story while I steal a bit of hay and grain for the horses?"

Lenore nodded, dashing the tears from her eyes and drying her wet face. Snowfire was her darling, and she was determined to see him fed.

Boldly she rode up to the inn door and dismounted, handing the reins to a stable boy. The landlord had come to the door, and behind him his wife, a slatternly woman, peered out at this unlikely traveler. Lenore drew everyone's rapt attention by telling them excitedly of an overturned coach on the road a short way back, filled with gentry wearing gold rings and velvet cloaks, crying out for help. "They said they'd pay well for assistance," she told the landlord.

The landlord, a fat man with small eyes, straightened to attention at the sound of the word "gold." He rubbed his hands together. "You, Eben," he told the boy. "You come with me now—ye can take care of the lady's horse later. My good wife will fix ye a fine supper, m'lady."

Lenore smiled winsomely at him. "Well enough," she said. "Meanwhile I'll walk my own horse to the stable. 'Twill limber my bones."

The slattern disappeared inside, and her husband and the stableboy started off at a fast clip down the road.

"Now you'll have dinner, Snowfire," Lenore murmured. She was walking him toward the stable when she met Geoffrey. He was laughing.

"I heard your last words," he said. "You've a natural talent for acting, Lenore."

She saw that he was holding a pie.

"I filched it from the kitchen window while the cook wasn't looking," he told her. "We'd best away to eat it before there's a hue and cry."

"Not yet," said Lenore grimly, leading Snowfire toward the hay where the bay was already contentedly munching. "We can allow them time for a few bites while you and I fill a sack with hay and one with grain."

They tarried as long as they dared and then rode swiftly away and found a little copse of trees near a small stream and shared the pie, which was kidney and very good, while the two horses ate their hay and grain.

"We can follow this stream a ways down," said Geoffrey, finishing his last bite of pie and licking his fingers appreciatively. "Walking through it will keep dogs from following our trail—in case the landlord takes offense at the loss of a pie and some horse feed."

Lenore got up abruptly. She thought she heard a distant baying.

A little farther on, they left the stream and climbed a low hill where Geoffrey surveyed the countryside.

"Does it look safe to you?" she wondered.

He sighed. "Who can tell these days?"

They walked their horses down to a country lane, but left it when they saw ahead a knot of Cromwell's soldiers and knew they'd be stopped and questioned. They plunged into a beech grove and soon were riding cross-country, and Lenore was quite lost. She hoped Geoffrey knew where he was going.

When they stopped and slept by a small spring, she was dead tired and fell asleep instantly. She did not see her tall cavalier stand smiling down at her.

Running for your life was a good bulwark against grief, Lenore found. Though she mourned for Jamie in the days to come, she found Geoffrey to be an interesting distraction.

She had become more curious about him as they rode. And although she had seen him looking at her sometimes in a way that made her blush and turn her head away, he had not laid a hand on her since that night when he had raped her.

She wondered if it was gratitude because she had not betrayed him at Boscobel, or if he thought she might run away and be caught and alert the countryside to his probable whereabouts. Or perhaps he was a man of his word.

"What do you do for a living?" she asked him once as they lounged beneath a tree, eating apples, seeing through its low branches a manor house with inviting mullioned windows that flashed gold in the sun—one of so many manors they dared not approach, for who knew the political leanings of the dwellers therein?

Geoffrey, about to take a bite out of an apple he had acquired in a raid on another manor house's storage bin, paused in astonishment. "I am a gentleman, Lenore," he said with just a touch of frost in his voice. "With the King, I've been enjoying the hospitality of those who would receive us."

"Beggars," she said bitterly.

"But royal beggars," he said in a blithe voice. "Come, Lenore, why this questioning? Are ye not satisfied with me? Have I not protected you thus far?"

"I see you have no trade and we will starve," she said flatly.

"Ah, that we'll not," he said, and his voice had a steely edge. "Not while this arm can hold a sword or a pistol."

She did not ask him what he meant. It had a comforting sound, and she had been buffeted enough—she was in need of comfort.

"We'd best get on," she said, rising and smoothing down her green dress over her yellow petticoat. "They may have seen us from the manor house when we crossed that open field, and all wayfarers are suspect now."

87

"You've learned fast," he said wryly. But he got to his feet and mounted his patient horse.

For a time they sought shelter in woods and deserted huts, finding food and drink and fresh hay and grain for their horses in "safe" manors which favored the King. This was a dangerous business, in which Geoffrey usually went on ahead to get the lay of the land, for sometimes the manors had changed hands' or were occupied by Cromwell's men. More than once they rode for their lives with musket balls singing after them. At one place they were told that the King had fled into the West Country, but now was safely got away to France, 'twas hoped. Everywhere they heard grisly stories of those who'd been taken, tortured, killed, or sent to barbaric lives of slavery in the Barbados.

On their wanderings, she learned Geoffrey's moods. Sometimes he was pensive, studying her with a wistful eye and sighing, as if he had some great decision to make. At other times, lighthearted ("Come along, Lenore, for there's a fair at yonder market town and none to know who we are—we can slip into the town and mix and mingle for an hour or two with the rest!")

At the fairs Geoffrey would look around him keenly and sometimes desert her for long intervals. He came back with money or food—once with a cloak. She did not ask him how he came by these things, but she was sure he engaged in dicing—a dangerous game for him, for he had little coin other than that he occasionally was able to borrow from sympathetic supporters of King Charles at "safe" houses, and such supporters were usually hard-pressed themselves.

But the fairs were few, the hardships ever present. Although they took the name of Daunt to cloak their real identities and let everyone believe them a married couple on the way to visit far-off relatives, there was always the danger of being discovered and transported to Barbados—or worse. For Lenore was haunted by the sight of crossroads gibbets with dangling bodies which now decorated the countryside as grim reminders of the cost of trying to overthrow a revolutionary regime.

They avoided the crossroads, for these were usually guarded by soldiery, but sometimes from a distance Lenore could see that the ancient stone markers which had guarded England's crossroads since time immemorial had been vandalized by Cromwell's troops. Noses were missing from the ancient stone faces, ears, and locks of curling stone hair. The face of England was changing beneath the Roundhead boots . . . as her life was changing. Sometimes it made her want to cry.

They had been riding aimlessly, changing direction to whatever seemed at the moment safest, but had gradually drifted south into Dorset, as they tried to avoid the roving troops who seemed to be everywhere.

"Faith, we've nearly been pushed into the sea," growled Geoffrey, frowning as they passed the ruins of twelfth-century Corfe Castle. He nodded toward the ruins. "Destroyed by Cromwell's army five years ago. Another mark against our great Lord Protector."

Lenore nodded in silent understanding. She knew what Geoffrey meant. Cromwell's Ironsides were pulverizing history under the hooves of their horses.

"Faith, I could use a drink," he muttered.

She knew a sudden sympathy for him, this man she had tried so hard to despise. For it was he who bore the heavy responsibility for their safety, he who had put his broad back between her and the flying balls from the Roundhead musketry. If he was edgy, she guessed the cause: he wanted her.

Though to her surprise, after that first night, Geoffrey had respected her grief. She had watched him suspiciously as the days went by, half expecting him to seize her unaware or from behind and take her by force. But he did not take advantage—not even when he came upon her unexpectedly when she was bathing in a stream near which they had pitched camp and she rose dripping and naked from her bath and almost blundered into him along the bank. His eyes had lit with a certain roguish delight, but he had turned away abruptly while Lenore dressed herself with trembling fingers. Nor had he spoken

89

of it when she appeared, red and embarrassed, but fully gowned.

It was a hard life, like that of the running deer in the forest, but it had its compensations. Sometimes on crystal clear mornings they feasted on a fat fish from the rivers, or a hare Geoffrey brought down. They lounged in shady groves at midday and ate and talked. Once, by a small fire hastily made in the shelter of a cliff, she sang village songs in a low voice while Geoffrey lay on his back and looked at the stars. Geoffrey told her of London, of Paris and life in the royal court. She marveled to hear him, and it made her see a great world outside, of which she had only dreamed. He made it seem near and close and reachable as she listened lazily to the sound of his deep rich voice beside her.

That Geoffrey wanted her she was well aware. It gleamed in his gray eyes as the days progressed, in the lingering touch of his hand when he happened to brush her. She was all too tinglingly aware of her tall cavalier. Less and less she was stabbed by thoughts of Jamie, reckless Jamie who had left his people for another country—and then ridden out to die for his own in the end. Before that dark wolfish face with its saturnine smile, the memory of Jamie faded day by day. And gradually Geoffrey alone occupied her thoughts.

What happened was glorious . . . and inevitable.

CHAPTER 5

From Corfe they rode west into Devonshire, skirting Lyme Regis and Sidmouth, for the soldiery were harrying the countryside there, seeking out Royalists to bring them to trial, and the roads were still unsafe for such as they. North of Exeter they crossed the River Exe, by night for added safety. Because Geoffrey grumbled that he was tired of fleeing the Ironsides, they turned southwest into the wilds of Dartmoor, beautiful and desolate. Pursuit in this rugged terrain seemed unlikely, and Lenore, whose grief was fading, although she did not yet realize it, could give herself up to enjoyment of the beauty of the wild countryside.

Hawks and ravens rode the skies above them, and red deer, startled, shied away from their path and disappeared across the coarse grasses into thick clumps of oak and ash. They passed dolmens and cairns, and skirted the edges of the great central swamp where five great rivers including the Dart and the Taw had their source. Since the weather had continued unseasonably warm, they pitched their camps below rugged granite tors that rose high and majestic above the plain. Here above tiny camp-fires they roasted the birds and rabbits Geoffrey brought down by arrow from a bow he had fashioned himself. This was a further precaution against discovery by prowling bands of soldiers who might be attracted by the sound of a shot.

As they rode south, Lenore had become more and more aware of Geoffrey's concentration on her. It made her uneasy, although she refused to show it. He was a strong, virile man and although he had been meticulously polite in his treatment of her since that first night, somehow she sensed that this brittle film of politeness which existed between them was about to snap and elemental feelings would be unleashed.

She noted how he found excuses to brush her—reaching across her to pick up his bow, or a stick of wood for the fire. Always she felt his touch go through her as if her body were a lute and a master musician had idly rested his hand upon the strings. It disturbed her that Geoffrey should have this incredible effect upon her, so much that now she backed away unobtrusively if he came too close. That he was aware of this she was sure, for there was something restive in his flashing glance that made her remember that first night when she had lain beneath him, struggling vainly until she had surrendered herself to splendor.

Came a night of big brilliant low-hanging stars and a big white moon that silvered the moor and turned the treetops into swaying silver lace. Somewhere from the trees a dove cooed sleepily, and an owl's wild call broke the silence. They were camped under great gnarled oaks, had dined on hare and cold stream water. Now their campfire was out; only the tang of its smoke remained.

Geoffrey had risen and was pacing restlessly about. There was something of the caged tiger in him tonight; all day she had noticed it. Now he came, his boots making no sound on the soft turf, and stood just behind her. It made her nervous having him so close, and she leaped up quickly to face him.

Although it was dark in the woods, the moonlight reaching down through the branches illuminated his broad-shouldered form, his aggressive stance as he stood there, feet planted with determination. Moonlight gleamed on his dark waving hair as he bent slightly from his tall height to survey her. That it illuminated her own rapt face, as well, she was not aware.

But Geoffrey was. He saw the amethyst lights flickering in violet eyes shadowed by dark lashes, her golden hair cascading in a shimmering shower around her bare shoulders. That moon of the moors had paled her molten hair to the soft gleam of yellow metal, he thought idly—the precious stuff men fought and died for. He was agonizingly aware how the silvery light highlighted the pearly tops of her round breasts. God, how she stirred him! She with her insolent walk and that flung challenge in her eyes. The throbbing memory of how it had been to hold her in his arms made his loins ache with desire. He had given her his promise that he would not take her against her will, but of late her soft, relaxed gestures, the smiling way she regarded him when she thought he could not see her, had told him that if he took her it would not be against her will, but something she desired as much as he, whatever her soft lips said about it.

He straightened his broad shoulders and took a deep breath. She had reproached him for not respecting her grief. Well, he had respected her grief. Week by week he had waited for that grief to abate, for the sad distant look to leave her face. But now—his blood rose in him, pounded impatiently in his temples as he looked at her—now he would wait no longer, brook no refusal.

"Come here, Lenore," he said lazily.

She smiled warily but did not move.

A moment later his long arm had reached out and hauled her close against his chest. At the very touch of her a thrill went through him and—yes, he thought he felt her tremble, too.

Lenore had known this moment would come. But she had pushed away the thought, nervously. Now a breathless tension possessed her that made her throat dry. The

93

buttons of his coat cut into her soft breasts and she moved restively.

"Why d'ye not obey me?" he asked, his voice casual as he toyed with a lock of her long hair.

This was the moment she'd dreaded, feared—*wanted*. She was a free woman, no longer handfasted, and he a free man. But she would not be made his easily.

"I'll obey no man," she said, tossing her head so that her bright hair shimmered and fell along his arm. "And certainly not you."

He laughed and tilted up her chin to smile down into her reckless face that regarded him steadily, for all her heart was beating with blows that sounded in her ears like drums.

"Faith, I think you mean that," he murmured, and her senses swam as his lips came down on hers in a warm, compelling kiss. Probing, his tongue forced open her lips and quested within. Her breath came faster and she was trembling as he let her go. But still she stood firm and straight as a young sapling, not yielding in his arms.

"A whole month we've been on the run, you and I," he murmured as, lingeringly, he let her go. "Yet still you fight me. Why?"

"I'm not yours," she said unsteadily.

"Think you not?" As abruptly as he had let her go he pounced on her again, and this time Lenore struggled almost in panic to be free of him. But this time there was no escape. He held her in a firm grip and with his free hand tugged at her bodice till it departed her shoulders and glided toward her waist. Her young breasts burst free of their bounds as her chemise ribbon broke, trembling as she twisted away from him.

With an easy gesture he swept her back against him and buried his face in the soft white curve of her neck where it joined her smooth shoulder. Then downward inexorably his lips moved until they took possession of one trembling, snowy breast.

Now he had lifted her skirts, and the moonlight silvered her long thrashing white legs. She made one last desperate

94

effort to be free of him before they fell together, like falling leaves, to the soft forest grass in the shadow of a great gnarled oak.

All the time they had ridden together, she had denied to herself the torrents of emotion that had been unleashed in her that first night Geoffrey had taken her in his arms. She had steadfastly refused to admit that she could feel the very pressure of his gaze, that his lightest touch thrilled her. But now her senses swayed and tumbled as his questing hands moved her to passion, and she felt herself yielding, yielding to the force of his will, the strength of his arm, the power of his desire for her.

Then the floodgates within her burst, and torrents of emotion cascaded and roiled within her. Bright passion drove her recklessly forward, like a leaf tossed upon wild rapids that burst through high, narrow-walled cliffs. His every touch spurred her on, and the world slid away, forgotten, to be replaced by a dream landscape. There was no reality but this—this wild, sweet rapture she had found in his arms as their bodies locked together and strained and tumbled on the soft earth.

She clung to him, every sense alive, flaming with desire, wanting him, needing him, yearning toward him. And she murmured small incoherent things as her body quivered and her back arched and she was borne up in ecstasy to some high bright world beyond the lacy treetops where summer never ended and winter never came.

And when at last she floated down and lay beside him in the dappled moonlight, she knew that her love for Jamie had been young love, a young girl's love born of dreams and hoping, but that what she felt for Geoffrey was something else, a woman's full-blown passion that burned white-hot and constricted her chest and interfered with her breathing and shook her slender body as if a hurricane battered at her and heightened all her sensations to wild and reckless peaks.

As she rested there in languorous silken bliss, something perverse and as old as Eve made her sigh, "You promised you would not take me against my will."

Geoffrey rolled over on one lean arm to consider her gravely in the moonlight. "Tell me," he challenged, "that what I did was against your will."

"No," she murmured honestly, amethyst lights flickering from her shadowed violet eyes. "It was not against my will, Geoffrey."

He laughed softly and dragged light triumphant fingers across the pink tips of her breasts, and when she quivered and her eyelids fluttered shut, he planted a kiss on each trembling nipple and lay back in luxurious contentment alongside her.

Beside him, Lenore shivered—but not from cold.

She knew that tonight she had found her lover, the one man out of all the world designed for her alone.

When at last he rose with a sigh and offered her his hand that she might rise, too, when he bent and very tenderly kissed the top of her head, and wrapped her in his cloak against the dew, and lay on his arm and gazed on her with a kind of wonder, it was more than handfasting, more than her reckless promise to Jamie, more than she had ever felt for any man.

For to Lenore this was no trial-for-a-year marriage that would only be a true marriage if it lasted for a year and a day. She knew now why she'd fought him since the moment they met—it was her own overwhelming attraction for him she'd been fighting. She'd been fighting herself—and he knew it, had known it from the first. And now all her defenses were down and she was his. Utterly. Completely. Forever.

Though the vows were unspoken, they were wed that night on the wild moors. Even though they were fugitives and dared not legalize it in a kirk, to Lenore it was a marriage that would outlast her life.

CHAPTER 6

For two days and nights they lingered in their sheltered camp in Dartmoor, Lenore and her lover. There beneath the frowning high tors with the strong west wind blowing, they sought each other's arms and made love again and again—and Lenore had never felt so free—or so fulfilled.

Geoffrey, whose gray eyes held a kindling light as he watched her performing even the smallest chores about their makeshift camp, asked her where she would like to go next—it was all one to him, and doubtless they'd be harried wherever they went, but winter was coming and they could not winter on the wild moors, for snow would soon be sifting down on the bogs and icy winds howling over the heath.

"A bridal gift?" smiled Lenore. "A new place?"

"A change of scene is all I can give you," said Geoffrey huskily. "Though God willing, one day I'll do much better by you."

"I am content with these scenes," sighed Lenore, look-ing up at the gnarled oak above them, the great tree that had sheltered them on the night of their silken joining, and past it to the high tors rearing into the sky. "But you are right, we cannot winter here. Still—I remember long winter nights in the Cotswolds when frost made a fairy-land of the forest and my mother—oh, I was very little then—told me stories about King Arthur and his knights. Are we not very near the coast? Think you we could visit Tintagel Castle where Arthur was born?"

At this shy request, Geoffrey's brows shot up. "I've been there. 'Tis some six or seven leagues west of Launceton. But would you not rather visit Camelford, which is but two or three leagues distant and which men say is ancient Camelot?"

"No, there might be soldiers there," she said hastily. "But surely not in a ruined castle."

" 'Tis an easy wish to grant," he smiled. "I had thought you might ask me to take you to Paris or to Rome—for which, unfortunately, I have not the passage money."

Lenore, unaccustomedly shy with him this morning, having shared one of the secret longings of her childhood with him, looked down and plucked at the hem of her worn skirt. She would never have asked Geoffrey for something beyond his reach; in time he would know that about her, of course.

Leaving the tors and heath and treacherous bogs of Dartmoor behind them, they set out. Into the wild reaches of Cornwall they plunged, where the southwest coast of England reached out into the sea toward the Scilly Isles and ancient circles of crude stones stabbed stern fingers at the sky. Rugged Cornwall, whose roots were lost in antiquity, where the Phoenicians had sailed their frail craft to take on tin and copper, where men had worked the deep mines since time immemorial. Cornwall, which the Celts had wrested at last from the iron grip of Rome, only to yield it in the time of Athelstane to the Saxon axe.

Moving by easy stages, camping on the way in quiet, out-of-the-way spots, they reached the cliffs at dusk and laid up in a small clump of stunted trees near Tintagel.

Once again they had reached the coast.

The next morning they rode down to the ancient ruins

of Tintagel Castle and sat for a while on the cliffs over-looking the blue sea. Lenore, drifting in a honeymoon of contentment with her lover, smiled dreamily as she considered the ancient stones of Tintagel. This fortress stronghold was the birthplace of Arthur, King of Britain, hero of a hundred legends. Husband to the lovely, faithless Guinevere...

"Beyond is Ireland," said Geoffrey with a careless wave of his hand.

Lenore's violet gaze spun over the gull-swept sky and the distant reaches of the wild seas. *I love him,* she thought, turning a tender, shadowed glance toward the dark, stalwart man who bestrode the bay horse beside her. *This melting feeling I have whenever I look at him is called Love. It has melted the ice around my cold heart, and I will never be cold again....*

She did not say that, of course. She said simply, "It is lovely."

Geoffrey nodded. How could he know that inwardly Lenore was likening herself to lost Guinevere, who had turned from golden safety to a dark, exciting stranger—Lancelot. Geoffrey was her Lancelot and she his Guinevere . . . and she longed to hold him in her arms this very moment and tell him how many ways she loved him.

With luminous eyes, she eased from Snowfire's back. Geoffrey, sensing her soft mood, smiled down at her and dismounted, leading the horses to a sheltered place among the ancient lichened stones, a place where soft grasses blew invitingly in the sea wind. And while their horses cropped the clumpy grass, they made love there, touching each other tenderly and with love in their eyes and in their hearts. Quivering, thrilling, a sob caught in Lenore's throat as her twined arms pulled him fiercely to her and they lay in a trembling tangle of arms and legs on the soft grass. Lenore's body pressed vibrantly against Geoffrey's, and her love was as soaring as Guinevere's—and tinged with guilt, as Guinevere's must have been, for she'd been brought up in the kirk, and this man she'd taken for her own without benefit of clergy. Not even the half-status of handfasting was theirs to claim. . . .

Later, with dreaming eyes, her body thrilling with memories of the time just past, she strolled with Geoffrey along the low stone wall that curved about the rugged, windswept cliffs, looking out to sea where dragon ships once roamed. He matched his long stride to hers; her skirts whipped in the wind and her red-gold hair streamed out behind her. Lenore felt in her secret heart that she could have spent her life at Tintagel and was certain that the magic of the days just passed and her day here on the cliffs of Cornwall would be with her always.

Completely in tune in every way, here in this storied countryside that had seen so much of England's rich history, they forgot they were fugitives and walked hand in hand down to the base of the rocky cliffs. Lenore, fresh from her lover's arms, took long deep breaths of the bracing sea air, smiled down at starfish and sea urchins trapped in the tidepools, touched the algae-eating limpets that clung to the cliff's rock face, and stretched out her arms for very joy.

At dusk they bought a plump pilchard from a smiling, weatherbeaten fisherman and cooked it over a fire in a sheltered place among the rocks. The night wind blew her hair softly and scattered sparks like fireflies as she cooked it. She looked up to see Geoffrey watching her fondly.

"What are your parents like?" she asked, pushing back the locks of hair that fell down around her flushed face.

He laughed shortly. "My father is a stern, tall man with a voice like stones crunching together. 'Tis said I resemble him in nothing but his height. He disowned me for my dissolute ways—for wenching, for gaming, for following the King—all manner of reasons. But the real one's that we disagreed on Cromwell. He's sure Cromwell will hold the country, and he wants to be on the winning side. My older brother's his darling—he's everything I'm not."

"And your mother?" she pursued, frowning. "What does she say?"

"I never knew my mother. She died when I was born, and my father never talks about her. He married again almost immediately, and I was brought up by his new wife. She's childless but she too prefers my brother."

"But surely you have a portrait of your mother? You know what she looked like?"

"No. To be sure, there was one, but my father burned it—along with all else that would remind him of her. It seems they had some falling out shortly before my birth and 'tis thought he pushed her down the stairs and brought on my birth prematurely. Anyway, he drove her out and 'tis said she died then or shortly after. Mayhap she cuckolded him. I'll never know, because his new wife made a clean sweep of the servants."

"Oh, I cannot think she cuckolded him," protested Lenore, shocked.

" 'Tis possible," he shrugged. "My father in a rage once told me 'twas where I'd gotten my bad blood. I've always assumed I resembled her—which could have contributed to his dislike of me."

"You might have asked her people what she was like," said Lenore, feeling sorry for this abused and cast-off wife whose forbidding husband had a voice like gravel.

"She had no living kin. Only a guardian, and he was an old man who died before I was three years old. She was from Northumberland. A dour country. I'd not blame her if she flirted a bit, coming from a bleak place and marrying a man old enough to be her father and as grim as her native hills!"

"You don't hate your father," smiled Lenore, reaching out fondly to touch his coat sleeve. "You only pretend to."

"No, I don't hate him." He sighed. " 'Tis the other way around. Watch out, you'll drop the fish in the fire."

"Never," said Lenore, with a deft gesture holding it just the right height above the flames. " 'Twould have been better if we could have wrapped it and packed it between the hot coals."

"I'd starve if we waited for that. Faith, I'm hungry enough to eat it raw!"

She laughed and deftly served him his portion on a trencher of clean-washed flat rock. "Careful. 'tis hot," she warned.

"Ye've taken well to the roving life," he approved her, taking the food from her with some care, testing it with an experimental finger and drawing it quickly away. "Some women might have died from the hardships of our journey. You," he added with a grin, "seem to thrive on it!"

Lenore leaned back against the rocks, letting her portion cool a bit. "And would you have liked me better," she challenged, "had I been some simpering French lady you met while serving your King?"

He gave her a startled look. "Why d'ye ask that, Lenore?"

She shrugged and tucked her feet up under her. "I but wondered if you preferred breeding to health," she said tartly.

"I prefer you," he said in a grave voice. But he was silent as they ate. Lenore, watching him covertly as she picked at her fish, realized his father's disavowal must have hurt Geoffrey more than he cared to say. She would make it up to him, she promised herself.

After they'd eaten, with the fire burning low there in their sheltered place in the rocks, with the shapes of the grazing horses dark against a starlit sky, they moved like the incoming tide into each other's arms, and Lenore's wild spirit responded fiercely as Geoffrey made love to her.

There was an unleashed violence in him tonight, a rough possessiveness, and she guessed it was brought on by this talk of home. His fierce caresses twanged through her like the quivering strings of a mighty harp, and she fitted her body to his as a scabbard fits a sword and tried to show him in every little way that she was his . . . his forever . . . his alone.

Remembering how he had cursed their pursuit and often wished himself across the Channel with the King, she murmured against his dark hair, "I would go with you anywhere, Geoffrey. To France, if that is your wish."

As if she had flicked a raw place, she thought he winced. Then he seized her in so fierce a grip that words were forgotten as, thoughts aswirl, bodies locked, they spun toward the distant stars in a fiery eternity of passion and fulfillment.

Afterward, she lay dreaming within the magic circle of his arms, her being full and contented. She would have something to tell Geoffrey soon, something that only she knew, but there was no hurry.

I am going to have a child, she thought as she drifted off to sleep. *A son. And I will name him Geoffrey.*

CHAPTER 7

They roved northeast again, gloriously in love, shunning the towns and taking pleasure only in each other's company. They skirted Bridgwater and Taunton and rode on a day of blue skies with the shadows of clouds tinting the landscape, past ancient Glastonbury Abbey.

Here was the famous Glastonbury thorn which bloomed at midnight on Christmas Day. Here was the fabled Isle of Avalon. It pained Lenore to see men busily quarrying stone from the beautiful hulk of the Abbey, where Henry VIII had ordered the last abbot hanged. Entombed somewhere beneath its stone floor, legend said, lay Guinevere with her golden hair—and Arthur, the King she had loved and deceived. And where was Lancelot? A cold feeling invaded Lenore, though the sun was warm. Those golden lovers had seemed so real to her at Tintagel. Now, staring soberly at the lichened stones, she was reminded that even lovers die.

"There is a hawthorn here," she said moodily, "that blooms at midnight on Christmas Day."

She turned away disconsolate when Geoffrey told her the Puritans had cut down the thorn tree during the Civil War.

"It will bloom again," Geoffrey comforted her. "It will send up sprouts. Thorns are hard to kill."

"I've seen enough of ruins," sighed Lenore. "Sometimes it seems to me all England is a ruin—all the tops knocked off the crossroads markers, houses blown up and burned and looted."

"Your mood will improve with a good dinner," predicted Geoffrey cheerfully. "We'll push on. There's a market town up ahead."

They pushed on, but Lenore's mood of depression did not improve. She was beginning to feel sick in the mornings now and sometimes queasy at odd times through the day. Her morning sickness confirmed her belief in what she had not yet told Geoffrey—that she was pregnant.

They pressed east, toward Salisbury. They were more impudent now, less afraid, for England was tiring of its witchhunt for Royalists, and this was evidenced by fewer soldiery on the road, less interest in strangers. At a market town they paused and, because Snowfire was fast, Geoffrey raced him in an impromptu race that was held. He was beaten by a slender lad on a big black gelding.

" 'Tis your weight," Lenore told him wearily. She was wrapped in a cloak they'd traded for stolen apples and her curls were pulled up in a plain linen coif that had been thrown in. "Snowfire's a small horse—too much weight on his back slows him down."

Geoffrey realized the plain truth of what she said, and was very thoughtful for the remainder of the day.

Hearing Salisbury was still occupied by troops, they swung through the countryside in a lazy half-circle, heading toward Wells, which lay at the foot of the Mendip Hills, and where they had heard a fair was to be held.

Lenore had been scarcely able to touch her breakfast, but she began to feel hungry as they approached Wells and buoyed up by anticipation, for fairs had always been gala days for her. Farm lasses waved from lumbering carts and gaily dressed rustics strode along the dusty road or bestrode plodding farm horses as they neared the city. It reminded Lenore pensively of Twainmere, when she had put on her best dress and her notched red-heeled shoes and ridden into nearby towns on a cart to stroll about, flirting, on fair days.

She thought the west facade of Wells's beautiful twelfth-century cathedral, with its over three hundred statues, the most breathtaking sight she had ever seen, and sorrowed that Glastonbury Abbey had not been so preserved. She was jolted to awareness by Geoffrey's murmured, "Can ye really make Snowfire limp, Lenore?"

She gave him a startled look. "Limping" was just one of the many tricks she'd taught Snowfire on long summer days in the Cotswolds. Now, wondering why he should desire it, she gave Snowfire a murmured word as signal, and they ambled through town with Snowfire conspicuously favoring his right forefoot.

Geoffrey was well satisfied. "Let me do the talking," he muttered, taking the lead. Swaggering in the saddle he rode up to a group of men at the fair who were about to race their horses for the prize of a fat goose.

"Which nag d'ye think will win the goose?" he drawled. "For I've a mount can outrun them all."

All eyes turned brightly to this braggart. Most of them were shrewd country eyes, used to squinting at the sun and at sharp cattle dealers, and now they saw in this tall stranger astride an indifferent-looking mount a chance for a wager.

"Wilt bet on it, fine sir?" asked a wiry farmer, patting the flanks of a big roan. "I'd place my money on Hobbs's horse here."

Geoffrey gave the big roan a scathing look. "Faith, is that the best ye've got to run against me?" he drawled insultingly.

At this insult to his horse, the bristling owner, a man called Hobbs, stepped forward. "My roan's beat ever' nag he's come up against!" he cried. "See for yourself, I'm about to race my roan against yon big gray."

"For the goose?" asked Geoffrey in a bored voice.

"Nay, 'tis for a wager," said Hobbs. "I'm betting my

roan beats the gray by four lengths." He was a big, bulky man, and he threw out his chest a bit as he said that.

Geoffrey laughed. "I'll watch the roan run," he said contemptuously. "If he's mettle enough, I'll race him then."

Hobbs glared at him and stomped away. Quickly the course was cleared and the impromptu race begun. The gray's rider was a man of even bigger hulk than Hobbs and the two big horses with their heavy riders thundered down it, but it was immediately plain that the gray was no match for the roan, who left him behind by five lengths.

"Snowfire may not be so fast," worried Lenore.

"Hush," growled Geoffrey in a barely audible voice. "I'm tiring that great beast."

She subsided. Hobbs cantered back and leaped down with a swagger. "Never been beat!" He gave the big roan's flank an affectionate pat.

Geoffrey gave him a supercilious look—such a look as caused Hobbs's beady eyes to redden with wrath in his big heavy-jowled face. "Not good enough," said Geoffrey coolly. "Why, I'd not waste my time riding against you!"

" 'Tis afraid ye'll be beat, ye are!" cried Hobbs in a fury.

Geoffrey's gray eyes gleamed. "Why, the lass with me could beat you," he sneered. "And on the poor half-lame nag she's riding!"

Lenore straightened up, and her violet eyes widened. So *she* was to race Snowfire against that big roan!

"An' do ye have yellow gold that says so?" bellowed the belligerent Hobbs. "Or is it all talk that ye are?"

"Five golden doubloons that she beats you!" said Geoffrey in a cold voice, planking down a small purse that had a heavy ring to it.

Lenore quailed. That small purse contained only copper pennies. If Hobbs should demand a count—!

But Hobbs was too furious for that. Undeterred by the size of the wager, he tore loose a leather-thonged pouch from his waist. "Hold the stakes, Amos!" He thrust the pouch into the hands of a gray-bearded farmer who'd said nothing as yet. "And mount up! Man or maid, my roan can beat 'em!"

Geoffrey thumped his pouch down into Amos's hand with a deep frown that forebade inspection of its contents. Amos took it with a shrug that said it was not his duty to meddle.

By now they had collected a small crowd of interested spectators who elbowed each other for a better look at this rash newcomer who'd challenge the supremacy of Hobbs's big roan.

Lenore was feeling queasy again; she had a need for air.

"If I'm to ride," she muttered, "take charge of my saddlebags, Geoffrey, for they're extra weight." Obligingly Geoffrey tossed them across his own saddle.

She took a deep breath and stared soberly at Hobbs's mount. Snowfire was fast, but the big roan was rangy and had a longer stride. Giddily, she feared for the outcome.

"I'll ride bareback!" she declared ringingly, sliding down from the saddle. Geoffrey cast an uneasy look at Hobbs, who might have protested this change except that Lenore flung him a contemptuous look. "Unless you're afraid a mere *maid* can beat you!" she called derisively.

Stung, Hobbs glared at her. "I'd fetch you over here and paddle your pretty bottom for that barb, mistress—save that I'm going to beat you soundly in the race!" He guffawed and slapped his big thigh.

Geoffrey had her saddle off now and Lenore, with the world reeling slightly about her, peeled off her cloak and tossed it to him. There were appreciative murmurs from the crowd at the sight of her thin tight-fitting green dress which outlined her delicious figure, more murmurs as she tucked it up so her yellow petticoat showed.

She took off her shoes and stuck them in Geoffrey's pocket, and Hobbs yowled, "Wouldn't ye like to take the rest off? We could use a Godiva here!"

There was a chorus of lusty catcalls at that, and Lenore saw a muscle tighten in Geoffrey's hard jaw. She touched his arm for warning and her dark Cavalier gave her back a grim look. He was not enjoying Hobbs's jesting with her, she knew. She but hoped he would keep his temper,

108

for with only pennies in that purse, their circumstance was desperate, she knew.

Her head was clearing a bit and she was reasonably sure she could hold her breakfast down, at least for the span of the race. The course had been cleared now, with women shooing children to the sidelines and people lining up along the stalls to watch.

Lightly she vaulted to the saddle. "Wish me luck," she muttered.

From the crowd nearby came a clear laughing masculine voice. "Here, my lady, use this on him!" And someone tossed her a light whip. Lenore—who would never have used a whip on Snowfire—closed her fingers around the whip and acknowledged this token of good will with a brilliant smile. She could not see the donor, but she had a swift impression of a pair of crystal eyes that glinted at her from a laughing face that sported a golden Vandyke beard.

Seeing her mounted, and already the darling of the crowd, Hobbs paused insolently for a parting shot before bestriding his horse. "Ye'd best hurry, mistress, before those dark clouds overhead loose the rain upon us," he taunted. "I wouldn't want ye to claim 'twas the muddy course that made ye lose!" His loud guffaw was only lightly echoed by the crowd; plainly big Hobbs had made his weight felt around here once too often.

Lenore looked up apprehensively. The wind had risen, and there *was* the damp smell of rain in the air. Snowfire would have less chance on a muddy course against that great beast. Anxiously she studied the sky where thick-packed dark clouds had obscured the sun.

"Mind him not," said Geoffrey sharply, and then leaning close on the pretense of checking her bridle. "If ye lose, don't stop—turn and ride south, I'll join ye," he muttered so that only she could hear.

Lenore caught her breath. So if she lost he meant to run for it, knowing he could not pay his wager! She cast a glance at him. He was tightly surrounded by a pack of farmers and weighted down by her saddle and saddlebags. How could he break free from that crush? If he even tried it—assuming Hobbs and the farmers didn't beat him to death as a welcher—there were plenty of off-duty Roundhead soldiers moving through the crowd who'd be alerted and maybe would ask them for papers. . . .

She felt cold sweat trickle down her back, and the faintness came over her again. With an effort she overcame it, and with an irritable gesture, seeking more air, knocked back her coif, which fell off. She let it go and shook her head to clear it, which caused her red-gold hair to tumble down, looking almost molten against the darkening sky. Men gazed at her beauty longingly, and women studied her enviously and whispered, but Lenore was unaware of it. Her mind was awash with terror, though none of it showed on her lovely, almost haughty, countenance.

If she lost—oh, God, she must not lose!—they'd be in dire trouble.

Trying to conceal the trepidation she felt, she walked Snowfire up beside the big roan, who turned an evil eye toward her and kicked out. Snowfire skipped away with an angry look at his antagonist. Lenore knew the big horse was making him nervous; he was making her nervous, too.

She clenched her jaw and alongside a jeering Hobbs she waited tensely for the starting signal, seeing before her the dusty track and at its end two men holding a ribbon suspended between them that served as finish line. Beside her she could hear Hobbs chuckling; it was an evil sound. Feverishly she tried to remember how Hobbs had ridden against the gray. She had not been paying much attention; she'd been feeling ill, and her mind had been preoccupied with Geoffrey. But it seemed to her Hobbs had veered suddenly to the left down there where the way was narrow and lined with stalls selling live geese and chickens, and that the gray had faltered there. Was there perhaps a rough spot in the course, a rut made by a cart that Hobbs had forced his antagonist toward? The gray's rider had come back looking not only glum but angry; perhaps Hobbs had tricked him as well as outridden him. She squinted her eyes down the course, already darkening as the cloud cover overhead deepened, and cursed herself for not having taken note of it earlier.

The course, the line of stalls, the hawkers, and the crowd all swung around her in a slow circle.

Oh, God, don't let me faint! she thought despairingly. *For then the race will be forfeit and Geoffrey will stay to help me and be trapped!* She closed her eyes and prayed.

With a snap her eyes blinked open. The signal had been given, they were off! She was almost unseated as a nervous Snowfire leaped ahead. For a moment her heart lurched with joy, but then the big roan pounded up beside her and Hobbs turned to laugh in her face.

Down the course they thundered, neck and neck, on a sudden gust of wind that blew leaves and scarves and ribbons into the air. Lenore, her senses swimming, tasted acrid dust as the wind stung her cheeks to scarlet. With her bright hair streaming straight out behind her and her yellow petticoat billowing up so that her white legs flashed, she clung desperately to Snowfire's mane and urged him on.

In their headlong run, she realized suddenly that the big horse beside her was bearing her to the left, dangerously close to the line of stalls where people waved and shouted encouragement as they went by. Her senses quickened. To the left—why to the left?

Abruptly Hobbs's intention became clear to her, and her eyes widened in fright. Midway down the course, where live chickens and geese were being sold, was a deep rut caused by a lumbering cartwheel in some recent rain —and across it, protruding carelessly onto the course like a bar, was a wagon tongue! Hobbs was edging her over, trying to shove her into that, and if Snowfire hit it, his legs would be broken and she'd be flung headfirst into the wooden side of the big fruit wagon that separated the chicken stalls from the geese!

In a moment of bright terror she knew why the gray had faltered and let the big roan pull out so far ahead. The gray's rider had pulled him up at the last minute—as Hobbs intended her to do—or die!

A vision of Snowfire, broken and falling, and herself

pitched through the air to oblivion came to her—and simultaneously another vivid picture, this one of Geoffrey, bound and bleeding and being dragged to a tall gibbet.

"Get over!" she cried fiercely, striking out at Hobbs with her right arm.

Hobbs gave an ugly laugh and drove the big roan horse against her. Snowfire reeled with the impact but righted himself and plunged on. Lenore felt her leg go half numb from its contact with Hobb's bony knee. With a laugh Hobbs veered away to let them recover. He was playing with her! He meant to make her give up so the crowd would make sport of her while he crowed in glee!

In moments they would reach the narrow place with the rut and the heavy wagon tongue protruding like a bar before it. If Hobbs kept his present distance they'd sweep harmlessly by, but she had no hope he'd do that. She knew she was looking death squarely in the face, for he was sure to rush her again. There was no time—the decision was now!

In a desperate flash it came to her that Hobbs was wearing long sharp spurs—the fiercest she had ever seen, though she had not seen him use them and the roan's sides were unmarked.

Her expression hardened. Yes, she could do it! And she would—for Geoffrey's sake!

"Coward!" she cried, leaning over to flick her whip toward that jeering face.

Hobbs, quick as tinder, responded as she'd guessed he would. Jaw jutting out, he rode for her again—on a collision course that would almost certainly send her headlong into that wagon tongue. But her taunt had thrown off his timing and made him turn the roan a little sooner than he'd meant to.

As he came in range, she lifted her whip high in the air and with all her force brought it down into Hobbs's snarling face—and as he flinched back, throwing up an arm to ward off the blow and shifting his weight unsettlingly on the roan's back, she drove her right foot violently against Hobbs's left ankle so that the shining

112

point of that vicious spur struck sharply into the big roan's side.

The roan, on his own account, had just turned his head, showed his white teeth, and bit at Snowfire. At the sudden unexpected assault of the digging spur on his left side, combined with Hobbs's sudden shift of weight and the whip singing over his head, he skidded, reared up on his hind feet with a wild swing to the right, and almost went over on his back in a cloud of dust. Hobbs, cursing, was almost thrown from the saddle.

At the menace of those big teeth, Snowfire, already skittish, and now maddened by this terrifying turn of events, gave a half-human scream and leaped high in the air, clearing the rut and wagon tongue and grazing the big roan's pawing forefeet as he broke to the right, landed almost on his knees, and took off like the wind, his tail waving in the big roan's face.

Lenore, choking on dust and clinging to his back like a burr, turned her head to see that Hobbs had finally got his mount under control and was thundering off after the flying pair.

But Snowfire had had enough of his huge antagonist. He showed the roan a clean pair of heels, running fast as the deer of the forest. Lenore, leaning low over his neck and with tears of pride trembling on her lashes, was hard pressed to keep him from running into the next county. When they broke the red ribbon at the finish line, Snowfire, with his featherweight burden, had beaten his heavy-laden antagonist by four lengths, and the crowd went wild.

The feeling of nausea had left her now. Head high, smiling in triumph, Lenore galloped back down the course toward Geoffrey on a trembling Snowfire, his eyes rolling, his limp forgotten. And all the way people cheered her and waved scarves and applauded.

She had almost reached the place where Geoffrey stood beaming at her when a hoarse baritone voice boomed out, "The maid's not human—no, nor her horse, neither! I saw him limp through town a while ago, and now he runs like the wind!" And another voice chimed in on a high

113

excited note: " 'Tis no maid at all, tis the Angel of Worcester! Don't you remember, Hank? We were bringing up a fresh horse into the battle and we saw her ride by!"

The Angel of Worcester . . . A sigh went through the crowd like the rustle of dry leaves. For by now all knew the story of the flame-haired woman on the white horse who had galloped through the battle into Worcester and disappeared. Abruptly pandemonium broke loose as men jumped forward to get a better look at Lenore, who flinched back, flinging Geoffrey a wild look.

"Ride!" shouted Geoffrey, sweeping up the stakes from Amos's astonished hand and landing astride his bay horse almost in one smooth gesture. Striking out with the heavy saddle in his right arm, swinging the saddlebags with his left, he lay about him, scattering those who would have jumped forward to seize his bridle.

Into the path he cleared plunged Lenore. Snowfire followed Geoffrey's mount nose to flying tail as the crowd gave way in panic before this pair of demons, men leaping hastily to right and left to avoid being knocked down and trodden. A bright flash of lightning zigged through the sky and the crash of thunder added to the panic and covered the pounding of their horses' hooves as they plunged into a side street before pursuit could be mounted.

Down twisting cobbled streets and narrow alleys—deserted now, for everyone was at the fair—they tore, pummelled by big drops of rain that had begun to splash down. But in the distance over the steady patter of rain Lenore could now hear the thunder of pursuit, and she winced. Snowfire was not equal to a long-distance run. He'd come all the way into Wells carrying her, and now he'd run a hard race—he'd never make it!

She careened around a corner with the wind whipping her hair and saw Geoffrey beckon from up ahead. Lenore reined in and watched doubtfully as he leaped off the bay, ran up the stone steps of a church, and swung open the big peaked wooden doors. She frowned and hesitated.

"Come on," he called desperately. " 'Tis our only

chance!" He was leading the bay horse inside as he spoke.

Lenore dismounted, tossed back her long damp hair, and led Snowfire up the slippery stone steps and down the center aisle of the empty church. His hooves rang on the stone flooring and echoed eerily from the vaulted ceiling lost in dimness above them. Beside her the bay horse gave a lonesome whinny as Geoffrey closed the doors on the pouring rain outside and joined her, a tall shape in the dimness.

"It does not seem right," she murmured, looking up with a little shiver at the great vaulted ceiling and the stained glass windows, dark and murky against the rain.

"Sanctuary in churches," Geoffrey said flatly. "An ancient Saxon right. I claim it."

"But to bring horses into a church!"

"Did ye not know that horses were stabled in Worcester Cathedral during the Civil War, Lenore? They—" Geoffrey's voice cut off abruptly as outside the sound of hooves thundered by, combining with the pelting rain to make a tumultuous sound like demons trying to get in.

"I suppose—under the circumstances . . ." she said haltingly.

Geoffrey's eyes gleamed in the darkness. "They've gone on by," he said with relief. "It did not occur to them to look for us here. You see what I mean by sanctuary?"

She might have appreciated his humor more had not a sudden bolt of jagged blue lightning chosen that moment to strike the church steeple. Lenore screeched and clutched Geoffrey as the stained glass windows were lit with a sudden fearful brilliance, illuminating the church's interior as if it were day. Snowfire and the bay both reared up in terror as a roll of thunder shook the building and stones from the broken steeple bounded in a thunderous avalanche over the roof and down to the cobbles below. Geoffrey seized the maddened bay's bridle, nearly receiving a kick in the head from a pawing forefoot, and Lenore, who had only managed to catch her fingers in Snowfire's mane, was dragged halfway down the church aisle before he came to a trembling halt.

She patted and soothed him while Geoffrey brought up the bay, eyes rolling and ready to rear again. Lenore winced herself as the vivid lightning, striking again through red stained glass, streaked a slash of red down Snowfire's snowy head. For a moment it looked like blood gushing from a wound. She hugged Snowfire in a sudden rush of worry for the gallant horse—none of this was his fault.

"We'd best leave," muttered Geoffrey. "People may come to investigate the damage to the church."

They walked their skittish horses through the church and out a peaked side door into drenching rain. The thought came fleetingly to Lenore that the muddy hoof-prints their horses had left on the church aisle would further feed the legend of the Angel of Worcester—the gullible would be saying she'd ridden into church and disappeared again! And this time doubtless in the company of a demon! She sighed and bent her head to avoid a wind-whipped tree branch, gasped as it poured a stream of water down her neck, and followed Geoffrey, sloshing through the rain. She was soaked through before they reached the tent-like shelter of some big oaks that lined the way to the vicarage stable. As they entered, another bolt of lightning struck nearby and lit up the interior brilliantly. It was deserted, save for an old bony gray horse —probably the vicar's mount—who looked at them with momentary curiosity, whinnied once, and returned placidly to munching his oats. Lenore tossed back her wet hair and looked about her with relief. For the moment they were alone in a cozy world with the rain beating outside and only a couple of dripping roof leaks within.

"Looks safe enough for a while," said Geoffrey grimly. "I doubt me those who come to the church will notice our tracks—they'll be too occupied with viewing the steeple, what's left of it."

Guided by the lightning flashes, Lenore led the horses to the water trough, calling to Geoffrey to pitchfork down some hay. He climbed the wooden ladder to the hayloft and dropped the hay down through a big square hole cut in the flooring for the purpose.

"That's enough," she said. " 'Twill be all they can eat."

"Oh, just a bit more for our backsides to lie on," he protested. "For we'd best stay downstairs with our mounts, in case we have to leave suddenly!"

"All right, but get some grain from that bin while I curry Snowfire—he's very hot and steamy from running and I don't want him to catch cold." She hugged the white horse, burying her face in his heavy mane, and her voice was husky. " 'Twas Snowfire brought us through."

Geoffrey's sigh was inaudible against the pounding rain, but he got the grain, and as Snowfire ate, Lenore worked with brush and curry comb until his white hide glistened. Geoffrey, meanwhile, curried the bay. Snowfire gave a low whinny and nuzzled her as she finished.

"What happened midway down the course, Lenore?" Geoffrey tossed aside the curry comb. "I couldn't see, for a fellow waving a big hat got in my way, and when I brushed the hat aside, I could see Hobbs was nearly up-ended and Snowfire was leaping in front of him."

"Hobbs tried to run us head-on into a wagon tongue that stuck out over a rut," explained Lenore tersely. "He tried to crowd us into it."

"My God!" Geoffrey stared at her aghast. "Lenore." He bent down from his great height and took her by the shoulders. His voice was rich and deep. "I want you to know I never thought there was any danger in your ride—just that you'd be lighter and more apt to win."

"I know." Lenore leaned against that broad chest and sighed. Tense and keyed up from recent happenings, she had only just begun to realize how weary she was. "It doesn't matter, Geoffrey. It's over now and we have money again."

"I'll not risk you again," he promised, his voice deep timbred as he held her to him.

Lenore, thinking this no time for lovemaking when the vicar's servants might at any time come out to the stable to see how the gray horse fared, twisted away from him. "Where do we spend the night?"

"Far from here, I hope," he said, letting her go reluctantly. "We'll slip out of the city at dusk with the homeward-bound crowd."

"We cannot leave in these clothes," pointed out Lenore. "We'd be recognized at once."

"Aye." Geoffrey waved his arm as a flash of lightning illuminated some old clothes hanging on a nail. They looked ragged enough to drape over scarecrows and perhaps that was what they were intended for. "Those should disguise us."

Lenore shuddered. "Oh, I couldn't wear those—they're filthy!"

"Better filthy than dead," said Geoffrey grimly. "The grime we can wash away once we're clear of Wells, but death has a nasty permanence."

Grimacing, she took the big ragged shawl he handed her, held it with two fingers and said, "Ugh!"

"Put it on," advised Geoffrey with callous cheerfulness. "If I can put on this ragged red cloth cloak, you can wear that!"

She held the shawl at arm's length. "But won't everyone recognize Snowfire anyway?" she protested. "He's so—so *striking*."

"Easily remedied," said Geoffrey with a heartless grin. "I'll splash some mud on his legs as we leave and we'll drape those old horse blankets over both horses." He indicated a pile in the corner. "Meantime, I saw the remains of a fire someone had built under the lean-to shed out there—doubtless they scorched the roof, but 'twill serve our purpose." He went out and returned with a handful of ashes. Over Lenore's anguished protests, he proceeded to turn Snowfire's snowy head and mane into a mottled gray.

"In the dark, no one will be able to tell the difference. He's a gray horse now," he declared cheerfully.

Lenore thought Snowfire looked indignant. "What about the bay?" she asked doubtfully.

Geoffrey shrugged. "Wells is full of bay horses. He'll attract no notice. But bind up your long hair, Lenore. *That* no one could miss!"

Swiftly she twisted her damp hair into a thick coil around her head and draped the big shawl over her head. "You might pretend to be drunk," she suggested, "and sprawled over your horse. That way they won't see your face."

"Good," he said. "And *you* can sport a black eye that I gave you while drunk!" He rubbed the ashes around her right eye until it looked very bruised, stood back critically to consider her in a lightning flash. "We're indeed an indifferent-looking pair," he said with satisfaction. "We don't look like people anyone would wish to get close to—let alone touch!" He laughed.

"I don't find it very funny," said Lenore, thinking how she had just curried Snowfire and now he looked terrible. "I would we could get it over with—think you it is dark enough to leave?"

" 'Tis dark enough," he said quietly. "For the rain has quenched the light. And if we're careful to attract no attention, we can be a pair of farmers returning home from the fair. Few will notice us in the rain."

Grimly Lenore pulled the rough wool shawl around her. Already it was making her skin itch. "Then let's get on with it."

As they went through the stable doors, the rain stopped as the thunderstorm took itself elsewhere. Lenore did not know whether that was an omen for good or ill.

CHAPTER 8

In the gathering darkness the pair slipped into a narrow alley behind the stable and managed to avoid the church. From thence they blundered their way toward the main thoroughfare, finding easy passage through the muddy streets until they reached the press of home-returning fair-goers plodding soddenly toward the city gate. Unobtrusively they joined this flow of humanity, Geoffrey lolling as though drunk across the bay's back. The rain had given the air a bitter chill, and Lenore had reason to give thanks for the extra warmth provided by the big tattered shawl which was draped over her head and enveloped her to the ankles. She looked down at Snowfire, glad to see him covered by a big horse blanket, but looking dirty and woebegone to her eyes, so used to seeing him white and glistening.

Around them people sloshed along, talking companionably about the fair, and just ahead a farm family plodded along in a cart. But Lenore kept her head down, her great shawl clutched about her, hoping to escape notice in the procession.

If only they would move faster! But the pace slowed and slowed, finally coming almost to a halt. Past the high farm cart she saw that up ahead loomed the city gate. Beyond that gap in the walls lay the dark road—and freedom.

But there was a bar to freedom. A lantern swung at the city gate, and Lenore, her hands clammy, saw that people were filing through and a young trooper, backed up by several more who lounged in the background, was questioning each one.

"Can you see what's holding us up, Mister Boone?" queried an old woman behind Lenore.

"I think they do be looking for the Angel of Worcester, Mistress Lennox—her that won the race today," a tall-hatted farmer responded patiently.

Lenore stiffened. This was no casual check for Royalists, then. Those troopers were looking for *them!*

Behind her the old woman cackled. "If ye mean that young woman who rode the white horse, she looked to be no angel to me!"

"Ye'd best keep your voice down, Mistress Lennox," warned the farmer nervously. "For tempers are tricky today, what with the cloudburst and all, and they may take it into their minds to punish scoffers by questioning everyone at length. Then we'll be here till cockcrow!"

Beneath the scratchy woolen shawl Lenore felt perspiration trickle down her neck. Questions . . . a vision of the rack loomed up in her mind, and herself screaming in agony as she was broken upon it. The picture faded to a bloody red as behind her a younger voice interposed eagerly, "I did not see the Angel, Mistress Lennox. How was she in appearance?"

"About the size of that woman ahead," said Mistress Lennox, and Lenore felt as if an arrow had just entered her back. Mistress Lennox was indicating *her.*

"I was told she was very fair," muttered the farmer, "as an angel should be. But very tall and stately. 'Twas

121

said her hair was sun-gold and she wore a green dress."

Lenore thanked God for the darkness which obscured the narrow green line of her skirt which showed beneath her great shawl. Nervously she studied the lantern ahead. That young trooper was bending and staring into people's faces as he talked to them, shining the light in their faces. She prayed he would not push back her shawl the better to see her face, for if the lantern light were to fall on her golden hair . . . !

Behind her Geoffrey lolled in apparent helplessness, mumbling a snatch of bawdy song off key, as he lay along the neck of the bay horse. His long legs stuck out from the shapeless tattered red cloak he had thrown over his own, and the hat which rode so perilously on his drooping head looked as if it had been trampled by an army. But Lenore sensed the tension rising in him as just ahead the farm cart was stopped for questioning. The farmer gave crisp answers; his wife beside him was sleepy and muttered her answers. Lenore saw the guard flash the lantern in her face and play it over the three sleeping children piled together on the hay in the back amongst some bags and kegs of vegetables.

"Pass," said the trooper at last, and Lenore, walking Snowfire forward under the stone gateway with Geoffrey and the bay close behind, froze as Mistress Lennox's strident voice rang out clearly.

"The Angel of Worcester," she insisted stubbornly, "was not tall and stately. I tell you she was the size of that young woman riding up ahead."

The young trooper who held the lantern could not have helped hearing. And now he was alerted to the fact that Lenore was the right size. Should he swing that lantern in close and peer beneath the shawl and sight her red-gold hair . . . !

Lenore flung caution to the winds. She came down off her horse like a spitting wildcat. "Call me no more names this night, John Daw!" she shouted in Geoffrey's direction. "For I'll take no more from you, drunken lout that you are!" Holding her shawl tight around her throat with

122

her left hand, she whirled and seized the lantern from the astonished trooper's hand.

"See that?" she yowled in the thickest West Country accent she could muster. She thrust her face almost into his, holding the lantern so high that the light fell more over the top of her head than her face. "See what my husband did to me this day?" she bawled. "Hit me, he did! And just because I said he'd had too much ale and emptied out his tankard on the tavern floor! Took offense and hit me, he did!"

From behind her came Geoffrey's voice, sounding thick as it interrupted his mumbled drinking song. "To be married to a shrew . . . !" he hiccupped. " 'Tis only on fair days I get me drunk, 'tis only on fair days. . . ." His voice petered out in maudlin fashion and he slumped forward in apparent insensibility on the bay's neck, one long arm dangling.

Lenore gave an angry shriek. " 'Tis a lie!"

"Your name, mistress," said the startled trooper sternly, stepping back a pace and recovering his lantern. His vexed frown showed that domestic quarrels were no concern of his.

Lenore advanced on him threateningly. "Prudence Daw's my name. And this big oaf, sprawled drunk and useless across yon horse, is my husband John. We live half a league down that way"—she stabbed with her finger—"and down the narrow lane as far as you can throw a butter churn." Her voice rose. "I can see you're taking up for John!" She shook her finger in the young man's face so close he jumped back for fear of his eyes. "I can tell—you *look* like you're sorry for him! Why are all the men so sorry for my husband? *I'm* the one people should be sorry for, for 'tis me who had the bad sense to marry him, lackaday!"

The trooper, who was young and confused, flushed under this attack. "Mistress, I said nothing to—"

"Nay, but you *looked* it!" squalled Lenore. "You men always stick together! Like as not *your* wife is at home right now slaving over washtubs and stewpots with half

123

a dozen little ones clinging to her skirts and another on the way—"

"I've no wife at all!" gasped the trooper. Behind him the other troopers were chuckling.

"What!" screamed Lenore. "All the spinsters wasting away in this parish and you, a great hulking fellow, are out wenching in the hay instead of getting you honest wed! For shame! Shame, I say! Shame! You—"

But the young trooper had had enough of Mistress Prudence Daw. "Pass!" he roared, giving her a rough push that sent her reeling away from him. He gave Geoffrey's horse a hasty slap calculated to move it on faster.

Lest he remember he hadn't looked into Geoffrey's face and mend the oversight, Lenore let Snowfire go on ahead a few steps, then turned as Geoffrey came through and darted back to shake her finger in the trooper's face once more. "Your day will come!" she cried menacingly. "Bachelor that you are!" She almost spat the words. "Some woman will straighten you out!"

Amid howls of laughter from his fellow guards, who were vastly enjoying their comrade's discomfiture, the trooper shouted, "Pass, woman! Get you gone!" Lenore stomped off, muttering, climbed aboard Snowfire and rode away, leading Geoffrey's bay.

She hadn't realized how frightened she was until she hurried their pace a bit, passing the farm cart at a wide place in the dirt road. Then she realized how icy the wind seemed against her face and knew it was beating against drops of perspiration. She had felt trapped there at the city wall, and her heart had known the terrors of a winged thing beating helplessly against a cage.

Now she turned to look at Geoffrey and saw that he was regarding her from his prone position with one eye open—and that eye glimmering with wicked amusement; his shoulders were shaking with mirth. "In truth, you've missed your vocation!" he gasped. "You should have been an actress—you near frighted that young trooper out of his wits."

"Did I?" asked Lenore in a shaky voice. She tried to laugh, but found she was shivering.

Suddenly from the now receding city gates came a chorus of shouts from which the words "After them!" reached Lenore with a sickening jolt. They'd made it through, but they'd aroused suspicions—probably that old woman who'd been behind them in the crowd had said something.

At the commotion, Geoffrey straightened up like a bent sapling suddenly released. "Ride!" he called to Lenore grimly and darted past her, leading a weaving path around some startled farmers, then darting suddenly off the road into the shelter of some trees, losing his hat to a low branch.

Behind them Lenore could hear a discordant clamor as some farmers joined in the pursuit. Voices called excitedly; there was a muffled thunder of hooves in the mud, and a couple of wild musket shots. She thanked God for the darkness which gave them cover, although it was dangerous plunging through the dark forest.

Her shawl whipped back, twigs tore at her hair, a branch stung her face as she raced on. Snowfire's breath and her own steamed in the frosty air, and the cold wind tore at her throat. There was a nightmarish quality to this flight through trees that loomed up and zoomed by to right or left. They had been so light-hearted riding into Wells. Now once again they were running for their lives, with naught before them if they were caught but torture and death—or transportation and a life of slavery. Lenore bent her head low over Snowfire's flying mane and urged him on. Gamely he responded, and Lenore comforted herself that at least the horses had had food and a bit of rest in Wells.

Always before they'd eluded pursuit fairly easily, but this time whenever they thought themselves free of their pursuers there was an outcry from some new direction. All night they fled before their pursuers, and Lenore was reeling with fatigue when just before dawn broke Geoffrey led her cautiously into a clump of trees, parted some brush, and showed her a great dark gaping hole in the hillside.

"I know this place from my boyhood," he said, dismounting, "when I visited a great-aunt who lived near here. 'Twas a secret place where I hid when I did not wish to be found."

"Your aunt, is she still alive?" asked Lenore, dismounting and studying the entrance. She had always been frightened by caves and had no desire to enter this one.

"Long since dead, her property sold," he said. He pawed in their saddlebags. "We'll need candles, and I dare not strike flint until I am well inside lest the light be seen by the wrong eyes. Do not follow me, Lenore, until you see a light within."

Shivering, Lenore waited until she saw a wavering light from deep within the cavern. Then, leading the two horses, their hooves ringing on the cavern's stone floor, she headed toward the light, catching up with him and stumbling along as he led them deeper and deeper down a twisting path between huge boulders that opened up suddenly into a great echoing chamber, its ceiling lost somewhere in gloom above them, but filled with eerie, long-reaching stalactites and stalagmites. By the wavering candlelight they seemed to move and glitter, and from somewhere came the drip-drip-drip of water trickling, the source that had created these majestic stone icicles.

Lenore slumped wearily down on a stone hummock and studied the cavern. Perhaps, she thought wearily, her tired thoughts becoming fanciful, this was Merlin's crystal cave. They had reached the end of their strength, the end of their luck. Perhaps Cromwell's troops would catch them now and hang them out of hand; perhaps this was the place where lovers died.

Geoffrey found a small stone grotto just off this spacious vaulted room and called to her. She staggered up and entered it through a narrow way composed of two great rising stone cones, and so hidden that it was almost like a low box just offstage in a theatre.

"We'll be quite snug here," he said, his voice for once showing strain, and even through her own numbing fatigue she realized how tired he was and her heart went out to him. "Even should they search the cavern they'd be unlikely to find us for we could crouch down behind the stones and the horses could be well hidden in the short passage behind that screen of rocks just there." He indicated with a nod, carefully setting down the candle in a little depression in the floor.

Lenore studied the stubby candle in fear. "We have only two candles," she murmured. "Suppose—suppose they go out, Geoffrey? Think you we can find our way out again through this maze?"

"Find our way out we certainly will," he told her energetically. " 'Tis long since I've been here, but I remember these first passages well enough. And to make sure you don't catch your death in those wet clothes, I'm off to find us some firewood to build a fire, for 'tis cursed cold in this place."

Lenore, whose teeth were chattering, said, "I'll go with you." She had sunk down on the cold stones, but now, afraid to be left alone in this great echoing place, she staggered again to her feet.

Geoffrey hesitated, but seeing the beseeching look in her eyes, he relented. "I'll tether the horses to this stone post so they'll not wander off and fall through any holes in the flooring. We'll bring back firewood." He took off his cloak and wrapped it around Lenore. "Ye look cold," he said.

She did not deny it.

Quickly they retraced their steps, and Geoffrey wedged the candle in some broken rocks so that only the weakest of light lit them to the entrance. Outside the world seemed almost unnaturally quiet and a handful of frosty stars, looking clean-washed by the rain, beamed down.

"Perhaps I should look for a spring," Lenore suggested. "We've a bit of food with us, but we'll need water to wash it down."

"Sit in the entrance and wait for me," said Geoffrey quietly. "Remember, I know this cavern. A short way behind the great room is an underground stream. We will not lack for water, nor will the horses." He was off, cat-like, into the dark, and Lenore, bone tired, sank down and rested her head on her arms. She was almost asleep, though half freezing, when the sound of a twig breaking beneath his booted foot announced Geoffrey's return. He was carrying a huge armload of broken branches and Lenore stood up, wavering on her feet.

"I'll help you with that," she offered. She reached out to help him with his load and suddenly the stars whirled around in a wild circle and retreated into blackness.

Lenore had fainted.

She came to in the grotto, with a crackling fire beside her and Geoffrey kneading her hands and feet, trying to warm them. The firelight played across his dark hawklike face, gave rich highlights to his gleaming dark hair, and lit the concern in his gray eyes.

"Are you all right?" he asked sharply.

"Yes." She stirred, realizing he had wrapped her in his coat as well as his cloak, and was but thinly clad in the pervading chill of the cavern. "You must take back your cloak, Geoffrey." She sat up dizzily.

"No." He pushed her back, eyeing her keenly. "This fainting of yours . . . have you not something to tell me?"

She hesitated, blushing. "You have guessed?"

"Aye. Stupid of me it was not to realize it before, since you've been pale and wan so many mornings. When will the baby come?"

"I—I don't know. Early in June, I think."

He studied her, the fire making golden lights dance in his gray eyes. "The first night I took you?"

"I believe so," she said, hurried.

His voice softened and he reached out to caress her hair with a gentle hand, smooth it back from her flushed face. "I'd not have let you ride today had I known, for it could have brought on your time too soon. Lenore"— he pressed his face into her hair and his voice was muffled, hoarse with emotion—"I am grateful."

Moved, she clung to him and tears swam in her eyes and almost but not quite spilled over her long lashes. And to think she had been half afraid to tell him!

He slid under the cloak with her, his arms wrapping about her warmly. Lenore moved against him, loving the feel of his powerful body.

That night he took her with a tenderness that made her feel more loved than all the wild nights they had known together.

This is how it will be, she thought blissfully, rubbing her cheek against his. *When we are married, this is how it will be.*

When she woke, the fire was out and the darkness about them was absolute. She knew moments of terror while Geoffrey, cursing, worked with his flint to light the only bit of candle they had left. Stiff with cold, but refreshed from their rest, they made their way to the entrance and found to their surprise that it was already dusk. All day they had slept soundly in the depths of the cavern.

At the entrance there was a sudden rustle of wings behind them and a great wave of screeching bats flew past them from the cavern to darken the sky for a moment.

Lenore stifled a scream and fell against Geoffrey. Had she known those creatures were in there with her . . . !

" 'Tis all right," he comforted, encircling her slender shoulders with a protective arm. "The bats fly out in the evening to feast on the night insects of the fields. By day they sleep in the cavern depths."

"How do you know so much about bats?"

"As a boy I was of an adventurous nature, exploring bogs and holes and thickets—any place that was forbidden. Not only this cavern did I explore, but others. Once I was lost for two whole days in a cavern."

"Two whole days . . ." she whispered, shuddering.

He smiled. "By now I think our pursuers will have tired of looking for us where we are not, and be back to chasing their neighbors' wives and daughters—the ordinary pursuits of normal men!"

He was trying to rally her, and she gave him a wan smile. But when they had wended their way into the starlit valley below and the horses were grazing hungrily on a convenient haycock some farmer had piled up in his field, Lenore looked past her tall Cavalier at a pale new moon and asked, "Where do we go now, Geoffrey? What road is open to us?"

"I have thought on it," he said, "and there seems but one answer: we'll to Oxford. In your condition 'tis the best solution, for I know a woman there and her house should be safe for us."

"A—woman?" asked Lenore faintly.

He smiled at the inference and leaned down to kiss her lightly on the lips. "My old nurse," he said. "She left us long ago to go and live with her son in Oxford. If she's still alive, she'll welcome us."

But not approve of your alliance to me, a woman who bears your child but not yet your name, thought Lenore with a sinking heart. Her anxiety showed on her face.

"Come, come." His smile was reassuring. "You'll like Oxford, save that it's damnably damp and cold."

Their progress through the countryside had changed, for she had not known Geoffrey to use such caution as she now saw him exercise, taking no chances with her at all, leaving her hidden in copses and behind rock outcroppings while he tried for food at out-of-the-way cottages and woodcutters' huts where word of fugitives would be slow to penetrate. Lenore knew this new care of her was due to her pregnancy, and took vast pride in it.

The weather was cold and crisp now, and Lenore, her face cleaned of ashes in a crystal-clear spring, rode swathed in enough old clothing to make a ragbag. But Geoffrey kept her warm and well fed and tried to amuse her as they made their way by a stealthy circuitous route toward Oxford.

Once near a tiny hamlet they walked their horses through a shallow ford and drew up beside a small stone church that made Lenore think pensively on marriage and how her unborn child would need a name.

"What is it?" asked Geoffrey, reining up as he saw her halt and sit her horse, wistfully gazing up at the low steeple with its single bell to peal for weddings and funerals and all the great events of village life.

" 'Tis a church," she said softly, looking up through gnarled oak branches to which red-brown leaves still clung, at the gray stone walls, tracing a path to the wooden doors that must have opened to admit a hundred brides. . . .

From his hawklike face his gray eyes studied her, their expression inscrutable. Suddenly he leaned over and slipped an arm around her waist. "Lenore, I know what you're thinking," he murmured. "And God knows I would marry you this very day, but—I cannot. I already have a wife."

Lenore stiffened. She turned a stunned gaze toward him. "A wife?" she asked in a faint, incredulous voice. "Did you say a *wife?*"

"Aye, a wife," he sighed. "I had not meant to shock you, but—"

"Not meant—!" Bright spots of color stained her cheeks. "Did you think I would take it calmly?" she cried. "When it is your child I carry in my body?"

He winced. "At first it did not seem important to tell you," he admitted, frowning.

"And then it was too late, I suppose?" She studied that dark loved face bitterly.

"Just so." He bent down to kiss the lobe of her ear. It was a gesture meant to soothe her, but Lenore jerked away as if his touch had seared her.

"And this woman?" she demanded in a tight voice. "This *wife* of whom I have been so late to hear—where is she? Why, is she, not I, riding beside you and sharing your lot in caverns and hovels?"

Geoffrey frowned. "You are right to be angry, for I should have told you of her. She is in France. 'Twas an arranged marriage, Lenore. Some friends of mine, knowing my impoverished state, sought to better it—they found me an heiress."

An heiress! Lenore flinched. "And where is your heiress now?"

"I left her with her family when I took ship for Scotland with the King."

A wife . . . in France. Lenore's fingers were clenched white and her head was whirling. She fought to keep her voice under control. "Have you not heard from her?" she asked tightly.

"Not once. She was eager to wed me, was Letiche, for she thought I was possessed of a fortune—and I leaped to the bait, for I thought *she* had one." His laugh was grim. "Furious still is Letiche, I've no doubt! She'd thought to wear ropes of pearls as my wife—and I thought to inherit a duchy, no less!" He sighed. "The French are full of guile."

"So are the English!" choked Lenore. "I'll not stay with you another day!"

She shook off Geoffrey's restraining arm and dug her knee into Snowfire's side. Startled, the white stallion took off as if the devils of hell were after him. Geoffrey yelled after her, but his bay could not catch her racing mount. She rode on blindly, unaware of the biting wind that whipped her face, conscious only of a deep pain stabbing somewhere around her heart. *Married!* Ah, she'd never thought of that. Never. Geoffrey had seemed so . . . so wild and free and unshackled. And desirable.

And—hers.

Leaves brushed her cold, tear-stained face as Snowfire, filled with alarm by Geoffrey's shouts and Lenore's wild weeping, veered from the rutted cart track into the forest, but Lenore did not care where he took her or what happened to her. Geoffrey had given her a deep wound that she would never forget or forgive, and all her bright dreams of wedding vows exchanged, of a flower- and rush-strewn way to the church, were shattering one by one like crystal goblets flung away by careless merrymakers, and the bright shards were her glistening, heartbroken tears.

For her there would be no circlet of myrtle, no jeweled betrothal ring or enameled hoop, for her no bride-ale or leaping over the stile . . . never for her.

Snowfire swung sharply left to avoid an onrushing tree trunk. Lenore, her feet not even in the stirrups, put a hand up to her tear-blinded eyes and a low-hanging branch swept her from the saddle to land in some heavy bushes. She lay there, sobbing.

Moments later Geoffrey thundered up. He was white to the roots of his swinging dark hair. "My God, are you hurt?" he cried, disentangling her from the broken branches of the bushes.

"Let me be," she said in a shaken voice, striking away his helpful hand. She dashed away her tears, looking to see where Snowfire had gone. Only now had he come to a halt in the distance and turned back to look at her questioningly. With a convulsive movement she sat up and tried to untangle her hair, which had come loose from its pins and was tangled with the twigs and leaves.

"You might have thought of the child you bear," he said accusingly. "Before you chose to bolt!"

"So might you!" cried Lenore on a gust of fury. "For it will not have a name!"

He winced. "Lenore," he said. "Listen to me—"

"No, I will not listen to you!" she shouted, jerking her hair free with an effort and giving a cry of pain as some strands of it, wrapped around the twigs, were pulled from her head. "At least *I* did not deceive *you*, Geoffrey! I told you I was handfasted—but you did not tell me you were married!"

"You did not ask me." He was imperturbable again as he reached out and set her firmly on her feet; he kept his grip on her though she struggled angrily to be free, slapping at his hands. "Now listen to me." His voice was hard as steel. "Nothing is changed between us, Lenore. I have a wife in France who'll ne'er set foot in England. I no longer go by the name of Wyndham, but by the name of Daunt. And to the world you are my wife—Mistress Lenore Daunt. When our child is born it will bear that surname—Daunt. And bear it proudly, I hope. Save that I cannot take you to the church, Lenore, I'll be your faithful husband, I swear it. And we can live together as man and wife."

She studied him from tear-bright, disillusioned eyes. "Do you feel nothing for her, this French girl?" she demanded huskily.

"We were married but a week before I left the country. She was hot for my arms until she found I'd no fortune.

Then she turned me out of her bed and berated me like a very termagant. Believe me, I was glad enough to go. Lenore, Lenore, I tell you it will make no difference between us. You'll bear my child and I'll hew to you henceforth."

I should leave him, she told herself bitterly. A man who would lie to me, who would use me thus! But even as the thought crossed her mind she felt herself weakening. The truth was—*she did not want to leave him. She wanted to stay forever by his side.*

She covered her flushed face with her hands. "Why did you not tell me, Geoffrey? Why let me think—?"

"I could not bear to see the look on your face I see there now," he said simply, his dark face fraught with the anguish he felt for this golden angel he loved. "But today when you looked at the church with such yearning, I knew I could keep the truth from you no longer. Can you find it in your heart to forgive me, Lenore?"

Her hands dropped away, and she saw that his sober, hawklike face was near and close, his stern lips only a kiss away. She could feel like a throb in her veins the pressure of his concern for her, of his desire for her—yes, of his love for her. For that was love she read in his worried gray eyes.

His voice deepened. "Humbly I beg your forgiveness, Lenore, for you will always be the wife of my heart."

Something in that rich tone tore painfully through all the barriers she had thrown up against him, broke down all her well-guarded defenses.

"Oh, Geoffrey, it will take getting used to," she said in a blurred voice.

He sighed. "That I know. But at least there is truth between us now. Wait here, I'll bring back your horse."

Lenore stood mechanically pulling twigs from her hair and watched him go. Watched that straight, arrogant back, that swinging stride—the walk of a vigorous man in his prime. A man who had had many women—and who along the way had married one of them. A man she would never cease to love . . .

Her hands clenched convulsively. Nothing was changed,

134

she told herself dully. Nothing was changed. She loved him as much as ever, and he loved her. Only now there was this Frenchwoman, this Letiche, who bore his name. They had lived together for a week in France; suppose Letiche bore him a child? Oh, no, that would not happen, it would be too awful. Lenore turned her head away and let the wind fan her hot wet cheeks.

I love him, she told herself fiercely, even while something inside her wept. *He is mine.* And again, with grim determination: *nothing has changed between us.*

Ironically, next day they chanced on a country wedding procession, their path to the church strewn with rushes. The bride, a fresh-faced village girl with shy eyes and long fair hair, was clad in the traditional russet, with a circlet of corn-ears around her head.

Brooding, Lenore paused to watch and was reminded of Meg's wedding, which had been very merry. A flowery garland had barred the couple's way at the cottage gate, and the bridal pair had had to jump it or pay a forfeit. Tom had cleared it readily, but Meg had jumped over and caught her heel in her russet gown and would have fallen had not Tom leaped forward and caught her in his arms.

Lenore remembered the adoring look in Meg's eyes as Tom Prattle swept her up in triumph and carried her over the threshold of his cottage, how Meg had pledged him everlasting love by dipping a sprig of rosemary in the wine they drank at the end of the ceremony . . . and within a month Tom had been reeling home drunk and knocking over bowls and cream crocks onto the hand-stitched house linen with which Meg had lovingly filled her bride-chest.

Lenore sighed, turned her back on the procession, and galloped after Geoffrey, who had gone on ahead. Perhaps marriage wasn't everything. Perhaps the important thing was to find a man who loved you and stay with him, whether the banns were posted or not.

For a flashing moment she remembered Jamie, who at another village wedding had won the bride's garters and drunk too much bride-ale. Golden, faithless Jamie . . .

135

She cast a sharp look of appraisal at the dark warrior who rode along beside her. Was he any better?

Ah, she had to believe he was . . . she had to, for 'twas his child she carried in her body.

Lifting her chin, she rode on. *Nothing has changed,* she told herself defiantly. *Geoffrey loves me—he will always love me. Nothing has changed.*

Geoffrey turned to her. "In Oxford," he promised, "everything will be better."

Better? Lenore gave him an odd look. Could anything ever be better than the close idyllic relationship they had shared in the lonely forests, the wild moors? They would be enjoying civilized life again, that was true, but—better?

For a moment, like Lot's wife, Lenore looked back, treacherously, at what she had lost. Like yesterday's roses, shedding their petals, memories drifted through her mind, blowing softly, fleetingly, through the doorway of a past on which the door was now closing. Sharply, almost with physical pain, she recalled the splendor of the mornings beneath the high tors when she had waked warm and blissful in Geoffrey's arms with only the wild sky and the soft earth around them, and stretched out her arms to greet the new day and found them filled— with Geoffrey and his love for her. Like flower petals drifting down a stream—lovely but swiftly gone—bright pictures floated by: of herself standing beside Geoffrey with the sea wind whipping her hair on the ruined heights of Tintagel Castle, looking out across the sea toward Ireland, and for a magic moment half believing that he was Lancelot and she his Guinevere. Riding with him beside her through endless virgin forests to little woodland clearings where they warmed themselves by tiny campfires and sought each other's waiting arms—wonderful secret places where they and their love were alone with God.

Would Oxford be better? She hoped so. Fervently she hoped so.

BOOK
II

THE
MISTRESS

PART ONE

THE TOAST OF OXFORD

Oxford, England 1651–1652

CHAPTER 9

Through a drizzling rain they rode north across the Berkshire Downs to Oxford, that ancient Saxon city which had once stood on the frontier between Wessex and Mercia. Here the River Cherwell, flowing south, joined the Thames on its meandering journey eastward toward London and the sea. Southeast lay the beechwoods of the Chiltern Hills and to the northwest rose the Cotswolds, where Lenore had left her young dreams.

Wet and miserable, Lenore hardly saw the vista of Oxford rising ahead of her. Instead she kept her eyes bent on the rutted road where their horses' hooves found uneasy footing on the slippery clay. She did not care that here in the palace of Beaumont, Richard the Lion-Heart had been born, or that Sir Walter Raleigh had been educated here—she had been sick again this morning and now as they slogged through the cold mud, she felt that she would never again be dry or warm.

The rising spires of this alien city gave her unease. Oxford was not a village like Twainmere, she realized with a sudden sense of panic, it was a center of learning and commerce. Physical comforts they might have here, but in other more important ways their lives would change, and with a flash of insight she knew it would not be for the better. Hunted though they had been, in a way these past weeks they had wandered through a dream world, Geoffrey and she. Here in Oxford they would be surrounded by other people, people who would change and shape them; they would no longer be—like Adam and Eve—alone in their private Eden.

More than that plagued her. A feeling of dread, a sense of doom, of something waiting . . . waiting. Oxford had been here all along, but Geoffrey had carefully avoided this refuge. Why?

She gave him a narrow look. What hadn't he told her?

"I see no soldiers," he observed, reining up to survey the road ahead. "The countryside must be tired of hunting down Royalists."

"Yes," said Lenore bitterly. "Soon Cromwell's Ironsides will have killed them all or transported them to the Barbados as slaves!"

He shot her a troubled glance. She had had a bitter tongue ever since she had learned of his French wife. He sighed. After all, who could blame her? "You'll feel better," he assured her, "when you've sat a while by a warm fire and dried your clothes."

Lenore gave him back a scathing glance. "Then don't dawdle here talking about it," she said, sneezing. "Let's on!"

Geoffrey narrowed his eyes for one more keen look up ahead, but the countryside appeared to be peaceful.

They slogged on.

Just before they crossed the Thames, the rain stopped and the sun broke through the clouds, flashing gold upon the city's honey-colored Gothic spires and towers. But when they rode past Christ Church it had started raining again, and the city they entered was wrapped in a depressing gray gloom.

"Charles I held his last Parliament here," Geoffrey

commented as they clip-clopped down High Street. "Here Cromwell beseiged him during the Civil War."

For a moment their eyes met, and she knew they were both wondering if the murdered King's son, whom Geoffrey had followed overseas and finally to defeat and rout at Worcester, would ever reign in England as Charles II.

But safety, more than politics, nagged at her in this old university town.

"Think you we are safe riding in so openly?" she wondered as they negotiated the sodden, rain-emptied streets. "Should we not have waited until dark?"

Geoffrey shrugged. "We've not been stopped—perhaps because the weather is uncommon cold and wet; it may be those who'd harass us are huddled in warm taverns. Though, faith, 'tis no wetter than I remember Oxford to be." He frowned as he noted Lenore was shivering and cut abruptly toward an inn where small-paned windows glimmered from the fire within. He alighted and over her protests swung her off her horse and carried his bedraggled lady over the mud into a warm firelit common room. There he left her, drying her skirts before the fire, and went to make inquiries as to the whereabouts of his old nurse.

Facing the roaring fire in the big stone fireplace, Lenore suddenly felt eyes upon her and turned her head, her face flushed with the heat, to note that a young man had strolled into the empty room and now stood at gaze, feet wide apart, admiring her. She blinked, for his was quite the handsomest face she had ever seen. About Geoffrey's height, though thinner, he had an arrogant bearing, a pale complexion, and a head of thick hair the color of caramel satin. He was foppishly dressed in honey-colored velvets with more Mechlin at his throat than the law allowed, and he was taking in the details of her trim figure with a pair of languorous caramel eyes.

Before this bold inspection, Lenore hastily lowered her skirts and turned her back primly to the fire, regretting that since his entrance she could not lift her wet skirts so that her bottom—chilled and tired from riding—could feel the bracing heat. She sighed and went over and sat down rather stiffly at a table.

A pretty vacant-faced girl flounced in from the kitchen with a blackjack of warm port for Lenore and gave the new entrant a delighted glance.

"Hello, Dorothy," he said to the girl as she passed. "Bring me some ale to warm the liver, for we've had naught but rain these three days past."

The girl Dorothy hastily set down the black leather tankard before Lenore, forgot her, and turned her full attention to the newcomer. "Right away, Master Gilbert," she said in a flustered voice, and Lenore thought, in shrewd amusement: *Dorothy knows our Master Gilbert. Rather too well, if the look she gave him is any indication!*

Master Gilbert gave Dorothy a familiar pat on the rump as she passed him on her way back to the kitchen, and she jumped and giggled and swished her brown linsey-woolsey skirts away from him. Master Gilbert turned his bright inspection back upon Lenore, who looked pointedly away from that slender, handsome face, the skin almost girlishly perfect and showing no sign of the weathering a soldier, for instance, might have. *Too pretty,* she thought contemptuously, but when Dorothy returned and Master Gilbert engaged her in conversation as he drank his ale, Lenore stole another look at him. More maids than Dorothy would find this vision attractive, she admitted. And he must have courage, too, to wear his hair so long and his clothes so fine—although in truth many of the Lord Protector's cohorts—including his own wife, if gossip was to be believed—dressed finely, so Puritan drabness had not reached everywhere in England!

The wine warmed her and after another stint of standing by the fire, her back pointedly toward Gilbert, now working on his second ale, she began to feel quite restored, but worried about what might be keeping Geoffrey. It was a relief when at last the oaken door swung open and Geoffrey strode in, cloak swirling about his lean legs. He cast a keen look about him, and so relieved was Lenore to see him safe returned that she jumped up

—not noticing that the handsome fop nearby had hastily turned his back at the sound of the door creaking open.

"What news?" she asked eagerly.

"Bad news, I'm afraid," he said in a low voice. "I found the house where she'd been living readily enough, but she and her son have been gone these twelve months. 'Tis reported they've joined the Quakers and have crossed the sea to the American Colonies." He was peering intently over her shoulder as he spoke, and his puzzled face suddenly cleared. "Gilbert!" he cried in a strong voice. "Gilbert Marnock!"

Master Gilbert of the caramel hair swung around, and his handsome face mirrored disbelief. He leaped up and came over to clap Geoffrey on the back. "Geoffrey! Lord, I feared it was one of my creditors seeking me! 'Tis a pleasant surprise!"

Geoffrey wrung the proffered hand. "What brings you to Oxford, Gil?"

Gilbert's winsome smile lit his sunny countenance. "My parents knew not what to do with me, so at long last they decided to give me an education!"

Geoffrey threw back his dark head and laughed. "Faith, they took their time about it! For we're the same age! But what of the Lady Millicent? You were to marry her, I thought."

A grimace passed over that handsome face, and a lace-cuffed arm lifted as if to brush away cobwebs. "How like you to remind me! When the Lady Millicent recovered from her long-standing malaise sufficient to wed, her father had already plunged into the King's cause—and as you can imagine, it brought him down. Her fortune's none so fair these days. As for me, though I've fled the betrothal, I've not yet begun my studies here—and may not, for I've no taste for books, as you know."

Lenore watched this scintillating fellow, puzzled. Was he then a fortune-hunter? But Geoffrey turned his broad smile toward her. "Lenore, this is my cousin—Gilbert Marnock."

Instantly Gilbert made a lavish leg to the lady. "So fair a face I have not seen in Oxford, Mistress Lenore," he said gallantly, with a ring of truth to his voice. "Have you come then to make our gray skies sunny?"

"She has come," said Geoffrey dryly, his voice lowering, "as I have—to find a safe hidey-hole until this hue and cry for Royalists dies down."

A slight change in the expression of those languorous caramel eyes told Lenore that Gilbert Marnock had upgraded her from courtesan to aristocrat in his mind. She gave him a dazzling smile.

"We heard you had come over from Holland with the King, Geoffrey—but word reached Marnock Hall that you'd died in Worcester."

" 'Twas an exaggeration," smiled Geoffrey. "As you now perceive."

Gilbert shot a glance toward the kitchen door. "This is no place to talk. Dorothy's a good lass, but after a couple of tankards she'll tell any likely lad all she knows, and add a dollop of imagination to boot! We'd best adjourn to my lodgings—right next door."

Minutes later they had climbed the wooden stairs of the half-timbered Tudor house next door and were entering the most cluttered lodgings Lenore had ever seen. A tumble of handsome clothing and books and tankards and trenchers were strewn everywhere.

"Come ye in!" cried Gilbert hospitably.

Geoffrey removed Lenore's still-damp cloak and pulled off his own soaking one, hanging them on an overcrowded nail in the door. Gilbert tossed piles of his clothes from the room's two chairs into the nearest corner—already heaped high. With a careless velvet arm he cleared a small oak table top and dug from the clutter of a cupboard not only wine but three silver goblets which he polished on his velvet sleeve. Lenore, shivering from the contact with her damp cloak, accepted her goblet gratefully and felt the hot liquid warm her body. Still digging in a heaped-up jumble, Gilbert came up with a box of sweetmeats which he offered to Lenore with a careless, "My mother sends them down to me from Marnock Hall—she thinks me monstrous underfed." And then, seating himself gracefully on the edge of the oak table with one long leg dangling, he took a sip of wine.

" 'Tis good to see you again, Geoffrey," he said in a hearty voice, although his gaze did not leave Lenore's bodice. "A fascinating tale we heard of you—of course, we discounted it."

Geoffrey raised his dark brows quizzically.

"We heard you were not only dead, but risen! 'Twas reported your ghost was seen at the Wells Fair consorting with the Angel of Worcester—that lovely naked lady who rode in like Godiva to aid the King!"

"I was there," murmured Geoffrey, with a humorous look at Lenore.

Lenore's color heightened, and her round breasts rose and fell in indignation. Was she never to be rid of that ridiculous story? It had even reached Oxford!

Geoffrey leaned back in his chair, stretching his long legs in their muddy boots. To Gilbert's curious, "Where've ye actually been, Geoffrey?" he sighed.

"Running," he said, downing his wine and accepting another. "Running the length and breadth of England, Gil. Faith, I'm tired of it! But with the hue and cry dying down a bit we'd hoped to find safe lodgings in Oxford. But I find my old nurse removed to the Colonies. I looked for Ned Bight but was told at his lodgings that he's away and may be gone the night."

"Ned's courting a girl at Marston across the Cherwell. He may be gone for days! At any rate, he's likely to linger until his betrothed's family throws him out."

"So that's the way of it? Think you he will marry her?"

"Like as not. He says he's been thinking of settling down."

Lenore listened in surprise. Geoffrey had *friends* here. It occurred to her to wonder why he had not sought refuge in Oxford before, instead of scurrying about the country.

Geoffrey gave Gilbert a steady look across his wine goblet. "Know you of a safe house here, Gilbert?"

The resplendent Gilbert thought about that, turning

his silver goblet around in his hand. "For the two of you?" He nodded toward Lenore.

Geoffrey inclined his head.

"And this lady is. . . ?" began Gilbert delicately.

"The Angel of Worcester," said Geoffrey dryly. Gilbert turned a startled look at Lenore, but Geoffrey leaned forward, and the look in those steady gray eyes bade him be silent. "She's also my wife," he said in a steely voice. "We're going by the name of Daunt—Geoffrey and Lenore Daunt."

"Yes, of course—your wife, Mistress Daunt," Gilbert agreed hastily.

Lenore felt herself reddening again. That Gilbert knew about Geoffrey's French wife she felt certain from something fleeting in his gaze as he looked at her. "I was fully clothed in Worcester!" she said stiffly. "Wearing this same green dress!"

"Of course," echoed Gilbert, his caramel eyes losing a bit of their languor and glinting at her. He bent to pour her more wine and she saw that at close range they were flecked with gold—disturbing eyes; their tan-gold depths reminded her she was not wed to Geoffrey. "Tom Burgh's rooms are for let," he told Geoffrey. "For Tom's going home to wed an heiress—no more scholastic life for him!"

"Sensible of him," agreed Geoffrey laconically, and Lenore felt another unhappy pang. For Geoffrey had believed Letiche to be an heiress.

Night found them lodged in Tom Burgh's old lodgings off Magpie Lane. Gilbert had declared the house a "safe" one, and indeed Mistress Watts, the landlady, looked every inch a Royalist with her shabby fripperies and bows and curlicues and bedraggled wig. She was a wiry little woman with sharp dark eyes and a fringe of dusty-looking curls above a narrow, hatchet-like face. Though she peered at her new tenants somewhat curiously, she asked no questions, merely accepting the money which Gilbert gave her, stepping in front of Geoffrey with a flourish to do so. Startled at that, Lenore learned from a low-voiced conversation she overheard between the two men that this was part payment on a small sum Gilbert owed Geoffrey from some long-ago game of chance and which he called a "debt of honor."

She mentioned this to Geoffrey that night as she made ready for bed in the small but cozy room, sighing with pleasure at the fire roaring on the hearth which shut out the damp and cold. " 'Tis few gentlemen would remember a debt of honor so long," she observed.

A small cynical smile played around Geoffrey's mouth. "I had long ago written it off, as I'm sure Gil had, but— he had an urge to impress you. 'Tis your lovely face stirred his memory."

Stepping out of her dress, she straightened up in her chemise and gave him an indignant look. "*I* think your cousin is a very fine gentleman!"

"All women think so."

"*And* he was thoughtful enough to give me these sweetmeats!"

There was an odd light in Geoffrey's hard gray eyes. "Gil's also very sound of wind and limb," he murmured. "Have ye not wondered why he was not at Worcester?"

"Perhaps he was detained," she began, and Geoffrey gave her a droll look.

"By his studies? Which he's not yet entered on?" He shrugged. "Ye'd best to bed, Lenore, before yon fire goes out."

A bed . . . a real bed! Lenore gave him a winsome smile and drew aside the heavy woolen curtain that separated the sleeping alcove from the main room. Few luxuries did these barren rooms contain, but that big bed made up for everything. With a sigh, she pulled back the coverlet and heavy quilts and slid luxuriously between the sheets, blissfully curling her bare toes against the wrapped hot brick she had placed inside to warm the cold bedding. How long had it been since she had slept in a real bed? She had almost begun to believe that beds were but a memory, that nights were spent in forest glades, in caverns, tucked into convenient haymows or shivering in deserted sheds.

"This is wonderful," she murmured. "Geoffrey, stop banking the fire and come to bed."

Nothing loath, Geoffrey strode across the uneven flooring and climbed in beside her. She opened her arms to him lazily and curved her body languorously to his. Poor and hunted they might be, not even proper wed and with an uncertain future, but tonight, warm and cozy between fresh clean sheets, Lenore felt as if she'd been carried over a threshold. These rooms at Mistress Watts's off Magpie Lane were her first real home—with Geoffrey, her beloved Cavalier.

CHAPTER 10

Lenore slept late and woke to find Geoffrey gone. Lazily she stretched in the unaccustomed luxury of a bed and studied the room beyond the sleeping alcove by daylight. Last night by the light of a single taper and the red glow of the fire the room had been filled with mysterious shadows, but the hard morning light showed her that it was plain but clean. The leaded casement windows had a satisfying sparkle. The meager rug that graced the floor was faded from Turkey red to a rich pink. The large cupboard would be more than sufficient for their few possessions. And since breakfast would be brought up to her on a tray by Mistress Watts's indifferent servant girl, and they would sup of evenings downstairs with Mistress Watts herself, that sturdy wooden table and assortment of chairs would be quite sufficient for their needs. Through an open door she could see their other smaller room—hardly more than a dressing room and containing only a corner cupboard and a bench. With

151

the woolen curtains drawn across the bed alcove, both rooms could serve to receive guests.

Cheered, she jumped up and dressed, shivering in the cold. Geoffrey must have gone out early and expected her to rise very late, for no fire burned on the hearth. She had finished dressing and was combing out her long red-gold hair when a knock on the door announced her breakfast, and the servant girl, who was Welsh and whose name was Gwynneth, scuttled in with a tray.

The girl gave the cold hearth a scared look, begged Lenore not to tell Mistress Watts she'd "forgot it—lor, she might be dismissed!" and hurried away to bring up a bucket of hot coals and some faggots.

"There's no hurry," said Lenore graciously and wrapped herself in her cloak to enjoy the porridge and clotted cream and apple puree on the tray.

Gwynneth had taken the tray away and the newly made fire was already knocking off the chill when Lenore heard footsteps climbing the wooden stair and ran on light feet to the door. Expecting Geoffrey, she tossed her cloak aside and would have flung the door open when a strange voice in the corridor stayed her hand.

"Your wife?" exclaimed the strange voice. "You mean you've brought Letiche over from France, Geoffrey?"

"Her name is Lenore," was the stern rejoinder. "France is as may be. I've chosen to forget my name is Wyndham. Here I go by the name of Daunt, and I'll thank you to remember it, Ned."

There were some more muttered words but Lenore, her eager hand reaching for the latch, snatched it back and shrank against the wall in humiliation. She was twisting her fingers together and trying to straighten out her confused thoughts when there was a light tap and the door opened to admit Geoffrey and a stranger.

"Lenore, this is my old friend, Ned Bight," said Geoffrey, with a careless wave of his arm. "Mistress Daunt, my wife."

Getting a grip on herself—for they must not know she had overhead—Lenore turned and regarded the new-

152

comer steadily. She saw a carelessly dressed young man of medium height. He stood with an easy grace, and a wealth of brown hair cascaded down onto a worn brown velvet coat. Wilting yellow-starched lace cuffs, muddy boots which wouldn't have gleamed even on a sunny day—yet it was his smile that attracted her, a bright beaming flash that showed friendship and a row of even white teeth.

"Mistress Daunt." Faultlessly, Ned Bight made her a leg. "I know not by what good fortune Geoffrey secured such a bride."

Lenore winced inwardly. How smoothly Ned had carried it off—no hint here that he knew she was but a mistress! She gave him a stiff little smile.

Geoffrey seemed not to notice her reserve. He sat Ned down and engaged him in a long conversation about a number of people Lenore had never heard of. She sat with her back very straight, her hands crossed firmly on her lap, and regarded them with a level gaze. When Ned finally rose to go, he promised to send Lally over as soon as she was recovered from the distemper which was going around—a bad cold.

"And who is Lally?" Lenore asked Geoffrey when Ned had left.

"I haven't met her, but Ned tells me she's the daughter of a captain in the Guards. Her father died of apoplexy when she ran away with a young officer in the regiment. Before they could tie the knot, he got drunk, fell in the river, and drowned. Lally found herself 'ruined' and with nowhere to turn, for none of her relatives would have her. Ned has a kind heart. He took her in."

Lenore looked away. Her voice was remote. "Does Ned plan to marry her?"

"I don't think so. As a matter of fact, I don't think Lally expects him to. She knows about the girl he's wooing in Marston."

So Lally did not expect Ned to marry her. Lenore turned squarely to face Geoffrey. "For three months now we have been driven hither and yon like foxes before

153

the hounds—yet all the time you knew we would be safe in Oxford," she challenged him. "Why did we not come here before?"

He frowned. "No place was safe for us, Lenore—Oxford no more than any other."

Lenore's knuckles clenched white on a chair top and her violet eyes flashed amethyst lights. "I will tell you why," she said in a tight voice. "You did not bring me to Oxford because you had friends here. You were afraid one of them would tell me about your French wife!"

"Lenore." Geoffrey would have taken her arm but she shook him off.

"You did not tell me about her until you decided to come here!" she accused.

"What does it matter?" he demanded in a rough voice. "All will honor you as if you were in truth my wife. Either that or"—his eyes held an evil flicker—"feel the point of my sword!"

Lenore felt stunned by the question. To have all his friends *aware* that she was not his wife—and he asked if that *mattered!* Smouldering, she turned away from him, coldly presenting a proud shoulder and a haughty profile to his gaze.

"We'd best buy a new pair of shoes for you, mistress," he said dryly.

"I don't need new shoes," said Lenore in a muffled voice. It was untrue; her shoe soles had long since succumbed and her once-pretty shoes were stuffed with odd bits of leather and parchment in a vain attempt to keep out the rain.

"We'll to the cobbler's. 'Tis close, so there's no need bringing our horses from Mistress Watts's stable." Geoffrey held out her cloak.

In silence Lenore slipped into it, and in silence accompanied him down the wooden stairs and out onto the cobbles. There they ran into Gilbert Marnock, just approaching the door, his honey-colored velvet cloak complementing his long caramel locks. Gilbert smiled broadly and made a sweeping leg to Lenore. "Mistress Daunt, Geoffrey—I come to see how you fared."

"We fare very well, Gilbert." Geoffrey gave him a cool look. "And we'll fare even better when Mistress Lenore has visited the cobbler and been outfitted with a new pair of shoes."

Gilbert's head inclined gravely, and his lazy gaze wandered over Lenore, seeming to penetrate her cloak, her dress—even her chemise. "A dainty foot," he commented. "'Twill be the cobbler's good fortune to have shod it!"

Something perverse in Lenore made her smile flirtatiously up into that narrow, handsome face and swing her skirt negligently so that more than a little ankle showed. "Dainty or not, 'tis true I've need of shoes." She stepped by Geoffrey and took Gilbert's proffered arm.

Gilbert flashed Geoffrey a triumphant look and together the three of them walked to the cobbler Geoffrey remembered as a good one, though Gilbert strongly recommended another, saying Ned's doxie had recently purchased a handsome pair of imported chopines there. At this careless reference to Lally, Geoffrey frowned, but Lenore tossed her head. Suddenly hard to please, she could find nothing she liked at Geoffrey's cobbler and insisted on visiting the cobbler of Gilbert's choice, only three doors away. There, in the little shop that smelled of leather, she immediately chose an impractical pair of high-heeled red satin slippers. Geoffrey looked doubtful at this choice and had the cobbler bring her a pair of velvet clogs with cork soles six inches tall to slip on over her slippers "against the mud." Lenore was grateful to him, but still too angry with him to say so. She swished out of the shop in her new shoes and clogs, not looking where she was going as she chattered to Gilbert—and promptly collided with a fat, elderly man just reeling out of an alehouse. Yet to learn that Oxford was a town of daytime tipplers, Lenore was knocked back against Geoffrey, who reached out a long arm to steady her.

"Fool!" cried Gilbert. "Watch where you're going!"

His lace-cuffed arm shot forward, and a hard slap from his open palm tumbled the old fellow backward so that he landed on his back in the muddy street, a look of abject bewilderment on his face.

"Your pardon, young sir!" he bleated. "I did not see the lady!"

"The toe of my boot will improve your vision!" cried Gilbert, drawing back his foot. But Geoffrey, who had righted Lenore, grasped him by the arm. "'Twas an accident, Gil. Have done with him, lad!"

They hurried away down the street, with Gilbert angrily insisting the fellow should be taught manners and Geoffrey grimly retorting that brawling in the streets would bring them attention that they could ill afford.

"I had forgotten you two were wanted by the law," admitted Gilbert.

"Well, keep it in mind, if you please. Unless you choose to see Mistress Lenore dangling from some gibbet!"

Halfway to their lodgings, Gilbert spied a friend and parted with them, promising to catch up. When he did not, the Daunts stalked home together, Lenore testing her new shoes on the cobblestones.

"Do not encourage Gil in his peppery ways," Geoffrey cautioned her sternly. "Or your head may be forfeit to your lack of sense."

Lenore still had not forgiven him for this morning. "At least *he* would have fought for me," she said in a mutinous voice.

Geoffrey gave her an impatient look. "Gil challenged an old man he knew would not fight. Could you not see that? Where's your common sense?"

Driven too far, Lenore whirled on him. "I left it outside Worcester—where you left your honor!"

She was instantly sorry, for his face turned gray. For a moment he towered over her and she quailed back, thinking that he would strike her down. But he got control of himself and slammed out, muttering, "Better by far had I left you to the Ironsides!"

Lenore flinched, sank down on a hard wooden chair

156

and burst into a storm of weeping. She was drying her eyes when Gilbert arrived, showing surprise to find Geoffrey gone.

Lenore considered him through wet dark lashes. Geoffrey had implied that Gilbert was a coward. She would ask him directly. Her question was blunt. "Why were you not at Worcester fighting for your King?"

If he was startled by this assault, Gilbert did not show it. With an elegant gesture, he brushed a speck of dust from his velvet sleeve. "I was in indifferent health and down with a bout of chills and fever when the King rode south. I recovered and was on my way to Worcester when news of the defeat reached me. There was no point in continuing on—I returned home."

Lenore was satisfied with that answer. It became apparent that Geoffrey was not.

When he returned that night, Lenore apologized. "I was angry," she said stiffly, and Geoffrey returned her a curt nod.

"It is forgotten, Lenore." He studied her for a moment from under dark brows. "I have arranged with Mistress Watts to have a dress made for you. Of russet wool. You are too thinly clad in that dress, lovely though it is. You will need the wamth of wool to endure an Oxford winter."

She felt shame flood her. She had been thorny and intractable, while Geoffrey was thinking only of her comfort.

"I asked Gilbert why he was not at Worcester," she said quickly, as a way of changing the subject.

Geoffrey's brows shot up. "Ah, then he was here after I left?"

She ignored the overtones of that remark in her eagerness to tell him of Gilbert's chills and fever. " 'Twould have been madness for him to continue on after he had learned of the defeat."

Geoffrey smiled grimly at her. "My caramel-haired cousin has many endowments—not the least of them an imperishable charm for women, but valor is not one of them. He straddles the fence with a foot in Cromwell's camp and one in the King's and plans to ride easy with the winner."

"How can you say that?" demanded Lenore hotly. "You've no proof!"

"No, but I know Gilbert. When we were lads, we once faced a wild boar in the forest. We were armed only with bows and arrows, and 'twas a full-grown boar. I could not loose my arrow because Gilbert was squarely in the way—but he would have had a clear shot. Instead he stood rooted to the ground until I knocked him aside to save his life, for the boar was charging. My arrow struck the boar in the snout—but the boar struck me also. I was fortunate that he tossed me over the branch of a tree where I clung until rescue came. I bear the scars of it yet."

She remembered a grisly scar on his right leg, an "old wound" that he had dismissed as being "of no importance." "And what of Gilbert?" she asked faintly. "Was he injured also?"

"Nay, Gilbert took off running and launched himself at a low cliff. He scrambled up the rocks and made it back to the manor."

"He brought you the rescue party!" she protested.

"The rescue party did not come from Gilbert," he said evenly. " 'Twas a party of hunters chanced by and staunched the wound and saved me from bleeding to death. Gilbert must have been ashamed of his part in the encounter, for when he reached the manor he informed his parents that we had become separated in the woods, he knew not where I was. I did not inform them differently when the hunters carried me in."

Lenore's violet eyes widened. "I shall charge him with it!" she cried.

Geoffrey took her by the shoulders. His voice was very stern. "We live here by Gilbert's sufferance, Lenore— Gilbert's and others like him. Oxford is a town full of turncoats, men of great words and little deeds. Gilbert is friendly with both sides, and a word from him can bring us to ruin."

"But he is your cousin and loyal to the King!" protested Lenore.

"True he is my cousin, but loyal he has never been—to anyone. There was a maid at Lapham—"

She turned unsteadily away. "I do not want to hear."

But now she felt uneasy about Gilbert, whose gaze in her direction had been much too hot, and who knew along with Ned that she was not truly Geoffrey's wife. It would take getting used to, being in Oxford.

The next day Lally called.

She was not what Lenore had expected.

Lally was very tall, reed slender, with a face that could not be called beautiful, though some might call it arresting. Her coloring was lovely—slate-blue eyes and pale ash-blond hair. She had a rich, low drawl, a determined walk, and a lighthearted attitude toward the world. She came striding into Lenore's lodgings, handsomely dressed in plum-colored wool and carrying a dark forest-green cloak across her arm.

"I'm Lally," she said simply, extending a gloved hand. "And 'tis good to meet you, Lenore. Ned's told me so much about Geoffrey, they're such good friends—as I'm hoping we will be. Ned tells me you've been hotly pursued and could bring no luggage, so I brought you this cloak, for Oxford winters are cold indeed, and the wind will pierce you to the very bone!"

Lenore was touched by this gift and hastened to make Lally welcome. As they talked, she felt herself observed by calm, worldly eyes. In this daughter of the regiment, she was instantly certain she had found a friend.

"I'm not married to Ned," Lally told her frankly over her second cup of chocolate. "Not even betrothed. He's my protector, for 'twas my bad luck to lose both father and would-be husband at near the same time. But we don't love each other, and Ned goes courting to Marston once a week—and sometimes twice!"

Lenore was fascinated. "The young lady there, does she—?"

"Know about me?" Lally laughed. "No, I doubt she

does, for who would tell her? Not Ned, certainly. Ned presses his suit with her, and if her family does not object, they'll be married in the spring."

"But then you. . . ?"

"Will find a new protector." Lally shrugged. "Though none so easygoing as Ned, I've no doubt."

"Don't you worry?" wondered Lenore. "About the future, I mean?"

Lally's slate-blue eyes were suddenly empty. "I lost my future when the river swept my Kevin away before he could wed me. But"—her arm moved as if to sweep away cobwebs and she rose suddenly—"many merry days lie ahead, and I mean to enjoy them. Christmas is coming, remember!"

"You mean they dare to celebrate Christmas here?" exclaimed Lenore in surprise, for celebrating Christmas was outlawed under the stern Puritan laws.

Lally laughed and picked up her gloves. "Some of us will, you'll see! Now don't forget, tomorrow night you and Geoffrey are to sup with us. We've rooms across town—Geoffrey knows the way. No, I'll let myself out, I want to say hello to Mistress Watts."

From the window, Lenore watched Lally's plum-colored skirts sweep across the cobbles. Lally's head was high. She had a determined walk, a determined look in her eye, a determined set to her firm jaw. Somehow Lenore thought Lally would pick up the pieces and straighten out her life someday.

In the meantime—Lenore picked up the dark green cloak Lally had left, which was of warm wool and nearly new—in the meantime, she knew she had found a friend in Oxford.

When Geoffrey returned, she made no mention of her earlier upset, nor did he. She told him instead of Lally's invitation and showed him the green cloak, whirled around in it for his inspection.

"It suits you well," he approved. "Green becomes you." And then he wrapped his arms about her, cloak and all. "Lenore," he said, emotion deepening his voice, "you are my life. And all will honor our child."

Shame washed over Lenore. Geoffrey was caught in a trap as well as she. He loved her—and would marry her, was he but able!

"I'm sorry," she whispered against his deep chest, hearing the rhythmic throb of his heart. "Oh, Geoffrey, I do love you so."

He swept her up and bore her to the alcove with its big bed. They needed no supper that evening, for they feasted in their own garden of earthly delights. Arms wrapped around each other, they lay comfortably beneath the piled-up quilts in the big bed and laughed and made love and talked and again made love until warm exhaustion overcame them and they fell asleep with their legs companionably intertwined and their hair mingling on the pillow.

Lenore woke after a bit to find her left leg grown numb and eased sleepily away from Geoffrey. As she moved she cast a look upward at the shaft of pale light that struck through the leaded panes. A white moon rode the sky, and Lenore smiled up at it.

Marriage might be beyond her reach, but joy she would find in Oxford town. . . .

The next night she and Geoffrey dined with Ned and Lally at their lodgings, which consisted of three large rooms rather handsomely furnished. Besides brandy and cider, Lally—who was very up-to-date—served the new "China drink," as tea was called, and Lenore had her first taste of it. "I think I do prefer it to the West India drink, don't you?" smiled Lally, referring to chocolate.

Lenore, ignorant of both until just now, nodded bright agreement. It was just coming to her that she was an unsophisticated village girl and this was Town.

As the lamb pie and fritters and baked potatoes and pudding and jelly were served by an elderly serving woman in somber gray with a stiff-starched apron, Lenore found herself envying Lally—so self-assured in her rustling taffety dress of a becoming orangy shade that set off her pale hair. Lally must have spent two hours on that elaborate hairdo. Lenore was abruptly conscious

161

of her own simple hair style. Her mouth set in a rather grim line. Geoffrey must not be ashamed of her—she'd have Lally teach her how to do her hair like that!

She was distracted from these thoughts by the banter of the two other guests, both Oxford students with Royalist leanings. One was named Michael and one named Lewis, and she spent most of the evening returning their quips with banter of her own. They found her enchanting; both thought her astonishingly beautiful and went away to spread her fame abroad.

The next day Michael, who had been especially smitten, showed up at Mistress Watts's handsomely dressed in red (Lenore was to learn that he always wore red) with a bottle of good wine, smuggled from France, as a housewarming gift. And while he was still stammering in the doorway, Lewis showed up with fruitcake his mother had sent him. Lenore ushered both young men into her lodgings and made them welcome.

Geoffrey was astonished to return home and find her laughing and entertaining as if their barren rooms were a brace of spacious withdrawing rooms equipped with liveried servants at her beck and call. That he approved this little tableau was obvious, for he stood a moment at gaze and then a faint smile spread over his countenance.

"We are honored that you chose to visit us so soon," he told the uneasy students, who looked abashed to be caught visiting his lady while he was out. They were nearer Lenore's age than his, but he made them welcome by joining them in a glass of wine.

Afternoon also brought his cousin Gilbert Marnock with his burnt sugar hair and meticulous grooming and glittering smile. Gilbert stayed all afternoon and offered to take Lenore sightseeing about Oxford in a sleigh as soon as it snowed.

"I see we are not to be lonely," laughed Geoffrey, when they had all gone and Lenore tripped down to supper in Mistress Watts's common room beside him.

And it was true. Soon their rooms were packed every day, with every chair taken and some perching in the windowsills or standing about. Lally had made haste to introduce Lenore to Oxford's Royalist sympathizers, and the beauteous "Mistress Daunt" became the fashion, the shabby lodgings off Magpie Lane humming with raillery and laughter.

Lenore was glad of their company, and she felt Geoffrey was glad, too, to find her a social success. But sometimes when she was clearing away the tankards of the departed guests, crumbing the table and setting the chairs back in place, she thought of all that she had lost. Wistfully she remembered those long wonderful days with Geoffrey in the shadow of the high tors. And when the wind whipped in from the west, bringing with it the tang of sea salt, she remembered Tintagel and was saddened. Material comforts she had now—and she needed them, for next June her child would be born—but she'd have traded all the comforts in the world to have Geoffrey all to herself again . . . the way it had been.

Generally she had little time for such thoughts. Michael had volunteered to help her improve her penmanship, bringing over quills and ink and parchment, and she spent hours under his guidance with his cherubic face smiling down at her. Lewis had shyly brought over two of his precious books with worn leather bindings, which she read whenever Geoffrey was away overnight. Lighthearted Lally was teaching her clever new ways to arrange her shining red-gold hair. Gilbert had volunteered to teach her the newest dances from France. ("He learned them in brothels," Lally leaned over to confide. She laughed. "He knows not if they be from France or Holland—or Spain, for that matter!")

Lenore was delighted to learn the new dances, and clad in the russet wool Mistress Watts had had made up for her at Geoffrey's direction, she swung about the floor with Gilbert. The music was provided by a couple of students who played the *viola da gamba,* and the Daunts' rooms rang with forbidden merriment as feet stamped and skirts whirled and Lally and Lenore, their faces flushed, danced the afternoons away.

Sometimes Mistress Watts came up to caution them that the music was too loud, it could be heard clear around Magpie Lane, and they might get in trouble with the law—but mostly she let them alone. Mistress Watts's heart was with them; she had been young in Royalist England when dancing and games were a way of life, and she had no heart for this stern Puritan England that strove to quench all joy.

By now Gilbert was almost a fixture in the Daunts' establishment, lounging about with his long legs draped over a convenient chair, watching Lenore from lazy heavy-lidded eyes as she laughed and talked with Lally and Ned and their friends. Sometimes it made her nervous to look up and find him watching her, for Gilbert had a magnetic personal charm that had nothing to do with love. His mocking gaze reminded her that he was a man and she was a woman, young, desirable, and with Geoffrey gone, perhaps . . . available.

For Geoffrey was often gone overnight now and sometimes longer on mysterious tasks, and she was lonely without him. She suspected he had turned to dicing or betting on cockfights in nearby hamlets, but always he returned with enough money to keep them going. Gilbert knew of his frequent absences and would capitalize on it if he could. Relentlessly he pursued her as a dancing partner, and on those days when Geoffrey was gone, he was so conspicuous in his attentions that it embarrassed her.

Finally one day when Geoffrey had ridden out, she decided she must do something to discourage Gilbert. Adroitly she managed to avoid dancing with him, always whirling away with another partner as he approached. She thought Gilbert had got the point at last when he turned with a shrug and asked Lally to dance, but when that dance was over, he headed in her direction once again. Ignoring his advance, she quickly turned to Michael and asked him if he thought her penmanship had improved—and when Gilbert joined them, she fled to the window.

Gilbert sauntered across the room, following her. He would not have done that, she thought rebelliously, had Geoffrey been here. When Geoffrey was present, Gilbert treated her more circumspectly and the music was kept toned down sufficiently so that it could not be heard in Magpie Lane—but with Geoffrey gone, everything got out of hand.

At the window she stood her ground and faced Gilbert, her face impassive though a little flushed. As usual, he was tremendously fashionable, setting the styles for Oxford's hot young bloods. Today he was wearing one of the new "jackanapes" coats of heavily embroidered greenish-gold satin, cut so short as to expose half a hand-span of yellow silk shirt between his coat and his loose-flowing satin knee-breeches of a deeper hue. The pale lemony slik lining of the breeches was gathered at the knee into a band and garnished with forest-green ribands. Although the other young men present were wearing wide-topped boots with yellow-starched lace boothose, Gilbert—who had hired a sedan chair to avoid wading in mud—sported beneath his lemon silk stockings square-toed shoes with flat lemon satin bows and rather high lemon heels that made him even taller. At his neck was a carefully careless froth of Florentine lace. Even his buttons were distinctive: a stag rampant, green enameled on gold. He always wore buttons with a stag design. Geoffrey had told her that Gilbert had designed that stag himself and had the buttons made up in dozen lots by a London firm—always with the same stag design but enamelled in different colors, on a gold or silver ground, to match his costumes. They were a hallmark of his meticulous grooming. Now he leaned back against the wall like a resplendent peacock spreading his feathers. Extravagant he might be, and possibly but a few steps ahead of the bailiff for his tailor's bills, but it was a very glittering picture he presented, she had to admit, lean and graceful, with his narrow, handsome face surrounded by long shining caramel curls.

She steeled her heart against him.

165

Those eyes considered her lazily, raking her delicious figure and settling on her slightly heaving bosom. Hot gaze never leaving her, he took out a gold snuffbox, the top enameled in a stag design that matched his buttons, and delicately took a pinch of snuff.

"Geoffrey leaves ye too much alone these days, Mistress Lenore," he murmured in a voice so low none but she could hear it. "Would ye not welcome a quiet supper at the Crown? I'd take a private room, so your presence there would not be remarked."

A private room . . . his meaning could not have been more clear. Supper for two, some wine—and seduction. She yearned to give him a sharp rejoinder, yet . . . she must not have a falling out with Gilbert; that might be dangerous.

"In Lally's company I would be glad to sup with you at the Crown," she said, managing to keep her voice calm. "Whether in a private room or no. But I could not sup with you alone, Gilbert. As Geoffrey's cousin, you must know that."

He sighed. "Aye, Geoffrey's women were ever faithful to him." The snuffbox closed with a snap.

Geoffrey's *women!* Lenore ground her teeth inwardly at that slap, but she kept a bland smile on her face. Obviously her rebuff had rankled.

"Perhaps another day will find you in a warmer mood," he said coldly and went over to where Lally was standing, engaged in conversation. Lenore stared after him. She was skating on very thin ice, for she had almost given him the scathing answer he deserved.

She did not tell Geoffrey about the incident when he returned that night. She had noted how thoughtfully he looked after Gilbert these days. But after that she took great care not to offend Gilbert; she was scrupulously polite—but she took equal care not to brush his arm as she served him and her other friends glasses of wine. For Gilbert's body seemed to send her a special message, and she felt a kind of uneasy shock when she brushed him. It disturbed her, for in spite of his shortcomings she found him attractive—as Lally plainly did—and there were nights with Geoffrey gone when her arms felt empty and she tossed restlessly, unable to sleep, wishing for arms to hold her. Geoffrey's arms, of course—no matter how many nights he left her alone, she would not falter in that.

But Gilbert's treacherous smile told her daily that there would come a time when she would slip—and he would be waiting.

"I see your admirers are writing sonnets to you now," Geoffrey remarked dryly when he came home one day to find a bit of sealed parchment inscribed to "The Fair Lenore" slipped beneath the door.

Lenore laughed. "They mean nothing by it—'tis something to do."

Deliberately he broke the seal and read aloud:

> *So fair is she, so sweetly made*
> *That if Lenore were mine,*
> *I'd take her in a woodland glade*
> *And need no stronger wine.*

He studied it. "I'd say the writing is Gilbert's."

"Nonsense." She snatched the parchment from him. " 'Tis more like to be some foolish lad who's seen me shivering on my way down the High Street and is practicing his sonnets to win some blushing maid back home!"

There was no laughter in Geoffrey's searching gray gaze. "Gilbert was always good at sonnets . . . and other things."

Lenore flounced away from him. "There's no need to be unpleasant. I've told you I don't know who wrote it. Where were you last night?"

He shrugged, and shook out some coins upon the table. "For your purse."

She scooped them up hesitantly. "I have never asked you how you come by these, Geoffrey."

"No, nor should you," he said curtly, and went back and threw himself upon the bed. "I'm dead tired," he said. "Should any of your admirers call, have the goodness to draw the curtains and let me sleep."

167

She frowned. Geoffrey had no reason to be jealous of Gilbert, for all that Gilbert made little effort to conceal his ardent pursuit of her. Nor could she, after Geoffrey's warning not to fall afoul of Gilbert, ignore him. She felt trapped between them.

She said haltingly, "Geoffrey, about Gilbert, I—"

He turned and opened one eye to regard her. His brows were exceedingly straight, his voice stern. "Gilbert shows you too much attention when I am gone. Ned has remarked it."

Oh, so Ned had remarked it, had he? Guiltily she remembered Gilbert saying as they rested from dancing a lively *gaillard,* "Ye should be kinder to me, Lenore, for are we not . . . cousins now?" His voice had been lazy and his fingers had reached out and tucked back a tendril of her bright hair that had come loose during the dance. She had given him a shadowed, troubled look from under dark, silky lashes, turned and seen Ned looking straight at her. Had he heard? Had he told Geoffrey? Was that what had brought this on?

She took a deep breath. "But you wanted me to be friendly with him because you said he could be a danger—"

"I wanted you to be polite to him, Lenore. No more than that. I do not propose to share you with my cousin Gilbert Marnock."

Lenore gasped. "How *could* you say such a thing? How could you *think* it, Geoffrey? I've never—" She was sputtering with indignation.

He sat up, his broad shoulders looking very broad, his face dark and grave, and threw back his head so that his thick, dark hair rippled like heavy silk. He sighed. "Lenore, I'm accusing you of nothing. I am warning you that you must be careful of Gilbert. 'Tis entirely possible you've never met a man like him. He's very clever."

"Oh, I've met clever men," she said bitterly. *"And* devious ones!"

He reached out and seized her wrist. His fingers were like steel bands. "Don't deliberately misunderstand me."

168

"Oh, I understand you well enough!" She tried to pull away from him, and he opened his fingers and let her go.

"Let Lally have two strings to her bow if she chooses," he said. "Let the gossip be about her—not you."

Lenore was startled. "Does Ned say that Lally and Gilbert—?"

"No," he said dryly. "Ned has eyes only for his lady in Marston and is blind to what goes on in Oxford. But I have eyes in my head, Lenore, and when I am here, I see who Lally dances with, who she flirts with."

And when you are not here, Gilbert dances not with Lally, but with me, thought Lenore uneasily. *You may know that, too. Doubtless Ned has remarked it!*

"We will stop dancing," she said, guilt making her voice sharp. "I will tell our friends—I will tell them that it disturbs Mistress Watts, who could end up in the stocks —as could we all—if it were to become known she allows dancing in her house. You need trouble yourself no more about my dancing with Gilbert, Geoffrey!"

He was watching her a little sadly. "Lenore, come here —'tis not right that you should feel so. You must understand that we are attracting too much attention in Oxford." His voice had a coaxing note, and in his gray eyes there was a glimmer of warmth and of desire. She knew if she approached that big bed now he would reach out and sweep her up in his long arms and claim her, and she would melt and meld with him in joyous surrender. It was a dizzy prospect, but her pride was too wounded to let her follow her heart.

"I am going out," she said bitterly. "Perhaps a walk in the cold air will clear my head and I will see your accusations in a better light."

She half wanted him to leap up and seize her before she could clear the door, to laugh at his suspicions, to drag her protesting to the big bed and stroke her wriggling body to warmth—but he did not do so.

"As you please, mistress," he said, his jaw hardening. "I'll thank you to let me sleep."

Lenore, already affixing her pattens, leaped up, flung on her cloak, grabbed her shawl, and swept out with a swish of skirts, throwing the shawl over her head as she left.

She hurried along the cobbles, breathing the cold damp air from the valley. Scrambled about her among the twisting streets were the big buildings of the university. But Lenore cared not a fig for that institute of learning. Not all of its courses, she felt, would teach her what she needed to know about men. *That,* apparently, must be learned the hard way—by bitter experience. Who would have thought Geoffrey would be so jealous of Gilbert?

Her pace slowed thoughtfully. Perhaps Geoffrey had a *right* to be jealous of Gilbert! Could it be that all unthinking she had showed him favor? Meaning nothing by it, of course, but only trying to be pleasant in the face of his obvious blatant interest. She loved to dance with him—could that have been misinterpreted? By Gilbert as well as by Ned? Her lovely face grew sober. She would walk a narrower path, she would please Geoffrey.

But as luck would have it, when she returned to her lodgings off Magpie Lane, almost at the door she met Gilbert. He was advancing on her rapidly from the other direction, and he waved to her to wait for him. Reluctantly she did so. He came up to her, cloak flying open, his cuffs and coat resplendent with stag-enamelled buttons.

"Ah, there you are!" he said breezily. "Ned and Lally are right behind me. And we shall have music, as well, for Harry and Fred have promised to come over and bring their *violas.*"

"Gilbert," she said anxiously, following him perforce up the stairs which he was mounting two at a time with long booted legs. "It might be as well if Harry and Fred did not play today. Yesterday we disturbed Mistress Watts quite a bit and—"

Gilbert had swept open the unlatched door to their lodgings and was ushering her inside. With his hand on her back, she was propelled into the room.

"I see Geoffrey's not home yet," he said comfortably, drawing off his gauntlets as his eyes swept the room. She saw that the curtains to the bed alcove were drawn; Geoffrey must have drawn them, to sleep. Desperately she opened her mouth to speak, but Gilbert cut her off airily with, " 'Tis convenient for you, Lenore, having Geoffrey away so frequently."

"It is *not* convenient!" cried Lenore wildly, afraid Geoffrey might be lying awake behind those drawn curtains and drawing his own conclusions from this conversation. "And Geoffrey *is* here. He's just come home, he's tired and trying to sleep—and you're disturbing him!"

"Nonsense, you'd not have been out strolling had Geoffrey just come home," said Gilbert coolly. "And he'd have had the sense to bed you first, no matter how far he'd ridden. I'll prove you wrong, Lenore!"

He strode to the bed and as Lenore watched in horror, flung the curtains wide.

The bed was rumpled but empty.

"Faith, it looks like you've been enjoying a tumble with some likely lad, from the way 'tis rumpled—or is that the way Mistress Watts keeps house, Lenore?" He eyed her speculatively.

"Gilbert!"

"So no more talk of Geoffrey, who's probably twenty leagues away at this moment! We'll have dancing and music today—though, by heaven, we need no music, you and I!" He grabbed her and danced around with her, and she pulled away.

"No, Gilbert!"

He laughed. "Come now, Lenore, be not so cold—we're cousins now, remember? Let's have a cousinly kiss before Ned and Lally get here!"

Lenore drew back her arm to slap his face, for she knew by the look in his eyes that he was going to kiss her, whether she would or no. But abruptly he stepped back from her, his startled gaze fixed on something over her shoulder.

She turned to see what had wrought this sudden change in him.

Tall, sardonic, and with a very cold expression in his steady gray eyes, Geoffrey had come out of the small room and now stood in the doorway.

"So that's how it's done when I'm away, Gil?" he said. His voice was almost gentle, but there was something in it, some undertone, that made Gilbert hastily take another step backward.

"No need to be hasty, Geoffrey," he cried. "I did but seek to dance a measure with Mistress Lenore here!"

"So I see—and a kiss for good measure?" Geoffrey advanced on him with a nasty look. They were both tall men, and at that moment to Lenore's frightened gaze they looked as tall as towers, but Geoffrey's broad shoulders seemed to broaden further, his deep chest to expand as he strode toward his cousin.

"Mistress Lenore invited me up!" cried Gilbert in an aggrieved tone.

"I don't doubt it," said Geoffrey kindly. Before Lenore had a chance to feel relieved at this forbearance, seemingly from nowhere Geoffrey's hard right fist swung up and caught Gilbert neatly on the jaw with enough force to send him hurtling into the doorway—and into Ned's arms, for he and Lally had just arrived.

"Ho, there, Geoffrey, what's this?" cried Ned, staggering back and nearly colliding with Lally, who skipped nimbly backward to avoid him.

"He's gone mad," muttered Gilbert, his handsome face distorted as he tried—not too hard—to leave Ned's restraining grasp and surge back toward Geoffrey.

"Not so mad that I couldn't remember your taking ways, Gil." Geoffrey had folded his arms and stood calmly, legs planted well apart in a firm stance, watching his cousin with some interest. "That little love-pat I just favored you with was a recommendation that you mend your manners where Mistress Lenore's concerned."

"I've shown Mistress Lenore nothing but respect— always!" shouted Gilbert, his face white with rage save for a dull red mark on his jaw.

"That I don't doubt, either," said Geoffrey softly. "Else she'd have been quick to complain to me. This is a recommendation for your behavior in the future."

"God's teeth, he's gone out of his mind!" cried Gil. "Let me away from this madman!" He tore loose from Ned's grasp and hurtled past Lally down the stairs. They could hear him fuming as he went out and the front door closed with a crash.

"Now what was that all about, Geoffrey?" asked Ned, coming into the room and peeling off his gauntlets. Behind him Lally watched with sparkling eyes. A true daughter of the regiment, Lally loved a good fight. "Do *you* know?" Ned turned to Lally.

"No, but knowing Gilbert, I can guess," laughed Lally.

Lenore gave her friend a reproving look. "Geoffrey feels that we make too much noise with our music and dancing, and when I told Gilbert we should not have the *violas* today he seized me and started to dance me around the room. Geoffrey came out and"—she gave him an angry look—"behaved like an idiot!"

"Gil needed a lesson, Ned," Geoffrey said calmly. "I gave him one. Can we offer you some wine?"

"Faith, I'll need it for strength if I'm to catch the bodies you send flying through the door," said Ned in a rueful voice, accepting a glass, which Lenore had poured with shaking hands. "Do ye think 'twas wise to offend him, Geoffrey?"

Geoffrey frowned and ran a hand through his dark hair. "Not wise, perhaps, but called for, Ned. Gil thinks all women fair prey." He looked speculatively at Lally, who stiffened a trifle and took a fast sip of wine.

"Yes, I've watched him with Mistress Lenore," said Ned frankly. "He does pursue her, though she does nothing to warrant it—to that I can testify."

Lenore gave him a grateful look.

"D'ye think we should leave Oxford, Ned?" sighed Geoffrey. "Gil's treacherous—I know him of old."

Lenore gasped. Leave Oxford in winter, with hardly any money, and herself with a baby due in June?

"Surely you cannot believe he would denounce you?" Ned sat bolt upright. "If I thought that . . . !"

"He'd do worse if he'd a mind to," said Geoffrey calmly. He turned his glass around in his hand and studied it. "I'm debating whether he'll consider it to his advantage to do so."

"But if he should do such a thing, 'twould implicate us all—himself as well!" cried Ned. "For we've all helped the King's cause to some extent—we would all be undone!"

Lally gave them both a worldly look. "There's no need to talk of leaving Oxford," she said with spirit. "Gil will not turn ye in to the Ironsides, Geoffrey, if that's what ye're thinking—not if he's interested in Lenore, as you believe. For to do so would implicate her, and he'd not like to see her hang from a gibbet!"

Geoffrey gave Lenore a thoughtful look. She tossed her head rebelliously. "There's much in what you say, Lally—and the countryside does not lend itself to travel in this season. The mud was so deep I could hardly get back to Oxford."

"You can patch it up with Gil," said Ned uneasily. "I'll speak to him for you."

"Perhaps the less said the better," mused Geoffrey. " 'Twas not too hard a blow I gave him." Lenore thought how Gilbert had skidded across the floor and crashed into Ned—she shuddered. "He's bruised—as well he deserved to be—but I was careful not to break his jaw. And he knows I have friends here who would take it amiss if he makes trouble."

"Lenore can be pleasant to him," said Lally instantly. "She can treat him as if nothing has happened, and it will be all right, you'll see."

"But if there's to be no dancing—as Geoffrey wants," said Lenore, troubled, "won't Gilbert feel that's a slap at him?"

"There'll be *less* dancing," corrected Lally. "What do you say, Geoffrey? Wouldn't a sharp cut-off cause rumblings?"

He gave her an amused look, as if half suspecting she wanted the dancing to continue for her own amusement, which Lenore felt was probably true! "A pity the King did not have your counsel at Worcester, mistress—for your guile might have carried the day!" Lally laughed, but he added a note of caution. "Just so ye do not all end up in the stocks, for while the rest of you might eventually be let out of them, I fear Mistress Lenore would go on to the gallows."

Lenore was chilled as she was again reminded that they were wanted Royalists in Puritan England. The frivolity of the life at Oxford had almost made her forget it. "I will be more careful of the music, Geoffrey," she promised quietly. "I will keep the noise down."

"Perhaps you'll help, too, Ned?" suggested Geoffrey. "I've need to be away so much."

"Whenever I'm in town," Ned agreed instantly. "And when I'm at Marston, Lally can help."

He did not notice the slight grimace that passed over Lally's face. "Some more of your delicious wine, Lenore," Lally said gaily, holding out her glass. "I feel a need to be warmed by spirits!"

Quickly Lenore refilled her glass. She gave Lally a compassionate look. For Lally it was a cold world; she'd need of something to warm her in this cruel life.

The next day Lally swept in, in her orangy velvets, and caught Lenore alone. "Well, that was a close call yesterday!" she said in a significant tone.

"What do you mean?" asked Lenore, puzzled.

Lally leaned down to peer at her. "Do you mean to say you're *not* having an affair with Gilbert? But he led me to think . . ."

"I most certainly am *not* having an affair with Gilbert!" snapped Lenore, her cheeks burning. "No matter what he told you!"

"Oh, he didn't exactly say it," murmured Lally, adjusting her plumed hat. "I guess I assumed . . ."

"Are *you* interested in Gilbert?" Lenore shot at her.

Lally was thoughtful for a moment; her hands, adjusting the orange plumes, were still. "He amuses me, Lenore, and . . . and I must think of the future." Her face hardened as she said that. "Well, no matter." She shrugged. "We'll fix it all up, anyway."

Lally's method of "fixing it up" was to take Lenore for coffee on a sunny day at the Crown. There they encountered Gilbert, who had been studiously shunning the Daunts' lodgings. At first he gave Lenore a smouldering look, but Lally waved him over and he warmed to her banter. Soon he was laughing with them, leaning back so that his resplendent clothes showed to best advantage. He insisted on paying for the coffee. Lenore saw that his jaw, though slightly empurpled, was mending fast. She smiled at him with a sweetness she did not feel and told him they missed him.

"That was a good beginning," announced Lally with satisfaction after they left. "By the end of the week, tempers will have cooled, and I'll have you and Geoffrey for supper and arrange for Gil to drop in afterward—and they'll be civil to each other, you'll see. You can borrow something of mine to wear. It should be low-cut. Gil likes low-cut dresses. We want him to see how lovely you are at my table by candlelight. And you can mention again, with a little pout, that we all miss him—no, say you take it amiss he's been avoiding you these afternoons, for he's the best dancer among us. He'll be enchanted. For he's vain of his dancing and loves to be flattered. And of course he'll realize he certainly can't see a sweet thing like you get put in the stocks—or hanged. He can't denounce Geoffrey then, even if he's a mind to—it would pull you down with him, don't you see?"

Lenore did see. But the seeing of it made her glum. It meant she dared not offend the offensive Gilbert.

By the following week everything was much as it had been, except that the music in the lodgings off Magpie Lane was toned down, dancing there was not quite so frequent, and young Mistress Daunt carried on in dread of her future.

Placating Gilbert was perilously akin to flirting with him—and that Geoffrey would not brook. But as Lally had said, she must heal the breach. Lenore was on a collision course between Geoffrey and Gilbert—and she knew it. But puzzle though she would, she could think of no road to travel but this one, wherever it led. Once again Gilbert was hovering over her whenever Geoffrey was gone, Gilbert with his theatrical clothes, his exciting touch, his wicked almost demonic beauty.

In panic, Lenore almost wished she had been born ugly. Then she would not have attracted Gilbert. But then —then perhaps she would not have had Geoffrey. It came to her suddenly that one paid a price for everything in life, and the price of beauty—to the possessor of it—might be high indeed.

CHAPTER 11

Just before Christmas a great snow fell, weighing down the ivy and frosting Oxford's stately towers with white. Ordinarily Lenore, who loved skating and winter sports, would have welcomed the snowfall as a respite from the mud, but Geoffrey had ridden off to the south, destination unstated; he had been gone several days and she feared this heavy snow might have closed the roads and that he would not make it back to Oxford in time for Christmas.

She was leaning pensively against the leaded window, staring out at the swirling white flakes, when she heard a jingle of sleigh bells and saw a sleigh drawn by two prancing black horses turn off Magpie Lane and come to a sliding halt in front of Mistress Watts's house. Gilbert, smartly clad in a fur-trimmed tan cloak, was driving. He looked up, saw her at the window, flashed her a smile, and waved a gloved hand. She watched him leap out, caramel curls tossing as he landed on hard-packed snow, and heard his tan boots clatter up the stairs.

"I've hired a sleigh and come to take you for that tour

of Oxford-in-the-snow I promised you!" he told her exuberantly as he pounded on the door.

Lenore threw the door open and gave him a doubtful look. To be pleasant to Gilbert in mixed company was one thing, but to drive out with him alone before all Oxford—when his low, intimate voice, his encroaching manner, his hot looks made it so clear he wanted her—she doubted Geoffrey would care for that!

Gilbert moved past her into the room with a masterful stride, cloak swinging, snow sticking to his boots. "We're off to pick up Lally," he said carelessly, as if he sensed her doubt. "I promised her a sleigh ride as well."

Lally! That made it all right. Geoffrey could not criticize her for sleigh-riding in Lally's company. Hastily Lenore put on her velvet clogs, slipped into her deep green wool cloak, and threw over her head a red shawl Geoffrey had brought home from one of his prowlings.

Mistress Watts came out of her lodgings as they ran downstairs and stood in her doorway. She was clutching her blue shawl around her, and her big white cat was purring and arching its back and rubbing furry sides against her faded taffety skirts. " 'Tis too cold for such frolics!" she exclaimed with a shiver. "Even Puss here seeks the hearth in this weather!"

Lenore laughed and blew her a kiss. " 'Twill be my first sleigh ride this year!" she declared gaily. "If the horses can stand the weather, I can!"

Mistress Watts shook her head and watched them go.

The sleigh was a graceful one, painted red, with a curving front and long runners. Expertly Gilbert handed her in and joined her. He arranged a blanket so that it swathed them both from foot to waist, and she forgave him for tucking her in so tightly that her skirted thigh was pressed against his neat fawn breeches—for it was indeed bitter cold and their breath fogged up in the stinging air. Gilbert flourished his whip and they were off around the corner into the hard-packed snow of Magpie Lane. She did not see the narrow look of satisfaction Gilbert gave her, for this sleigh ride would mark the first time he had gotten her out publicly without Geoffrey. She was too happy with this glittering white world and the merry tinkle of the sleigh bells to notice. How she loved sleighing!

Down the curving High Street with its towers and spires they sped, the cobbled gutter that ran down the center of the street looking sugar-frosted. They passed other sleighs with laughing occupants, and struggling carts and lone riders, bundled up, breath fogging the air above the horses' manes. Hugging the shelter of the buildings, women tipped past on tall pattens and men trudged purposefully along with snow crusted on the shoulders of their short cloaks and spilling over their wide-brimmed peaked hats. People were out, Christmas shoppers fighting the drifts to bring home fat geese and sugarplums and expensive oranges—for tomorrow was Christmas Eve.

"But—this is not the way to Lally's," she protested, when Gilbert swung off the street and reined up beneath some snow-laden concealing branches that almost but not quite dropped another blanket of white over them.

"Did you think it would be?" Those hard tawny eyes considered her from beneath sleepy lashes as he dropped the reins and turned toward her. "What need have we of Lally's company?"

Lenore recoiled. She had been so eager for a sleigh ride she had not even considered this treachery. Lally was not waiting for them—Gilbert had but lied to her to get her alone! Instantly she struggled to toss back the blanket so she could leap out of the sleigh, but Gilbert's long arm pulled her back easily.

"Now, as I see it, ye've two choices, Lenore," he said in a cool voice, his tan leather glove tipping up her angry chin so that her wide violet eyes looked directly into his own. "Either ye ride with me to a convenient inn where we will get to know each other better. Or ye set up a great howl betwixt here and there and alert all of Oxford that ye rode out with me and we had a lover's quarrel."

"Wrong," she said steadily. "I've yet another choice." For over Gilbert's shoulder she had glimpsed Lally— magically Lally, her pale hair caught up beneath a tall beaver hat, her beaver muff crushed to her orange velvet bosom, trudging along in her pattens with her orange skirts held up. Head down, she was walking fast over the hard-packed snow. "Lally!" she shouted. "Lally!"

Lally turned, bent down to peer beneath the overhanging snow-laden branches, and smiled in delight. "Why, what are you two doing here?" she exclaimed, and then the smile abruptly faded as she saw Gilbert's arm encircling Lenore's rigid shoulders, faced his sardonic smile.

"Gilbert has hired a sleigh!" cried Lenore merrily, for though Lally was her friend she could not afford a chance word to Ned that might be repeated to Geoffrey. "We were just coming over to get you when a great cart near ran us off the street. We retreated here and have been rearranging our blanket. There, that's better!" She gave Gilbert's arm a push. "Won't you come for a drive with us?"

Lally hesitated. "I was on my way to buy sugarplums."

"We could drop you off," suggested Gilbert.

"All right," said Lally. "For I'm meeting Ned at the Crown for supper—he'll be back from Marston by then."

"Oh, no," insisted Lenore, her voice growing desperate. "Forget the sugarplums. Come with us, do—we can all end up at the Crown and make a party of it!"

Lally laughed. "Why not? You've convinced me I don't need sugarplums." She turned a bland face to Gilbert. "I'd enjoy a sleigh ride, Gil." She waited for Gilbert to get out, gave him a gloved hand, picked up her orange skirts, and climbed in beside Lenore. "Where's Geoffrey, Lenore?" She turned to give Lenore a penetrating look as Gilbert rearranged the blanket.

"Still away," admitted Lenore, her cheeks uncomfortably hot under Lally's bright scrutiny.

"Not back yet?" Lally was indignant. "But tomorrow is Christmas Eve! He leaves you too much alone, Lenore."

Her voice held an undertone of warning, and Lenore sighed. " 'Twas because I was so lonely I leaped into the sleigh—when Gilbert told me we were to pick you up at your lodgings."

Lally's worldly smile was as sardonic as Gilbert's. "At my lodgings . . . Well, Gilbert's a forgetful lad, he should have sent word by messenger, and I'd have been there."

"I clean forgot," murmured Gilbert, and Lally laughed.

"Did you now?" she scoffed.

So Lally understood the situation perfectly!

But that was no reason why she should be deprived of the pleasure of her sleigh ride! She'd been cooped up long enough! Lenore's cheeks were still bright with anger, but she was determined to enjoy this treat now that Lally was here to make it respectable.

Sandwiched between Lally and Gilbert, her shawl draped over her bright hair and her legs pressed against Lally's orange velvet skirts on one side and Gilbert's fashionable fawn-breeched legs on the other, Lenore snuggled down beneath the blanket wrappings with a sigh of comfort and took in great draughts of the frosty air.

For all he'd been outwitted, Gilbert took his defeat in good part. Snapping his whip high over the horses' heads, he took them for a merry ride over the snowy streets of the old walled city. Through big swirling flakes that drifted down lazily to melt on their eyelashes and sting their cheeks to red, they rode on long silent runners—past Christ Church, which had been founded by Cardinal Wolsey.

"The meadow path on the north side is called Dead Man's Walk," Lally told her, and when Lenore wondered why, Gilbert said it was because Jewish funeral processions used to pass this way to reach their synagogue which had once stood almost where Tom Tower stood today. Those Jews could afford memorable processions, he grinned; they'd charged interest of forty percent!

Lenore studied Gilbert covertly as their sleigh bells tinkled past Tom Quad, the grandest quadrangle in Oxford, its snowy cathedral spire on the east perhaps England's oldest. She missed what he was saying about it. It puzzled her that a little while ago this caramel dandy had been going to take her, willy-nilly—and now, completely without malice, so far as she could see, he was doing his best to entertain her, like any cavalier with a lady.

Could that be Lally's influence, she wondered, or had Gilbert just given up?

Beside her, Lally, her gloved hands kept warm by her

beaver muff, dodged a snowball tossed by a laughing tot who jumped up and down, shrieking with glee. Straightening up, she pointed out the Magdalen Tower, which had been a watchpost during England's Civil War that had brought Oliver Cromwell to power. Staring upward, Lenore reached up to brush the snow from her red shawl with near-numbed fingers. Lally frowned and told Lenore her hands must be freezing, Geoffrey should buy her a muff.

Gilbert, wheeling the black horses expertly about to avoid some snowballing children who were fighting a mock war from their mounded snow forts, said carelessly, "I'm giving Lenore a fur muff for Christmas."

Lenore flashed him a startled look, for fur muffs were valuable. She hoped Geoffrey would not make trouble about it, for Gilbert would assuredly be angry if she rejected his gift.

"You should not do it," she said simply. "For I've naught to give you. These are lean days for us."

"It gives me pleasure just to see you." Gilbert smiled down at her from heavy-lidded eyes. "And a muff you shall have."

Lenore gave him a long, slow smile of winsome beauty. Perhaps this was Gilbert's way of making amends, his way of saying: *At last I accept the fact that you belong to Geoffrey and there is nothing I can do about it.* Perhaps this attempt to get her to an inn had been in the nature of a last try for what he had once called in a hoarse whisper her "sumptuous body." People changed—even Gilbert. They might end up being friends after all.

She was in a warm mood when they reached the Crown Inn at Cornmarket, finding it crowded, for none of the roads to the north were passable at this time of year and many students had waited too late to journey home and must spend their Christmas season in Oxford. Friends across the room waved tankards at sight of them, and a table was hastily set for them in a corner. Lenore was glad of the great fire blazing on the hearth, for the cold air had chilled her, and she stamped her clogs on the stone floor to restore her circulation.

Lally cast a quick glance around the crowded room.

183

"Ned isn't here," she said in disappointment, sliding onto the bench beside Lenore.

" 'Tis the heavy snow. He'll make it," Gilbert assured her, and raised a gloved hand to wave at some new-comers. "Ho there, Michael! Lewis! Join us."

Glad of the extra company, which made it doubly obvious to all that she'd not been out sleighing with Gilbert alone, Lenore squeezed back to make room. Michael, with his cherubic face, his brilliant red garments crusted with snow, and awkward Lewis, stumbling over a protruding boot, threaded their way through the crush and pulled up chairs at their table.

Lenore was hungry and ate heartily, but Lally seemed subdued and only picked at the good dressed crab and hare soup and wild fowl which Gilbert ordered. Midway through the meal Ned came through the door, clad in a great Manderville coat and gauntlet gloves. He brought a great gust of snow with him, and Lally's face lit up as she moved her orange skirts to make room for him beside her on the long bench. He'd barely made it from Marston, Ned told them blithely, for it was snowing hard all the way—in truth, he might have stayed the night in Marston but the house was so jammed with visiting relatives, there for the Twelve Days of Christmas, that they'd no room even to sleep him in the attic!

Lally's bright smile faltered a little at that and she was silent for a while, picking aimlessly at the food on her trencher. Lenore promptly inquired as to the depth of the snow, and Ned said he'd seen nothing but the tops of men's hats—their bodies were buried in drifts! At this jovial exaggeration, the party became very merry. Soon Lally too began to laugh almost hysterically at the jokes that flew about. Lenore studied her from beneath shadowed lashes. She had noted a tenderness in Lally's gaze when she looked at Ned which belied her cheerful, offhand "We don't love each other." Lenore guessed that Lally was caught up in something too big for her and was ruefully determined to play the game out, wherever it led. She had to admire Lally's aplomb, counterfeit though it might be, as she lifted her glass in a toast to Ned's Marston lady which Gilbert callously proposed.

Even Michael looked a bit startled at that, and he and Lenore promptly engaged Lally in conversation, covering Gilbert's blunder. Lenore liked Michael. His brown eyes sparkled and his new red coat already bore the stains of wine, for Michael was careless in his ways. His cheeks were pink as a girl's in the cold weather, his cherubic countenance adoring as he watched Lenore. Bumbling Lewis watched her avidly, too, and Lenore basked in their devotion, for it was hard to face Christmas without Geoffrey, and her sagging spirits needed a lift.

As if realizing that he had offended Lenore by this mention of Ned's betrothed before Lally, Gilbert, whose rum-soaked mood was expansive, now showed off his knowledge of local lore. His distinctive enamelled buttons glittered on his fawn satin coat and cuffs as he beat his tankard on the table for emphasis and told them in a loud strident voice that Will Shakespeare, the playwright, whose plays, though forbidden, were sometimes seen around Oxford and would be again—he winked broadly —had stayed here at the Crown on his way to the Globe Theatre. Hence, yearly on Shakespeare's birthday, he informed them with a hiccup, they drank malmsey here.

"Naturally," Michael piped up in his strong high voice, with a delighted smile at Lenore. "Since Will Shakespeare was godfather to the landlord's son!"

Somewhat discomfited at young Michael's superior knowledge, Gilbert turned to Lenore. "And where is Geoffrey gone to this time?" he asked with asperity. His voice carried piercingly across the room.

Lenore tried not to look concerned at this blunt question, though she feared for Geoffrey, perhaps at this very moment being pursued down icy roads, blundering through great drifts. "I do not try to hold Geoffrey too close," she answered with an indifferent shrug.

"Wise of you," commented Lally dryly. "Though I don't think Geoffrey would mind if you did!"

Gilbert's laugh rang out discordantly. "Geoffrey always

had the devil's own luck with women—and now he's found an Angel!"

They all laughed at that, but Lenore looked about her uneasily, for not all in this room tonight were Royalists, and she feared Gilbert, the worse for drink, might drunkenly propose a toast to the Angel of Worcester. But Ned, perhaps sensing the same thing, quickly ordered another round in a loud voice, banging his tankard on the table, and the subject of Geoffrey and his Angel was quickly forgotten. But it had served to remind Lenore of Geoffrey's warning, that Gilbert was mercurial and could be dangerous.

Even though Michael and Lewis tried to rally her with droll stories and quips, her joy in the evening was quenched. She felt she had endangered Geoffrey by being here. Later, when Ned, Lally, and Gilbert dropped her off at her lodgings, Gilbert offered to "see her up." She shook her head, and Lally reinforced that by saying reprovingly, "Nay, 'tis nearly curfew—Tom bell will be tolling! We'll be caught out by the watch!"

Lenore threw them all a bright smile and ran to Mistress Watts's front door through snow that was up to the tops of her tall clogs even though it had been shoveled clear when she'd left earlier. From the open doorway she blew them a kiss, quickly closed it, and ran past her landlady. For, nightcapped and curious at the jingling bells and laughter, Mistress Watts had come out into the hall. Lenore ran past her up the stairs before she could be taxed with idle questions as to Geoffrey's whereabouts.

As she closed the door of her lodgings behind her, she heard all the way from Christ Church the Great Tom bell —loudest in Oxford—reverberate, sounding curfew. Its hundred and one peals, carried on the swirling snow, had a mellow sound . . . it was five minutes past nine o'clock then, for that was when Great Tom always tolled. Lenore stood at the window, watching the sled's departure through frosted panes, hoping they'd safely avoid the watch. When it had disappeared around the corner into Magpie Lane, she sighed and went over and stirred the red coals on the hearth with a poker until yellow flames leaped up. Gwynneth must have been keeping the fire going all day, for the room was not cold.

She studied the yellow flames wistfully. Christmas would be lonely without Geoffrey. She could only hope that he would return in time—and if he did not, that it was snow and not the Ironsides that deterred him.

Lenore was still working at rebuilding the fire when a scratching at the door announced Mistress Watts's cat, who regularly called on the lodgers for tidbits. Poor thing, she thought, Mistress Watts must have latched her door, forgetfully leaving the cat outside in the freezing cold corridor! When she opened the door, the cat, a big white tom, rushed inside and rubbed against her legs, purring vigorously. Lenore laughed and rubbed his furry neck with gentle fingers.

"There should be a bite for you somewhere, Puss," she said, tossing him a scrap of ham from the cupboard and going back to building the fire.

The cat gobbled the ham and looked up brightly with big lamplike golden eyes, hoping for more.

"Puss? Where are you, Puss?" Mistress Watts, calling in a low scolding voice from downstairs.

Lenore opened the door. "He's up here, Mistress Watts."

"Ah, you're a wicked Puss!" Energetically, Mistress Watts flopped up the stairs in a pair of slippers and picked up the cat, holding his big furry body against the faded rose taffety of her ample bosom. "If Puss bothers you, Mistress Daunt, just you boot him out! Lord, it's cold in this hall!"

She scurried back downstairs and Lenore smiled at the retreating figure. She turned back to working on the fire. She got the fire up to a blaze and went to bed.

It did not occur to her that she had forgotten to latch the door.

CHAPTER 12

Lenore dreamed of Dartmoor. They were campéd again in the shadow of the high tors. She could hear the night birds calling. A great gnarled oak spread twisted branches overhead and Geoffrey was beside her, warm, wonderful, murmuring words of love in the moonlight. His strong arms held her and his lips caressed her; there was a sweet wild clamor in her blood, a stirring of the senses as her woman's body roused to passion.

She awoke slowly, sensuously, coming out of a deep warm sleep to find strong arms about her, hands intimately caressing her. Geoffrey was back! Luxuriously she sighed and opened her eyes. The fire had burned down, but there was enough of a glow for her to see that the head pressed into her shoulder had not dark locks but light.

This was not Geoffrey!

Panic seized her. She gave a violent involuntary lurch away from the arm that held her. But her attacker must have been expecting that, for his grip tightened painfully, and the scream that rose in her throat was abruptly silenced by a scarf that was thrust roughly into her mouth to gag her.

Choking and desperate, she fought her unknown adversary. His head lifted, and looking up with wide, terrified violet eyes she could see who it was—Gilbert! A Gilbert with red-rimmed glittering eyes and reeking strongly of ale. There was no chance to reason with him, for the gag he had stuffed into her mouth, and which almost stopped her breathing, enforced her silence except for the moans and gasping breaths that escaped her as she struggled.

"Lenore." Gilbert had half risen above her flailing, writhing body, but now his hands seized her shoulders in a painful grip and brutally he pressed her down upon the bed. His tousled caramel curls fell down upon her face, fell into her eyes, making her blink as he deftly dodged the blows she tried to rain upon his narrow handsome face. "Lenore," he panted, "let be. 'Tis not as if ye were a virgin, nor yet an affronted wife—we all know ye're Geoffrey's doxie!"

She managed to give him a sharp kick that temporarily numbed the toes of her right foot. He gave a short yelp, and his weight fell on her. Abruptly he let go of her shoulders, seized her wrists, and savagely yanked her arms up over her head. With his other hand he administered a sharp slap that made lights dance before her eyes, and his foot slapped down on her right ankle, holding it paralyzed.

" 'Tis me, not Geoffrey, ye want," he told her thickly, and she realized then how very drunk he was. "Ye want *me!* All along ye've wanted me, enticed me—admit it!"

With a bitter, strangled sob, she turned her head away from that drunken face, writhing beneath him in an attempt to free herself. Her ankle was twisted painfully beneath his foot and she moaned, hardly audible above his rasping breathing. Half suffocated in his brutal grip, she could hear her chemise tear, feel the fabric lightly burn the skin of her buttocks and back as it was ripped from her violently. The bedclothes had long since departed, slid to the floor as they tussled back and forth.

Naked now, she fought him, her body smooth and supple in the light of the dying fire. Almost suffocated, she tried to dig a knee into his groin, and he drew back a hand that had been squeezing her breast and slapped her again on the side of the head, this time so hard that for a moment the world swam away from her and she sank into momentary darkness.

Out of the dark she fought her way back inch by inch, aware only of a terrible necessity to survive, to fight. Something was holding her, something she must somehow escape! Comprehension came slowly, forcing its way into her ringing head. Gilbert rode atop her, Gilbert drunk and determined. The gag was choking her, she must have air. But now—oh, God, now he was jerking at his trousers, her hips were pinioned powerless beneath his, he was—he was—!

"Mine," he muttered on a hot breath into her ear, as his male hardness made its savage entrance. "Mine at last!"

Tears streamed down her face as he took her. In wild grief she tried to stiffen, tried to make of her very flesh an inert barrier to show him how much she despised him. But her resilient woman's body that fitted so easily into the crook of a man's arm betrayed her. Against her will she found herself relaxing, against her will she felt her senses quicken and wild darting responses race along her nerve ends as Gilbert relentlessly probed her most sensitive, secret places. Shamed and bitter, her breast heaving as she fought him and that more powerful adversary—herself—she felt herself yielding, yielding.

At her involuntary response, Gilbert's head lifted again and he stared down at her. For a moment of agony that would be forever seared into her memory she looked up into that narrow, handsome face, gilded by the firelight, and saw there a look of triumph. Tears of rage blurred out his image, but she heard his low, drunken laugh.

More gently now he lowered himself back upon her, handling her more like a woman than a body to be punished. His long fingers no longer bruised, but caressed, sensually. Though he kept her wrists tightly manacled in his fingers, he explored her naked body with his free hand, savoring the delights of her, pinching, probing, making her wince and moan. Delighted with this evidence of passion, he moved within her with a lazy rhythm, impudently caressing the silken flesh that quivered in fury and desire at his touch.

Such shame as she had never known filled her. Oh, God, that she could not control this quickening! That she should melt against him until his passions were so roused that he seized her with renewed violence. His pace increased to a pulsing feverish rhythm that swept her along like a leaf over bouncing rapids and exploded over a high waterfall into a deep gorge that left her falling, falling, until she lay spent and bitter, violated and used.

He flung off of her with a low oath, tossing back his damp curls. "You're splendid, Lenore! Superb!" He ran a hand down over her body as she twisted away from him, rolled off the bed, and gained her feet, jerked the suffocating gag from her mouth.

"Geoffrey will kill you for this," she said in a low dangerous voice.

Gilbert laughed—a reckless sound. He lay on his back in her bed, naked and wet with perspiration in the cold room. "I think not," he said carelessly. "Who will tell him? You? A woman who goes to bed, leaving her door unlatched?"

Lenore's face whitened. Shaken, she stared at him. Had she done that? Had she indeed forgotten to latch the door after she let the cat out? It must be true, else how could Gilbert have got in?

"Then _I_ will kill you!" she cried hoarsely, and flung herself forward, striking at his groin with her fist.

He caught her arm, swung her body onto the bed, and jerked her upright as he rose to a kneeling position on the bed. His angry face was thrust into hers. "Play me no tricks, Lenore, or I'll teach ye a lesson ye'll never forget!"

"If you hurt me," she panted, "Geoffrey will want to know how I come by my bruises!"

"True." He considered her dispassionately, and she saw that had sobered him. "But then ye'd have to explain to him how I chanced to be here, and I'd tell him 'twas by your invitation."

191

"Geoffrey will believe *me*," she said in a tight voice, trying to break free of him. "He will cut you down like a dog, Gilbert—even if you swear I left the door unlatched for you!"

Gilbert shrugged and let her go. She fell away from him, slid off the bed, caught hold of a chair back to get her balance. She straightened up and his insolent eyes raked over her naked, panting body. "Mayhap Geoffrey would believe you," he said in a cold voice. "But you'll tell him nothing, Lenore. For if you do, I'll alert the authorities to Geoffrey's activities and he'll be arrested before he can do me any mischief."

"Get out," she said thickly, reaching for her torn chemise and clutching it against her with trembling fingers, to ward off his gaze. "Get out before I kill you myself!"

His laugh was low and nasty. "You'd best be careful in your manner toward me," he warned. Swiftly he rose and adjusted his flowing trousers around his lean legs. Bitterly she guessed he had left his boots in the hall and tiptoed in, once he had ascertained the door was unlatched—that was why she had not heard him. With a graceful gesture he brushed back his thick golden hair and picked up his fur-trimmed cloak and hat. " 'Twould not do for Geoffrey to suspect we are lovers, Lenore—I do but warn you." He paused thoughtfully. "We'd best not meet here in future. 'Twould cause comment. My rooms, I think."

With a sob, Lenore reached down and picked up the closest thing within reach—her shoe. With all her force, she hurled it at his head. Gilbert ducked, caught the shoe in one hand, and tossed it contemptuously away from him. He stood before her, arms akimbo, a tall, glittering figure in his fawn satins, the angular lines of his face made satanic and evil by the light of the dying fire. His voice held a note of menace.

"You are *my* doxie now," he growled. "Ye'd do well to remember it."

"I am *Geoffrey's!*" she flashed.

He shrugged indifferently. "I do not object to sharing you with him." He sauntered to the door and stood a moment looking back at her as she crouched by the chair, holding her chemise like a shield in front of her. His tone was deliberate, cold. "You'll keep your silence about this night, mistress—and about all the nights to come." Like stones, the words fell crushingly on her ears. "You will do it because you'll remember—even as the hot words rise to your lips—that I hold Geoffrey's life in my hand."

"May you rot in hell!" sobbed Lenore.

"More like, I'll find paradise in your arms," he sneered. "You'll change your mind when you have thought on it."

Then he was gone and Lenore dropped her chemise and threw herself at the door, latching it with shaking fingers. Naked and trembling, she leaned against it. She could hear the small scuffling sound as Gilbert sat on the stairs pulling on his boots, then soft footsteps tiptoeing down the stairs. Plainly Gilbert did not mean to compromise her with Mistress Watts.

No, having had her once, he meant to have her again. Doubtless he planned to fill in for Geoffrey whenever he was away! Tonight he'd be slipping like a shadow through the streets, carefully avoiding the watch—but next time he meant to have her spend the night in *his* rooms, returning her with the dawn!

Shame and mortification such as she had never known flooded over her so that she sagged against the door. This could not be happening to her! A sense of doom pervaded her, dragging her down. Geoffrey was away somewhere prowling the roads. Who knew when he would be back? Perhaps he was never coming back, perhaps he was lying in the snow at this very minute, his blood staining the white snow red. . . . She swayed in terror at the thought.

Abruptly she sneezed—and realized that she was not only naked but freezing cold. The fire was almost out and the embers gave little warmth. Shivering, she found her chemise. It was so badly torn she cast it aside and instead wrapped herself in her shawl and fell into bed, hiding her face in the pillow as dry sobs wracked her body.

She was still awake when the first light pinked the sky.

Grimly she faced the dawn and the cold hearth. Gilbert had wanted her—and he had taken her. Now that he had taken her, it had but warmed his ardor. She had little hope his threats were empty or that this drunken romp would be the last he would try with her.

The alternative? To tell Geoffrey and let him revenge himself on Gilbert. Ah, but she could not do that, for Gilbert would exact his revenge first and expose Geoffrey's activities. That would mean the gibbet for Geoffrey.

In silent agony, she rocked back and forth in the bed. *What . . . could . . . she . . . do?*

Her bitter musings were interrupted by Gwynneth, Mistress Watts's serving girl, who came up to build the morning fire. When she had it blazing, she laid down the poker and asked Lenore if she was ready for her breakfast.

"I want bath water first," said Lenore. "Lots of it."

"But the room be cold yet," protested the maid. "If ye wait till after breakfast—"

"Now," said Lenore harshly. She felt as if Gilbert's touch clung to her everywhere, and it made her skin crawl. "Tell Mistress Watts I'll want clean sheets today. I'm—I'm expecting my husband back." It wasn't true, she had no idea when Geoffrey would return, but it was an acceptable reason for changing sheets on the wrong day of the week.

Gwynneth gave her a puzzled look and scurried away muttering that Christmas Eve was no time to be changing sheets!

The hot bath in the small metal tub which Gwynneth set in front of the hearth made Lenore feel better. While Gwynneth changed the bed linen, she lingered in the tub, scrubbing herself until her flesh glowed bright pink, rubbing herself dry on the linen towels Gwynneth had brought her. She dressed slowly, ignoring the breakfast tray Gwynneth brought up. "I'll eat later," she promised. "Would you ask Mistress Watts for a needle and thread? No, don't bother, I'll ask her myself."

She squared her shoulders and went downstairs. Best to know at once if Mistress Watts had heard any unusual sounds in the night, or had seen Gilbert slipping out. Mistress Watts was bustling about, preoccupied with preparations for Christmas, and gave Lenore the needle and thread

194

with an absent smile. Lenore could detect nothing in her landlady's manner to indicate knowledge of the nocturnal activities of young "Mistress Daunt" upstairs. Perhaps, even if she had heard something, she had paid no attention, for she had two student tenants who lodged in the back and came and went at all hours—it was because of them that the front door was never locked. As she left Mistress Watts and went out into the hall, both students strolled by, nodding a civil greeting, and Lenore bore her needle and thread back upstairs with a sigh of relief. No trouble from that quarter, then.

There remained, of course, the sticky problem of Gilbert and what to do about him. Lenore walked to the window. Bleakly she gazed out through the little leaded panes into the snowy alley below. She turned away with a sigh. She had a chemise to mend—Geoffrey must not return and find it torn like that. It would make him wonder.

Lenore was not very proficient with her needle, and mending the torn chemise took her a long time. Finished, she held it up and surveyed it critically. She had been more skillful than usual. Geoffrey might not notice, so neatly was it mended—even if he did, he would assume it had been torn in some less dramatic way. As she laid it down, her gaze fell on the untouched breakfast tray.

She must eat, Lenore told herself abruptly. Not for herself, but for her unborn child—Geoffrey's child. Hardly tasting, she forced down the gruel, now cold and congealed, the milk in the pewter tankard, and took a dispirited bite out of the red apple from Mistress Watts's basement bin.

Restless and upset, she yearned to throw on her green cloak and red shawl, slip into her clogs, and take a brisk walk in the snow. But—Gilbert and his sleigh might lie in wait around the corner of Magpie Lane. And how would she explain fighting with him in the street if he stopped and tried to put her into the sleigh by force? For that matter, how did she know that he was not on his way over now to pay a "call" on young Mistress Daunt?

A shudder went through her, and she hurried downstairs with the breakfast tray—for she did not want to open the door, believing it was Gwynneth come to clear the dishes, and see Gilbert standing there instead. She returned the needle to Mistress Watts, thanked her and said, "I'm not feeling well; I intend to sleep all day so—so I'll be rested for Christmas. If you should see anyone about to mount these stairs, would you ask them not to disturb me?"

Mistress Watts gave her young tenant a sharp look, for this was the first time such a request had been made of her. "Ye do look flushed," she said with a frown. "Do you need something from the apothecary? Or perhaps ye should be bled. Dr. Micaw says the humors—"

"No, no, 'tis nothing—I am but tired." Lenore hurried back upstairs and latched the door.

Tomorrow was Christmas, and Gilbert planned to give her an expensive present—a fur muff, which she dared not refuse. Doubtless he'd exact a price for it!

In blind rage, she struck the pillow on her bed with her fist. Gilbert's head would not lie there again! It would not!

She threw herself onto the bed and tried to think, but her hammering thoughts gave her a headache, and she looked wan and pale when Gwynneth knocked. "Mistress Watts thought since ye not be feeling well, ye might relish supper up here."

"Thank you, Gwynneth." Lenore opened the door to admit the little maid, who set the tray down and turned to go. "And thank Mistress Watts, too. Have you a family, Gwynneth?"

"Six sisters and three brothers—living," Gwynneth told her proudly. "We would be sixteen of us all told—had all lived, but six did die at birth or soon after. My youngest sister is two years old."

Two years old! No wonder poor Gwynneth had to work long hours. "I wish you a merry Christmas, Gwynneth," Lenore told her soberly, wondering what she could find to give the girl tomorrow. "And I'll bring the tray down myself—tomorrow morning."

The girl brightened. "As soon as I've finished clearing

196

up supper, I'll be away home—we're roasting chestnuts tonight!"

She looked so happy at this unusual treat that Lenore swallowed as she watched her go. The lot of girls like Gwynneth was hard, a life of drudgery from childhood, and nothing to look forward to but more of the same. While she—! Drudgery would not be her lot—shame, more likely, or a short merry dance on the gibbet! She lifted her chin defiantly as she latched the door behind Gwynneth and heard the girl's feet tripping lightly down the stairs. She would find a way out of her troubles. *Somehow.*

Dutifully, Lenore ate the pork pie and pasty which Mistress Watts had sent up, and downed the cider which accompanied it. With the food her sagging spirits rose a little and she sat by the window watching the snow flake down. Would it never stop snowing? she wondered irritably.

A scratching and mewing outside the door announced Mistress Watts's cat, eager to be out of the cold corridor and inside in the warm. Automatically, Lenore went to the door and opened it. The cat rushed inside and rubbed against her legs, purring. Lenore fed him the remains of her pork pie and sat soberly watching him eat. With satisfaction the big white cat licked his furry jaws, manicured his whiskers, washed his paws, leaped to the bed and took a complete bath with an energetic pink tongue for a wash-rag—and then settled down for a sleep in the warmest spot—curled up in a furry ball by the hearth.

Lenore watched him soberly. Mistress Watts was kind, and so her cat was in out of the snow, but there were many cats with cold wet paws shivering beneath icicled eaves tonight—many who would not survive the night. And perhaps children, too.

She covered her face with her hands, and a deep sob escaped her. She had not only Geoffrey to think about, but her unborn child—she owned a duty to that child, too. The awful events of last night washed over her afresh, sickening her all over again. If she told Geoffrey what Gilbert had done, his face would turn white and he would seek Gilbert out and kill him—and she had no doubt

197

Gilbert would make good his threat to expose Geoffrey as a Royalist and a highwayman before he died. Even should he not do so, the law was strict—Geoffrey would be caught and hanged for Gilbert's murder. In the afterwash of that tragedy she would be taken, would plead her belly as convicted women usually did, her child would be born in jail and they would hang her later—or transport her to a life of slavery in the Colonies. And her child—if it survived the grim life of the orphanage—would have no more chance than Gwynneth and her brothers and sisters. None at all.

Arms wrapped about her knees, Lenore rocked with misery. The latch—such a little thing, she had forgotten to latch the door. But would Geoffrey ever understand that? Would Mistress Watts, for that matter, believe her? Why, she would ask reasonably, had Lenore made no outcry? Why had Gilbert not had to batter the door down? She would believe Lenore had made a tryst with him, that they were secret lovers who had had a falling out. Even Geoffrey might believe it—and that she could not face.

With a start she hurried to the door, checked and rechecked the latch, and shoved a chair against it. Then she went back to bed and after a time fell into an exhausted sleep. She woke once to think she heard a discreet tapping.

"Lenore." Gilbert's voice, low and urgent.

Lenore stiffened. He was back! She got up, ran barefoot to the door, and spoke with her face pressed against the panel.

"Go away," she whispered. "Or I'll call Mistress Watts and be damned to you!"

There was a muffled curse on the other side of the door. Then he must have swung on his heel, for footsteps clicked rapidly down the stairs.

Lenore returned to her bed and lay staring into emptiness, seeing how it would be. . . . His threats were not empty—they were real and terrible. Last night there had been a warning in those hard caramel eyes in the firelight, and more—there had been steamy desire. She had waked something in him that would be hard to control.

She turned to stare at the window—a lighter square in a dark room, where snow was drifting down. Oxford, which at first had seemed so wonderful, their first real home together, had closed in about her with cold white arms. The lodgings off Magpie Lane which had seemed so idyllic had become a trap.

The big white cat, disturbed by Gilbert's knock, rose and stretched his long thick-furred body luxuriously, then he leaped onto the bed and with eyes closed in bliss rubbed a furry cheek against hers. His whiskers tickled as she scratched his soft neck, and he curled up beside her in contentment.

Lenore lay on her back stroking him, staring bleakly at the little leaded panes, and took what comfort she could from the rasping purr beside her.

She knew not how it would end, but she could not risk Geoffrey's life—nor could she risk the life of her unborn child by starting out now into the deep-drifted snow, penniless, cold, and wanted by the Lord Protector's harsh law. She took a deep breath, and her delicate jaw grew as grim as it had another time when she'd steeled herself to ride through the battle at Worcester. She would not lie with Gilbert—nor did she mean to endanger Geoffrey. She would think of something.

In the meantime she had no choice but to play the game out.

Wearily she closed her eyes—and sat up almost immediately at the soft calls from below of "Puss! Puss, where are you?"

"Up here, Mistress Watts." Lenore opened the door to call downstairs, and Mistress Watts scurried in and picked up the big white cat from the bed.

"I woke and found him gone," she apologized. "I'm sorry to wake you up like this, but something woke me— I don't know what—and I looked around for Puss. Bad Puss!" She gave him an affectionate shake. "Giving me a scare like that!"

Lenore could guess what had waked her—the sound of Gilbert closing the door as he slipped back out into the night. "You didn't wake me," she assured. "I couldn't sleep."

"Oh? Well, I'm sorry to hear that, I'd hoped you'd be feeling better." Mistress Watts, in her heavy woolen wrapper, carried Puss to the door and set him down in the corridor, where he stretched and yawned. "Will ye be up for Christmas?"

She meant, would the servants, busy as they were, have to carry her Christmas dinner up to her. "I'll be downstairs for Christmas," Lenore promised grimly.

"Good. Well, then I'll just take that tray. Come along with you, Puss, giving me such a fright—I did think you were locked outside and turned into an icicle by now! Mistress Daunt, ye've let that fire die down too much— ye should put a log on it, or ye'll be freezing before morning."

Lenore sighed, and latched the door after her landlady's departure downstairs. Christmas Eve . . . at least she had gotten through the day without incident. She squared her slender shoulders. Tomorrow Christmas must be dealt with.

Shivering now, she stayed up for a while. She put fresh faggots on the fire until it blazed brightly, and then a heavier log. Gradually the cold room grew warm, and she lifted a hot brick from the fire with tongs and carefully wrapped it, placed it in the bed to warm it. At last she banked the fire on the hearth, took off her dress and petticoat, and with a light woolen wrapper thrown around her chemise, took a last barefoot walk over the cold, uneven floorboards to the window, where the snow had piled up on the sills so that she could scarce see out. It had stopped snowing now and a cold moon rode the skies, making the narrow street below almost as light as an overcast winter day.

Lenore leaned forward, her breath frosting the panes. Around the corner from Magpie Lane, floundering through the deep piled-up drifts, struggled a bay horse, his head and mane whitened with snow. And on his back with the wind whipping his dark serviceable cloak was a tall rider —Geoffrey.

Unmindful that she was barefoot and the stairs were icy cold, Lenore ran downstairs and joyfully threw open the front door. Geoffrey, himself well coated with snow, was just alighting, and he shook himself like a big dog and enfolded her in a snowy embrace.

"You came back!" Her voice thrilled. "Oh, Geoffrey, you came back for Christmas!" She hugged him, unmindful of the snow.

"Did you think I would not?" He ruffled her long streaming hair with a gentle fist. "Back upstairs with you, Lenore, for I've got to take care of my horse—he's near to freezing."

She nodded, her heart too full to speak, and ran lightly back upstairs. Tomorrow might find her world wrecked, but tonight—Geoffrey was back! She rushed about, plumping up pillows, lighting a taper, rewrapping another hot brick to warm the bed. There was a pitcher of cider, and a bowl of apples. She set those out and waited. Whatever had happened, she would let nothing spoil Geoffrey's homecoming.

Caring for the mount who had brought him through the blizzard took Geoffrey a long time, and Lenore was standing by the table in her wrapper when his booted feet came wearily up the stairs. He shook out his wet cloak and spread it over a chair before the hearth. Lenore hurried forward to help him out of his heavy wide-topped boots. She winced to see them clogged with snow, and kneaded the cold flesh of his near frostbitten calves with gentle fingers.

Geoffrey was seated on a chair by the hearth, and now he drew her to his lap with a contented sigh. "The drifts on the country roads are piled deep," he said. "The last two leagues I feared I'd not make it, for the horse was near done. But I did not want you to sleep alone on Christmas Eve."

Burrowing into his shoulder, Lenore managed not to wince. Had he come back a day earlier he might have found his bed occupied—by Gilbert! She put the thought away from her, sat up, and gave him a soft, mysterious glance from under shadowed lashes. "I am glad you came," she whispered. "For it would not have been Christmas without you."

For a moment there was a leaping hunger in his gray eyes. Then he leaned forward and planted a gentle kiss on her lips, stood her on her feet, and undressed, with Lenore helping to urge him out of his wet coat and trousers.

"I've been warming the bed with hot bricks," she told him eagerly, and he gave a low laugh, scooped her up, and carried her to it.

"You'll need no hot brick tonight, for 'tis myself will warm you," he promised her, throwing back the heavy quilts and plumping her onto the bed. "And there's a Christmas gift for you in my saddlebags—a velvet hat and muff."

Lenore caught her breath. She must mention it now lest there be trouble tomorrow. "Gilbert," she said with studied carelessness, "has announced he's giving me a fur muff for Christmas." She watched him in dread.

A frown darkened Geoffrey's lean face, and he shot her a sharp look. "A handsome gift," he mused, "from one who's never been known for his generosity in such things. Gil must indeed be smitten."

She bit her lip. She must be careful, careful what she said. Geoffrey must not suspect.

"He was probably just showing off before Lally," she improvised, blowing out the taper beside the bed. "Or perhaps he hopes I will intercede for him—he fancies her, you know."

"Does he now?" Geoffrey smiled. "Ned may have something to say about that!"

" 'Tis nothing Gilbert's said—and she has not spoken to me of it," said Lenore quickly. "But he hired a sleigh and took Lally and me for a ride yesterday—I think he thought Lally would not go with him alone." How cleverly she had distorted the facts! "Ned joined us at the Crown for supper—and Michael and Lewis were there, too." Her voice rushed anxiously on; she hoped Geoffrey would decide there was safety in numbers. "I am glad you are here to counsel me, for I knew not what to do—about

202

the muff. You had told me to be careful where Gilbert is concerned, but I fear not to accept the muff would offend him, Geoffrey. Truly I do."

Looking into her worried violet eyes, so frank and open to his gaze, Geoffrey suddenly checked and his brow cleared. "We'll accept Gil's muff," he decided. "For 'twould run about the sum he still owes me from that old debt. But you'll wear *mine*, mistress. And later, if you should decide to trade Gil's muff to Lally for something of hers you covet more, Gil will be none the wiser."

"I'll *give* his muff to Lally—after Christmas. For she gave me her green woolen cloak. And anyway"—her bright smile was one of relief—"velvet becomes me better!"

Geoffrey chuckled and slipped under the covers with her, his body feeling hard-muscled and still cold from the snow. "I had meant to take you for a sleigh ride myself, Lenore," he murmured, "knowing ye're childishly fond of snow!"

"There'll be other times!" She snuggled against him, fighting back tears that she should deceive him so, pressing warm kisses into the deep throb of his throat. "And I've a gift for you too, Geoffrey—I saved my coins to buy it. 'Tis—'tis an enameled ring. To bind you to me," she whispered, suddenly shy, for in truth she'd gone without things she needed badly to buy the ring.

The sinewy arms around her tightened. "You need no ring for that, Lenore, though I'll wear it proudly." His voice grew husky. "But the gift of yourself, Lenore, is the greatest gift of all."

Tears stung her eyes, trembled on her lashes. Tomorrow might find her dead or on the run—for in anger Geoffrey might well kill her as well as Gilbert if he found out. But that was tomorrow—she had tonight.

Forgotten was her sense of doom in that warm room in the firelight. Forgotten were all her forebodings.

She flung herself against Geoffrey with a violence that surprised him. "I love you so much," she whispered brokenly.

"Faith," he murmured into her white neck, "I should be

gone more often—if only to enjoy such homecomings!"

"You should never be gone from my side," she declared fiercely. "Not for one instant!"

He laughed and stroked her slender, resilient body, his fingers tracing a fiery trail of pulsing sensations along her spine, making her breasts quiver and her nipples tingle to hardness. Those fingers wandered farther, easing along her satiny hips, playfully stroking that small triangle of bright silken hair between her thighs until she shivered at his touch.

In silent happiness, thankful that he was home returned, she melted against him, feeling the fires of his passion warm her. *The gift of herself* . . . what heavenly words those were. . . . Through the heavy drifts Geoffrey had struggled to reach her—in time for Christmas. She would she had more to give him, but the delights of her temptress body would always be his to hold. Gently, silkily, with expert ease he entered her, and the linen sheets rasped against her bare legs and her body thrilled and clamored as his hands caressed her, explored her lovingly. From a luxurious sea of shared bliss, they rose and fell on mounting waves of stormy passion. Outside the white moon shone down on a crystal world, but inside all was warm and dark and wonderful.

Other gifts, more valuable in the world's eyes, they might someday give each other. But on this, their first Christmas Eve together, their greatest, most magical gift to each other was the fire in their bodies, and the love in their hearts. As she fell away from him at last, warm and sleepy and satisfied, and forgetful of their peril, Lenore knew that no matter what gift Geoffrey ever gave her, she would never truly wish for more than this—himself.

CHAPTER 13

The wind, whipping across a white winter landscape, had brought a biting cold, but the Christmas season at Oxford was as merry as Lally had promised. For Lenore, however, it was a terrible Christmas, all the gaiety and gladness shadowed by fear.

In defiance of the law, a dozen of the merriest Oxford youths (all of them with Royalist leanings) went together and purchased a Christmas goose, which was stuffed with chestnuts and oysters and roasted by Mistress Watts's cook. To this feast, Mistress Watts generously contributed a large plum pudding and Geoffrey, who had come back from his mysterious, snowy ride in funds, furnished chestnuts to roast before the fire. Young Michael brought sweetmeats his mother had sent him from their manor house south of Coventry, while most of the others arrived laden with wine.

Lenore's sense of doom had returned and pervaded what should have been a wonderful day, heightened as it was by callers and the giving of gifts. Lenore felt quite overwhelmed, for Lally arrived early, bringing her a pair of gay red wool stockings, and a new pair of gloves from Ned. Both gifts were badly needed and gratefully accepted, for her own stockings were much-mended and her hands in her threadbare gloves were near to freezing these days.

She presented Lally with an orange plume for her hat. Geoffrey had told her earlier that they had enough money to buy presents for everyone and they had rushed out, banging on closed shop doors and getting surprised tradesmen to come downstairs and open up for their late-bought gifts. Ned's gift of a pair of gauntlets must be given to him later, for now that the snow had stopped and the roads were passable, he was spending Christmas Day with his Marston lady.

Lally exclaimed impressively over the lovely plum velvet hat and muff Geoffrey had given Lenore as she whirled about the room modeling them for her. But Lally fell silent at sight of the enameled ring Geoffrey sported. Lenore knew what she was thinking—that a ring would not hold Ned, that perhaps nothing would hold him. Quickly she urged on Lally another glass of Christmas cider—hastily procured, along with sweetmeats, from Mistress Watts downstairs. Lally accepted the cider, but Lenore hadn't missed her sad, envious glance.

Lenore had a bad moment when Gilbert arrived bearing the muff he had promised. He looked startled to see Geoffrey, but he rallied and presented the muff with a flourish—it was of marten and very soft. Lenore had steeled herself to face him—the first time since that hot, shameful encounter in her bed. In silence she accepted this bitter gift. The soft brown fur seemed to sear her hands; she yearned to hurl the pretty muff into the fire. But . . . they were all watching—Geoffrey sardonically, Lally with narrowed eyes.

Gallantly Lenore lifted her head and gave Gilbert a cool, impersonal smile. "It's very lovely," she said in a lightly distant tone.

"As you are, Mistress Lenore." Gilbert fetched her a handsome bow, his honey curls falling foppishly forward.

"And from Geoffrey and myself." She handed him a

wrapped package and Gilbert took it warily, as if it might blow up. The gift was one of the gay colored knitted woolen scarfs which they had hastily bought for all their student friends this morning.

Before he could properly thank her, Lenore shoved a glass of cider into his hand and the door swung open to admit Michael—handsomely garbed in a new red velvet cloak—and his friend Lewis. Michael surprised Lenore by giving her a length of warm green wool, which she exclaimed over, saying it would match her cloak perfectly—and Lally told her that together they'd manage to make it up into a dress. Lewis shyly gave her a bit of Florentine lace, and Geoffrey raised amused eyebrows at these tokens of devotion from her ardent young admirers—and at their exuberant joy at being presented with colorful woolen scarves by young Mistress Daunt.

"You'd think Lenore wove them herself," Lally laughed, but her slate-blue eyes were sad.

Then Mistress Watts came hurrying up the stairs with a white linsey-woolsey petticoat for Lenore, so that she might face the rigors of Oxford weather rather better. Lenore was glad she had bought a bright shawl for the kind landlady. "And a tidbit for Puss," she added, handing Mistress Watts a small wrapped package containing salmon.

They all laughed at that, and Mistress Watts hastened to tell them that Puss expected Christmas presents "same as anyone," and confided that she always spiked his Christmas milk with a bit of spirits.

"Should Puss get too drunk, Mistress Watts, let him stagger on his paws over to my lodgings," Gilbert said. "I've a fondness for strays." He was looking at Lenore as he said that, and she flashed him an angry look. He was standing beside the window looking very rakish in bronze silks, his weight supported on one foot as he lounged against the wall. As she met his sardonic gaze, he shifted his weight so that his other hip was thrust forward and a lean bronze silk thigh was thrown into high relief in the bright winter light reflected off the snow. His easy smile was knowing, and raked over her as if he had stripped her down to her chemise and already was tossing back her skirts. Before that cool, insolent look, remembrance flooded bitterly over Lenore, and she turned quickly away, to find Lally watching her with a penetrating gaze.

"Has Gilbert been bothering you lately?" Lally whispered.

"No, of course not," Lenore lied with an innocent look. "Why should he?" Her shrug said: *one rebuff should be enough.*

"Oh, I don't know—he's very persistent and I just thought he might. Well, I must be going."

"Don't go, Lally," urged Lenore. "Stay with us till time to dine—'twill not be long."

" 'Twill be very long," corrected Lally. "I remember last year 'twas late at night before all was ready! We were near to starving before the goose was carved. The Great Tom bell had already tolled curfew, so we'd no choice but to stay the night sleeping on the floor in Mistress Watts's common room!"

Last year . . . so Lally had been with Ned a year, at least. Lenore had not known it had been so long.

"I'll be back." Lally rose and pulled on her gloves. "Tonight is a festive occasion, and I mean to dress for it!"

What Lally meant became clear that evening when she made a sensational entrance on Gilbert's arm. He was resplendent in honey-colored velvets frosted with Mechlin, and she was every bit as spectacular in a deep red velvet gown cut shockingly low. Her ash-blond hair was magnificently done, every hair swept up in place. From her soft kid gloves to the tips of her velvet pattens she was a fashion plate, and she bore in her arms great sprays of holly for Mistress Watts's table decoration.

Lenore felt plain by comparison. She was wearing her usual russet wool, full-skirted, with a starched white linen collar and cuffs edged in point. For a moment she gazed wistfully at her flamboyant friend. And yet—she looked down at her dress; she remembered that Geoffrey had arranged with Mistress Watts to have this warm woolen dress made shortly after their arrival in Oxford and had surprised her by its early completion on the first bitter cold day. "Of russet wool to complement your hair," he had said gravely as he presented it to her, but she had suspected him of choosing that color out of sentiment, because russet was the traditional color of country brides' dresses.

She looked up again, from fingering the russet material. Lally might be garbed in rich velvets, but her slate-blue eyes were unhappy, and the fashionably dressed man on her arm was not her lover. While she. . . ! Lenore gave Geoffrey a soft look. He was everything to her—and she to him.

Christmas dinner was a happy occasion, marred for Lenore only by Gilbert's presence. Although several times before dinner he had tried to corner her, she had managed to avoid him. True to Lally's prediction, the sun had waned before the meal was served, but Mistress Watts had been reckless in her use of tapers, and the beamed low-ceilinged common room downstairs blazed with light. Wide-topped polished boots scuffed over the clean-scoured stone floor and masculine voices made a low hum, for with the exception of Lenore and Lally, Mistress Watts's guests were exclusively male.

At one side of the room a Yule log burned brightly on a great hearth with an iron crane above it from which hung a great iron pot. The aproned cook was tasting the oyster stew from this pot with a long-handled iron spoon, and the goose was being turned on a spit by Jack, the stableboy. The warm hearth emitted a mouth-watering aroma. Potatoes were baking in their jackets in the ashes at the edge of the roaring fire and pitchers of cider sat in the deep windowsills waiting to be poured into pewter tankards.

Gwynneth, aided by her younger sister Dora, who had been hired for the occasion, were arranging pewter knives and trenchers and tankards and linen napkins atop the improvised "dining table." This was a number of long boards supported by carpenters' "horses" and covered with an assortment of odd-sized linen tablecloths—for Mistress Watts's linen chest was inadequate for the entertainment of so many guests. The holly Lally had brought had been arranged into three handsome centerpieces spiked with candles and spaced down the long board. And although some of the students' cuffs were frayed and their boot soles worn almost through, Lenore thought she had never seen so glittering a company.

She was seated between Geoffrey and red-coated Michael (who had vied with Lewis in a friendly scuffle to sit beside her) and directly across the table from Lally—and unfortunately across from Gilbert also, for he was squiring Lally this evening.

The steaming oyster stew—served in wooden bowls and eaten with pewter spoons—was rapidly consumed, for by now the guests were ravenous. Then the Christmas goose was brought to table on a huge pewter charger and received a cheer from the company. Lenore smiled as she watched an elderly admirer of Mistress Watts carve the goose with obvious trepidation. He lived across the street, and had gallantly contributed the chestnut and oyster stuffing.

Seeing her suitor was nervous at carving before so many guests, Mistress Watts attracted their attention by saying loudly, "I've a rare sight for you, a trick I've taught Puss here." She ordered Gwynneth to bring up a low stool and place it beside her, and the big white cat obediently jumped atop it, his head and half his body now showing above the table. "I've trained Puss to eat at table," Mistress Watts announced in an important voice. "See? He'll eat every course, won't you, Puss?"

A round of exuberant applause greeted Puss's quick demolishing of a small bowl of oyster stew, but the noise frightened the cat, who jumped down from the stool and sought an empty windowsill where he licked his paws and gazed balefully at the company.

But Mistress Watts's elderly suitor gave her a grateful look for diverting attention from his clumsy efforts at carving and her kindly eyes twinkled back at him.

As the goose was served, Lenore leaned forward to speak to Lally, and saw that Lally was staring somberly down at her hands, her fair head bent a little and reflecting the candlelight, while Gilbert argued with the student on his left.

Sensing Lenore's compassionate gaze upon her, Lally looked up and her slate-blue eyes hardened. *"You* have a muff for each hand," she said bitterly. "While I—!" She broke off, but Lenore knew it was not muffs Lally was talking about.

Except for one or two bad moments when Gilbert looked across the table at her with unadulterated lust in his gaze, Lenore found herself enjoying the occasion. Geoffrey was at her side and witty remarks flew back and forth as the guests stuffed themselves. The servants ran about, flush-faced and bright—they'd been nipping at Mistress Watts's French brandy in the pantry. That brandy had been smuggled into Oxford up the Thames and so had arrived duty free. Lenore was glad the servants were having a good time of it, even if the service was careless— glad, too, that she'd remembered to buy them baskets of red apples for Christmas.

The meal progressed. The goose and pease and hot baked potatoes, bursting in their brown jackets, were consumed along with a large amount of cider. Then the stable-boy proudly brought forward the great plum pudding, flaming on Mistress Watts's treasured silver tray. They ate it with a thick wine sauce, drank wine and brandy, and uproariously toasted each other's health—and as they grew drunker and more reckless, the King's. Lally matched the gentlemen, glass for glass. Lenore watched her anxiously, for Lally in her daring red gown was too merry tonight, her forced laughter too shrill. Gilbert, too, was watching Lally with heavy-lidded eyes, watching her flushed face and the strand of ash-blond hair that had come loose from her intricate hairdo and which she irritably pushed back to lift her glass again and stridently toast "All of Royal England!"

Gilbert drank with the rest and looked across the table. "Took ye the white horse on your journey this time, Geoffrey?" he asked carelessly. But before Geoffrey could answer, he added "Nay, I suppose not—a white horse shines like a beacon in the darkness, but a bay horse slides into the shadows well."

"What are ye saying, Gil?" Geoffrey's voice was lazy, but a pair of cold gray eyes challenged his cousin.

Gilbert shrugged. "Only that mayhap the bay does keep ye safer from . . . *highwaymen.*" He emphasized the word and laughed discordantly; Lenore could see that he was getting very drunk.

Geoffrey studied his cousin, obviously making allowance for Gilbert's drunken state. "I've managed to hold my own with the gentlemen of the road thus far," he said in a level tone. "Perhaps my luck will hold a bit longer."

"Aye, 'tis luck we all need." Gilbert's gaze played mockingly over Lenore, and she flushed and turned pointedly away. He shrugged and turned back to Lally. When Michael said something that turned her attention that way again she saw that Gilbert's drunken gaze was bent fixedly on Lally's heaving red velet bodice. Lenore—though relieved at this respite from Gilbert's unwelcome attentions—could not help feeling angry with Ned. His Marston lady had expected him to spend Christmas Day with her, of course, but—his lonely daughter of the regiment needed him as well, and her heart might well break because of him.

When, after dinner, Gilbert and Lally slipped away early, Lally weaving on her feet and being supported by Gilbert, whose condition was almost as bad, Lenore's shoulders jerked spasmodically, and she made a convulsive gesture as if to stop them.

" 'Tis not our affair," Geoffrey murmured in her ear, seeing the direction of her lowering glance. "Each must make his own bed, Lenore, though sometimes 'tis thorny sleeping in it."

"But—can't she see him for what he is? Corrupt?"

"Women have always forgiven Gil his corruption," Geoffrey sighed. "He has a pretty face."

"*I* do not find him pretty," snapped Lenore.

Geoffrey laughed. "Then you're in the minority."

"I just don't want to see Lally hurt," she sulked.

"Nor do I. But Lally's a grown woman—yes, and a worldly one. She'd not appreciate your clucking over her like a mother hen."

Around them now the wine was being poured by unsteady hands, spilling over pewter tankards, drenching lace cuffs and splashing onto the clean-scoured floor as the young bloods clashed their tankards together and roared out forbidden Christmas carols. The very walls rocked with "God Rest Ye Merrie Gentlemen" until Mistress Watts's eyes rolled in her head in fright as she sought vainly to quiet the singers. Lenore was hard put to avoid several roguish youths who sought to kiss her beneath the mistletoe Mistress Watts had hung from the beams to snare the attentions of her elderly admirer.

When the guests had all departed—three of them were so drunk they had to be carted awkwardly through the snow to their lodgings in wheelbarrows, to Mistress Watts's distress (she muttered that the neighbors "would think she was running a bawdy house"), and Lenore was once more alone in her upstairs lodgings with Geoffrey, he went over to stir up the fire and Lenore came up behind him and wrapped her arms about him.

"Our first Christmas together, Geoffrey," she said in a soft voice.

He put down the poker and turned about, taking her shoulders in gentle hands. "Pray God the rest will be better ones," he said huskily. "And celebrated in a home of our own."

"Oh, do not say that!" She hugged him. "For a finer Christmas I have never known!"

"God's grace sent you to me, Lenore," he said simply, his lips brushing her bright hair which she had loosed to cascade down about her shoulders. "For surely I do not deserve you."

For the moment Lenore had forgotten Gilbert, and her laughter brimmed with confidence. Roguishly she cuffed his face. "Deserve me? Certainly you don't deserve me, but I'm a foolish woman and I love you as you are!"

"Come to bed and prove it!" His white teeth glinted in a wide smile and he pushed down the neck of her chemise

213

and pressed a warm kiss into the gleaming whiteness of her bared shoulder.

"Look, Geoffrey, it's snowing again," she murmured as he carried her to the big square bed. "The town will soon look like a wedding cake!"

For a moment she felt his muscles stiffen, and she rushed on to say something else. Marriage was a subject they avoided now, as if it were treacherous ground where they must never tread. Once they were abed and fondling, her foolish remark was forgotten as their love flamed on this cold, unforgettable Christmas night.

CHAPTER 14

During the Twelve Days of Christmas, winter tightened its icy grip on Oxford. All Christmas week Geoffrey did not leave her side and with Geoffrey home, Gilbert prudently avoided Lenore—for he had a healthy respect for Geoffrey's sword arm. She saw him once, when Geoffrey took her skating on the frozen Thames. He was skating arm in arm with Lally, and they made a handsome couple, scarves flying, their breath frosting the air and their noses red with cold. Seeing them together sobered Lenore because she knew that room had been made for Ned at Marston and he would be staying there till Twelfth Night, which left Lally to spend the holidays alone. Lenore knew she should have been grateful Ned was at Marston, for Gilbert's new fascination with Lally gave her a respite, but she could not help feeling sorry for her friend, whose sad face haunted her.

Lenore loved the icy crystal weather and Geoffrey affixed her pattens and together they explored the old walled city afoot. She found it to be a long narrow town built upon a gravel bank, with a crossroads at the center. The Roman roads had passed Oxford by, a wind-whipped pink-cheeked scholar told them pleasantly when they stopped to rest in the shelter of an ivied wall—the Romans, from bitter past experience, mistrusted roads built on swamps.

Happy to be with Geoffrey on these walks, Lenore hurried along beside him, laughing at the cold, for she was muffled to the ears. Scrambled about her among the twisting streets were the big buildings of the university. But commerce as well as learning were important here, Geoffrey told her, for as soon as the ice broke, barges would ply up and down the Thames, carrying wool downriver from the Cotswolds for the looms of Oxford, and wines upriver to the old walled city from France—and sometimes, for the militant, arms. At taverns where they stopped to warm themselves on bitter days, they shared tankards of hot buttered rum and sometimes beef or mutton pies.

During the whole of that enchanted Christmas week they were gloriously happy.

Early in January, Geoffrey rode out. He would be gone a fortnight, he told her. He was not. He returned three nights later and limped up the stairs leaving a bloody trail. Lenore, who'd been prudently staying downstairs with Mistress Watts on the grounds of an indisposition—actually to avoid Gilbert in case he tried to pay her a call, heard the outer door open, heard limping footsteps ascending the stairs, seized a lighted candle and ran up after him in time to open the door to their rooms as he sagged against it.

"What happened?" she cried, frightened at the sight of his white face.

"I've been shot," he said grimly. " 'Tis only a leg wound, but it opened as I dismounted, and I fear that my blood stains the snow outside. 'Twill cause questions. Would you go down and scrape up the bloodstains from the snow and wipe them from the stairs, Lenore? And stable my horse?"

216

"But your wound—!" gasped Lenore. She set the candle on the table and ran to help him to a chair.

"Go now." Geoffrey waved her away. "*Now*, Lenore!" He staggered to the table and leaned heavily upon it for support.

Lenore hurried away to do his bidding, but from the landing she heard a heavy thud and rushed back to find he had slid to the floor unconscious.

Lenore had had practice binding up Meg's wounds when Tom Prattle had come home drunk and beaten her. Now she moved quickly and with dispatch. She brought Geoffrey to, weak from loss of blood. She removed and tossed aside the bloody scarf that bound his wound. Somehow she got his boot off and with water from the pitcher she washed the wound, bound and stanched it efficiently with clean linen napkins. Once that task was done she slipped down the stairs and out into the frozen moonlight and quickly removed all evidence of blood from the snow—and from the stairs. After that, she stabled and fed the bay horse.

When she came back in and closed the outside door, Mistress Watts had wakened and stuck her head out. "Is anything the matter, Mistress Daunt?" she inquired sleepily.

"Nothing at all," lied Lenore in an easy voice. "Geoffrey is back, so I'll spend the rest of the night upstairs."

"Back so soon? That's good." Mistress Watts yawned. "No, don't come out, Puss—I can't be chasing you!" Hastily she pushed back a furry white paw and closed the door, and Lenore fled up the stairs to Geoffrey.

He had got himself over to the bed when she got back. He was lying fully clothed and exhausted across it, his wounded leg stretched out and his other booted one dangling over the edge of the bed. Lenore pulled that boot off, too, slid a pillow under his head, threw the coverlets over him, and wrapped a warm brick for his feet.

"Ye're a good nurse," he gasped, beads of sweat frosting his forehead as he moved his injured leg to a more comfortable position. "One would think ye'd been battle-trained, Lenore."

She glowed with pride, held up his dark head and poured some brandy down his throat, took the glass and then sat down on the bed beside him, smoothed back his dark wavy hair and asked him how he'd come to be shot.

'Twas cursed bad luck, he told her. A friend of his father's had recognized him at an inn and—glad to see him—had blurted out his name in greeting. 'Twas too well-known a Royalist name not to cause remark. And his way out of the town had been barred by soldiers, hastily summoned by the Puritan innkeeper. He'd fought his way through—Lenore shuddered to hear—and lost them on well-trampled roads. None had followed him here, he was sure of it.

Lenore held that well-loved head to her breast and thanked God he had made it home to her.

All January Geoffrey convalesced, passing off his condition as a distemper of the lungs. Since Oxford was filled with distempers of the lungs at this season, his story was readily accepted. Lenore was glad to have him with her, but their funds were running perilously low. Mistress Watts did not press them for the rent, and once without Geoffrey's knowledge, Lenore even borrowed a small sum from Michael, who came over shivering, with his red cloak clutched around him and two woolen scarfs wrapped around his neck. Oxford had the worst weather in the world, he assured Lenore gloomily—July and August were the only frost-free months this miserable town had. There'd once even been a snowstorm right in the middle of summer term, and he for one found it unbearable! He had no plans to spend another winter here, but would return to his home near Coventry in June.

Lenore had to laugh at so much gloom, but even she found the weather irksome. Winter had indeed closed down on Oxford town. January was a gray month with fall after fall of snow. Snow perpetually covered the city wall with its high walk for sentries and its bastion. Snow drifted down on ivied towers and warrens of medieval cottages, on shops and stables and taverns, iced the streets and made work shoveling for day laborers with red noses and patched clothes. Snow almost closed the cobbled alley called Magpie Lane, where in better weather footfalls echoed after dark, and hampered the efforts of young Mistress Daunt to get some exercise by walking about the city with Lally. Fast sleighs glided past them over the hard-packed snowy streets and sleigh bells tinkled in the frosty air. The Thames stayed hard-frozen—the Oxford students called these lovely upper reaches of the river, romantically, the "Isis"—a river goddess. Lenore would have gone skating there with Lally, but Geoffrey objected, lest she fall on the ice. Lenore gave him an impatient look—she was a good skater. The sound of sleigh bells, reaching them from Magpie Lane, made her yearn to ride out on Snowfire over the hard-packed snow, but Geoffrey sharply forbade that, lest it bring on a miscarriage. Lenore fretted at that, but she arranged with Lally to exercise Snowfire, and spent long hours petting and currying Snowfire in Mistress Watts's warm stable—and giving attention to the bay, too, who had brought Geoffrey home to her through the blizzard. The stable boy was fond of the bay, and exercised him for her, but he was afraid of prancing Snowfire, who had once inadvertently kicked him.

For Lenore this time of Geoffrey's recuperation was like a truce in a battle. Time seemed to hang suspended for her. Geoffrey's constant presence was a bastion against Gilbert—although as the month wore on and her pregnancy became more apparent, Gilbert gave her an angry, sulky look when he passed her trudging down the High Street with Lally. He seemed to take her pregnancy as a personal affront, for he pointedly eyed her stomach and after that brief encounter almost ceased to notice her altogether. Lenore had the uneasy feeling his attentiveness would return once the baby was born, and she was slender again, but that was a long time away, and she refused to think about it—their circumstances might be much changed by then.

Lally was amused by Gilbert's sullen manner. "Don't mind him," she blithely counseled Lenore. "Gilbert hates women who are increasing—can't stand the bulge. Last year he sent poor Millie Tippert away to the country to have hers, said he couldn't bear to look at her ungainly form—and *he* was the father!"

Lenore shuddered. "Where is she now?"

"She died in childbirth. There was a terrible storm, the farmhouse where she was staying was on the river-bank, and with the flooding it became an island—the midwife couldn't get through and the farmer's wife got hysterical, didn't know what to do. It must have been awful."

"I don't see how anybody could even *speak* to Gilbert after that!" cried Lenore. "It was all *his fault!*"

"Of course." A cynical smile curved Lally's mouth. "But Millie had her revenge posthumously. She was lonely in the farmhouse and she felt cut off, so the night before she died she sat down and wrote a long letter to Gilbert's mother complaining about the way Gilbert had treated her. The farmer saw that it was delivered, too—he'd felt sorry for Millie. Gilbert's mother read it and flew into a passion—Gilbert said she was positively *livid* with rage—he was supposed to come home, but she refused to let him—said he could jolly well stay in Oxford for another two years until he'd learned how to behave! That's why he spent Christmas here—he can't go home until she decides to forgive him."

"I hope that's never!" said Lenore with vicious emphasis, although in truth she'd have been glad to see Gilbert through the city gates at any time.

"It wasn't because of what he did to Millie." Lally gave her an amused look. "It was because of what she was. Millie was a laundress, and Gilbert's mother couldn't abide his taking up with a low-class doxie!" Her laughter pealed.

Lenore was appalled. She gave Lally an uncertain look, but Lally shook her head ruefully. "You're very innocent of the ways of the world, Lenore. Perhaps that's what Geoffrey saw in you—oh, I didn't mean that," she added hastily, for Lenore had broken stride and stiffened.

Lenore relaxed. Lally was, after all, her friend. But she knew it would be even harder for her to be civil to Gilbert after this.

They stopped at a coffee house for warmth and refreshment. It was forward of them to come in unattended, but Lally knew the proprietor's wife, who promptly whisked them back to a small private room where they enjoyed steaming coffee and little wheaten cakes. The proprietor's wife bustled away, leaving them sitting companionably at a small wooden table, beside them a window with small leaded panes that gave onto a stable with icicles dripping from the thatched roof.

Lally was watching her brightly, and Lenore cast about for a way to break the awkwardness that had arisen between them over the story of Millie. She could scarce say she had another reason, as well, for hating Gilbert! Her hand passed nervously over her white collar, smoothing it, and brushed a lump half-concealed by her bodice —she had her subject: eagle-stones!

This morning Mistress Watts seemingly had at last discerned that Lenore was pregnant. She had been remarkably slow to discover it—Lenore suspected her landlady guessed they were not married and thought Lenore might not wish to admit she was bearing Geoffrey's child. But this morning Mistress Watts had hurried upstairs with a silk bag of eagle-stones, which her wealthy cousin in Bath had brought home from abroad. This, she told Lenore importantly, her scanty curls bobbing for emphasis, was a very efficacious charm which had helped her cousin in Bath through two difficult pregnancies. The silk bag must be worn on a ribbon around Lenore's neck until two or three weeks before the baby was born—just to make sure all went well at the birth.

Lenore had accepted this well-meant gift with grave thanks, threaded a ribbon through the eyelets of the silk bag and put it around her neck immediately. She was uncertain as to the efficacy of charms, but one could not afford to take chances. Charms were popular with pregnant women. Women in the Cotswolds wore them, too— Meg had worn several supposed to give her an easy delivery, but whether they had helped her was debatable, for she had miscarried all the same.

Now Lenore eagerly pulled the silk bag from her bodice and displayed it to Lally. "Mistress Watts gave me these eagle-stones to make certain a good birth. Think you they will help?"

Lally, stirring her coffee, stared at them with a kind of fascination; then she shuddered and turned away. "Eagle-stones did not help *me*," she said shortly. "My baby died. In Stratford, the day he was born."

Lenore's violet eyes widened. She had not known Lally had gone so far with her Kevin. . . . It helped explain why Lally's strait-laced relatives had been unwilling to take her in after her father died.

"That surprises you, doesn't it?" challenged Lally grimly, swinging about to face Lenore. "You've wondered about Ned and me. The baby was Kevin's, but 'twas Ned saw me through it—though it ended badly all the same."

"No—I never wondered," said Lenore, hastily taking a swallow of near-scalding coffee.

"Of course you did. Everybody does. They can't understand why I stay with him, filling in the time until he marries. But—" she bit her lip and frowned. "I wanted *you* to understand, Lenore."

"You're very good to Ned," Lenore said soberly. "I've often felt he should wed you instead of some ninny in Marston."

"Ned likes small pretty brunette women," Lally informed her in a brittle, hopeless voice. "Not long, stringy ones like me. And her name is Lavinia."

Lenore felt called upon to protest. "I don't even like the name Lavinia," she said hotly. "And you have the carriage of a queen, Lally. Geoffrey often comments on your spirited walk."

Lally laughed bitterly. "But not on my pretty face, I'll wager." She looked out the window at the hanging icicles. " 'Tis unsettling, but I've grown fond of Ned these past months we've been together. When he marries—God's teeth, I'll miss him!" Her voice roughened.

Lenore gave her a sympathetic look. She had a very good idea of what blond, fashionable Lally was going through.

"Perhaps Ned will change his mind," she suggested hopefully.

Lally's harsh laugh stung her. "Not till after he's wed Lavinia and bedded her," she said bitterly. "*Then* when the thrill of the chase is gone, he may miss me—he may want someone to talk to. But I'll be gone, for I won't be able to sit by and wait in hopes he'll come back to me for an hour, a night. . . ."

"Where . . . will you go?" Lenore wondered.

"I'll find a new protector, as I once told you I would," Lally replied in a determined, hard voice.

Gilbert, thought Lenore with a pang. That caramel head was often bent over Lally's fair one these days. "I wish spring would come," she sighed.

"Ned will marry Lavinia in the spring," Lally reminded her, studying her hands.

"I'm sorry," said Lenore in a contrite voice. "It's just that I hate being cooped up indoors so much, and I suppose I'm impatient to hold my baby in my arms—" she stopped lamely, for Lally's face had twisted for a moment.

"It's all right," Lally told her softly, pressing a hand down over Lenore's on the table. "It hurt terribly at the time but—I'm over it now."

Lenore suspected no one ever got over it.

This conversation with Lally made Lenore all the more conscious of what she had—a strong man's arms to comfort her, a strong man to love her—and his baby on the way. Geoffrey mended fast, and at night their bodies responded vibrantly to each other in a perfect union. By day they found it easy to laugh off the gloom of others who found the continued cold depressing.

It was only lack of money that plagued them.

The next time she trudged with Lally through the snow, they met Gilbert coming out of an alehouse. He made them both a sweeping bow, but his smile was for Lally.

"If you make a leg so handsomely in this weather,"

223

Lally cautioned him lightheartedly, "you are apt to land on your backside in the snow!"

"You and Mistress Lenore seem to keep *your* footing," was Gilbert's cynical rejoinder. He was looking at Lally's muff—which was the one he had given Lenore for Christmas and which she had promptly presented to Lally on the pretext that "after all, you're exercising Snowfire for me." His lazy gaze passed over Lenore's plum velvet hat and muff—Geoffrey's Christmas gift—and his voice held an edge of spite. "I see from Mistress Lenore's fine clothes that Geoffrey must have found a way to live without working—certainly his father is not supporting him, has refused to see him, in fact. I heard through an aunt that Geoffrey traveled a great distance to see his father but was turned away at the door."

Lenore flushed and bit her lip. "Your aunt must have been misinformed," she said icily.

Gilbert's laugh was a trifle unpleasant. "You've no need to worry, Mistress Lenore," he told her smoothly. "Geoffrey's tough—he'll be back on the road soon enough. He's never let a wound hold him back for long," he added on a taunting note.

Lenore cared little that Gilbert was implying Geoffrey was a highwayman, for she doubted he could prove it—but it frightened her that Gilbert had guessed Geoffrey was wounded. "I don't know what you mean," she said carelessly, her hands gripping inside her velvet muff. "Geoffrey has an indisposition of the lungs—not a wound!"

Lally gave Gilbert an angry look. " 'Tis too cold to stand here talking nonsense," she said crisply. "We bid you good day, Gilbert."

When she returned home, Lenore taxed Geoffrey with it. She did not look at him as she pulled off her gloves and spread out her cloak before the fire. "Gilbert believes you've turned highwayman." When he said nothing she turned and faced him. "Tell me how you were wounded, Geoffrey—the truth."

"It was as I told you," said Geoffrey. "Be damned to Gilbert!"

She studied his face, that dark, loved face with the steady gray eyes. They were looking at her now, with tenderness. She sank down on a chair. "Oh, Geoffrey," she said in a hopeless voice. "What are we to do? We have no money, no—"

"Come here, Lenore." Very tenderly he enfolded her in his arms. "My leg is almost mended. Trust me. I will find a way for us."

He would need to, she thought sadly. Their situation was fast growing desperate.

In February rain fell soddenly and melted the snow and everyone—Town and Gown alike—caught cold. Candlemas was marked more by deep slush than revelry, and the city of towers became a dismal place of stuffy noses and hacking coughs and gloomy, wet, cobbled streets. On winter mornings vapor rose all around the city from the numerous rivulets about the river.

Geoffrey, up and mended, was now gone most of the time. He told her once gravely that he was trying to arrange a "living" for them. She wondered what he meant, and surmised he might be trying to arrange through relatives for a pardon and perhaps to borrow enough money to buy a commission in the army, for soldiering was the only trade he knew.

That he was unsuccessful in these attempts was apparent, for he came home through the gray winter mists looking grim and had little to say about where he had been or what he'd been doing. But he brought with him little trickles of money, enough to keep them alive, and now as she grew big with child, she was grateful. For with the baby coming, she no longer felt capable of riding the boggy winter roads and shivering through the nights in caverns and barns and chance hovels.

Now that her advancing pregnancy had—happily—made her repugnant to Gilbert, Lenore had lost her fear that he might try to repeat his performance of just before Christmas. She hated the sight of him and gave thanks that he no longer frequented her lodgings.

In the meager rooms off Magpie Lane, young Mistress Daunt held uneasy court, for she was always edgy these days, feeling that Geoffrey was off somewhere taking some great chance and instead of riding home might be brought back to her in a cart—for burial.

Michael was her most frequent visitor, for with her advancing pregnancy, the rash young men who had written her love sonnets drifted away to woo likely tavern maids, and Lenore, save for her visits from Lally and occasional dinners with Lally and Ned, on those infrequent occasions when he was not at Marston, was much alone. She spent long hours practicing her penmanship under Michael's guidance until even Geoffrey admitted her much improved, and she read borrowed books until her candle guttered out.

It was a pleasant respite from the miserable weather when Michael would come swinging over in the afternoon in his red cloak, bringing with him a bottle of wine and sweetmeats sent from his ancestral manor south of Coventry. He seemed bent on entertaining her, and would regale her by the hour with stories of bloody riots between Town and Gown which had been erupting since medieval times. Lenore didn't know whether to believe him or not when he told her that on one occasion hooded country folk had swarmed into Oxford bearing a black flag, killed sixty students, and scalped some of the chaplains. It was not, he conceded, chewing thoughtfully on a sweetmeat, the university's finest hour.

Sometimes Mistress Watts joined them, trudging upstairs with the big white cat purring in her arms, to tell them with sparkling eyes and a tremor in her voice of the wild days during the reign of Charles I when university courts had banished lewd women and arrested night-walking citizens. She recalled how Charles had made Oxford his headquarters during England's Civil War. Why, the town had been like a garrison, with New College turned into a magazine, and All Souls into an arsenal, New Inn Hall a mint, and the King himself at Christ Church, where the main quadrangle was turned into a cattle pen! How the town had rallied to his cause, then, with undergraduates throwing up great earthworks! Things were different now, she sighed. Lenore understood her longing to speak of these things, for they were memories of the days of her youth.

But being indoor so much chafed Lenore.

"Mistress Watts warns me I should not go out in this weather," she complained to Lally one day. "And in truth I grow so ungainly that I may pitch forward on my face on the cobbles—on wet days I fear to go out in my clogs for fear I will slip, and not to wear them would drench my shoes!"

"Stay indoors," advised Lally.

"That is very hard for me," sighed Lenore. "For I am a country girl and used to fresh air."

With the flowing green cloak to hide her condition, she continued to prowl the town on good days, sometimes walking all the way to Port Meadow, the pastureland which lay just to the northwest of Oxford. Now in the winter, damp mists lay over Port Meadow, which was owned by the Freemen of Oxford and was grazed by ponies and cows, frequented by flocks of ducks and geese and other birds. From its soggy ragwort and thistle-sprinkled grass the towers of Oxford rose in the distance in immense majesty, and Lenore would pause, shivering, to admire them.

Geoffrey heard of these prowlings and sternly ordered Lenore to stop going out alone—it wasn't safe. Did she not know there were footpads about?

"In daylight?" she asked wearily.

"Take Lally with you," he said.

Lenore gave him a resentful look. "Lally's busy enough exercising Snowfire—I can't take up all her time."

"Then get Michael to accompany you. He's a bright lad, and too cautious to let you get into trouble."

Lenore was over-surfeited with Michael's adoring company already, but when the weather moderated a bit, she relented and let him take her walking beneath the sycamores and wych elms and mulberry trees. Honestly believing Lenore would be interested in anything that interested him, Michael took her to the Ashmolean Museum to see the famous unicorn's horn, and Guy Fawkes's lantern and near it the bulletproof hat with its iron lining which had been worn by John Bradshaw when he presided over Charles I's trial. Lenore studied it and shivered.

The Lord Protector, men said, was an evil man, but . . . Michael had casually shown her the old gate where Cranmer, the Protestant Archbishop of Canterbury, had been burned to death by Bloody Mary's Catholic regime. The fires of burning Protestants had lit up the countryside then . . . no wonder sturdy Englishmen had brought the Lord Protector to power, they wanted an end to the burning. But now she looked at that bulletproof hat and thought of the beheaded King and shivered.

Michael's eyes had danced at that. He loved gruesome things and spoke of them with relish.

Lenore went home from that excursion sighing, wondering if all men were children at heart.

She found Lally waiting for her, sitting on the edge of the table, swinging one long leg and looking very depressed.

"I came over to show you my new blue velvet gown." Lally stood up and swung around so Lenore could view this new creation. Then, dispiritedly, "No, I didn't. Ned's gone to Marston again, and I had a falling out with Gilbert over that ridiculous barmaid, Dorothy. Oh, Lenore, I don't know what's wrong with me these days. I—"

Lenore poured her a glass of wine and handed it to her silently. "Perhaps Gilbert is what's wrong, Lally. Had you thought of that?"

Lally shot her a look. "You're wondering why I bother with Gilbert, aren't you?" she asked softly. "Ned isn't even married yet and . . . here I am, slipping around back streets with Gilbert."

Lenore's rising color was an admission that she had indeed wondered.

"I'm the kind of woman who has to have—someone," said Lally dispassionately. "Arms to hold me. If not Ned's—someone else's. Mind you, I love Ned—I never told anyone that before, not even Ned. But it's true, Lenore, I do love him. When Kevin was drowned and my father died, it snowed soon after and it was bitter cold, I thought on death. It seemed to me the answer was out there in the snow. I could just walk and walk until I

228

froze to death and all my troubles would be over. I actually started out across the fields, trudging along through a white, faceless world. I remember growing sort of numb and sleepy and slowing down and finally I couldn't move any more and I thought, *This is death. Soon it will all be over.* Suddenly I felt someone slapping my face, and I came to and I was looking up into Ned's face. I'd never seen him before. He'd been riding across the fields, taking a shortcut to see some friends, and he found me lying there in the snow. He brought me back to his lodgings and warmed me—with rum and hot broth and with his own body, he made me want to live again. And when he learned my story, he helped me through with the baby—and then he brought me with him to Oxford. I've been very happy here, Lenore. But now that—that I'm losing Ned, I have to look around. Gilbert isn't the man I want, but he's witty and well-dressed—and he makes me feel like a woman. And sometimes I need that." Her smile was wistful. "I wanted you to understand, Lenore, because you're my friend and I care what you think."

Lenore felt a lump rise in her throat. Quickly she poured Lally a glass of wine.

Absently, Lally accepted the glass and toyed with it. "There have been times this winter," she said, her slate-blue eyes clouded with bitter reflection, "when it was bitter cold and Ned was in Marston and I have looked out through the frosted panes and yearned to go out and just keep walking, walking in the snow until the hurting stopped and I grew numb and dropped down and down and down. . . . Freezing's an easy death, they say."

Lenore stared at her. Worldly and witty, Lally had been through so much. "What stopped you?" she asked, her mouth dry.

Lally gave her a rueful smile. "At the last minute, I always found a shred of hope to cling to. That's what Ned's done for me, I suppose, given me hope. I'm a victim of my sometimes optimism. It's kept me going."

"Lally," Lenore's voice was husky and sincere, "I wish with all my heart that Ned would marry *you.*"

229

"So do I," shrugged Lally. "But 'tis not like to happen."
She sighed. "It's growing late, I must go."

In the gathering dusk, Lenore watched her friend walk
around the corner into Magpie Lane, a solitary figure
hurrying home to a cold hearth—and a colder bed.

CHAPTER 15

With the spring, the wind off the Downs brought with it
the scent of damp woodland, meadow wildflowers, and
a promise of summer to come. With the spring, the face of
Oxford, a city set amid the floodlands, changed. Hawkers
came swinging into the town, selling the dead swans and
moorhens they'd snared on baited eelhooks in the nearby
Thames. Yeomen farmers walked about, gypsy caravans
with bright painted carts lumbered through the streets,
their horses jingling with fancy trappings. The market
abounded with fish and fowl and venison, and from the
swampy land the wonderful gardens overshadowed with
huge oaks and sycamores and wych elms sprang to life,
and a breath of warmth ruffled the ivy that clung to the
honey-colored stone towers.

As Lally had gloomily predicted, Ned and Lavinia, his
"Marston lady," were married—first a civil ceremony ac-
cording to the law, and then another ceremony at home in
Marston "to make Lavinia feel married," as Ned said

happily. To this home ceremony Geoffrey and Lenore were invited.

"Are you going? To Marston?" a forlorn Lally asked Lenore.

"No," Lenore said moodily. "My excuse is that my delicate condition won't let me make the trip, but the truth is I couldn't stand it, seeing Ned marry somebody else when he should be marrying you."

"Oh, please go," Lally urged with a break in her voice. "Ned actually told me I could go if I wished, that he'd pass me off as a distant relative." She tried to laugh, but it didn't quite come off. "But I couldn't bring myself to. I couldn't bear to see it but I—I want someone to tell me about it. How—how it goes, and whether Ned seems happy." There were tears in her voice, and Lenore almost cried, too.

Though large with child by now, Lenore reluctantly assented to Lally's pleading and together with Geoffrey attended the wedding. She wore her russet wool gown and green cloak and the plum velvet hat and muff Geoffrey had given her for Christmas, for the weather was still unstable and the day dawned damp and cold. She and Geoffrey crossed the Cherwell by ferry with some of Ned's friends. On the opposite bank they were picked up by the bride's family coach and went on to Marston. The jolting coach made Lenore feel slightly ill, and she was not prepared to like Marston. She found it a swampy town, filled with fingers of the Thames, where white swans rode the placid waters like a bevy of brides.

The manor house they rode up to in the jolting coach was small but elegant, of red brick turned greenish by the damp climate, and approached by a flight of mossy stone steps. Geoffrey kept a firm grip on her arm as she negotiated those slippery steps, and Lenore gave him a grateful look.

The heavy oaken doors swung open and they found themselves inside a handsome wainscoated hall, stone-floored and sparsely furnished. At one end a bright fire crackled on a large stone hearth, moderating the spring dampness. Lenore would have headed at once for that fire, but Ned and his Lavinia came forward to greet them.

It was the first time Lenore had met Ned's Marston lady, and grudgingly she found she liked the small, buxom, bright-eyed brunette, who kissed her warmly and made her welcome.

"Ned, now that I've met Mistress Lavinia, I realize what a fortunate man ye are!" Geoffrey gave Ned a hearty slap on the back. Ned grinned idiotically, but Lenore, with a pang, thought of Lally and how disconsolate she must be today. Gilbert had stayed in Oxford with her, and for once Lenore was glad Lally had Gilbert—Lally would need arms around her this night.

"Cheer up," Geoffrey whispered as they followed their hostess into the big withdrawing room to the left of the hall, where the mullioned windows were heavily draped with handsome green damask. A number of guests milled about there, their bootheels grinding into the big Oriental carpet which had traveled half across the world and up the Thames and into the heart of England. "This is a wedding," he reminded her in a low voice, "not a wake. We owe it to Ned to be cheerful."

Lenore gave him a wan look. It was a wake to her. But she rallied a little as she drank warm wine and ate sweet cakes with the other guests. They drifted out into the hall and saw a group of new arrivals, the women wearing plumed hats. People flitted up and down the heavily carved acanthus scroll staircase. Many guests were to stay the night, but she and Geoffrey were not; along with others from nearby Oxford, the family coach would be taking them back to the ferry.

"I do not like weddings," muttered Geoffrey at a moment when no one was near. "Had I been in Ned's boots, I think I'd have come out on the Puritan side, for once, and said 'Let be' after the civil ceremony!"

Lenore gave him a scathing look. For once she lined up on the side of Lavinia, the Marston lady. "The poor girl wouldn't feel married!" she protested.

"She'll feel married enough when their first child comes along!" said Geoffrey. He looked abruptly sorry he'd said that, and Lenore sighed. There was always this awkwardness between them on the subject of marriage and—it wasn't right that it should be so. Their love for each other was as sturdy and sure as any marriage could be. She watched the little bridesmaids flit by with wistful eyes. They looked so young and fresh—so innocent and so happy.

She was still pensive when she went in on Geoffrey's arm to partake of a hearty meal of cold ham, haunch of venison, boiled leg of mutton and capers, flour pudding and sturgeon—all washed down with white and red wine, beer and cider—and so many tarts and pasties that Lenore felt stuffed as a Christmas goose.

Some of Ned's relatives were very late in arriving—among them his brother—so the ceremony was held up awaiting his arrival. Lenore, because of her condition, was given a cot in a corner of one of the upstairs bedrooms to rest in. She found herself unable to nap, for people came and went, greeting each other, hugging each other, eagerly giving news of friends. Many of the women's clothes were quite beautiful, with pastel silks and satins garnished with lace and plumed hats and pearl necklets. Lenore in her plain russet wool felt quite out of it.

After her rest she went back downstairs and found Geoffrey standing among a group of friends from Oxford, drinking wine.

"Ned's brother—still not here?" she asked him.

"They fear his coach may have lost a wheel—'tis known he was on his way, for there are those here who passed him on the road."

"How long will they wait?"

Geoffrey shrugged. "Faith, they seem in no hurry. The knot is already legally tied, and this ceremony is just a garnish on the cake." He turned and smiled as Lavinia came by and told them prettily that the ceremony was sure to be so late they'd never reach Oxford before curfew and of course they must spend the night here at Marston. At first Lenore demurred, but Lavinia insisted, smiling prettily with her small Cupid's bow mouth, her voice persuasive. "And you haven't seen my house linens—or my wedding gifts!" she told Lenore merrily, taking her by the arm.

"Every stitch of my linens is mine—I made them all myself, yes and embroidered them, too! Ned is so proud of me! The flax was spun here and the wool is from the Cotswolds—Ned tells me you're from the Cotswolds, Mistress Lenore."

Lenore admitted it.

"All those beautiful green hills and the flocks of white woolly sheep!" cried Lavinia ecstatically. "How could you bear to leave it?"

Lenore smiled and forbore to enlarge on her manner of leaving. She couldn't imagine Lally making that remark or looking at her in that lost, starry-eyed way. She wondered what Ned's married life was going to be like.

Then she found herself looking at the handsome collection of bridal gifts. The little silver cup she and Geoffrey had been able to afford was lost among massive candlesticks and handsome silver bowls, but Lavinia raved over it at length. She had never *seen* anything so beautiful! Lenore knew Lavinia meant well, but it all made her sad. She was glad when Lavinia rushed on to gush over somebody else.

At last Ned's brother arrived, covered with mud and with a wild tale of an overturned coach and some hastily procured help to drag it out of the mud—a large undertaking, as it turned out, for it was tightly wedged between a boulder and a tree and when righted was found to have lost a wheel. But at least now the ceremony could proceed.

Lavinia looked so joyful that she could now be "proper wed" that even Lenore had to smile. Lavinia retired to her room, waving to Lenore to come along with her. There her mother and sisters and female cousins helped get her into an elaborate costume, all of white. Sewn all over it were knots of colored ribbon—after the ceremony the young men would pull these off and wear them as bridefavors in their hats. Everyone gasped at Lavinia's gloves, which were of delicate lace-trimmed leather with tiny seed pearls sewn into rosettes. When Lavinia was ready—her mother having combed her long, dark hair down loose and set on it a circlet of myrtle—Lenore and the others went downstairs and waited for Lavinia to come floating down.

When she reached the bottom step, Lenore caught Geoffrey's eye from across the room. He raised a gauntleted glove to her (Ned had given all his friends fringed gauntlets as marriage tokens, as was the custom). Like the other guests, Lenore was now wearing a brightly colored scarf, and she adjusted it as she walked over to him.

This was a country wedding, and blithely free of the strictures of Puritanism save that the bride would wear a plain gold ring instead of a jeweled or enameled hoop. Beside Lenore, an elderly lady in a regal plumed hat and stiff brocades muttered, "*I* would have had Ned give me a jeweled hoop, had *I* been Lavinia."

"I think I would have been content with gold," sighed Lenore.

The woman gave her an odd look, and Geoffrey said in a vexed voice, "Mistress Lenore has lost her ring—when she pulled off her gloves as she came in from skating. But —I intend to buy her a better one, with jewels to match her eyes!" He squeezed Lenore's hand.

The plumed hat bobbed in approval—and then forgot her, for the bride was coming down the stairs.

A ring . . . Geoffrey meant to give her a ring. Wistfully Lenore remembered the gimmal rings used in the Cotswolds, rings that were separated into two parts—half given at betrothal to the man, half to the maid. Then both halves were united into one ring at the church. As a little girl she had been determined to wear such a ring. Now she knew she never would, but perhaps . . . one with blue stones to match her eyes. Her gloved fingers—which had felt no need of a ring in the wilds or Dartmoor—felt suddenly quite naked, and she twisted them together during the ceremony.

Ned looked so happy . . . not a thought of Lally in his merry gaze. To get her mind off Lally, Lenore studied the bride's crowning circlet of myrtle, which she wore so proudly over her long, dark hair. It reminded her of Meg's circlet of myrtle—though this wealthy bride wore white and Meg had worn russet, as became a village girl.

Lenore sighed. She should not attend weddings. They

reminded her of all that she had lost and all that would never be hers.

After Ned and his Lavinia were pronounced man and wife, all present drank wine with sops in it—and Lavinia shyly dipped in a sprig of rosemary "for everlasting love" before she drank. She giggled as the ribbons were stripped from her gown by eager hands and stuck rakishly into the gentlemen's hats.

Afterward the guests—hardly hungry, for they had already been well stuffed—were seated at long boards covered with linen and embellished by tall silver salts and with a centerpiece of holly and ate their way through a banquet of some fifteen courses. Lenore could hardly force herself to touch another scrap, but Geoffrey and the others seemed to enjoy the roast duck and roast piglet and bullock's heart and boiled fowl, and urged on her the roast beef and oysters and cheese and plum and apple tarts.

"Geoffrey," said Lenore, laughing, "if I eat any more, I will burst!"

He grinned. "Ned's in luck. His bride's family sets a good table!"

Wine flowed so lavishly that as they left the table many of the guests were already weaving, their tongues slurred. But the merriment continued, and that night they all drank the traditional sack posset which was made of spiced wine and milk and eggs and sugar. Voices rang as they toasted the bride's health, the groom's health, the health of all present. And at bedtime, as was the custom, the bridemen gaily pulled off the bride's garters. Lavinia had previously untied them, with much giggling, so that the dangling ribbons hung down and were easily grasped ("else they might grasp my knee instead!" she had cried merrily). Lenore fastened Geoffrey's to his hat, as did the others, and went with the bridesmaids to the bride's chamber, where they helped her undress. With a half-scared look, her eyes enormous, Lavinia climbed into the great feather-bed, sinking down into it as if in a white-capped ocean.

After that the bridesmaids retreated, passing with much giggling the groom, attired for bed with a nightcap hanging down over one eye and being escorted to his marriage bed by unsteady-footed friends.

"Ned will ne'er survive it!" grinned Geoffrey. Lenore gave him a wan look. Lally was the one who might not survive this wedding—Ned and Lavinia would be fine, she thought sadly.

No sooner were the couple in bed together than the whole company poured into the room to wish them happiness and drink their health once again. Lenore, exhausted, was glad when the curtains around the great fourposter were finally drawn and the party withdrew below stairs for an evening of revelry. There would be no honeymoon, she knew, for Ned would stay here with the bride's family for a time, and then he would take her to the new house his father was building for them in Somerset on land he had purchased for Ned.

The wedding guests so overflowed the house, and so raucous was their merriment, that sleep was impossible and they made their way back to Oxford, yawning, via the family coach and the ferry at dawn. Lenore knew she looked haggard. Exhausted, she let Geoffrey undress her and put her to bed as if she were a child.

Tenderly he kissed her forehead and drew the coverlet up about her neck and offered her a glass of wine. Lenore shook her head and smiled at him through a daze of fatigue.

"Lenore," he sighed, taking her hand and looking down at her ringless fingers, caressing those fingers as he spoke. "There will be better times for us. When the child is born and you can travel distances again, what say ye to America? In the Colonies a man can indenture himself for, say, four years—and after that he's free again and can make a fortune if he's a mind to."

Lenore's eyes opened wide. For a moment fatigue left her and she felt excited, as she had in the Cotswolds on fair days. The American Colonies seemed far away and hospitable and beyond the law. Who would care there if Geoffrey's name was Wyndham or Daunt? Who would know that he had a French wife?

"I'd like that," she said honestly. "Oh, Geoffrey, I'd like that so much."

"I'm trying to arrange it, but 'tis devilish hard without money."

Lenore was smiling as she went to sleep.

Geoffrey had dressed and gone out before she awakened, but she opened her eyes to a loud banging on the door. "Lenore, open the door—Gwynneth had your tray ready and I've brought it up."

Lenore got up and opened the door. Lally brought in the tray and set it down, then straightened up to confront Lenore. Her face was white and drawn. "Is it done, then?" she asked tensely. "And is Ned happy? Oh, Lenore, do you think he will be happy with her?"

Sleepy and disoriented, Lenore stared at Lally. Her rose silk dress was so shimmery, her slate-blue eyes so sad. Lenore pulled up a chair for Lally and went back to sit on the bed. She ran a hand through her long hair.

"It is done," she said. "They are married and"—she studied Lally's mask-like white face—"I think he will be happy with her," she added hesitantly.

"Tell me about it—and eat your breakfast." Lally sank down on the bed studying her gloves; she did not look at Lenore.

"I'm not hungry," sighed Lenore. "Lavinia is pretty and . . . and rather silly. But I think she loves Ned; at least, she seemed very happy."

Lally winced.

"There was a great deal to eat and drink—far too much, and most of the guests were reeling or sleeping it off in corners when I left. Lavinia wore the handsomest bridal gown I have ever seen," Lenore continued. "It was white. All the guests wore beautiful scarves in bright colors, and Ned gave his friends gloves like these." She nodded at the fringed gauntlets Geoffrey had received, which were tossed carelessly on the table beside the tray.

Lally turned to regard them. "Ned always had good taste," she murmured.

"And a deep pocket," said Lenore on a note of

asperity. "His father has bought land for him and is building them a home in Somerset."

"So the wedding went well?"

"Yes. The bridesmaids carried rosemary branches—gilded. The ring was plain gold. There were beautiful wedding gifts, and a great deal of dancing and pledging the bride's health, and that night—"

"I think I have heard enough," said Lally in a thick voice. "I only wanted to—" her voice shook—"to know if you think Ned will be happy. And you have told me he will." Suddenly she turned a tormented face to Lenore. "Is—is Lavinia very pretty?" she asked hoarsely.

Lenore nodded, swallowing. "She is a little thing, with a great deal of dark hair and bright eyes and a tiny mouth. She seems lost in her rich gowns, they billow about her, and she smiles a great deal—and giggles. Yes, Lally, she is very pretty."

"I am glad for him," said Lally in a broken voice. She brushed her hand across her eyes and rose. "Ned wanted to provide for me, but I have already made my arrangements."

"You—you have?"

"Yes." Lally moved rapidly to the door. She almost blundered into it, and Lenore guessed her vision was blurred with tears. "I am moving in with Gilbert." She ran through the door with a swish of rose silk skirts and closed it quickly behind her. There was a sound of finality in the closing of that door.

Lenore's heart ached for her. She hoped Lally would find happiness with Gilbert, but she doubted that was possible.

Geoffrey came home, bringing her a pouch of apples—for just before arriving in Marston she had expressed a mad desire for apples. She was full of fitful fancies where food was concerned these days, suddenly dying for a potato or something more exotic at odd hours—and sometimes losing her taste for it, even before it could be procured for her.

She was pleased that Geoffrey had remembered her ardently expressed desire for apples—even though that desire had now departed. Carefully she arranged them in a bowl, polished one against her petticoat, and bit into it. Geoffrey sat down across the table facing her.

"Did you really mean what you said about going to the Colonies, Geoffrey?"

He flashed her a quick smile and polished an apple on his sleeve before he answered. "And would ye like that?"

She nodded.

"Then I must find a way to make it possible." He leaned back, rested a booted foot on a nearby bench, and frowned. "Money is an obstacle, even if one is not so nice in the way one comes by it."

She did not press him. To show too much eagerness might lead him recklessly into danger. Meanwhile there was to be an even more important event—the birth of their first child, conceived on their first, memorable night of loving.

CHAPTER 16

Lenore, who had felt so well during the bulk of her preg-
nancy, now found herself nervous and short-tempered and
full of aches and pains. She felt incensed that as her waist
thickened and she moved about with difficulty, the wild
young lads had all fallen away, leaving only young
Michael, with his cherubic face and dog-like devotion,
who came over and sat with her on the excuse of tutoring
her in penmanship. Even bookish Lewis now occupied
himself elsewhere.

Feeling ill much of the time, her fingers all thumbs as
she tried to work on the baby's layette, she was brusque
and quarrelsome with Geoffrey. He bore it well, blaming
it on her condition. But on gloomy days she fell to brooding about his wife in France and imagined Letiche sailing
for England and converging on Oxford to whisk Geoffrey
away. The unlikelihood of such an event comforted her,
but the thought that it *could* happen gave her world a
sour flavor. Sometimes the wine of youth was turned to
vinegar.

Lally—now living with Gilbert—stopped by sometimes, but she was dispirited, not her former breezy self. Once she sported a purple bruise beneath her right eye and replied shortly to Lenore's query that she had fallen. Lenore was sure Gilbert had struck her, and she worried.

"Ned and Lavinia have left Marston—they have gone to Somerset," she told Lenore in a dispirited voice. "He was in Oxford today, and I saw him for a moment. He is very busy overseeing the building of their new home. He said he missed talking to me." She sounded wistful.

Lenore had thought Ned might miss talking to spirited Lally after scatter-brained Lavinia's giggles. "You should forget him," she counseled sternly.

"Easy to say," murmured Lally. "Lenore, the reason I came by today is there's a play being given this afternoon in a barn outside town."

"A play?" Lenore was fascinated. Although plays were strictly forbidden in Cromwell's England and the Puritans had closed the theatres, she had learned in Oxford that there were threadbare roving companies of strolling players who still wandered the back lanes when the weather was clement and held their plays in forest glades, in barns, even in caves. But these were of necessity furtive gatherings, for should the strict Puritan authorities descend on them, they well might fine the audience and whip the players out of town tied to a cart-tail. "I've never seen a play, Lally," Lenore admitted.

"I know 'tis near your time, and with Geoffrey away you hesitate to go out," said Lally. "But there'll be a cart to take a group of us there, and I'd take it as a favor if you'd accompany us, Lenore. You see . . ." she hesitated and her slate-blue eyes were clouded. "I'm not getting along well with Gilbert."

Lenore's gaze flew to Lally's black eye.

"And it's not the first time," Lally muttered. "Although 'tis the first time the bruise *showed*."

"*Leave him!*" cried Lenore fiercely.

"That's what I must decide," said Lally in a weary voice. "But in the meantime, it would help to have someone . . . along with me today." Her voice faltered a little.

243

"You see, Lenore, it hurts Gilbert's pride that I still love Ned. He can sense it. I suppose that wounds a man."

"Certainly I'll go with you," said Lenore warmly, and Lally gave her hand a quick squeeze and left, promising they'd be back to pick her up.

In the big barn that warm afternoon Lenore sat on a pile of hay beside Lally and watched the play—her first. On her other side a pair of lovers whispered and giggled, never took their eyes off each other, and so missed the entire performance. On Lally's other side Gilbert sulked, rarely laughing even at the actors' best sallies. Lenore watched with rapt attention as the players—all men, though some were dressed in skirts portraying women's roles—wearing their ordinary clothes, presented Will Shakespeare's *A Midsummer Night's Dream.*

But the gaiety of the performance was spoiled for her when, in the general buzz of conversation between acts, a name jumped out at her from someone speaking just behind her: "Letiche d'Avigny," and someone else said, "You mean Letiche Wyndham?"

They were speaking of Geoffrey's French wife!

Lenore sat straighter and then hunched down as another voice muttered sharply, "Hush! Can't you see—?" Lenore scrounged down in the hay and tried to make herself smaller; not for worlds would she have looked behind her to see who was speaking. Lally, who'd been talking to Gilbert in a low tone, turned and asked anxiously, "You're so flushed, Lenore. Do you feel all right?"

She snapped resentfully, "I'm fine," and Lally looked surprised.

But for her the play was ruined. She hardly heard the rest of it and yearned for it to be over. She only nodded when, at the end of the performance, Gilbert seemed to have mellowed and Lally murmured a "thank you" in her ear as the returning party of playgoers let Lenore out at Mistress Watts's in the gathering dusk.

She walked cumbersomely upstairs and opened the door to her lodgings to find Geoffrey waiting for her, hands clasped behind his back, pacing the floor. He swung

244

toward her as she came in, looking exceedingly tall and with a grim expression on his dark face.

"Where've ye been?" he challenged. "Mistress Watts said ye rode off in a cart. I knew not where to seek you."

"I went to a play with Lally and some others," she defended.

"A play!" he exploded. "Lally must be mad! Faith, had the authorities got wind of it and taken actors and audience together in their net, think you they would not have questioned you? 'Tis your life would be forfeit! So Lally is carting you around to plays these days! Does she not know how often such performances are raided?"

"Well, nothing happened," said Lenore in a sulky voice, pulling off her gloves. Actually the jolting ride in the cart had made her feel a bit ill.

He was not to be put off. "Since I cannot always be here to protect you, promise me you'll do nothing rash when my back is turned."

"I do nothing rash whether your back is turned or not!" she flashed. "I wait, wait, wait to have your baby! I'm so awkward I can hardly get around. I'm *tired of waiting,* Geoffrey! And," she added accusingly, "someone in the crowd mentioned *your* French wife."

He looked taken aback, but Lenore, ill and irritable, put her hands to her throbbing temples. "Tell me of Letiche," she said in a hard voice, "for all seem to know more of her than I do!"

Geoffrey sighed. His face looked drawn. "I have told you about her, Lenore."

"Tell me again."

"Lenore, you flay yourself with these thoughts. 'Tis—"

She swung on him like a tigress, her face white, eyes blazing. *"Tell me,* Geoffrey! I have a right to know more about this woman whose very existence denies my child a name!"

"She does not concern you!" he shouted, flung out and was gone for three days.

Feeling desolate, as if Geoffrey might never return, Lenore struggled out and clumsily walked the cobbled streets. She had begun to think much on death. It could

245

be she would die when her baby was born . . . in this city where so many had died before her. Her thoughts were morbid. Oxford was a bloody place. Here in St. Frideswide's priory all the Danes in the city had once been collected and burned alive. Here the murdered Fair Rosamond, Henry II's beautiful mistress, lay buried, her epitaph calling her the Rose of the World . . . and in an unmarked grave somewhere lay Amy, wife to Robert Dudley, that favorite of Queen Elizabeth, who perhaps had had her hurled downstairs to her death in a fit of jealousy.

Mistress Watts sensed Lenore's despondency and had Gwynneth bring her up a hot posset, saying it would give her strength. Cooped up in her lodgings, Lenore fretted, for with her new unwieldy awkwardness, walking tired her. She wandered downstairs and fell into conversation with the cook. The cook had been married ten years and wanted a child. She dipped out a cup of soup from the kettle with a long iron dipper and sat down and told Lenore earnestly that she was drinking the waters—sold at a guinea a bottle—of the holy well behind the little church at Bimsey, said to make women fertile. 'Twas so expensive, she sighed, that if she did not become pregnant soon, they'd have no money to buy a christening gown! She looked at Lenore's girth enviously.

Lenore sipped her soup and listened. Mistress Watts came in and tried to entertain her, briskly maintaining that the house next door was haunted by the ghost of a Puritan housemaid who had been deserted by her Cavalier lover and had died of a broken heart. Lenore gave her a wan smile. She had no assurance at the moment that she too had not been deserted by her cavalier lover.

Lally came by, bearing a beautiful long gown for the baby made of fine linen trimmed in lace. Lally's bruise was fading, she sported a bright, brittle smile and walked with a challenging swagger. Lenore saw how happy she was and brooded about this change in her friend.

She slipped into a terrible despondency, feeling herself as much a prisoner in her upstairs lodgings as those unfortunate university prisoners lodged in the old prison of

246

Bocardo, from which everyone maintained there was no escape. She had seen them lowering collection boxes on long strings, hoping for alms, and had even sent up in compassion a few pennies she could ill afford to give away, when she had chanced to walk by. Even the time she spent in the stable with Snowfire did not cheer her very much.

And so passed the late days of her pregnancy, with the world outside bursting into blossom and Lenore's own heart heavy as she waited for her child to be born.

Though he had left her in anger, Geoffrey came back in a very different mood. She did not hear him ride up, did not even hear his footsteps on the stairs, for she was dozing, lying awkwardly on her back on the big square bed. His touch must have waked her, for she opened her eyes to find him looking down at her as he smoothed back the hair from her pale face, and the expression in his eyes was very tender. "Lenore," he said, "I was wrong to fling out and leave you. I realize that you do not feel well, that you are on edge, that this waiting—especially in our uncertain circumstances—is hard for you. If it is Letiche you wish to hear about, I will tell you of Letiche."

Repentant, now that she had got him back, she reached up and put her fingers against his mouth to silence him. "I have no need to hear, Geoffrey—I was angry."

"Nay, perhaps you do. I thought you understood, but if you do not—a friend of mine told me the d'Avignys were wealthy; I saw for myself how Letiche dressed, how she lived in Brussels. And the d'Avignys were said to have a finer house by far in their native France—in Paris. Little did I know that her parents had spent all their substance to launch Letiche into society in hopes of a rich marriage for her! My friends contrived that I would seem rich myself, with rumors of great estates in the West Indies. Her mother convinced me that little Letiche would inherit the d'Avigny estates near Boulogne, which I knew were extensive. We rushed to one another's arms, each believing the other to possess a great fortune. Came the reckoning, after we were wed. When I admitted I was penniless, Letiche's mother set up a great wailing. A doctor had to

247

be called. It all came out at her bedside then that they'd nothing, either—the great estates near Boulogne were indeed d'Avigny estates, but they belonged to a widowed uncle with two strong young sons of his own! So even though Letiche was an only child and his favorite niece, there was really no dowry, nor any chance of our making our way together."

"And you left her for that? Because she was not rich?" mumbled Lenore.

"Nay, I'd not have left her for that. 'Twas not Letiche's fault that her mother told lies, or that I hoodwinked them. Letiche berated me, 'tis true, but . . . I deserved it. I know not what would have happened had not her mother snatched her from the house and left me with the debts we'd incurred in our brief marriage. I left within the week, and I've neither seen Letiche nor heard from her since. I'm sure the d'Avignys pray daily for word of my death to reach them so Letiche can marry again and bring them the fortune they seek."

"She's—pretty?" This had been plaguing her, but the words came out with an effort.

"Letiche is small and dark and has a round face and a bubbly laugh. Some would not call her pretty, but she has a certain comeliness."

Like Ned's Lavinia, thought Lenore. *Small, dark, bubbly.* Not pretty like Lavinia, perhaps . . . but his wife. Lenore kept her head bowed as she thought about that.

"Have you ever written to her, Geoffrey?"

"No." His answer was emphatic. "Nor do I think she'd relish hearing from me. Lenore, you must know I consider you my wife—and you would be my legal wife, could I but arrange it. And I will guard you and the child you bear me as tenderly as if the words had been spoken over us in some vast cathedral."

"Oh, Geoffrey, I'm so ashamed that I doubted you!" Blinded by tears, she flung herself into his arms. "What more could I ask than that?"

"A great deal more," he said, holding her close, gently caressing her golden hair. "And I would that I could give it to you, Lenore."

" 'Tis only that I'm so tired of waiting to have the baby," she sighed. "It makes me irritable, it makes me say things I do not mean."

Geoffrey's arms tightened warmly about her. "Someday," he promised, "things will straighten out for us, Lenore. I've not led much of a life, but once our child is born"—his voice grew rich, telling her how much this baby meant to him— "I promise we'll mend our affairs. There are places where such as we can make a new start . . . The Daunts of Williamsburg, how does that sound to you?"

"The Colonies? Then you meant what you said about going there? 'Twas not just idle talk to cheer me?"

" 'Twas not idle talk. I've been scheming to arrange it. So far all has fallen through, but next week there's a man —a planter, Lenore, who's visiting relatives just three days' ride from here. 'Tis said he's in England looking for an overseer for his Virginia plantations and will pay a good price for the right man. He cares not for politics, but if I impress him well, he could arrange our passage."

Williamsburg . . . far from Letiche, far from France, far from the iron grip of the Lord Protector. "Williamsburg," she murmured, nestling into his arms.

"What troubles me," he admitted, "is that this is the last week of May. Next week will be June. The baby could come while I'm away, but—'tis my only chance to see this man, Lenore. He stays with his relatives but a week."

"I'll be all right," said Lenore staunchly. "Lally will come and stay with me. I'll send her word after you've gone."

He nodded, and held her in his arms for a long time. "You're so brave," he murmured half to himself. "If aught should happen to you . . ."

"Nothing will happen to me, Geoffrey," she insisted.

When Geoffrey rode off, Lenore sent a note to Lally at Gilbert's lodgings.

And received word that Lally had left Gilbert, left Oxford. She had taken only her clothes and her meager jewels. No one knew where she had gone.

To Lenore it was a crushing blow. Lally gone . . . she

had counted on having Lally around when her baby was born . . . she had gone without even saying goodbye. Gilbert must have done something awful to her to make her leave abruptly like that.

Now, for the first time, Lenore felt not merely gloomy, but frightened.

I will not have the baby until Geoffrey gets back, she promised herself nervously. *I will barely move around. I will sit very still and eat little and drink little, and Geoffrey will come back and I will have someone to cling to when the pains come.*

At other times she cursed herself roundly for a coward and deliberately got up and walked about, ate heartily, and told herself that she could do it all alone if necessary.

As it happened, she very nearly did.

She was sitting on a chair by the window, looking out at the rain pattering down from a gray sky, when she saw Michael in his red cloak swinging up the wet street. She sighed. She did not feel at all well, she did not feel like hearing horror stories of terrible times between Town and Gown, nor did she wish to practice her penmanship, which she was sure he would suggest, even though she had grown very passable at it by dogged effort and Michael had even bragged of her progress to Geoffrey. Moving cumbersomely, she went out onto the landing to call down to Mistress Watts that she was unwell today and was not receiving visitors.

Always alert for a meal, the white cat, who had been attentively crouching at a mousehole in the upstairs hall, turned to look at Lenore. The mouse saw its chance and ran out almost under Lenore's feet. She jumped aside with a little cry and collided with Puss, streaking forward intent on the chase.

Trying to dodge the running cat cost Lenore her balance. Her foot caught in the hem of her skirt as she teetered on the top step. She tried vainly to grasp the newel post as her weight, heavy to the front due to her pregnancy, toppled her. With a wild scream she tumbled down the stairs, arriving at the foot just as Michael opened the door.

His face turned white at the sight of her lying there in a crumpled heap, and Mistress Watts, who had heard Lenore scream, came running out. "What have you done to Mistress Daunt?" she cried fiercely.

Michael was taken aback. He gave Mistress Watts a wounded look. "I've done nothing to her. I was coming to call, and when I opened the door she was falling down the stairs." Anxiously he bent over Lenore. "Is she dead, do you think?" he asked fearfully, studying her unconscious form, afraid to touch her.

"Nay, 'tis her time has come, that's all. Let us hope she has broken no bones in her fall. There, you see, she's coming around now"—this as Lenore moved and groaned and opened her eyes—"can you get her upstairs by yourself, or shall I call the stable boy?"

"I can—do it—myself." Panting with effort, for he was not very strong, chunky Michael managed to pick up Lenore and stagger up the stairs with her in his arms. There, under Mistress Watts's clucking supervision, he laid her very carefully on the bed.

"Thank you, Michael," said Lenore weakly. She gasped as a sharp pain went through her.

"Don't talk," said Mistress Watts crisply. She adjusted the coverlet. "I'll send for Mistress Rue, the midwife."

"I'll go for her—'twill be quicker." Michael was obsessed with a need for action. He darted away.

"On Mount Street," Mistress Watts called after him.

Michael, just rushing out the front door, called back something unintelligible and kept going. But he had misheard. He hurried to Blount Street through a heavy shower that soaked him through and searched for Mistress Rue in vain. In rising panic, he blundered about the wet streets and finally ran back over the slippery cobbles to announce in an almost tearful voice that he could not find her. But Mistress Rue was already there, for Lenore's shrewd landlady had seen the state of upheaval Michael was in and had prudently sent her stable boy running to Mistress Rue's.

" 'Tis all right, all right," she assured Michael, for she

was quite pleased with herself that Mistress Rue had arrived so speedily.

"You mean she's here?" he asked incredulously, wondering how this miracle had come to pass.

"Indeed she is," Mistress Watts smiled as Michael slumped down exhausted. "Mister Daunt favored a doctor, you know. 'Twas I persuaded Mistress Daunt to insist on a midwife." In this she had been assisted by Lenore's experiences in Twainmere. "Midwives assisted at the birthings in Twainmere," Lenore had told Geoffrey stubbornly, "and 'tis after all up to me to have this child—neither doctor nor midwife can do it for me."

"And a woman will be more comforting than a man," Mistress Watts had chimed in to add, as she walked by the door and overheard their conversation.

She chose to forget that Geoffrey's dark brows had formed a straight line and he had gone over and closed the door rather hard, although at the time she'd sniffed and thought he should be grateful that she could provide such a good midwife.

And see how well Mistress Rue was doing! She had arrived, fat and bustling and energetic and wearing a large gray linen apron. "What, is Mistress Daunt already in labor?" she'd demanded, tossing her wet cloak to Gwynneth. "Then all the knots about the place must be loosened at once—in the kitchen, indeed in all the rooms!" The woman had foresight. Rushed as she was, she'd bethought her to snatch up an old garment—one that might have been new during the Old Queen's reign—"for luck" to wrap the newborn child in. Ah, this midwife was worth her salt indeed, and would never neglect any of the necessary childbirth charms!

Mistress Watts hurried upstairs. "Ye be lucky!" she beamed. "Mistress Rue is here."

"Where—is she?" gasped Lenore, pale and perspiring from her last bout with the fierce labor pains that had seized her.

"Down in the kitchen seeing that all the knots in the place are loosed."

Knots? What was this about knots? Another great pain struck Lenore, and she cried out. "I care not a whit for charms!" she gasped when she could speak again. "Only that my baby be born alive and healthy! Tell Mistress Rue to forget about knots and come upstairs at once!"

Mistress Watts sputtered. So shocked was she by this lack of proper feeling for time-tested charms that she withdrew from the room altogether in a huff and went back downstairs and slammed the door to her quarters.

"Your husband's very young," Mistress Rue observed to Lenore when she finally finished with the knots and went upstairs. For she'd glimpsed Michael sitting on the top step, looking tired and forlorn, and naturally assumed him to be the father.

Lenore gave the midwife a dazed look. She was just coming up out of a well of suffering.

"Never mind," said Mistress Rue, from out of her years of experience. "We'll get you through this, mistress."

But as the hours dragged by and Lenore's condition worsened, Mistress Rue began to look worried. She muttered that she had never placed great reliance in eaglestones herself. "But your husband might run to the church and demand the bells be rung," she suggested, brightening. "Indeed that often eases a difficult labor!"

Lenore, lying weak and pale between pains, said a little testily that the Daunts were of no consequence in Oxford and the bells would doubtless remain silent, no matter what they demanded.

At that declaration, Mistress Rue tore from the room and whispered something in Michael's ear. Michael, who had winced every time he'd heard Lenore groan, got up and went out looking dazed. He came back with a piece of frayed rope, which he silently handed to the midwife. She snatched it from him and went back into the bedchamber.

"We've had this from the bellringers." She waved the piece of rope at Lenore importantly. "It should do almost as well as having the bells rung." She tied the rope around Lenore's waist—rather tightly, for it was a bit too

253

short—and there it remained as a good luck charm until Lenore, screaming in agony, ripped her fingernails in tearing it off.

Mistress Rue clucked in dismay. "Now I must tie this back on," she insisted, moving to do so.

The pain had subsided for the moment, and Lenore gave Mistress Rue a baleful look. "If you even try it, I promise you I will claw your eyes out!"

Mistress Rue straightened up with a wounded look.

"Very well, Mistress Daunt, but if things go badly for you, I am not to be blamed!" She turned to Mistress Watts, whom curiosity had brought up the stairs again to see how matters were going. "She do be a bad patient," the midwife sighed. "I hope that she may not die, but I have attended at two birthings this past month where the ladies did die after they broke the rope—and they do say things happen in threes."

Mistress Watts clucked her tongue and gave Lenore a worried look. Michael, who had overheard this as the door opened to admit Mistress Watts, was slumped down on the stairs looking as if he too might expire. "Do you need more rope?" he croaked.

Mistress Watts turned to say impatiently, "Mistress Daunt refuses to use it."

"I do think he could do with a hot posset," Mistress Rue told the landlady, with an uneasy look at Michael. "Husbands do take on so at birthings!"

Mistress Watts forbore to tell the midwife that Michael was not the father, that the father was off on one of his many trips of which she so heartily disapproved—a man should be at his wife's side at a time like this! She brought Michael a hot posset herself; it was made of hot spiced milk curdled by ale, and he rallied as he drank it.

"Do you think she will live?" he asked in a tragic voice. "I heard what the midwife said."

"Keep your voice down," said Mistress Watts sharply. "And why would she not live, a fine strong girl like her? Mistress Rue is always looking on the dark side—but then, she sees so many as won't follow her instructions."

"But you heard her say Lenore broke the rope and tore it off!"

"Ah, but we've countered that with the knots we've loosened." She looked sharply at Michael. "Have ye any knots about ye?"

"I don't think so—yes, yes, I have!" Excitedly Michael scrabbled at his pursestring, a narrow leather thong, which he kept knotted for safety's sake.

"There, that may be what's been causing the trouble!" Mistress Watts told him triumphantly, when at last his awkward fingers had it untied, and Michael sank back, much relieved and feeling terribly guilty that the knot of his pursestring should have been holding back the birth.

It was a difficult birth. The hours dragged by, day slipped into night, and Lenore thought that terrible night would never end. She gripped the soaked bedding and fought down screams as her back arched in agony and her hand gripped Mistress Rue's with a pressure that numbed the midwife's fingers. She screamed for Geoffrey, and once for Meg, and could not understand the midwife's crooning answers. For a time the whole world seemed to turn to a hot blackness and there was only the pain, a livid leaping thing, knifing through her body as if to rend her apart. She came to, out of a long-drawn-out agony, in a red haze, dimly aware that the midwife was speaking to her.

"A fine lovely daughter ye have, mistress!" The fat puffing midwife was chortling. She held up the child as proudly as if she'd borne it herself. "I'll be calling the father to come in now—I do think he's gone to sleep out there on the steps. He'll be so pleased!"

"No—wait," murmured Lenore, reaching out for the baby, and the midwife handed the small precious bundle that was her daughter to her and went out to call Mistress Watts and Michael.

Weak and exhausted, with her face wet with perspiration and her hair plastered to her forehead, Lenore looked with wonderment at the small sweet creature she was holding so carefully.

She had done it! She had done it! She felt a thrill go

255

through her that was like none she had ever known. Her daughter! Out of that scalding night of pain, she held her daughter in her arms at last. Tears of joy trembled on her lashes as with a fierce sweet tenderness she cradled her baby.

She looked up in triumph, violet eyes aglow, as Mistress Watts entered the room. To the confusion of the midwife, Mistress Watts had just banished Michael sternly from the stairs and told him he could sleep in the common room downstairs, since curfew had long since sounded and the watch would get him if he left now. The midwife looked appalled at this, and turned to Michael as if expecting him to assert his rights.

"I'm not the father," Michael admitted sheepishly.

"Not the father?" Mistress Rue looked at Michael in bewilderment. "Then who's to pay me?" she demanded in a strident voice. "I'd not have come if—"

"Here, I'll pay you!" Hastily Michael pulled money out of his untied purse and counted out coins into the midwife's hand. "Is that enough?" he asked her doubtfully.

It was more than she'd expected. Mistress Rue closed her fingers on the coins and sniffed. An odd household, this! With a man who was not the father pacing the floor outside, and a woman giving birth who was so reckless of charms she'd near killed herself birthing! Determined to say as much, now that she'd been paid—and also that she doubted Lenore could have any more children—she followed Mistress Watts into the room.

There she found Mistress Watts almost in tears herself just to see the glorious expression in Lenore's violet eyes. With a rare instinct for a precious moment, kindly Mistress Watts hurried the protesting midwife away to let Lenore enjoy these first moments with her baby in private.

Raptly, by the light of a single taper, Lenore studied that small sweet face. What a great beauty she would grow up to be! she thought fondly. Already she was beautiful. *Her daughter!* It was hard to realize that she, Lenore Frankford, had a daughter! Although she had wanted a boy, had fully intended to name him Geoffrey, all thought of that was gone now, and the small pink child in her arms seemed the most desirable thing on earth. Her daughter . . .

I will name her Lorena, she thought dreamily. *For my mother.*

She cradled the baby in the crook of her arm. "You must grow up beautiful—and strong, Lorena," she murmured, cuddling the child to her. "For your father cannot give you his name, and you will have to fight the world for your birthright. I will help you." Gently she hugged the baby. "But most of it will be up to you."

Then she laughed at herself for trying to counsel a newborn infant, and went deeply, peacefully to sleep with Lorena warm and pink beside her.

It was the third of June, 1652. Outside the midnight bells were chiming in the rain.

CHAPTER 17

Michael bustled in the next morning, chafing because Mistress Watts had sternly denied him entrance to Lenore's lodgings until she had been served her breakfast tray. Had he but known it, he had also waited until Mistress Daunt had completed her morning toilette. She had combed out her long, bright hair, let it fall loose around her shoulders as she fed the baby, and when she lay back it spread luxuriantly over the pillow. She had wound the long gown Lally had given her for this occasion round and round the baby to keep her feet and body toasty warm, arranged the baby in the crook of her arm for viewing, and smiled as Michael entered the room.

He tossed his red cloak onto a chair and came and gazed at Lenore as she lay in the big bed with a kind of reverent awe. Lenore was touched by the look of wonder in his eyes. Michael had been a devoted friend, and she was positive he must have had a very bad night because of her.

"Isn't she beautiful?" she asked him, gazing fondly at Lorena.

Michael looked at Lenore, with her red-gold hair tumbled in shimmering masses about the pillow, her skin—from the long winter and being indoors so much—pearly and sheer. He swallowed. " 'Tis you who are beautiful!" he declared intensely. "Ah, Lenore, Lenore." He sank down on his knees beside the bed. "Sometimes I think I will die of love of you!"

Lenore looked at him in trepidation. She had known Michael loved her in a young, unformed way; that he had cherished secret thoughts about her she had long since guessed. But now to look at that woebegone cherubic countenance, flushed and earnest, and to hear his boyish voice blurting out such things. . . !

"Michael," she said, distressed, "you must not say such things to me—not even if you think them. You must remember that I am a married woman."

Though he reddened still further at this soft rebuff, Michael sturdily held his ground, impelled by desperation and by last night's very real threat of losing her. "Gossip has it ye are not married to Geoffrey, that he leaves ye alone while he prowls the highroads with a scarf over his face, seeking coaches to plunder!" The abject pain in his voice took away the sting of his words.

" 'Tis true we are not legal wed in a church, Geoffrey and I," Lenore said carefully, "but we are wed in our hearts, Michael—'tis a bond I cannot break, nor would if I could."

He looked so crestfallen that she reached out and touched his hand. "You are very young," she said gently, "and when—"

"I am older than you!" he interrupted defiantly.

In years, perhaps, she thought, but women of his age were having babies, while he was still at his books. She sighed. "Someday you will understand. Perhaps by then you will have met a girl who means as much to you as I do to Geoffrey."

His voice roughened in despair. "I want no other girl!

And you mean more to *me* than you do to Geoffrey! Ah, but say the word, Lenore, and I will take you away and shelter you and the babe—"

She put gentle fingers to his lips to silence him. "These things may be thought, Michael, but they must not be said," she told him sternly. "Your mother has great plans for you. I know, for you have told me so."

"I would take you home to her," he sulked.

And she would throw me out! thought Lenore wryly. She could well imagine the scene if young Michael showed up with the Angel of Worcester in tow—and carrying a newborn babe! "Your mother would faint at such an alliance," she reproved him. "Michael, I am honored that you love me, but—"

"But—you will stay with Geoffrey?" he finished for her.

She nodded, smiling a little sadly.

Michael sighed, got up off his knees, and dusted them off. She had the faintly amused feeling that he had been delighted to unburden himself of his feelings, but that he was also faintly relieved that she had not taken him up on his rash proposal.

"Wouldst tell Mistress Watts that I have finished with my breakfast tray, Michael?" This small errand, she felt, would give him a chance to retire gracefully and collect himself.

He gave her a pensive look. "I'll tell her on my way out, Lenore."

"Come back soon, Michael—I don't know what I'd have done without you." She pressed his hand, and he stood looking down at her with big reproachful eyes in his youthful cherub face, then clattered downstairs and was gone.

Not till after he had left did she learn from Mistress Watts that he had paid the midwife. It embarrassed her that he had done so, and she was sorry she had not known so that she could thank him.

The rain that had begun on the day of Lorena's birth continued to drizzle down. But word reached Oxford from muddy farmers who struggled through mired roads into the city with their carts that the rains were worse to the south. There it rained steadily for days and washed out all the roads. Lenore was not surprised that Geoffrey was late in returning, for he must have found his way blocked by torrential rains that made the roads impassable.

Lenore, at first unable to walk, began to mend. Her natural youth and strength prevailed, and by the time Geoffrey returned—slogging in from the south through deep mud that made the bay's chest heave with exertion —she was up and about, dressed in the green dress she had been wearing when she met him—although she had made herself a new white cambric petticoat. And in her arms was clutched her small daughter, whose frosting of pale hair haloed a small head and framed a small face of surpassing beauty.

What matter that Lorena's hair was pale and Geoffrey's dark? She was so proud of Lorena! She could hardly wait to exhibit her to Geoffrey.

It was midafternoon when he came in. The drizzle that had greened up moss all over Oxford had stopped at last, but the skies were still sullen, gray clouds chased each other overhead, and the air was damp. Lenore heard him running up the stairs three at a time, and her heart thudded with joy. Geoffrey was back!

Quickly she snatched Lorena up from the bed and seated herself gracefully on a chair by the window where the light would glow on her red-gold hair and Lorena's moonlight frosting. She had planned for Geoffrey to see them thus—a lovely sight for a new father, she thought.

The door came open as if blown by a gust. Lenore started, and the motion tipped the blanket she was holding down around the top of baby Lorena's head. Geoffrey strode in, tall and energetic, on muddy boots. His cloak was flying, and he tossed his hat on a chair and came toward her pulling off his gauntlets. His gray eyes lit up to see her sitting there, slender and beautiful again, with her bright hair agleam and her eyes shining in greeting.

"Lenore!" His voice was deep-timbred as he bent to kiss her. "And who's this? Don't hide the baby under a blanket—let me see his face!" He sounded so happy Lenore wanted to cry.

"*Her* face, Geoffrey," she corrected huskily. "We have a daughter."

Gently she drew back the blanket that had slid down almost obscuring the baby's eyes, and Lorena, who had been sleeping, opened her eyes—they were big and blue —and stared up in wonder at the dark, smiling visage that looked down into hers. The blanket slid back to show that small perfect head and the frosting of silky pale hair.

"A daughter!" Geoffrey stared down at the baby eagerly. Then his features stiffened, and his jaw seemed to harden into iron; it was a furious look he flung at Lenore.

"Her hair is white as hemp and her eyes are blue!" he accused her.

"All babies' eyes are blue," defended Lenore, encircling Lorena with protective arms.

" 'Tis not mine!" he cried, and she winced at the note of anguish in his harsh voice. " 'Tis the child of that fellow at Worcester!"

From the moment she'd seen the baby's coloring—so identical with Jamie's—Lenore had feared he would say that, but she had deliberately put the thought from her. "And is that so terrible?" she demanded. "You knew I was handfasted before you!"

"Yes," he said hoarsely, "I knew it—dàmn you! You've cheated me! Ye said the child was mine!"

Fury gave her strength. She leaped to her feet with the child clutched in her arms. Her body was rigid with rage and the agony of Geoffrey's betrayal. "How dare you accuse me!" she shouted. *"You with a wife in France!"* She fell to crying stormily.

He flung out, slamming the door so hard the house shook, and she heard his boots clatter loudly down the stairs.

Anger and disappointment and fright fought within her. She set Lorena down carefully, clawed at the casement, got it open, and stuck her head out. Geoffrey was just remounting the bay, who looked tired and woebegone.

"Where are you going?" she screamed.

"To France!" Geoffrey roared back at her and was off around the corner into Magpie Lane as if driven by devils.

Lenore slammed the casement—so hard the leaded panes nearly splintered—and fell back, covering her face with her hands, trying to control her sobs. Lorena, who until now had been quiet and bewildered, gave a sudden cry and Lenore picked her up. Wounded to the heart, Lenore grimly surveyed the tiny, perfect child in her arms through tear-wet eyes. What if Lorena did have Jamie's hemp-white hair and blue eyes? A beauty she was, so tiny and soft. Lenore held her and rocked her and wept afresh. This was *her* child, no matter who the father was! Hers to cherish, hers to love!

Never for an instant did she believe that Geoffrey meant his threat about going to France. But Mistress Watts, who had been just coming in from marketing when Geoffrey left, heard it and believed it and sent word on her own account to Gilbert. "For I know you are Mister Daunt's cousin," she wrote, "and that you would wish no harm to come to Mistress Daunt. Especially now that the baby has come."

Lounging in his cluttered lodgings, Gilbert read the note thoughtfully and crumpled it. Geoffrey gone to France, leaving the beauteous Lenore? He could hardly credit it! He got up and went on a tour of the taverns and found Geoffrey, lying drunk at a disreputable alehouse at Headington Quarry. Obviously Geoffrey had chosen a place where he would not be likely to encounter any of his friends. Gilbert went and stood over his tall cousin, stretched out on a bench and snoring lustily.

A very vicious smile lit Gilbert's handsome face. He fingered the jaw Geoffrey had struck, and thought of the delights of holding Lenore in his arms. There was a way to induce her to his bed, which Lally had so lately left and which was in dire need of warming these nights by someone better than drunken Dorothy, the tavern maid.

He turned about to go and speak to the tavernkeeper, a brawny giant of a man who watched him silently, great arms folded. As he did so his foot caught on a loose board. He tripped and was thrust against a wooden table before he could right himself. With a curse he got his footing again, never noting that the rough table edge had torn off one of his fancy enameled buttons. It had rolled unnoticed against Geoffrey's arm, which dangled to the floor from the bench.

Seeing the proprietor eyeing him, Gilbert thoughtfully dusted himself off and looked around him. Save for the snoring Geoffrey, he and the tavernkeeper were alone here.

"That long, tall fellow with the black hair." Gilbert's casual nod indicated Geoffrey's prone figure. "Do you think you could keep him drunk for a week?"

The tavernkeeper scratched his head with a stubby finger and studied this caramel creation with shrewd, practiced eyes. Gentlemen didn't often frequent his establishment, and here were two on the same day. The first had spun into the place in a fury and drunk alone, but this one with the hard caramel eyes—up to no good, he reasoned.

"Now that might be done for a price," he admitted. "But 'twould take an ocean of ale, for it took an ocean of ale to put him on his back there."

Deliberately Gilbert was counting out coins. They fell from his gloved hand with little tinkles onto a scarred wooden table top. At the sight of gold, the tavernkeeper's eyes glinted with greed.

"Here's the price," Gilbert said in a ruthless voice. "I care not how you do it, but keep him here for a week. He's not to know I ordered it, he's to see no one, talk to no one."

"I've a back room." The tavernkeeper's big hand swept up the coins. "Leastways, there's a curtain that separates it." He nodded toward some filthy hangings.

"Nay," said Gilbert thoughtfully. "That would make him suspicious when he wakes. Ye'd best leave him where he is—just keep pouring ale into him."

"Aye, that I will." The tavernkeeper winked. "A husband, I'll be bound? And you plan to frolic with the wife while he tarries here?"

Gilbert gave him a wintry look from flat caramel eyes.

"Just see that he stays where he is," he said with a thin smile. "And there'll be more coins for you."

As he left, the landlord—galvanized by this sudden wealth—was trying to pour ale down the unconscious Geoffrey's throat.

The first night Geoffrey was gone, Lenore frowned angrily and flounced off to bed. The next day she sought out Mistress Watts to ask if anyone had seen Geoffrey.

For once Mistress Watts's cheerful composure cracked. "Men!" she declared gloomily. "They'll be the death of us! If they're not off getting themselves killed in wars, they're home deserting us for other women! Though why any man would leave a face like yours is a puzzle."

"He already has a wife," said Lenore in a thick voice. She had a desperate need for someone to confide in.

"I knew that, my dear," said her landlady bluntly. "For all I knew your lover's name to be Wyndham and not Daunt, as he claimed. But I presumed you knew and did not care."

"I—cared," said Lenore haltingly. "But I—I found out about her too late." Ah, was that the truth? she asked herself wildly. Would she not have succumbed to Geoffrey's charms in any event? And where had it led her?

"Did . . . everyone know I was not his wife?" she asked painfully.

"All within the range of Master Gilbert's voice," was the wry response. "For I think he sought to supplant Master Geoffrey in your affections and did not wish to be thought dangling after another man's wife."

Lenore was overwrought. "Tell Master Gilbert for me," she said with suppressed violence, "that I hope he sinks into the pit!"

Mistress Watts sighed and tried to reason with Lenore. "This is no time to be taking on this way. Now that Mistress Lally has departed, 'tis surely Master Gilbert you must turn to now."

Such blazing anger gripped Lenore that she felt her head must melt. "I would as soon bed a demon—tell him that, too!"

"Then . . . where will you go? What will become of you?"

Lenore guessed this was Mistress Watts's subtle way of telling her the lodgings must be paid for, and a woman with a small babe had scant chance of earning a living.

"Geoffrey cannot have left me," she said, taking a deep breath. "He would not do that."

"Fine gentlemen have a way of leaving."

There was so much bitterness in Mistress Watts's voice as she said that, that for all her misery, Lenore cast a startled look at her landlady. That hatchet-face had once been young and piquant. Those eyes, melting . . . That dumpy figure had once been ripe and supple. Mistress Watts, too, had loved and lost. For a moment Lenore, who felt bereft herself, pitied Mistress Watts, trying to make do with her elderly suitor across the street.

"I must go and look for Geoffrey," she said abruptly. "He may be lying hurt somewhere."

Mistress Watts shook her head as determined young Mistress Daunt climbed the wooden stairs and returned again carrying Lorena, wrapped in a shawl. "You're not taking the baby?" she cried, scandalized.

"I must," said Lenore simply. "I shall walk all over town and inquire about Geoffrey—and I cannot keep coming back here to feed Lorena. She'd best go with me."

Mistress Watts was still shaking her head as her determined young lodger went out the door.

Into the town went Lenore, asking all of Geoffrey's friends if they had seen him. Encountering Michael on the High Street, she hailed him and asked him to help her in her search. Michael assented eagerly, glad to be of service to his adored Lenore. He looked in all the wrong places, earnestly searching the halls of the university, the Ashmoleum Museum, the Magdalen Tower, the churches. He seemed to think Geoffrey might be hiding from Lenore with a good book. Crestfallen, he had to admit he'd come up with nothing.

Lenore did not give up easily. She made the rounds of likely taverns and asked all his friends again. None had seen him for more than a fortnight, they swore—and all were telling the truth, for none of them frequented the disreputable alehouse at Headington Quarry, where Geoffrey was having more ale poured down his gullet every time he sat up. It did not occur to her to ask Gilbert, nor would she have gained the truth if she had.

Five days later, with all avenues of information exhausted, Lenore faced the bleak fact that Geoffrey was not going to return. And now the pain that went through her was of a different kind, but in its way as sharp and deep as the pain of Lorena's birth. Geoffrey was gone. He had deserted her in anger.

And without even a goodbye.

Her face must have reflected this terrible new certainty, for her landlady, when Lenore came downstairs asking as usual if Mistress Watts had heard anything, gave her a sharp look. "Your fine gentleman's really gone," she surmised. "Ach, that's the way they go—once the babe is born."

Lenore couldn't speak. She made her way unsteadily upstairs and sat down to think.

She couldn't stay here. That was plain. She had only a few coins left, not enough to pay for her lodgings—not enough to repay Michael for the midwife. Soon she'd be turned out. Mayhap she'd end up in debtors' prison. She had no trade, no way of earning a living except as a serving-woman—and even that would be difficult. For times were lean in England now, and soldiers, crippled in Cromwell's wars, limped about willing to work for a pittance, their wives reduced to slatterns who slaved for their keep, their children often begging on the streets for their very bread. Lenore shuddered. Her little Lorena must not come to that!

She could ask Mistress Watts for work—but that would mean supplanting poor Gwynneth, who so badly needed her job. And Gwynneth's meager salary would not furnish housing for herself and Lorena and stabling for Snowfire. And—and anyway, it would be very hard staying in Oxford and serving ale in some tavern—though she guessed she might find a job in one, for men liked to look at her as they sipped their ale. But in Oxford she would constantly run into friends of Geoffrey's, who would be embarrassed for her and pity her, and Gilbert could come and lord it over her. She ran a distraught hand through her hair. No, she would not stay in Oxford.

It did not occur to her to sell herself on the street, or to try to move in with Michael, who would have been glad to have her. Her mind didn't work that way. Instead, she pondered the possible alternatives of making her own way.

Her hands were clenched white in her lap. *I will not let him wreck me,* she told herself fiercely. *I will make my way alone.*

But how to do that? That was the problem.

At last she thought she had the answer. She would have to leave here, of course. But there were things to do first.

She sat down and penned a note to Michael, sending it by Jack, the stable boy. In it she thanked him again for all he had done and asked him for his family's address, since she knew he was soon to leave the university, and she wished to repay him the money he had laid out for her to Mistress Rue as soon as she was able.

Then she went downstairs and sought out her landlady, who was occupied with counting the spoons and looked up with a frown at Lenore's approach. "Two spoons missing," she muttered. "That careless Gwynneth! Probably thrown out with the slops!"

"I have not the money to pay what I owe you." Lenore came to the point at once. "And since Geoffrey has left me, I am not like to get any money here."

"Ye can stay without money," interrupted Mistress Watts with an expansive gesture that knocked the spoons to the floor. "Oh, dear—see what I've done! There's plenty of room, Mistress Daunt, and ye'll find a way, ye'll find a way." She was thinking that Gilbert, whose mother sent him money from time to time, would be glad to pay the bill for Lenore's lodgings—if not, some other young buck. And she would come to it, given time!

Lenore, helping her pick up the spoons, took her meaning and frowned. "No, I cannot do that," she said soberly.

"I know that you rent lodgings for your livelihood and cannot afford to have beggars such as myself occupying them. Do you chance to know where there's a fair being held, Mistress Watts?"

Mistress Watts straightened up and took the spoons Lenore held out. "A fair? Well, I did hear there was to be one at Banbury. Next week, I think—no, perhaps it is going on now."

"Then I'm to Banbury. I'll send you the money I owe you—if not from Banbury, from another fair."

Mistress Watts was aghast. Surely young Mistress Daunt did not propose to sell herself to the fair-goers—'twas known fairs were the haunts of prostitutes, who had rich pickings there of farmers and drovers on holiday!

"And now if I could ask cook to provision me for my journey to Banbury?" Mistress Watts looked taken aback, but Lenore reached in her purse. "I have enough money left for that."

"I'll tell her," said Mistress Watts, taking the money. "But I do think ye are making a mistake, Mistress Daunt."

Cook liked young Mistress Daunt for her spirited ways. She packed a big square of linen with brown bread and Cheshire cheese and apples and plum tarts and left it hanging over the newel post.

Puzzled by the urgent tone of Lenore's note, Michael hurried over and knocked at Lenore's door.

"Come in," she called over her shoulder, and glanced up as he entered. "Oh—hello, Michael." She hoped he wasn't going to try to persuade her to stay.

"Why, where are you going?" he burst out, seeing that Lenore was busy packing her belongings.

"Can ye not see?" asked Lenore irritably, without raising her eyes from folding a petticoat. "I'm taking my leave of Oxford before I pile up mountains of debts I can't pay and they send me off to debtors' prison."

"I could lend ye a little," he ventured, frowning.

Lenore straightened up and smiled into his eyes—albeit it was a wan smile. She was touched by Michael's offer, knowing how straitened were his circumstances. For all his fine clothes, Michael's parents kept him on a paltry allowance that allowed him few luxuries, and she felt deep in his debt already. "I couldn't do that," she said gently.

"Lenore," he said earnestly, his cheeks pink with emotion, "come home with me. I would be *so glad* to take care of you."

She patted his shoulder, looking ruefully into his flushed face. "I know you would, Michael, but . . . I couldn't."

"I know." He flinched a little. "I would promise not to touch you. I would remember that you belong to Geoffrey —wherever he may be."

She gave him a long, sad look. "No." Her mouth twisted bitterly. "Never again will I belong to Geoffrey. I belong to myself alone. As to where Geoffrey is, he's gone to France. He shouted that was where he was going as he left. I didn't believe him—then. But now I do."

Michael digested this. "Perhaps you might change your mind about me later?" he ventured. "Since you're a free woman at last."

Lenore turned away lest he see the agonized look in her violet eyes. Free? Would she ever be free of Geoffrey? Would a night ever pass with the wind sighing in the trees that she would not remember his lips, his burning touch, the strong masculine feel of him in her arms? She'd be alone . . . but not free.

Her lips denied it. "Yes," she said woodenly. "I'm a free woman at last. But"—from shadowed lashes she considered him, feeling compassion for his youth, his hopeless love for her—"I am not apt to change my mind about you, Michael," she added sadly.

"I see." He spoke hurriedly. "Can I help you pack, then?"

She shook her head. "I've little to pack, just what I can take in my saddlebags. Mainly I'm trying to clean up these rooms so they'll be no trouble to Mistress Watts and Gwynneth after I'm gone—she'll be wanting to show them to let." She was polishing the leaded windowpanes with a scrap of woolen cloth as she spoke.

"Where will ye go, Lenore?" Michael asked soberly.

"First, to Banbury, where Mistress Watts tells me a fair is being held."

"A—a fair?" he faltered, waiting for an explanation.

"Yes. I plan to race Snowfire there. That's how I'm going to support myself, Michael—by racing Snowfire at the fairs, wherever they are held."

"You—you mean to ride the length and breadth of England with a suckling babe in your arms . . . *racing at the fairs?*" He looked at her incredulously. "But the prizes are usually only a turkey or a small purse at best!"

Lenore nodded grimly. "I've had a taste of it. 'Tis not so much the purse or the fat turkey—'tis the wagers. I'll goad men into wagering good money because they cannot admit that a woman can beat them!" Her jaw hardened, remembering big Hobbs, who had tried to run her off the track at Wells.

"But—but ye've no money to wager!" he gasped.

"Pebbles will make a purse heavy," said Lenore. "And if I should lose, why then—why then, I will indenture myself to pay the debt!"

Michael was beyond speech. He looked at Lenore as if she had taken leave of her senses—a woman racing at the fairs, indeed! And wagering without money!

"At least, let me accompany you to Banbury," he pleaded. "For I'm quitting Oxford, as you know. I was going next week, but no matter, I might as well leave now."

"No," said Lenore absently. "Your mother will expect you home speedily, Michael. You must not linger at Banbury."

"But Coventry lies to the north of Banbury, Lenore. Banbury is on my way—I always stop there to eat cakes, Banbury's famous for its cakes!"

Lenore wasn't sure whether she believed him, but she knew she'd be very glad of his company as far as Banbury. Michael, at least, had stood by her. In the uncertain new life on which she was about to venture, it would be good—at least for a little while—to have a friend. Her smile was sad. "You are too good to me, Michael. I

271

would I could pay you for what you laid out to the midwife, Michael."

" 'Tis no matter." His voice was rough. "I was glad to do it, Lenore. I—I kept wishing the child was mine."

Lenore swallowed. His devotion was foolish but overwhelming.

"Michael," she said, "I will win enough at the fairs, I promise, to repay you all that you have spent on me."

"Win enough you may," he declared fiercely, "but you cannot make me take it!"

She smiled and leaned over and gave him a light kiss. His face flamed up as her lips brushed his. Later she was to remember that moment, and be so glad she had kissed him.

"I'll take you to a good dinner at the Crown and tomorrow we'll start out," he told her energetically.

Lenore shook her head. "I owe Mistress Watts too much already, and I mean to leave today. Cook has provisioned me. I am almost ready."

"But you cannot be in such a rush as that to be out of town," cried Michael, upset. "I'll rush home now and pack my saddlebags—the boxes can follow me later!"

"All right," Lenore assented. "I'll wait for you here, but do hurry, Michael. I like not the idea of spending a night on the road."

"There's a good inn," he began, but she waved him away.

"Hurry." She gave him a small push.

Michael had barely sprinted around the corner of Magpie Lane when Gilbert turned into it from a different direction. He has estimated his timing to be exactly right. With Geoffrey five days gone, Lenore should be at her wits' end, a ripe plum for the picking. Briskly he headed for Mistress Watts's establishment, slapped on his plumed hat, and opened the door.

"Not back yet?" he asked Mistress Watts, brows lifted in interested query, when he encountered the landlady in the downstairs hall.

"If ye mean Mister Daunt, that he's not," said Mistress Watts with tightly compressed lips. "And it's as well, I say, to be rid of him—a man who would leave his poor lady thus right after she's borne him a child!"

"True, true," agreed Gilbert piously. "And how does she take it—Mistress Daunt?"

"She has been very upset," confided Mistress Watts. "But now she packs, poor lady."

"Packs?" Gilbert was startled; this was one contingency that had not occurred to him. "Faith, I should dissuade her!" He hurried by the landlady, mounted the stairs on his high yellow heels, and knocked on Lenore's door.

Lenore had been burning her used parchment and trash on the hearth, preparatory to leaving. Now she was bent over, impatiently stirring the fire with a poker to make it burn faster. "Come in," she called over her shoulder, thinking it was Mistress Watts.

"Lenore, what is this foolishness I hear about your packing?" Gilbert came in and closed the door behind him, a foppish and elegant figure in honey-colored satins.

At the sound of that voice, Lenore straightened up, the red-hot poker still in her hand. She turned a malevolent face toward Gilbert, unaware that she looked very wild and beautiful as she stood there with her face flushed by the June heat and the roaring flames. "I am leaving," she said in a cold voice. "Kindly get out." Since he did not move to go, she walked toward him and seized the door handle as if to usher him through it.

"Lenore, Lenore." Gilbert's voice was indulgent. He moved toward the door and took her shoulder in a light grip. She flinched and jerked away. "Ye could move in with me. I'd accept the babe—"

Lenore seemed to grow taller. Her voice quivered with fury.

"At least I am spared that," she said grimly. "Now that Geoffrey is gone, I've no longer need to protect him from you! Let me not see your face again!"

"Lenore, you don't mean that." The caramel curls bent forward as he seized her shoulder again, insistently. "Think how it was with us," he urged. "Remember! I'd treat ye better than Geoffrey. Ah, Lenore, ye must re-

273

member the night ye spent in my arms—the joys we shared!"

In a wave of revulsion Lenore twisted away from him and drew back the poker. A moment later its red-hot tip had snaked through the air and landed with force on Gilbert's cheek. With a howl he fell back against the door-jamb, eyes wild as he regarded her, clutching his face with his hands.

"I have *longed* to do that!" she choked. "Get you gone, or I'll mark your other cheek as well!"

Gilbert turned and lunged through the open door. "I'll see ye hanged for this!" he cried, almost sobbing with rage and pain. "Think not ye can mark me and go scot-free! I'll tell the authorities who you are!"

"Tell them!" screamed Lenore, following him to the stair landing, poker raised threateningly. "Tell them who marked you! *Tell them why!*" Her angry voice followed him as he plunged down the stairs and into the alley, blundering around the corner into Magpie Lane.

When he had gone, she flung the poker away from her in revulsion. Pale and shaken, she swept up her baby in her arms and ran down the stairs, picking up the linen square of food the cook had left draped over the newel post as she went. There was no time to lose; she must take Lorena and make her run for it. Before Gilbert could make good his threat, before the authorities came.

"Tell Michael when he comes that I've ridden on ahead," she called to the open-mouthed Mistress Watts, who had witnessed Gilbert's headlong descent down the stairs with Lenore at the top brandishing the poker. "Tell him to ride hard and catch up with me—if he doesn't, I'll wait for him at the first crossroads. I'll remember to send you the money. Thank you for everything—and goodbye."

Running away with Michael! Mistress Watts was caught speechless. She stood and watched the beauty who'd been the toast of Oxford hurry to the stables and come back riding Snowfire. At that point she recollected herself and ran forward. "Mistress Daunt, Mistress Daunt!"

Lenore paused impatiently as Mistress Watts hurried

274

up and clutched her skirt. "I did not like to tell you before when you were so upset, but now that you're going, I'll not have another chance. I ran across Mistress Rue and she said she thought you'd been hurt somehow in your fall down the stairs and that ye were not like to have any more children."

"My fall? Or perhaps 'twas Mistress Rue's bungling," said Lenore bitterly. "Tying a rope around me while I was in labor!"

Mistress Watts looked shocked. "A good midwife she is," she protested, bridling. "The best in Oxford!"

Lenore gave her a sardonic look. "Mistress Watts, if you marry your suitor across the street and decide to present him with a child, I suggest you lock Mistress Rue out of your house—you'll do much better!"

"Well! Well!" Mistress Watts hardly knew what to say.

Lenore's face softened. "You've been very good to me, Mistress Watts, lending me your eagle-stones, and letting us make so much noise you might have landed in the stocks!" She leaned down and planted a quick kiss of gratitude on Mistress Watts's cheek, and the older woman beamed with pleasure and sniffled.

"Do you take care now, Mistress Daunt," she admonished Lenore.

Lenore took a deep breath. "Not Mistress Daunt— Lenore Frankford!" Her voice rang.

Mistress Watts looked nonplussed at this public declaration, delivered in the street. "Fine gentlemen do let us down," she said weakly.

"Don't they?" agreed Lenore in a hard voice. "Goodbye, Mistress Watts! Tell all my friends goodbye for me." She started to ride away, but Mistress Watts still clung insistently to her skirt.

"Suppose—suppose Mister Daunt comes back, after all?" she faltered.

"From France?" Lenore gave a short, scornful laugh. "Not likely! But if he does, tell him to go to the devil!"

She brushed off Mistress Watts's restraining hand, wheeled her horse and galloped away down the street, for tears were springing to her eyes and she did not want

Mistress Watts to see them—she did not want anyone to see them.

From the corner, Lenore turned and waved a hand at Mistress Watts, who still stood in the street bemused. For a moment her gaze lingered on the plain Tudor exterior of the lodgings that had meant so much to her. She was saying goodbye to her first home of her own where so much, both good and bad, had happened to her . . . the place where her little Lorena had been born.

Squaring her slender shoulders, she turned down Magpie Lane, keeping her gaze straight ahead. It was all behind her now: Oxford . . . all of it. She had a new life to make, and make it she must—not for herself, but for that small pink bundle sleeping in her arms. She must make a life for little golden Lorena.

She was galloping past Michael's lodgings—which lay directly on her way out of the city heading north—when a shout hailed her, and she turned to see Michael himself leaning out of an upstairs window. "Lenore, where are you going?" he cried. "Lenore!"

Reluctantly she reined in. "Catch up with me!" she called. "I must go!"

"I'm coming!" he cried desperately. "Wait!" He turned from the window and collided with Barney Claypoole, who had the rooms upstairs and who had come down to help him pack.

"What, won't she wait for you?" Barney's brown eyes were laughing at him.

Michael regarded Barney steadily from a cherubic face. Barney was always laughing at him. And now Barney had seen Lenore about to race by and would view his mad dash to catch up as ridiculous. He grasped his packed saddlebags and swung two more big bags over his shoulder. The weight made him gasp. "Ye'll send my boxes after me, Barney?"

"Aye," promised Barney. "But your boxes are like to catch up with you, so slow must ye go—a cart will catch ye, Michael, ye're so heavy-laden. I pity the horse!"

Weighted down, Michael dropped one of the big bags. "That one can come later," he groaned. "I told ye I'd

276

no time to procure a packhorse, my nag will have to carry these as best he can. Goodbye, Barney. 'Tis been fine sharing lodgings with ye, and I hope ye'll visit me in Coventry."

Barney wrung his hand, but his expression was still mirthful. "Think ye the lady will wait?" he jibed. "Mayhap ye'd best look to see if she's vanished!"

Michael never meant to return to Oxford, and Barney's home was almost at Land's End—'twas very doubtful their paths would ever cross again. How he'd longed to wipe that amused, lofty look off Barney's face! And now at last he had the chance to do it—with one bold lie. He took a deep breath. "'Tis only because ye're my friend that I tell ye this, Barney," he confided, throwing out his chest. "But Mistress Lenore is only displaying her impatience." He paused impressively. "We are running away together."

"What!" For once Barney was startled out of his supercilious attitude, Michael noted with relish. "Wait till Geoffrey hears of it! He'll crush you like a maggot!"

Geoffrey! Always Geoffrey coming between him and his precious Lenore! Michael felt jealousy pricking at him as it had so often in the past when he'd guided Lenore's quill pen across the parchment, feeling her barely concealed impatience for Geoffrey to be home. "Geoffrey can hear and be damned to him—in France or wherever he's gone!" cried Michael, coloring up. "Because by the time he hears of it, Lenore and I will be wed!"

"Ye're taking her home to your family?" demanded his friend incredulously. "A woman with another man's bastard clutched to her bosom?"

"If my family won't accept her, I'll take her beyond their reach!" Michael declared fervently. He staggered to the door with his bags.

"Here, let me help you with that!" cried Barney. "Where will you go?"

"That I must keep a secret," gasped Michael, spurning aid and bumping his way through the door.

Barney followed him downstairs with a respectful look. You could never tell what stuff a man was made of! Who'd have thought pink-cheeked Michael, who had mooned around Lenore like a lovesick calf until he was the laughingstock of Oxford, would have the courage to run away with her? What a story he'd have to tell at the tavern tonight! Fascinated, and hoping for more revelations, Barney pursued him out the front door. "Faith, I envy you, Michael!" he cried, overcome by admiration of this unsuspected boldness in his previously insipid lodging-mate. "Mistress Lenore's a rare beauty!"

"Aye, that she is!" agreed Michael, now adjusting his saddlebags with the help of a stable boy. "Wait, wait, Lenore!" he called despairingly, for she was already cantering up the street. Panting, he got himself aboard the horse, cursing as one more of his bags fell off. "Send it along with the boxes!" he bellowed. He tossed a coin to the grinning stable boy, who caught it dexterously, and careened off over the cobbles after Lenore.

Lenore heard his wail and turned her head. Seeing him in the saddle at last, she slackened her pace until his overburdened mount could catch up.

"Why are ye in such a hurry?" he gasped.

"Because I attacked Gilbert with a poker and burned his face for him—and he's threatened to call the authorities and prevent my leaving!" she told him tersely.

"Burned his face with a poker?" Michael was amazed. "Aye, Gil would take that amiss! Whatever possessed ye to do such a thing?"

Lenore had no intention of telling Michael that Gilbert had raped her. "He tried to force his attentions on me. 'Twas the only way I could think of to beat him off, for he is stronger than I am."

"Oh." Michael gave her a round-eyed look of great respect. He had half convinced himself as he caught up with her that they really were eloping, and now he had new proof of what a fiery woman she was. "Then we'd best hurry along," he said inadequately.

"Indeed we had," agreed Lenore, "if ye think that poor beast can hurry, weighted down like that!"

Michael looked unhappy, and she sighed and slowed her pace.

But as they walked their horses along the rutted road that led along the River Cherwell north to Banbury, she stopped and looked back for a last glimpse of Oxford. Like Lot's wife, she could not resist looking back at what she had lost. Under scudding clouds the river valley seemed dismal, gray—but suddenly a fleeting shaft of sunlight illuminated the honey-colored spires, and she caught her breath.

A fairylike place it seemed from here—beautiful, insubstantial, and unreal. Her expression hardened. As unreal and as insubstantial as Geoffrey's love for her had been! With a defiant toss of her head, she turned her face resolutely toward the north. Let all the gentlemen of England sail for France if they chose—*she'd* make her way at the fairs!

She touched Snowfire with her knee. Fit and rested and eager to run, he leaped ahead—and behind her Michael groaned. "Lenore," he cried, "my horse can't keep up with the pace you set!"

Vexed, Lenore slowed her pace to one that Michael's mount could match. Slowly they wended their way beneath the tall old trees that lined the lovely riverbank. Lorena was clasped lightly, firmly in her arm, and sometimes she crooned to her, or rocked her a little, or dropped a quick kiss upon the baby forehead or tiny reaching fingers. She looked soft at those moments.

But when she lifted her head and surveyed the road ahead, her expression changed. There was a hard new light in her violet eyes as she headed north on an eager, prancing Snowfire—a light that boded ill for any man who dared to love her.

CHAPTER 18

At the alehouse at Headington Quarry, the proprietor stooped over a tall man who lay in a corner, half on a bench, half off. He stirred the recumbent figure with his foot. "Time to go, sir," he said cheerily. And then when that prone figure didn't move, more loudly, "Time to go, ye beggar!" He had begun to suspect that the elegant gentleman with the toffee-colored hair who had given him money to keep this long, lean fellow drunk would never be back. Certainly there was no profit in continuing to waste good ale on a man who was too drunk to know what was going on. Best get rid of him, in case the authorities came snooping around, as they sometimes did.

Encouraged by the toe of a boot, Geoffrey came slowly back to life and bestirred himself from his drunken condition. He opened one bloodshot eye and saw the corner of a battered table near his head, and beyond that and above a low-slung ceiling. As he struggled to rise, a pain shot through his head like a hammer blow, and he groaned and sank back, resting one palm upon the floor to ease his descent upon the bench. Something hard and round bit into his palm and his fingers closed around it automatically. A coin, perhaps, dropped from his pocket? No, too sharp. Almost as a reflex, he stuck it in his pocket. Any motion hurt. With a groan he clasped his head, which seemed to have a steel band around it biting into his brain—but his questing fingers could feel nothing but his own flesh. Where was he? What day was this? Gradually he collected his wits, assessed the fact that he had a full complement of arms and legs, and sat up.

"How long have I been here?" he mumbled.

"Well nigh on a week," said his host grimly. "And I'd be glad to be shut of ye, as the sayin' goes."

A week! Geoffrey shook his head to clear it, and winced. His throat was dry, his condition filthy, and his head ached abominably. "What do I owe ye?" he asked, struggling up.

"Naught," said the tavernkeeper laconically (he had already gone through Geoffrey's pockets and removed all the coins). "A friend paid for ye."

Geoffrey looked surprised, but he shrugged and left the alehouse. The strong breeze, carrying with it a tang of salt, rippled his thick, dark hair. It was good to be out of that dark, foul-smelling place. He stood a moment stretching in the bright June sunlight, breathing in deep draughts of that bracing air, then reached into his pocket. He'd been very giddy in there, but was it possible that he had actually come out of the place with a coin?

He studied it in the sunlight as it lay in his palm. Not a coin, but a button—handsomely enameled and of a very distinctive design: a stag on a gold ground. One of Gilbert's. But . . . how had it come there? He had no memory of seeing Gilbert at the alehouse—though to be truthful, he had precious little memory of anything there. Still it was not such a place as his foppish cousin would visit. So how had it got there, lying so near his hand?

Vaguely disturbed by the discovery, he found his horse in the stable behind the alehouse (the proprietor had been afraid to steal his horse) and mounted. He forgot the button as more disturbing thoughts plagued him. The child . . . the child was not his. His face grew bleak as the memory of that bitter disappointment assailed him. In his rage he had blasted out at Lenore—he winced at the things he had said—and yet . . . now he asked himself, honestly could she have known? He had taken her that first night by force, in full knowledge that she was hand-fasted. How could he blame her?

By heaven, he was lucky that she had come to love him! He would go back, he would admit he was wrong, he would beg her forgiveness, he would make amends. Aye, he would even take the child and dandle it on his knee. For it was hers . . . as she was his. By heaven, he would protect them both!

And he had been gone a week since he had flung out! What must she think, hearing that he was drunk in an alehouse all this time?

His brow creased with worry, he rode rapidly back to his lodgings off Magpie Lane to right his grevious wrongs with the woman he truly loved.

He found those lodgings empty of Lenore's things, though his own were still in evidence, piled neatly on a table. She and the baby were gone. He whirled at a sound at the door.

It was Mistress Watts, her wig askew, her furbelows looking shabbier than ever. As Geoffrey's tall figure advanced on her, she fell back, looking scared.

"Where's Mistress Daunt?" he demanded.

"She's fled. Yesterday." And at his thunderous expression, "The authorities were here," she bleated. "For what she did to Master Gilbert's face."

"To Master Gilbert's face?" Brought up short by that odd remark, Geoffrey waited for illumination.

"Aye. Pinked him with a hot poker, she did. He ran down these stairs bawlin' and hollerin' what he'd do to her. He shouted he'd tell the authorities who she was! But all they told *me* was that she was wanted for assault."

Geoffrey's face hardened. He could well imagine what provocation would cause Lenore to do such a thing. And

282

she just out of childbed! There was a sword and baldric lying on the table, and now he buckled the strap of the baldric over his right shoulder so that his sword hung down under his left arm—convenient to his strong right hand.

Mistress Watts quaked as he swept by her. "A veritable demon he looked!" she told Gwynneth later, her hand on her palpitating heart. "I was afraid to tell him she'd left with Master Michael—I was afraid he'd cut my head off! And the way he slammed the door—'twas like to come off its hinges!"

Directly to Gilbert's quarters Geoffrey strode. Taking the stairs at three bounds, he kicked open the door with a booted foot and leaped inside. He seized the surprised Gilbert by the lace at his throat, twisting it cruelly.

When Geoffrey barged into the room, Gilbert had been sitting at his ease amid his usual clutter, leaning back in a chair propped against the wall. His long legs were stretched out indolently, booted feet resting on the edge of the table as he drank a glass of malmsey and brooded about the deviltry of a woman who would mark a man's face. He did not even have time to rearrange his legs before Geoffrey seized him. A screech rose in his throat, but that screech ended in a gurgle as he felt the chair knocked out from under him and the lace at his throat—it was strong and new and expensive—become a gallows knot cutting off his breathing.

A dark face that might have been the devil's own thrust itself juttingly into his, and he found himself gazing with terror into a pair of wild, bloodshot eyes. The voice that rang in his ears might have risen from the depths of hell. "Tell me what ye've done to Lenore!"

Choking, clutching at his throat, Gilbert, made an effort to rise and was forced to his knees. "Ye're mad," he gasped hoarsely, as the grip on his throat lightened enough for him to speak. "I've done nothing to her!"

He made an effort to twist free and was suddenly released. Geoffrey flung Gilbert from him so hard he bounced off the wall. As he staggered forward, Gilbert saw Geoffrey reach down into a pile of articles that had been carelessly swept off the table. From the clutter he found one of the collection of swords of which Gilbert was so fond. "Defend yourself," he said crisply, flinging it to Gilbert and almost simultaneously snaking out his naked blade and advancing upon his cowering cousin.

Gilbert picked up the sword in haste and leaped aside in a frantic attempt to ward off this new menace. He was no match for Geoffrey's sword arm, and he knew it. "She's fled you!" he cried in a voice that cracked. "Faith, none could blame her—look at you, already thirsting for my blood!"

"Fled where?" demanded Geoffrey inexorably, bringing his blade down with such mighty force that Gilbert's sword, which he had swiftly raised in an attempt to parry the blow, was immediately torn from his grasp and went clattering across the floor. For a moment Gilbert stood riveted and livid—and Geoffrey, his face entirely satanic, gave him a mocking smile and presented the point of his blade to his cousin's throat. Gilbert fell back and came up against the wall—that deadly point followed him.

"Before I dispose of you . . . speak!" growled Geoffrey.

Faint with terror, Gilbert looked into the devil lights that flashed at him like summer lightning out of Geoffrey's gray eyes. "She has fled with Michael!" he cried.

"With Michael?" Geoffrey's incredulous look turned into a contemptuous laugh. He pressed the point in a little deeper so that it drew a drop of blood.

Gilbert's face grew a shade whiter, and he gasped. "'Tis true!" he yelped. "I had it straight from Barney Claypoole, who has rooms above him. She came over to Michael's lodgings yesterday, Michael was all packed, and they rode away together." He felt the point leave his skin and relaxed a little. "Had you eyes to see," he added in an injured tone, stroking his bruised throat and wiping away the blood, "ye'd have readily seen Michael's in love with her. Why else spend so much time teaching Lenore to better her penmanship? Why else work with her over all those dull books?"

"Why indeed? echoed Geoffrey thoughtfully. "And which way did they go?"

"Michael told Barney he was for Coventry," said Gilbert sulkily. "I gather he's taking Lenore home with him."

Geoffrey looked startled. "I see you are wounded," he said grimly, sheathing his sword. He was staring at the court plaster on Gilbert's cheek.

"'Tis a boil," said Gilbert instantly. "I had to have it lanced. The surgeon has bound it up."

Geoffrey's gaze was ironic. "I know how it came to be lanced," he said in a low deadly tone. "I would like to hear your version."

Gilbert was sweating profusely now and looking from side to side for some means of escape. "Have done, Geoffrey!" he cried in desperation. "I but offered Lenore shelter for herself and the child when she told me you'd left her and gone to France! She took offense and gave me this!" Sulkily he indicated his cheek.

Geoffrey turned red-rimmed eyes of hell on his cousin Gilbert. Before that look Gilbert flinched. He tried to retreat and once again found himself backed against the wall.

"You of all people knew I had not gone to France," said Geoffrey in a steely voice. "Yet you did not tell her? You let her go away believing that?"

"I did not know!" gasped Gilbert. "I thought you were gone! She told me you were!"

With his left hand Geoffrey drew out the unusual enameled button with the distinctive stag design. "Have you lost a button from your coat?" he demanded.

"No—yes!" Paralyzed with fright, Gilbert looked from the button to that glowering face. "What does that signify? Where did you get it?"

"On the floor of an alehouse at Headington Quarry!" roared Geoffrey, flinging the button into Gilbert's face with force. "'Tis plain to me, cousin, that you had me drugged in some way—"

"I did not! Geoffrey, I swear—"

"So that ye could make a try for Lenore, believing she'd turn to you in my absence!"

"I did not! Michael has bilked us both, Geoffrey. He . . ." Gilbert was babbling now, his words almost incoherent, and they faded into gasping silence. He seemed to shrink before the towering menace above him.

Geoffrey smiled down at his crouching cousin, a terrible smile. "What's clear to me is that ye did something to Lenore bad enough that she struck you with a poker. Ye need fresh air, Gilbert—ye look to be choking!"

He pounced on Gilbert, seized him by the shoulders in a grip of iron. Words were bubbling out of Gilbert now. "Remember, Geoffrey—we are cousins!" he gibbered.

Cousins! In violent revulsion, Geoffrey hoisted him into the air and with all his force hurled him through the window, shattering the wood and leaded panes. Gilbert shrieked as his bones broke the panes and the casement, and there was a long-drawn-out howl as he catapulted through the air to the alley below.

Hoping sincerely he had broken Gilbert's neck, Geoffrey strode out of the place. He did not bother to look out the broken window into the alley where he had pitched Gilbert, and from which now rose a number of high-pitched screams and the sound of running feet. His mind was seething. It was ridiculous to think that Lenore had eloped with Michael. She would not! Still . . . he'd best ask Mistress Watts about it. One could put no credence in anything a liar like Gilbert said.

With fear in his heart that he had lost his woman —nay more than that she was, his life—he made his way back to his lodgings at an even faster gait.

"It must be true," Mistress Watts sighed, when Geoffrey confronted her with Gilbert's allegations. "For Mistress Daunt did leave word with me that Master Michael was to catch up with her, that if he did not, she'd wait for him at the first crossroads." She gave him an accusing look. "She believed you gone to France."

Geoffrey winced. Indeed it must have seemed like it when he'd been gone almost a week! "Should she come back, Mistress Watts, tell her I have gone seeking her." He paused, studying the landlady keenly, for he sensed she was holding something back. "Have you any knowledge of where she may have gone, Mistress Watts?"

"Ye'll not . . . harm her?" Mistress Watts asked in an altered voice.

"Nay," Geoffrey sighed. "I wish only to make amends."

"She did ask cook to provision her to Banbury—and told me she would send me the lodging-money from the fair there, or from some other fair."

Geoffrey frowned, and then his face cleared. Snowfire! Of course!

"But after Master Michael came over, she may have changed her mind." She bit her lip. "And when she left, I asked her what to tell you if you came back—and she said you could go to the devil."

So she had consigned him to the devil, had she? Geoffrey's expression was wry.

"Ye'll not—ye'll not harm her because I told ye that?"

He shook his head. "I deserved it. And as to the lodging money, I'll see ye receive it, Mistress Watts."

She watched him mount up, her faith in fine gentlemen somewhat restored.

But it was a grim face Geoffrey turned toward the north as he rode out of Oxford. He liked not the idea that Lenore might have changed her mind after speaking with Michael. She was proud, and if his apparent desertion of her had caused her to fall into Michael's arms, she well might turn him away when he found her.

That he would find her had no doubt. Gilbert had said Michael was bound for Coventry, and Mistress Watts had said Lenore planned to take in the Banbury fair. In either case, they'd have taken the Banbury road that led north along the Cherwell. They were only a day ahead of him, and Michael was no kind of rider. If he moved swiftly, he might even catch up with them, lying over at an inn on the way.

North along the Cherwell's beautiful riverbank he rode, making inquiries at all the inns along the way. Had they seen a young fellow garbed in red accompanied by a beautiful woman riding a white horse and carrying a small baby? A pair worthy of remark surely, yet none had seen them.

He passed tall haycarts pulled by sleepy-eyed lumbering oxen, and trudging farmers carrying pitchforks, moving sturdily along the roadside, big muscles rippling. He passed apple-cheeked country girls who looked at him with bright interest, and an occasional painted coach drawn by four or six horses. At one point, he rode down a green tunnel of overhanging branches where the trees pressed in upon the road. And midway down that tunnel he almost had to jump his horse over a deep depression some turned-over wagon must have dug in the mired earth. He looked at it grimly. A bad overturn, that. Someone could have been hurt, and it must have blocked the road in a place as narrow as this. He was distracted by a flock of sheep that poured like foaming water from a sheep track on the left and overflowed the road in all directions. They were being driven in from the Cotswolds and their baaing filled the leafy countryside with sound. They flowed around him like white-capped rapids, their woolly sides brushing his horse's legs, and the shepherd smiled at him for sitting his mount so still and letting the flock stream by. In desperation, Geoffrey even asked the shepherd if he'd seen a beautiful woman on a white horse, but he got a regretful shake of the head. Plainly the young shepherd would have liked a glimpse of the woman Geoffrey described in terse, vivid terms.

It was easy for Geoffrey to paint Lenore's picture in words. And his gray eyes betrayed his longing. He parted company with the shepherd, brooding about her. By heaven, how she had fitted into his arms! With a twisting pain in his heart, he remembered the silken feel of her slender body, her soft murmurings as he held her close, the agonizing sweetness as he took her. For a moment the summer air was filled with the fragrance of her hair, the sunlight blazing on a gilded coach ahead no brighter than its sheen.

But although he combed the road as thoroughly as he could and asked all likely travelers, though he stopped to inquire at inns and taverns and searched for her at Banbury where the fair was being held, no trace did he find of

Lenore. She seemed to have vanished from the face of the earth.

Haggard now—and with fear eating at him—he rode on to Coventry, dismounting at Michael's ancestral home, Maltby Manor, just south of the town. He found it to be a crumbling stone manor house, pleasantly situated on a little knoll amid a grove of beeches. The rotting outbuildings and air of general decay—no less than the ancient farthingale in which Michael's mother, the mistress of Maltby, was attired—attested to the fact that all their substance had been spent on their adored only son, Michael. On learning that he was a friend of Michael's, they ushered him in as if he were a prince and promptly supplied him with partridge and wine while the whole family gathered round to question him eagerly. Michael was not expected until next week—what, had he taken the road already?

Geoffrey assured them Michael had left Oxford.

"But we have not heard from him!" Michael's mother interrupted anxiously. "Are you sure he left Oxford before you and came up the Banbury road?"

"I am not sure he came by the Banbury road," said Geoffrey thoughtfully. "But that he left Oxford the day before me—of that I am sure, and I set no great pace, for all the way I stopped and inquired if any had seen him."

"And why?" This penetratingly from Michael's grandmother, a sharp old lady who sat bolt upright wearing stiff brocades and a yellowed ruff—obviously one she had worn as a girl, from its present state of dilapidation. "Why do you seek Michael in such haste, young man?"

They seemed so impoverished that Geoffrey was almost ashamed to eat the food they urged on him. " 'Tis not Michael I seek." He chose his words carefully. "But the lady Lenore who travels with him."

Michael's mother blanched. "T-travels with him?" she asked faintly.

"Aye," he said gravely. "She is my wife. She was under the mistaken impression that I had left her, and I think Michael gives her his protection on the way to . . . some safe place."

"And where would that be?" demanded the grandmother testily.

Geoffrey gave her a sad look. "If I knew, I would not be here."

"Oh," said Geoffrey's mother. "Oh, I see. But surely word will reach her through friends that you have not deserted her and—oh, I see, you believe it will not?"

Geoffrey inclined his head in assent.

"Perhaps he has taken another road this time," suggested Michael's aunt placidly, her cherubic face reminding Geoffrey sharply of young Michael.

Michael's worried mother threw her sister an impatient look. "It is not like him not to let us know," she said sharply. "And he should be here by now, if he left Oxford when this gentleman says he did."

"You see, Michael has always come straight home to us from Oxford—no dallying along the way," explained the wispy gentleman who was Michael's father, suddenly entering the conversation. He studied Geoffrey's worried face. "If Michael brings this lady here, we will promptly apprise her that you have been here seeking her," he said earnestly. "Where can we reach you?"

Geoffrey had been thinking about that, although he now had little hope that Michael would return to Maltby Manor anytime soon. Michael had always had with him a little money, provided by this poverty-stricken crew. It would be enough to provide a brief wedding trip, Geoffrey realized bitterly, should Michael's intentions be honorable. The thought gnawed at his insides. "Tell her I'll to Oxford," he told Michael's father. "And if she finds me not there, she can reach me through Ned—she will know where to find him. I will be in touch with Ned."

He thanked them for their hospitality, rose and escaped the bare, run-down surroundings that had spawned a cheerful young popinjay who—he drew his gauntlets on his hands with unnecessary force—had made off with his mistress.

He was about to ride away when he saw Michael's mother hurrying after him, impeded by her awkward farthingale. He halted and waited for her to catch up.

"You are not—you are not saying that Michael is—is enamored of this wife of yours?" she blurted, when she could catch her breath.

Geoffrey gave her a wintry look. "Such is Mistress Lenore's beauty that all men are enamored of her," he said savagely. "Michael no more than others, perhaps."

"But—but—"

"I believe him to be protecting her," he said shortly. "Perhaps from me."

He cantered rapidly away, leaving her staring after him, her face white and drawn.

Geoffrey's mind was working furiously as he rode away. Where could they have gone? Twainmere he discounted as impractical—Lenore would be afraid to return there with her lover. It was doubtful any of Michael's relatives would take him in. They might have gone to London, pretending to ride away as a feint, but actually slipping into a boat and floating down the Thames. If so, someone in Oxford might have seen them leave—Lenore with her bright hair and Michael in his red cloak would have made a memorable pair.

It occurred to him suddenly that Mistress Watts might know more than she had told him, that Gwynneth the serving-girl, with whom Lenore had been on friendly terms, might have heard her say something about her destination before she left—and he cursed his stupidity that he had not wrung them dry of information before he galloped off to the north. And that fellow who lodged upstairs from Michael, Barney—he'd seen them ride off together, according to Gilbert. Perhaps he'd have a clue as to where they might have gone.

Fast he rode back to Oxford. On his way back from Banbury he passed a crossroads marker. Above it some vultures were circling. A dead sheep, he thought, or perhaps a fox. He was impatient to get to Oxford and put those dark, circling wings from his mind.

Had he stopped to investigate, it would have changed the course of his life.

291

As it was, he went on to Oxford, riding in openly, impatient for news. He headed directly for Barney's lodgings.

But he had reckoned without Gilbert.

CHAPTER 19

When Lenore had branded Gilbert, he had rushed to a surgeon to have his face attended to. It would leave a scar, he was told calmly.

A scar on his handsome countenance! Gilbert had leaped up and staggered from the surgeon's house and gone running to the authorities intending to denounce her. But on the way a crafty thought had entered his head. He wanted to punish Lenore himself, and perhaps there was a way. . . .

Seething with rage and pain, he had charged her with assault upon his person. Once imprisoned, he told himself with demonic glee, she'd do anything to gain her release. His price for dropping the charge would be that she move in with him—and he'd keep her docile by threatening to denounce her as the Angel of Worcester. His caramel eyes glittered with anticipation. He'd stripe that pretty back of hers! Mayhap he'd even tie her up and brand . . . the sole of her foot, perhaps? For he'd no wish to destroy the beauty he intended to enjoy. Half his pleasure would be making her beg!

With a ferocious smile on his injured face, Gilbert accompanied the authorities to Lenore's lodgings. There a pale and shaken Mistress Watts stuttered that Mistress Daunt had ridden off, she knew not where.

Gilbert had given her a black look. He did not believe that—a woman with a small babe and no money! Lenore was in hiding. Well, he would find her himself!

On his way back to his lodgings, he ran into Barney. Barney, intrigued by the court plaster that adorned Gilbert's face as much as by the angry scowl that brought those caramel brows together, hailed him.

"Ye look like ye've been in a duel," he observed.

"An accident," said Gilbert shortly. It would hurt his pride to have Barney know he'd been branded by a woman. "What news?" he asked, to change the subject.

Barney laughed. He was full of news today. "Michael has run off with Mistress Lenore."

Rage broke over Gilbert like an onrushing wave. She had escaped him! Almost he rushed back to the authorities he had so recently left and denounced Lenore as the Angel of Worcester. But as the mist cleared from his eyes, he pulled himself together. He muttered something incoherent, flung away from Barney, and went back to his lodgings with murder in his heart.

There he quickly downed a brandy and sat down to plan. Perhaps she had not escaped him after all, this woman who had marked his face forever.

He touched the court plaster and winced. Barney had assumed he'd been pinked in a duel. He poured himself another brandy, and his eyes narrowed. He bethought him that he could indeed brag to strangers that it was an old dueling scar—even, in the right circumstances, that he had been wounded at Worcester; none would know the difference, and it would enhance his reputation. His mother had contemptuously called him "too pretty" more than once—this scar would give his narrow face character. On thinking it over, he could almost be glad it had happened because he could turn it to good account.

Lenore, of course, must not go unpunished. He thought about that, too, as the brandy burned his throat, and his lazy countenance was evil. He'd a mind to get her back and . . . there was a way.

Michael was a weak reed, he reasoned. He knew something of Michael's circumstances, enough to know that Michael always wore red because by having clothes of the same color, he could distract attention from a frayed cuff, a worn sleeve, by wearing some other garment that was dazzlingly *new*. Although Michael had pocket money, Gilbert was fairly certain the lad had no source of income other than his doting family.

Lenore was obviously without resources; if she'd had a place to go, she'd have taken Geoffrey there and had her baby. So she must go where Michael took her.

Even should Michael marry Lenore—and Gilbert thought him mad enough to do that—it would be beyond belief that Michael's mother would take in as a daughter-in-law, this cast-off doxie dragging another man's bastard.

So, Gilbert reasoned, times would become hard for Michael, his money would be quickly exhausted, he would abandon Lenore and scuttle back to the safety of his home near Coventry.

And at that point, Gilbert thought with a cruel smile, Lenore would be ripe for the taking.

He sharpened a quill, dipped it in the inkwell, and dashed off a letter to Michael at Maltby Manor, Warwickshire, in which he said:

"I know that you have run off with Geoffrey's doxie, Lenore, and knowing her fickle ways, must believe that you have now tired of her and returned home. Having lain with her myself—" he paused with the quill in the air; he wanted to say "on numerous occasions," but young Michael might not believe that; he sighed and began to write again—"I would account it a favor if you would apprise me of her whereabouts—and would send you my new 'jackanapes' coat which you so admired as a token of regard, upon receipt of such information.

Your obedient servant,
Gilbert Marnock."

He posted the letter and sat back with satisfaction to await developments.

Geoffrey's attack had come as a complete surprise. He had been so sure the doings at the alehouse at Headington Quarry would never be traced to him. And for Geoffrey to know that Lenore had branded him! In the agony of his burn and the horror that his handsome face might be marred for life, he had not even noticed Mistress Watts, her eyes popping, gaping at him from the downstairs hallway as he rushed out. Never had he thought that *she* might tattle to Geoffrey!

But Gilbert, for all that he had been found out, had in the end been born under a lucky star, and when Geoffrey threw him through the window of his lodgings, his luck had held. He had landed, not in the alley below, but in a tall-sided haycart parked beneath his window. The farmer who owned the cart had gone inside to collect for his hay in advance, for Geoffrey's landlord was careless with his hay payments for the stable he kept behind the house.

It was in this hay that Gilbert had landed—undoubtedly saving his life, for he arrived head first.

Hearing the crash of broken wood and glass and Gilbert's high-pitched shriek, the farmer, the landlord, and the cook all came running out to see in amazement Gilbert's flailing boots protruding from the mound of hay and weird inhuman noises issuing from its soft depths.

Sure he was dead and groaning loudly, Gilbert was pulled out. They brushed the hay off his handsome clothes —he struck one of them in a petulant rage as this was done—and stood him on his wobbly legs. There was nothing broken, but he presented a bloody sight, bruised and cut as he was from breaking through the stout casements with his body. That they were all minor wounds save one—a gouge in his other cheek where he had grazed a hidden pitchfork in the depths of the hay— attested to his luck.

"Geoffrey will pay for this!" he sobbed, putting shaking fingers to this new marring of his handsome face. "Geoffrey will pay!"

The landlord, secretly pleased at Gilbert's mishap, for he was an unruly tenant and slow to pay, was solicitous in helping Gilbert up to bed. There as the afternoon progressed his friends crowded around, clucking their tongues, for it was a self-serving tale Gilbert told them. Lenore had been bent on fleeing Oxford with Michael, he said—adding spitefully his own invention: Lenore's scheme was not to elope with Michael, as the lad believed, but to bilk him of what money he had, to steal his purse as he slept at the first inn they put up in, and make her way to London, where a woman of her endowments would have greater scope—she had bragged to him of this.

Amazed faces greeted this revelation, for they had all liked Lenore and loath to believe evil of her.

"'Tis true!" cried Gilbert, rising up in a passion at sight of those unbelieving faces. "When I remonstrated with her and tried to stop her—as indeed I should have done, being Geoffrey's cousin and Michael's friend—she flew into a rage and burned me with a hot poker and took off on the run with poor Michael!" He sank back upon his pillow and laid a listless hand upon his forehead. "When Geoffrey came back, he would not listen—he was sure I must have done her some injury that she had burned me! He threw me out the window and near killed me!"

His friends eyed each other thoughtfully. Gilbert did indeed seem to have reason for complaint—and the burn and cuts and bruises were there as vivid proof of his story. Though doubts lingered, young Oxford subsided before Gilbert's accusations. Geoffrey would turn up, some muttered, and they'd hear *his* version.

Sulking—and furious that both cheeks were wounded, for the pitchfork point had been dirty and the gouge festered—Gilbert convalesced with the aid of wine and Dorothy the tavern maid, who tended him faithfully. But when Dorothy brought word excitedly that Geoffrey had returned to Oxford, she had seen him riding toward Michael's old lodgings, Gilbert leaped out of bed, flung on his clothes in haste, and rushed past her. "I'll be back," he cried. "Wait for me!"

Gilbert raced for the authorities. His eyes took on a

297

wicked gleam as he ran—and a scared gleam, too, for he feared Geoffrey might hear that he had survived the fall and come back to finish him off! He composed his features as he explained to the authorities that he had recently learned, through family letters, that Geoffrey Wyndham, who in Oxford went by the name of Daunt, had fought for the king at Worcester. He sank down as if overcome as he said that, muttering that he had thought Geoffrey merely a rogue, but now it seemed he was also a traitor—and he had leaped up from his bed of pain to apprise them that Geoffrey was back and heading for Michael's old lodgings.

So it was that Geoffrey, when he clattered down the stairs after an unsatisfactory interview with Barney, found himself surrounded by a ring of steel.

Backed into the house by weight of their numbers, he fought them—up and down the wooden stairs he fought them, his sword blade flashing through the air to parry several blades that snaked at him. Wild-eyed, Barney watched the battle from above ("I've never seen a man fight like that!" he swore later in admiration) until a bullet fired at close range creased Geoffrey's forehead and he went down like a felled ox and woke up lying on a filthy pallet in the jail.

Lying in jail, slapping at spiders and fleas, kicking at rats, he had time to consider. For time was nothing here, as men waited in stinking cells to die or be transported.

But to the lean prisoner with the haggard face and the dirty rag bound about his wounded head, who lay in a room high up in the jail where desperate prisoners were kept, the days were haunted with memories of a winsome smile, the nights made restless as he tossed on his pallet longing to hold a certain fair body in his arms again.

Reluctantly now in the prison dimness, which cast a clear, hard light on his musings, he accepted what he had refused to believe before: Michael and Lenore had not headed up the Banbury road for Coventry, Lenore's story about provisioning for the fair was but a screen to hide the truth. Lenore had believed him gone to France and had eloped with Michael. She was lost to him!

Bitterly he speculated on where they might have gone. Most likely they had traded their horses for passage downriver to London and Michael had indentured himself to pay for ship's passage—as indeed Geoffrey had planned to do. For since Michael's disappearance had showed unexpected initiative, Michael might have other unsuspected resources—he and Lenore might even now be embarking on some tall white ship bound for the American Colonies, where his irate family would never find him.

He imagined her there, standing at the rail beside Michael, beneath billowing sails, while the wind rippled her hair, bravely embarking on a new life.

And the truth, he told himself painfully, though he had flinched to face it, was that Lenore was better off with Michael. He could offer his name—a good name and an old one—and blind devotion. Eventually, since Michael was an only son, he would inherit decaying Maltby Manor. The sale of it should ensure him a good position in the Colonies, and the bright-haired girl from Twainmere would be at last what she had longed to be—a respected wife.

If only he could have given her that . . .

He stood at the small barred window—so high that only a tall man might see out—and gazed out at Oxford's ancient spires, softened to tan by the haze. Somewhere in that jumble of buildings was Magpie Lane, and off of it an alley and a tumbledown Tudor building where he had passed some of the happiest days of his life. His hard gaze softened and grew wistful as he tried to locate the house where he had dwelt with Lenore.

They told him charges were being readied against him. Not only of being a Royalist and therefore a traitor to the Commonwealth, but they were also investigating a rumor that he'd prowled the roads as a highwayman these past months. Geoffrey gave them a ribald look when they told him that. On either count, his life was forfeit; this multiplicity of charges only amused him.

He gave little thought to the way he would die. All men died sometime, and it might be he'd escape the gallows yet. Instead his mind dwelt lingeringly on Lenore, and at night he dreamed that they were on the run again, camped beneath the high tors, and in the dying glow of their campfire he looked deep into her violet eyes and she moved silently into his arms—a lustrous woman, his alone. By day there was a whole treasure chest of memories to illumine his drab cell: the fire, the passion, the oneness that had consumed them both. Ruefully his waking mind traced every little inch of her sweet body. In the silence of his cell he could almost hear her sigh, and the little breeze that reached him through the bars reminded him of her gentle, delighted quiver as he entered her. His hard body ached with longing for the tremulous response he had always felt in her, and he groaned as he recalled too vividly an incurving waist, an outcurving hip, the maddening pressure of her firm young breasts against his hard chest.

How gallantly she had ridden beside him when they were hunted! How valiantly she had thundered to the finish on the makeshift race course at Wells—and returned flushed and triumphant that she had bested big Hobbs. He was proud of her, he loved her, and—a dry sob formed in his throat—though he deserved to lose her, dear God, he missed her so.

Now he would dance out his life on a gibbet and she would never know he had not meant the ugly words he'd hurled at her in pain and disappointment. That was what hurt most—she would never know.

Gilbert, resplendent in fawn satins, came to crow over him in the jail. Gilbert's bruises had turned from purple to yellow, his cuts—save for the festered one from the pitchfork—were healing fast, but the burn Lenore had given him with the hot poker was livid even in the little light afforded by the cell's small window on a cloudy day. Geoffrey took some satisfaction in the sight of that weal.

Though the jailer would have obligingly locked Gilbert in the cell with Geoffrey for a private interview, Gilbert hastily declined that and chose instead to speak to Geoffrey through the small grating of the iron door that held the prisoner secure inside.

300

"Ye made a mistake, Geoffrey," he taunted through the grating.

"Aye," Geoffrey agreed with a sigh. "I should have pitched ye through the front window onto the cobbles instead of through the side window into the muddy alley!"

Gilbert paled, and his teeth clenched. "Ye are about to die!" he stormed. "For no court will clear ye of both charges! Either ye'll hang as a Royalist or ye'll hang as a highwayman!"

"How can ye be so sure?" mocked Geoffrey. "Neither charge is yet proved."

Gilbert took a ragged breath and fought to compose his features. "I did not come here to quarrel with ye, Geoffrey."

Geoffrey laughed. "No? Then why did you come?"

"Because we are cousins and—"

"Faith, ye should have thought of it sooner!"

Gilbert edged nearer the grating. Seen through that square in the iron door, his face was crafty. "I am willing to forget that ye tried to kill me, Geoffrey, and do ye a last good turn."

Geoffrey eyed his cousin. "A draught of poison to speed me, perhaps?"

"Nay, do not jest." Gilbert lowered his voice confidentially. "I do not believe that ye know not where Lenore is. If ye will tell me her whereabouts, Geoffrey, I promise ye faithfully that I will go to her and tell her of your trouble so that she may slip into the jail and see you before the end."

Geoffrey gave a short laugh. "So that she may die with me? Is that what ye offer? Or perchance save her life by becoming your doxy?"

Gilbert empurpled. He smote the iron door with the hilt of his sword until it rang. "Guard! Guard!" he cried in fury. "I am finished with my interview with this prisoner! Sirrah!"

Lounging against the wall, Geoffrey favored that square of grating that showed his cousin's baleful face with a genial smile. "I am sorry, Gil," he began softly, and Gilbert turned an interested look toward him, hoping his cause was not lost, after all. "Sorry that I did not mark ye so well as Lenore," Geoffrey fetched a deep sigh. " 'Tis an error I'll correct one day—if I live."

Gilbert almost ran over the turnkey in his blind wrath as he charged out of the jail.

Geoffrey heard his departure and gave thanks for one thing—at least Lenore was clear of Gilbert's wrath. That Michael had taken her beyond Gil's reach was the one ray of sunshine in the eternal night that would soon descend on him.

His next visitor was more welcome.

Geoffrey had been resting in a corner of his cell, leaning against the stone wall and contemplating the spiderwebs that hung down from the ceiling. He looked up as a key turned in the lock and Ned's familiar form—plumper than he remembered—hurried through. In a bound he was on his feet and met Ned in the center of the room, clapping him on the shoulder in delight. Behind Ned the iron door clanged shut, and the turnkey's voice reached them. "I'll be within call—let me know when ye've done."

"Ned, I thought ye were in Somerset! Faith, ye've a paunch these days! I hope your lady's well."

Ned wrung his hand. "She's very well. I came when I heard ye'd been taken, Geoffrey. And as to the paunch—marriage is good to me; I'm well fed." He grinned at Geoffrey.

"I'll not ask ye to sit down, Ned—'twould ruin your clothes. But the air is better by the window. Ye'll have heard Lenore has left me."

"Aye."

"Is there any news of her?" Geoffrey eyed him anxiously.

"Nay, I've had none. She seems to have vanished—as Lally has." Ned's voice was melancholy.

Geoffrey was startled. "Lally? I did not know."

"Aye. I'm told she left Gilbert and none know where she has gone."

A tiny hope sprang up in Geoffrey—that Lenore might have sought out Lally, they might be hiding somewhere together—and was immediately quenched. Lenore had left with Michael, and he had not turned up, either.

"I think you must face it, Geoffrey," Ned said soberly. "Lenore has left you. Ye must look to yourself."

"That would be easier were I not in jail," said Geoffrey wryly.

Ned lowered his voice. "That can be remedied. I've a plan." Even as he spoke, he was disrobing. "Keep a sharp eye out for the jailer, Geoffrey. I've so much rope tied around me I can hardly move!"

"Faith, ye're a practical man, Ned!" Geoffrey's eyes lit up as Ned handed him a file and a short dagger. He kept his eyes pressed to the grating as Ned, panting, unburdened himself of a great length of rope. "I've yet another file in my other boot," he muttered, and Geoffrey chuckled.

"Ye're a walking arsenal, Ned! I'm surprised ye did not bring black powder to blow up the jail!"

"I've a better plan," Ned told him grimly, getting back into his clothes while Geoffrey stowed the rope and files and dagger beneath his pallet. " 'Tis dangerous, but—it should work."

He outlined his plan, and Geoffrey nodded. Then he frowned. "Gilbert was here to plague me, Ned. He'll try to stop us if he hears."

"Aye—I've heard the stories he spreads about Lenore."

Geoffrey said sharply, "What stories?"

Ned told him, and Geoffrey smote his palm with a hard fist and cursed softly. "I should have broken Gil's neck *before* I tossed him through the window!"

"I heard about that." Ned was amused. He began to pack some of the straw bedding into his clothes so that he would again have a paunch.

"Ye'll get fleas, Ned."

Ned shrugged. "Be easy about Gilbert, Geoffrey. He's had a falling out with Dorothy—you remember that tavern maid who used to be his doxie? He beat her black and blue, and she's swearing vengeance to all who will listen. For a few coins she'll manage to get him drunk for us."

Geoffrey nodded alertly. Except in matters of the heart, Ned always managed well.

"Ye're a good friend, Ned." Geoffrey's voice was deep. "I'll not forget this."

"I've not forgotten how you climbed a rotting tower to get me out of Wilby Hall that night when the place caught fire and I was trapped inside with a great cupboard toppled on top of me that I could not budge. All were against your climb, which they said was impossible —including the long leap you made from the tower to my window."

It was Geoffrey's turn to shrug. " 'Twas not so big a thing, Ned."

"No? Well, I thought it was. I was lying there half crushed with clouds of black smoke billowing around me —and you came through it with your eyes bloodshot and dragged me out and let me down the building with a rope. I had already consigned myself to the devil, and when I saw your face—"

"You thought 'twas he come to collect you," chuckled Geoffrey.

Ned slapped him on the back. "Take care, Geoffrey. We'll have but the one chance."

"Aye," Geoffrey wrung his hand. "We'll make it a good one."

"Let's hope no one bumps into me," muttered Ned, already scratching as fleas bit into him. "For my paunch will have an interesting crunch! I'll leave you now, Geoffrey. Jailer! Jailer! I'm ready to take my leave of the prisoner!"

When the iron door was unlocked, Geoffrey was seen to be reclining upon his pallet, looking melancholy. The iron door clanged shut.

Ned rounded up those Oxford students whose Royalist leanings he could count on, and they assaulted the jail— not with weapons but with music and song. The townfolk muttered about their unruliness—but then they were often unruly. They made enough noise that the rasp and occasional shriek of Geoffrey's file, sawing at the iron bars, went unnoticed.

When at last enough of the tough bars were sawed partway through—so that a good kick would finish them off—Geoffrey tied his scarf to the window of his cell and it floated out bravely on the afternoon breeze.

It was the signal. That evening a raucous crowd of students, inspired by Ned, appeared in the street at the other side of the jail. They seemed very drunk and carried with them a kettledrum and an assortment of iron pots on which they dinned and thumped with iron spoons and pokers. The attention of jailers and guards was thus attracted to that side of the jail. By five minutes past nine o'clock when the Great Tom bell began its hundred and one peals that announced curfew, the din was so great that Geoffrey was able to kick out the bars—they rattled down to the cobbles completely unnoticed—affix his rope, and start his dangerous climb down the stone side of the building.

In the dim alley below, a horseman had appeared with another horse on a lead. He jogged along slowly, as if on his way home at the sound of curfew. It was Ned—painfully conscious of Geoffrey's necessarily slow descent. He watched anxiously as Geoffrey came down the rope —and winced as fifteen feet from the ground the rope broke and Geoffrey fell rolling to the alley below, to end up almost under the hooves of Ned's horse.

The horse shied nervously, and Ned leaned forward tensely. "Are ye hurt?" he whispered, alarmed.

Geoffrey was already up and seizing the bridle Ned handed him. "Naught but a bruise or two," he said grimly. "I thank ye, Ned, for all ye've done. Now get ye gone so that ye are not caught in the net if I be taken!" He took the pistol Ned gave him, stuck it in his belt, and buckled on the baldric and sword.

"Wait, ye'll need this." Ned tossed him a purse, which Geoffrey caught. "There's gold in it." He gave his friend a troubled look in the dimness. "Where do ye go, Geoffrey?"

"God knows," Geoffrey flung back over his shoulder and galloped away. Ned had done enough for him, he thought—aye, more than enough; he would not endanger

Ned further with involvement in his plans. With luck he'd get out of Oxford and head southeast. It might be safer for him in the West Country, in Somerset or Cornwall or Devon. But—he wanted no reminders of Lenore. She was better without him, of that he was convinced— aye, being with him had held her back from the life she might have had: good wife to a good man. Not the life of a fugitive, which was all, God knows, he had to give her.

There'd been a thin chance for them there for a while; he'd hurried to Oxford over mired roads to tell Lenore he'd made the arrangements for them to go to America —but he had never told her, he'd seen the child and flung out . . . he deserved what had befallen him. And by now the ship that was to have carried them across the waters would have sailed without him—which mattered not, he'd no heart now to emigrate and work long, hard years of indenture overseeing the work on another man's plantation. For Lenore he'd have done it, and gladly, but for himself—he shrugged, he'd see what a man could do on the highroads.

Ned went back to Somerset, and though he was suspected of aiding in Geoffrey's escape—especially by Gilbert, who was loud in denouncing him—nobody was ever able to prove anything against him. Ned might indeed have been the source of the rumor that circulated around the taverns of Oxford: that the Angel of Worcester had flown to the windowsill of Geoffrey's cell and left him a rope and a file. It was just one of the many miraculous things now attributed to the woman who had "ridden in like Godiva to save the King at Worcester, and finding him fled had taken a dead man from the battle- field instead, breathed life into him, and vanished!"

Geoffrey made it out of town that night, using a ruse he had used before, and headed southwest, leaving be- hind him Oxford's stone spires, tall and pale in the light of a rising moon.

He never looked back—except once when he thought he heard sounds of pursuit. His memories of those months in Oxford were not concerned with the towers or their lodgings . . . they were memories of a woman, soft and sweet in his arms, a splendrous woman who had melded into his arms and into his heart. He would carry the memory of her with him all his tormented days.

For a while he turned highwayman, ruthlessly taking what he wanted where he found it, for life had been none so good to him of late and he was haunted by what he had lost. With a black scarf wound around his face and a steady pistol cocked and ready, it was a wintry pair of eyes indeed that he turned toward the scared coach travelers who had the misfortune to cross his path by night. There was a price on his head now, but he shrugged that off. Doubless he would die as he had lived—violently, in his blood on the highroad, with none to mourn.

And when he rode recklessly into market towns on fair days seeking a bawdy respite from the rigors of the road, and lost himself in the packed humanity that surged between the stalls, it was at the girls with red-gold hair that he turned his somber gaze, seeing in the flash of their bright hair in the sun a brief glimpse of the alluring woman he had lost. His face grew grim as he remembered. All that a man could want he had had—and thrown away. He cursed himself for his folly, and drowned his memories in wine.

It was a reckless face Geoffrey turned to the world now. He took ever more chances, for he cared little whether he lived or died. But a ball in the arm from an alert coach driver temporarily ended his career on the highroads. Mending, he drifted toward the coast.

At Dover, wise in the ways of the hunted, he fell in with a smuggler named Rice who brought French laces and French brandy across the channel duty free and pocketed a neat profit. On Rice's next trip across the channel—a dark, moonless night was chosen for the run—Geoffrey accompanied him. They were not lucky; midway across the channel the moon came out bright, and they were chased by a British revenue cutter. Almost in sight of the French coast, the cutter launched a nine-pound shot into their side. The next shot broke the mast —and when it fell, the heavy wooden mast caught Rice across the head and broke his neck.

Geoffrey did not wait for the cutter to come alongside. He went over the side and into the longboat. Fortunately clouds once again obscured the moon, and his going was unobserved. He rowed mightily toward the distant coast. A few cold stars were breaking through the murk when he pulled the longboat ashore in the surf and raked the empty coast with a keen, hard look. Without money, without friends, cast up on a foreign shore, something dogged in him refused to give up. He was determined to survive, and his first thought was how to get back to England. But what held England for him, indeed, what held any place for him—now that Lenore was gone? He might as well stay here!

But he knew a moment's sadness as he thought how, had things gone differently, he and Lenore might this day be landing on another coast—the American coast, ready to start a new life. He looked at the cold stars and hoped —with a pain like the twist of a knife in an old wound— that Lenore was happy with Michael, that he would make her a good busband and give her the kind of home she deserved.

Then he started a long walk toward a distant winking light that might be a candle in a cottage window, or might signify a town. As he strode along in the salt air, his mouth twisted into a grim smile at the irony of this landing on the French coast—he had made good the threat he never intended; he had gone to France.

PART TWO

THE

FORSAKEN

CHAPTER 20

On her sad journey north, away from the town that had become, in her heart and mind, her home, Lenore kept her head high, but her gaze upon the sweet summer countryside around her was bereft.

The long wild road she had ridden with Geoffrey was behind her now, the trauma of Wells, the sharp, brief glory she had known as "Mistress Daunt" in Oxford— and the bitterness, the lies. Love was behind her, too, lost somewhere in the ruins of her life. Lenore felt she would never again know the wild, fierce sweetness that had drenched her as she clung to Geoffrey, the wonderful fulfillment as a woman that had been hers as she rode beside him.

But . . . though she had lost so much, she had not lost all. Fiercely she clutched Lorena to her breast, soothing the pretty child with a swift kiss or a soft caress if she cried. "You will be good," she whispered brokenly to the baby, her lips brushing that small pink cheek. "Yes, and you will be beautiful—and your beauty will bring you good things, not harm as mine has done."

For that it was her beauty that had brought her to this cruel pass, she was certain. It was beauty that had made Geoffrey desire her, that had made Gilbert scheme to win her and finally to take her so savagely by force . . . beauty, too, that had made Jamie the Scot seek her for his handfast bride.

Like a quicksand made of pearls, her beauty had dragged her down—and now it had finished her. She was on the run again, this time alone, for Michael would leave her at Banbury. And although she had faced up to her future bravely, in her heart she knew the chances of a woman making a living racing and betting at the fairs was not good.

Lost, lost Lenore . . . sadly she watched her reflection float by in a still, shallow pool as they rode along the riverbank. A vivid shadow—Lenore, young and lovely as she rode erect and proud on her white horse, her fair face reflecting nothing of what she had suffered. Snowfire, after his long, tiresome winter and spring spent mainly in the stable, was undaunted and ready to run. It was difficult to hold him back to match the sedate pace of Michael's mount. So glad was he to have her on his back again that he danced and arched his white neck, tossed his silky mane, and whinnied to her in small, soft sounds. Lenore patted him ruefully and sighed. This was to have been such a wonderful time for her, these first weeks with the wonder of her firstborn in her arms and lean, sardonic Geoffrey by her side.

Michael was fretting because he had left with his baggage to be sent the clothes he wanted to wear to-morrow—and because he was grimly afraid the garter that held up his hose on his left leg was coming loose. His frenzied mind was checking over what was in his saddle-bags and bundles that flopped about his horse's back—no garters, he was sure of it. He would doubtless arrive in Banbury a figure of fun. Though he loved Lenore and would have followed her anywhere, he was already having second thoughts about this wild flight from Oxford and had little to say.

In her suffering, Lenore was almost oblivious to Michael's silence. She was used to Michael's doglike devotion and found it comforting. When she thought about him at all, she hoped vaguely that he would find some smiling girl with enough income to keep him in the red raiment he so loved and forget all about his infatuation for her.

As they rode along and Michael observed the beauty of the woman who sat her saddle so easily beside him—or more often just ahead, for it was difficult to hold back her prancing mount—his spirits lifted. He was secretly glad that Geoffrey had treated Lenore so shabbily, leaving her and going to France, for it had given him this chance to woo her and perhaps to win her. Any guilt he felt when she turned her head and he saw the shadowed pain in her violet eyes he dispelled with the airy thought that he would be *much* better for Lenore than Geoffrey. He daydreamed that she would give up this wild scheme of racing at the fairs and ride with him to Coventry, where his mother would see at once how beautiful she was and how he had to have her and immediately consent to their marriage. His father would mention bitterly the inroads Michael's Oxford education had made on their finances, how he had hoped to recoup through a rich marriage arranged for his handsome son, but he would come around if Mother did. Michael's father always came around to whatever his mother decided was best—like spending all this money on an Oxford education for Michael and dressing him like a peacock all in red so that people would notice him.

Lenore scarcely noticed Michael's wistful smile, his covert admiring glances. Immersed in bittersweet memories of Geoffrey, she swallowed painfully and said, "Yes, yes," to something Michael said, unaware of what his words were. Around her bees and cicadas hummed and songbirds flitted through the summer meadows, and great trees dipped leafy green branches into the reflecting water

313

at the river's edge. She had left Oxford as she had arrived, she thought wryly—unnoticed.

In that she was mistaken. Their departure from Oxford had not gone unnoticed. Hardly had they cleared the city gates when they passed a pair of riders, headed south. The road was well populated at that point. Produce-laden farm carts streamed into the city, and along the edges of the dusty road strode sturdy country lads, and occasionally broad-hipped, deep-breasted country wenches swung by carrying baskets of eggs and herbs and sometimes live chickens with their feet tied together, into town for sale. In the bustle of all this coming and going, Lenore, pre-occupied with her sad thoughts, did not notice the two riders—the big, coarse, black-bearded man and the small, sandy, weathered one—who reined in their horses and turned to stare speculatively after her and Michael.

This pair, whose names were Tubbs and Swan, had ridden in from Banbury, where—after a bad knife fight in which wiry little Swan had carved up a local drayman—the constable had warned them to leave before the fair started; drifters like them could give Banbury a bad name. So Tubbs and Swan had mounted up and were now headed into Oxford to see what pocket might be picked or what purse cut. A pair of cutthroats who'd long ago left all their scruples behind them, they were used to leaving places in a hurry. They'd been harried out of London, out of half a dozen towns since, so it was no novelty to be turned out of Banbury with their fair coming on. It had, however, put them in an ugly mood, and Swan, a wizened little fellow with coarse, sandy-red hair, a broken nose, and a slight limp, who was as quick with a dagger as any in Shoreditch, had been casting about him for easy prey on the road south.

As Michael and Lenore passed, he reined up. "Did ye see that?" he asked Tubbs in a low voice. "The wench and the stripling?"

"Aye," rumbled Tubbs, rubbing his matted black beard. He was a huge man with small, mean eyes and a voice that rasped almost painfully in his throat—souvenir of a barroom brawl in which he'd caught a flying bottle

314

in the Adam's apple. His gaze followed Michael's heavy baggage and Lenore's supple body thoughtfully. It was a tempting combination.

"A sight like that do heat the blood, don't it?" Swan was almost licking his chops as he looked after Lenore. "Now, there's a piece I'd like to get my hands on." He moved aside to avoid a passing farm cart. "The lad travels heavy—think you there could be something of value in those bags?"

Tubbs, who had been thinking the same thing, grunted. "The lad's armed with a pistol—I could see it."

"I doubt yon pink-cheeked lad can use it," sneered Swan. "Anyway, the girl's to my liking. How say you we turn about and ride north?"

The farm cart had now gone its creaking way, and there was a momentary lull in the traffic headed into Oxford.

"Not so far north as Banbury," Tubbs reminded him. "Or we'll land in jail."

"Nay, not so far as that. I say we take them somewhere twixt here and there—some likely spot. The wench reminded me of a tavern maid I knew in London—same color hair. She were a hot one. Not so pretty as this wench, though."

"I have eyes for the girl, too," rumbled Tubbs. "So if ye're thinkin' not to share her—"

"We'll share her," agreed Swan quickly, fingering his dirk as Tubbs's mean little eyes fixed on him. He had seen friendlier eyes on a charging boar. "But 'tis not to be like last time when ye was too rough and killed the girl afore I got my chance at 'er!" he warned in an aggrieved voice.

"Agreed," said Tubbs laconically. "We'll take care of the lad first and split up his belongings."

"And then we'll split up the girl!" finished Swan with an evil cackle and a flash of broken yellow teeth.

Heavy-handed Tubbs gave his companion a long, slow look from those little eyes. He'd been thinking of parting company with Swan before he got a dirk stuck through his ribs some night for some imagined grievance. The girl Swan spoke of had been but a young thing spitting curses. She'd given him a sharp kick—but he'd not meant to break her ribs when he'd crushed her to him angrily and thrown her young body to the ground beneath him. That she had died of it—well, that was the luck of the road, wasn't it? They'd got away clean, even though there'd been a great to-do about it, for the girl had turned out to be the daughter of the local magistrate. Now this bonny wench on the white horse, he'd be more careful with her, for she looked a rare piece, and it might be good for a wanted man to travel with a "wife" to draw suspicion away from him—at least for a while. Should he get in trouble, he might use her favors to get him out of it —and if he grew tried of her, he could always take her into London and sell her to a brothel. "Mother" Moseley or "Lady" Bennett could always use a pretty piece like her in their establishments, or any of the brothels in Southwark. Meanwhile he'd humor Swan. "Ye can have her first," he shrugged in an offhand way, spitting in the dirt at the side of the road.

Swan brightened. "Now, that's more like it," he beamed, bobbing his sandy head until his unkempt hair fell over his face. "And right handsome of ye!" He pushed back his hair with dirty fingers and slapped his huge friend on the back, noting again how ironlike were those great knotted muscles beneath the soiled jerkin. Idly he considered just where a dirk would best slip in—in case they had a falling out—for treachery came easily to him, and he'd a mind to have this hot-looking wench all to himself.

Up ahead Michael had decided to try his luck. " 'Twould be better if ye forgot Banbury and came to Coventry," he insisted. "The baby's so small—suppose it rains at the fair?"

"Then I'll find shelter," sighed Lenore.

"We have a big house just south of Coventry—you could stay in a spare bedroom. My mother would see there were clean rushes on the floor, and you'd like the view."

Lenore smiled at him. His next question was obvious;

316

she hoped to forestall it. "Thank you, Michael, but I—I couldn't. I must make my own way."

"If ye married me, there'd be no need to leave—ye could stay forever. 'Twill all be mine one day."

"Michael, you know your parents would never countenance your marrying me. What would your mother say?"

" 'Tis not what my mother would say that worries you," he discerned shrewdly. " 'Tis Geoffrey who stands in my way."

He was right about that, she thought wryly, and looked away that he might not see the answer so plain on her face. In her arms Lorena gave a little sleepy cry, and she busied herself with comforting the child.

"Am I not as good a man as Geoffrey?" Michael shot at her in an aggrieved voice.

How to answer that? "Michael," she groaned, "please do not talk so much about Geoffrey. How can I forget him if I am constantly reminded of him?"

Michael saw the sense of that, but for the moment it left him with nothing to say. He had been priming himself with arguments concerning Geoffrey, thinking up ways to disparage him, to convince Lenore how much better he could take care of her. It was slowly coming to him that she did not expect anyone to take care of her—that she meant to take care of herself. Now he bounced along with a frown on his pink-cheeked countenance—for he had never had a very good seat on a horse —and tried to think up new arguments to convince Lenore that she should marry him.

Lenore was glad of the respite. She would need her wits about her when she got to Banbury, and she did not want to arrive tired out from arguing with Michael. But unbidden her thoughts slipped back to Geoffrey, and she found herself brooding as she rode, only half seeing the road which Snowfire danced along.

Weighed down by her unhappy thoughts, it was some time before Lenore realized they were being followed. Michael, concentrating on what seemed to him the more important problem of pressing his suit, had become

317

accustomed to the pair of riders whose horses jogged along behind them just too far for a good view of them to be had, but Lenore's sense of danger—sharpened by her wild flight with Geoffrey through southwest England—had awakened.

Now that the traffic had thinned out and the road had become lonelier, for the twentieth time Lenore looked back. "Think you that pair mean us harm?" she asked, squinting at them in the distance. She looked restively about her, wishing for a farm cart—even one that would block the road and make passing difficult. " 'Tis unnatural that whether we speed up or slow down, they keep that same distance between us."

Michael frowned as he looked behind him. A vague unease plagued him. "We'll lie the night at an inn—we won't wait till dark, there's one up ahead that we'll reach well before sundown." It occurred to him that the remark made him sound timid—he doubted that would have been Geoffrey's reaction to the situation. "But ye've naught to fear," he added hastily. "Can ye not see I've a large pistol to deal with knaves who might try to harm us?"

"I see it, Michael, but—have ye ever fired it?"

He bristled. "Of course I've fired it! At target. And hit what I aimed at."

Lenore sighed. Like the two cutthroats who followed them in the middle distance, she very much doubted if Michael could hit anything he aimed at. She gave his overladen mount an impatient look—it was plain they could make no better time, and if the pair following chose to overtake them, they could do so at will.

Still, if they stopped at an inn before dark, all should be well.

"Ye'll be at the mercy of every robber and highwayman in the countryside—not to mention country rogues who might do you harm—if ye go from town to town with the fairs, whilst if ye married me—"

"Oh, Michael," wailed Lenore, "please *stop*. I do not love you, Michael," she added more gently. "And I have told you that before."

"But I love *you* enough for both of us," he said with ingenuous enthusiasm. "And in time—"

"We'll part at Banbury," said Lenore. "And in time you will forget me—soon, I hope. I would bring you no luck. What is that up ahead, can you see?"

They had been riding through meadowlands along the river, but now they had come to a heavily wooded area, overgrown with brush, and the track had narrowed so that sometimes they were scraped by branches even riding single file. It was as if a green foliage tunnel had closed around them.

"I think it's a cart," said Michael.

"I *hope* it's a cart," muttered Lenore, for squinting back, she had come to the panicky conclusion that the pair were gaining on them. Now she could see that the road ahead was solidly blocked; directly across it a huge wagon lay overturned and the six big draft horses that had drawn it stood disconsolately tangled in their reins before the wreck. Spilled from the wagon were several enormous pieces of oaken furniture and the driver, a big rough fellow in a worn leather jerkin, was standing on one edge of the deep rut that had broken his wheel, roundly cursing his luck.

Perforce they came to a halt before the wreck. Lenore looked at the broken wheel, the upended load, and felt sorry for the driver—the roads around Twainmere had been rutted sheep trails and she had seen many a broken wheel and helped to right many an overturned cart.

"Can ye move your horses so that we can go around?" asked Michael in a peremptory tone that reminded Lenore that Michael came from a manor house and was an only son.

The beleaguered driver did not relish that tone. He turned about, running a hand through his thick hair, and fixed Michael with a stern gaze. "I've got to take this load all the way to Southampton," he growled. "Furniture it is for my master, who's taking ship there for the Colonies—and me with it, if I can but get there. If ye'll help me move these chests and this cupboard, young sir,

319

perhaps I can get my wagon righted and out of your way."

Michael looked down at his clean red clothing, bethought himself of his left garter hanging by a mere thread, and then eyed with distaste the fallen furniture, now covered with road dirt. These draymen were a careless lot; could not this oxlike fellow have seen that rut plain before him? "I have a weak back," he said testily. " 'Twas injured some years ago in a fall—I can pick up nothing heavy."

Lenore turned to gaze at Michael with some interest. This was the first she had heard of a bad back—and the load with which he had staggered out of his lodgings in Oxford was sadly tiring his horse.

The wagon driver understood perfectly. His jaw hardened.

"Then, young sir and mistress, I'm afraid ye must take the track off to your left," he said curtly. "For ye cannot get past me—not with that great tree and the thorn bushes pressing in at the side of the road." He peered down the green tunnel behind them. "There look to be two sturdy travelers coming up who might help a man reload his wagon. Should they choose to help me," he added with a sour look at Michael, "they'll get through speedily."

Lenore, who did not wish to wait until the two sinister travelers, who paced them in the distance, caught up, turned and looked in the direction he indicated. She saw a faint trail that wandered off between the trees—a sheep trail, she took it to be, leading down from the Cotswolds. She looked back restively at the oncoming riders and her voice sharpened.

"Let's not wait, Michael. Let's take the track."

"Where does the track lead?" asked Michael, a little crestfallen at this detour.

"If you look sharp and keep turning right, 'twill lead you back to this road," said the driver. "It comes out at a crossroads that lies ahead."

"Come on, Michael," said Lenore crisply, for those dark silhouettes she could see behind them down that

320

long, leafy tunnel were fast closing the distance. "We can find a quiet place to rest the horses and have a bite to eat before continuing on."

Sulkily Michael followed her as she turned Snowfire down the almost indiscernible lane that led into the forest. She lost the feeling of fear that had nagged at her as they rode along to the sound of birdsong and the fragrance of wildflowers, for this was the kind of country she understood—sheep country on the edge of the Cotswolds.

"I think we're lost," said Michael unhappily.

"No. I've been watching the track. There's been no turnoff, and now the trail is veering to the right. Your horse is near to falling from all that weight, Michael, and I must feed Lorena. I can hear a brook tinkling over there to the left. Listen, can't you hear it? What say we find it and stop for a bite of bread and cheese?"

"All right," said Michael glumly. "But I still say we're lost. We'll end up spending the night in this forest."

"Nonsense." Lenore dismounted and located the brook. A tiny rivulet it was, clear and cold. It was fed, she guessed, by a spring. From it, they and the horses drank. On the shady leaf mould of its bank she spread a linen square and laid Lorena down upon it. The baby slept on. As she busied herself getting out the food that Mistress Watt's cook had packed for her journey, Lenore said over her shoulder, "You should take all those heavy bags off your poor horse, Michael—he needs rest more than we do."

Michael, bent over the brook dashing water on his hot face, muttered something unintelligible.

Lenore turned to fix him with a level gaze. "If your back is too weak to lift them off," she said evenly, "*I* will do it."

Michael reddened. He got up at once and fell to unloading his horse. Lenore smiled grimly as she heard him mumbling to himself.

"Now," she said with puckish humor, as he flung himself down panting beside her and she offered him some brown bread and cheese, "you can count yourself lucky to have escaped me! Suppose I had said yes to your offer of marriage!. What would your life have been like then?"

"In truth you do drive a man hard," Michael admitted, taking the bread and Cheshire cheese she offered him. "But"—he looked wistfully into her beautiful face—"I'd hope that once wed, you'd lighten your grip on the reins."

"Never," she told him, biting into the brown bread. "You should have helped that man with his overturned load, Michael. 'Twas unkind to leave him there in the road."

"You heard him say those two travelers would help him. Besides, it was his own fault that he ran his wheel into that great rut. 'Twas plain before him to see!"

"Some would say 'tis my own fault I'm where I am today," mused Lenore. "But I could still use a bit of sympathy for my plight!"

"Ah, I *do* sympathize with you, Lenore—"

"Only because you love me."

"What better reason?" he asked simply.

Lenore sighed. What better reason indeed? Who was she to criticize Michael, who was so childishly, so ardently in love with her? She fell silent, watching the horses graze as best they could, and she and Michael finished munching their bread and cheese and shared a plum tart.

She was suddenly aware that Michael was staring at her very wistfully.

"Lenore," he said in a husky voice, "we will part when we reach Banbury and—and I have never kissed you. I love you with all my heart, and I have never once kissed you."

His plea was so genuine, his face so earnest and sad that Lenore felt pity for him. She leaned over and gently pressed her lips to his.

Michael gave a great shuddering sigh and pulled her to him. He was awkward as he kissed her—and kissed her again.

Achingly she was reminded of all the nights Geoffrey had held her in his arms and she had thrilled to his touch. Remembering was a kind of sweet anguish that grew unbearable. She pulled away from Michael.

"I must feed my baby, Michael."

"Oh, Lenore, couldn't we . . . ?" His voice shook and his hand trembled as he touched her breast.

She flinched. "No, Michael, no."

"All right," he sighed, and hunched his shoulders away from her, a picture of abject misery. She gave him a hopeless look, wondering if this sort of behavior had got him his way at home. She supposed it had.

Briskly she moved over to where the baby lay, sat down beside her, picked her up very tenderly, and kissed her awake. Big blue eyes considered her gravely.

Then, deftly tossing a napkin over her breast to hide it modestly from Michael's view, Lenore fed Lorena. She was able to forget Michael, to forget Geoffrey, to forget the world for a little while as she rocked her baby in her arms, tickled her under the chin, and was rewarded by a small gurgling laugh. One by one she took up Lorena's tiny fingers and counted them in tune to a singsong nursery rhyme.

A bit sulky that there were no more kisses forthcoming, Michael stretched out by the brook with his hat over his eyes to shade his face from the summer sun slanting through the overhanging trees and rested as Lenore, leaning against a dark tree bole, sang her child a sad, sweet lullaby.

It was peaceful there in the woods with the birds singing overhead, but the slanting sun reminded Lenore that it was growing late. She got up and put the food away, and Michael again loaded up his weary horse. They mounted up—Lenore with Lorena sleeping peacefully in the crook of her arm—and rode on. For all that she'd told Michael they weren't lost, Lenore was beginning to be uneasy about finding the road again when just ahead through the heavy brush they saw the stone crossroads marker.

CHAPTER 21

Lenore frowned. Something wasn't right—the birds had stopped singing. Around them the air seemed still and heavy, somnolent and waiting.

Michael had no sense of danger; he brightened. " 'Tis the road at last," he sighed, urging his horse forward. "The inn should be—"

He never finished his sentence.

From behind the bushes at the roadside leaped two men. Lenore screamed. The big one—Tubbs—lunged at Michael, whose horse reared up and gave him time to drag out his pistol and cock it and fire it. The ball struck Tubbs in the chest. He gave a curse as he toppled, but his hamlike hand had latched onto the hem of Michael's short red cloak and he pulled the slender youth from the saddle as he went down. Michael's horse snorted and darted away, heading back down the road to Oxford, and the two men fell to the ground, locked in unequal struggle.

Swan meanwhile had leaped for Lenore's bridle, and

she had lifted her foot and given him a solid kick in the jaw that numbed her toes but sent him sprawling backward to stretch his wiry length by the roadside. As he toppled she heard Tubbs give a howl—Michael had kneed him. Now Lenore saw Tubbs bring his hamlike fist down with such ferocity on Michael's head that she could hear the crack when Michael's neck snapped and his head tilted at a crazy angle as he slumped over, dead.

Paralyzed by this turn of events, Lenore had no time to react to them, for Snowfire, rearing and terrified at this sudden attack, wheeled and bolted, almost unseating her. Back down the track they had come he ran wildly, and over Lorena's thin, frightened wail she heard big Tubbs howl, "Get the wench, Swan—I'm bleedin' half to death!"

Swan, on his feet again and cursing, ran for his horse and streaked off after Lenore.

Lenore, with the white stallion charging down the narrow track she had so recently traversed, looked back through whipping branches to see Swan thundering after her in wild pursuit. Snowfire was faster, but the track was treacherous at this pace. Lorena was wailing at the top of her voice, but Lenore was thinking fast now. She dared not return to Oxford, nor could she now take the road to Banbury with that great hulking brute waiting to cut her off at the crossroads. Just past the place where they had stopped for lunch, she had noticed a tiny track leading off to the left—another faint sheep track leading into the Cotswolds. It lay just ahead around a turn. She would have a chance to dart into that wall of greenery and lose her pursuer there—and if she did not lose him, she would be no worse off, for she dared not seek the main road.

She managed to turn Snowfire's head, and without hesitation careened off down an unknown trail.

It was a mistake.

Twenty feet down the track Snowfire caught his foot in a hole covered up with leaves and stumbled to his knees, throwing Lenore over his head.

My baby, my baby! she thought in panic as she sailed through the air toward a wall of green. Head bent and arms locked protectively around the bundled-up Lorena as if they had been a cage, she landed rolling in a bush. Thorns tore at her, she felt her head jerked violently as some of her hair was pulled out by clutching twigs, there was a sharp pain in her shoulder as a branch gouged her, caught and ripped the material of her sleeve—and then skidded harmlessly by as the material tore free.

She came up with a sickening jolt against a big tree trunk and for a moment lay there, gasping for breath. In terror she sat up, lifted her head to toss back the tangled hair that hung like a shawl over her locked arms, and unlocked those scratched, bruised arms to assure herself that Lorena—still squalling lustily—was all right.

"Hush, hush," she murmured in anguish, for those pounding hoofbeats were coming closer.

Behind her Snowfire scrambled to his feet and Lenore, on her feet now and prepared to remount, realized sickeningly that he could hardly bear his weight on his right forefoot. She'd never outdistance her pursuer now—and already he must be rounding the turn.

They could not run—they must hide!

She grasped Snowfire's reins, and putting gentle fingers over her baby's mouth to silence those strident wails, she led the limping white horse through a stand of poplars into a deep thicket. On she struggled through the heavy undergrowth, wincing at the pain that shot through her left shoulder, but managing to reach out bravely to protect both the baby and the horses's head from whipping needled branches.

After several minutes of this she paused to rest—and listen. No sound of hooves came to her through the patch of thorns behind her.

The silence worried her. Her pursuer could not have passed on—surely she'd have heard him thundering on up the track. But she'd best be still now, for the slapping branches she'd had to part to let them through had made some noise even though her shoes and Snowfire's hooves had padded almost silently over the soft, damp leaf mould underfoot.

In the oppressive stillness where even the birds had

326

ceased to sing, she cast an anxious look around her—and screamed.

From behind a tree Swan leaped, grinning, and plunged toward her. She could see his yellow teeth flashing past an intervening thorn branch. Dropping Snowfire's reins, her only concern now to save her baby, she ducked and slid through an opening in the green wall to her left, heard Swan's howl as he plunged full tilt into the thorn branch and the long needles tore into him.

Weaving through the heavy underbrush, she could hear his crashing progress behind her, his muttered curses, as she fought her way through the thicket, bending this way and that as she squeezed between tree boles, tore free of rope-like vines whose tendrils threatened to twine about her and hold her fast. Her breath was rasping in her throat as she broke free of the thicket into a tiny clearing. Her foot caught on an exposed tree root and she stumbled and went down heavily on her knees—once again breaking Lorena's fall with her bruised, scratched arms.

Before she could rise, Swan had crashed through the thicket into the clearing behind her, seized her by the collar of her dress, and was hoisting her, half-choked, to her feet. His arms were wiry and hard, and as if she were a puppet on a string he swung her around to face him with a triumphant laugh.

"Thought ye'd got away, didn't ye?"

"Please," gasped Lenore, "I've no money—"

"Money?" He laughed again. "Did ye think it was money I was chasin' ye for?"

Lenore swallowed. "I know people who live on this road," she told him fiercely. "They're due to come by any minute—and they have dogs and guns. You'd do well to let me go!"

"So-o-o . . . ye still have fight in ye." He leered down into her face. "I like a wench with fight."

Lenore flinched away from him, but her mien was defiant. His fingers were digging into her shoulders so hard she was sure there'd be a blue mark where each one pressed. The pain in her left shoulder sickened her, but she stood her ground.

327

"The people I know will pay you well if you let me go unharmed!" she cried, trying to buy time.

"Ye're a good liar, too," he approved. "Course that cart driver told us which way he'd directed you when Tubbs and I helped him move his cart so's we could get through. So we both know ye're a stranger to these woods."

Lenore felt she might faint.

Swan's jaw jutted closer. His voice grew surly and held a threat more terrible than any she had heard before. "Now ye'll give me no more trouble," he told her heavily, keeping a viselike grip on the arm with the torn sleeve and running a stubby finger down her flinching throat and between her breasts. "Ye might escape me, mistress, but yer baby won't. I could make do with *it*—if *you* get away."

Lenore's face turned so ashen that her violet eyes stood out as dark, horrified spots. With all that was left of her ebbing strength she edged her baby further from that yellow-toothed evil face thrust down into hers.

"Let me put the baby down," she said hopelessly. "Don't hurt her and—and I'll do what you want. Just so you don't hurt my baby."

"Thought you might." He grinned, but he kept his painful grasp on her arm as she turned and carefully placed Lorena in the bole of a hollow tree—he didn't trust her.

Lenore straightened up and faced him. Her gaze was steady, her jaw clenched. She might have been a woman going to the stake.

His greedy eyes roved over her as if she were a juicy roast he was about to devour. He licked his lips and studied her.

"I'll take ye here out of sight of the road," he decided. "And if ye're nice to me—*real* nice—I won't turn ye over to big Tubbs back there. He'll be meaner'n a bear 'cause he's been shot, so he'd rough ye up—kill ye, maybe. Me—I won't do nothin' ye won't enjoy!" An uncontrollable shiver went over Lenore. She kept her head high. "Course," he added on a note of warning, "do ye fight me, I'll remember how ye give me a kick in the face back

328

there and maybe break yer legs so ye won't go nowhere and I can take my time with ye."

Lenore's knees went weak at this threat.

"Do what you want," she said dully. "Just so you don't hurt my baby."

"Aye, now that's what I like to see—a docile wench," he said with satisfaction. "Lay ye down where ye are. Them leaves'll make a nice nest for us."

Slowly, wincing as her weight fell on her hurt shoulder, Lenore stretched herself out on the ground. The leaves beneath her were wet and smelled of leaf mould. They wet the back of her dress clean through, and she could feel moisture crawl along her spine. To her wide-staring eyes, it seemed that the devil himself stood above her, tearing open his dirty trousers.

"Ain't never seen nothin' like this, have ye?" he crowed. "Nothin' but weak nubbins of the gentry, I'll be bound!"

Lenore looked quickly away, and he snickered. At the sound her taut nerves made her muscles jerk and her breasts quivered. She looked back to see him staring at them, beads of perspiration forming on his forehead.

"You don't have to take your clothes off—now," he said thickly. "We can do that tonight. We'll have to run from Tubbs—he's hard to kill."

So he meant to take her with him! Her eyes dilated and her lashes were a dark fringe against her chalky skin. Her hair—full of leaves and twigs—had come down and was spread in a tangled shawl over the wet leaves. In the nearby tree-bole Lorena was wailing. The sound made Lenore feel sick. What would happen to her baby, once this monster had had his fill of her?

Desperation gave her strength. This man whose eyes goggled down at her had a dagger—it was stuck in his belt. She forced herself not to look at it, but to stare up into that lust-filled countenance. If she could but reach that dagger . . . !

She closed her eyes with an involuntary shudder as Swan lowered himself, chuckling, onto her and clawed up her skirts over her shrinking legs. "Ye're the prettiest

329

wench I ever had!" he declared in a husky voice, slobbering over her cheek as she turned her head sharply away from him. "Ain't no need to be afraid," he cooed ingratiatingly, clutching her hurt shoulder in a grip that made her cry out and left red weals where each finger pressed. Nearly paralyzed with pain, she slumped as he released his grip. "There, that's better," he said in a cruel tone. *"Relax!"* He slid one of his arms under her back, the other beneath her head, and his knee jabbed viciously at her locked legs in an attempt to wrest them apart.

"Lie still, damn ye!" he commanded fiercely—but Lenore, writhing beneath him, had got her right arm free. Now as he ripped at her bodice, exposing her breasts, she craftily worked that hand toward the hilt of his dagger. She cried out again as his lips closed suckingly over her right breast and both his hands violently clasped her bare buttocks, jerking her hips upward toward him. Lenore twisted in his grasp, but her hand was firmly on the dagger's hilt now. She moaned loudly to distract him—and pulled it out.

"Ye like that, aye?" he chuckled.

Lenore kept her eyes firmly closed that he might not read their murderous expression. By now his knee had wrested her legs apart and as he made to consummate their union she pressed suddenly toward him in simulated passion—to give her arm a better swing. Drawing the dagger back as far as she could, she plunged it hilt deep into his back.

Swan made a sudden strangled sound in his throat and rose up from her, clawing behind him. "Tubbs— damn you!" He staggered to his knees and Lenore managed to jerk her legs free as Swan looked wildly about for his erstwhile companion. His incredulous gaze turned to Lenore, who rolled away from him and gained her feet. *"You* done it," he gasped. *"You* done me in!" He seemed to wilt before her eyes, slipping down into the wet leaf mould. "You got to help me," he whispered. "If you don't, I'm done for."

How long she stood there gazing down at him, she did not know. He was a terrible sight, lying on his stomach

330

with the knife stuck into his back and blood oozing out. Worse, his head was twisted to the side so that he could look up at her out of the corner of one eye. "Help—me!" he gasped.

She stared down at him in revulsion. This monster had been about to violate her and do God knew what to her little Lorena. The memory of big Tubbs's hamlike fist smashing down on Michael's unprotected head swam up before her eyes. Once again she heard the snap as his neck broke. And Lorena's baby skull was so thin and soft.

She had not known her voice could be so cold. "You will live if God wills it," she said. "But not with *my* help!"

Swan groaned as she found his horse tethered to a tree and led it past him. Ignoring his cries, she picked up Lorena from the hollow tree where she had deposited her. Soft and warm in her arms, Lorena's wails subsided to hiccups as Lenore cuddled and petted her. Lorena had never seemed more precious to her than she did at that moment. Closing her eyes, she gave thanks to a merciful heaven that she had been spared to see her through to safety.

Lorena had quieted by the time she found Snowfire and led him back to where the gray mare stood. Carefully she mounted the unfamiliar animal—she could not afford to be bucked off with a baby in her arms.

"Ye can't take her!" cried Swan piteously. "Ye can't take my horse! I'll bleed to death!" He lapsed into a storm of curses.

She did not even give him a backward look. All the pity she had left she gave to Snowfire. His leg was swelling now. "Come along, Snowfire," she said gently. "We must away from here before the big one comes looking for us." As if he understood, the white horse—who had begun the day so gaily—limped after her as she set off on the gray mare along the unfamiliar trail that must, she guessed, lead into the Cotswolds.

Twice she changed direction, taking off on stony trails where she'd be hard to track. Sometimes she looked back to give Snowfire a compassionate look and murmur an occasional word of encouragement. His leg must be very painful by now, she knew, but he kept plodding along after her valiantly.

After riding a long while, she felt safer and sat for a moment, silent and listening. Lorena was asleep again. No sound but the wild birds and humming insects of the dusky summer forest broke the stillness. Nearby she could hear a little stream tinkling, and the last of the light gilded the tree branches to gold.

She drew a deep sighing breath. She must have lost any pursuit by now. Indeed big Tubbs might still be waiting at the crossroads for his confederate to return. She remembered how he had struck Michael, and a sob went through her.

Behind her Snowfire looked very woebegone. His leg was badly swollen now, and she dismounted and found the stream and led both horses over the softest earth she could to its bank. There she laid Lorena down gently and watched Snowfire and the gray mare drink their fill. She tore strips from her petticoat and gently bathed Snowfire's swollen foreleg and wrapped it carefully. Then she took off her clothes and washed her whole body in ice-cold water, wincing as her scratches hurt with renewed fury and her left shoulder ached.

It was not much, but the bath made her feel as if she'd washed Swan's filthy touch from her skin.

And then, half-dressed, she sank down and wept for a boy who had loved her and would never drain a tankard with his friends or wear a stylish red cloak again. Michael might be alive had he not dashed madly out of Oxford to follow her.

But she could not afford the luxury of a long weep. There was more to be done. She finished dressing, combed the twigs from her long hair, made a pillow of her saddlebag, ate a little, and fed her baby, crooning as she did so and holding her with a terrible tenderness, for she had been so very close to losing her . . . so close.

That night in the tiny copse she slept beneath a tree with Lorena cradled in her arms—at least, she tried to sleep. Her shoulder throbbed dully. Once she dozed and the wild cry of a loon startled her awake. The night sounds of hunting owls, small screeches, and slip-slaps in the water of the gurgling brook brought her to instant alertness. Was big Tubbs nearby? Had he found her? She clutched Lorena to her more than once and muttered a prayer.

Though Lenore did not know it, she had nothing to fear from big Tubbs. The letting of his own blood by Michael's pistol ball had cleared his angry head, and he quickly realized that he must get rid of Michael's body. He stuffed a dirty handkerchief into his bleeding wound, which he judged none too bad since the buckle of his baldric had deflected the ball. Systematically he went through Michael's pockets, pocketed his coins, and finding them too few for his liking, gave Michael's inert body a kick. Michael did not feel it; he'd been dead for some time. Tubbs yearned to leave him where he was, but this was a crossroads and someone might happen along at any time and raise a hue and cry. Unceremoniously he dragged Michael into a thick clump of bushes nearby and threw a couple of tree branches over him—animals, he thought grimly, would take care of the rest.

From this chore, Tubbs straightened and peered down the road. Michael's horse and baggage were nowhere in sight—probably halfway back to Oxford by now. Torn with a desire to follow the horse—at least the beast would have value, even if the baggage proved worthless —Tubbs began to curse. He dared not follow the horse, for he half expected Swan to run away with the girl— and she was worth more than the few coins he'd garnered from the dead lad in the red cloak.

Grimly, he mounted and set off down the track in the direction Swan had disappeared.

"Swan," he called cautiously as he rode along. And again, "Swan?"

At last he heard a weak voice answer.

"Here. Over here."

Following the voice, he blundered through the thicket into the little clearing where Lenore had left her attacker. Tubbs came to a surprised halt at the sight of Swan's body sprawled out with the dagger sticking in his back.

"Help me, Tubbs," cried Swan desperately. "The wench done me in!"

Tubbs gave a low whistle as he dismounted. "Did a good job on ye, didn't she?" he marveled admiringly. "Clean to the hilt! How d'ye feel, Swan?"

"Bad," muttered Swan. "Real bad. Draw the knife out careful, Tubbs. Mind you staunch the wound."

"Aye." Tubbs was imperturbable.

He leaned forward and Swan gave a banshee screech as the knife was drawn out of his back. "Staunch it!" he sobbed, seeing Tubbs sit back, wipe off the blade on the leaf mould, and stick the knife in his belt.

"Staunch it!" wailed Swan.

Tubbs pulled out a handkerchief and stuffed it casually into the wound. "Ye'll be all right," he said. Squatting on the ground, Tubbs rocked back and forth on his feet and surveyed his injured friend. "Where's your horse, Swan?"

She took it," said Swan vengefully. "Wait'll I find that wench! Just wait!" He tried to move and gasped with pain. "Here, help me up, Tubbs."

Tubbs rose. "I can't take ye up on my horse, Swan. We'd break his bloody back."

Perspiring with the effort, Swan had managed to rise to a sitting position. "But ye can't leave me here!" he panted.

"Nay, I can't—ye'd talk if they found ye," muttered Tubbs. "Well, I guess ye'll have to go, Swan."

Swan was shaking with relief. He'd thought big Tubbs meant to leave him to die in these woods.

"Maybe this stick will help ye—something to lean on." Idly big Tubbs picked up a heavy tree branch.

Swan saw this primitive cudgel cudgel poised above his head, screeched, and tried vainly to duck. The branch caught him in the temple and he plunged forward with a rattle in his throat. After a moment, he stopped twitching and lay inert.

Tubbs went thoroughly through his friend's pockets, took everything of value, and was about to depart when a frown crossed his heavy features. He and Swan had been seen together at Banbury—indeed the constable there had warned them both to depart before the fair. If Swan were found dead here, he'd no doubt be held accountable for his murder. He sighed. A man couldn't be too careful. Reluctantly he dragged Swan's body back a ways into the woods. Finding a soft spot of earth, he used Swan's knife to dig him a shallow grave, rolled him in, and covered him up with earth and leaves. Some animal might find him there, 'twasn't likely people would—at least not until he, John Tubbs, was well out of this part of the country.

He remounted then, headed back to the crossroads, and hurried back along the road to Oxford. On the way he caught up with Michael's horse, took what he wanted from Michael's baggage, and sold the horse in Oxford. He laid up there at a brothel until his wound was healed and started out again, for he was uneasy that one or both of the bodies might be found and there'd be questions he'd not care to answer.

He made his way without incident to Bristol—save for cutting a purse or two on the road—and there he was "pressed" into the navy and died from a blow with a marlinspike when he got into a fight with the second mate.

There were none to mourn him, and sullen Tubbs died without confessing any of his crimes. Swan's grave was never found.

Tubbs had got away with both murders, for he died without being suspected of either. But he'd left Lenore with a sticky problem, although she didn't know it for some time.

CHAPTER 22

Morning dawned bright and beautiful. A soft stillness enveloped the countryside, and the birds' songs were muted and sweet. A sky of brilliant blue with soft, floating white clouds could be glimpsed through the canopy of branches overhead. Around her was the chirp and hum of tiny living things going to work with the new day. Lorena gurgled up at her and reached up a tiny hand. Lenore kissed those tiny fingers and got up and washed her face in the ice-cold stream.

In the purity and beauty of the morning she found it hard to believe in the reality of yesterday's events. Surely they were all a nightmare and would be forgotten soon, melted away by the bright sunshine.

But a limping Snowfire and the gray mare were both grim reminders. As was her shoulder whenever she moved. And she knew that back at the crossroads lay Michael's body and along that wooded track behind her a wounded man. . . . It was a somber-faced woman who nursed her child and soothed it. Afterward she ate an apple and sat and stroked Lorena pale, downy hair and tried to plan for the future.

Racing at the Banbury fair was impossible now, of course. Snowfire's leg was hurt, how badly she could not tell, but it would be a long time before he could run again. The gray was a passable riding horse but not built for speed. Mentally assessing her assets, her eyes fell on the gray mare's saddlebags. She had not thought to look in those; automatically she had thought of them as belonging to somebody else. Now ruthlessly she checked through them, finding several pins—which she promptly used to pin her torn dress together—a dirty pack of cards, a bottle of rum, a dirty shirt, and—something hard. Her heart leaped, hoping it was money. But it was not. The object was wrapped in a small linen cloth, and when she unwrapped it an amethyst ring fell into her hand. Amethysts were highly regarded, and Lenore looked at it speculatively. Stolen, of course, but there was no way she could return it. Perhaps she'd be able to sell it. . . . With a sigh she put the ring in her pocket, kept the bottle of rum, and threw away the rest. It was a thoughtful woman who made ready to begin her journey once more.

The horses were hungry, so as noon approached and she saw a hayfield with only the rooftop of a cottage visible over the rise beyond, she dismounted and walked Snowfire and the gray carefully toward it, keeping a wary eye out for the farmer. Snowfire's limp was a little better today, but she hated to make him use that leg at all. At the edge of the little field she stopped and let the horses graze on the hay. It was stealing, she knew, and some farmer would no doubt curse her for it—unless he believed a wandering deer had done it—but she was at least careful to keep the horses on the edge of the field so their hooves did not trample down the upstanding hay. Snowfire nuzzled her gently, as if in appreciation of a good meal, as she remounted the docile gray. When she rode away he limped after her.

She no longer feared pursuit by Tubbs, for the cross-roads grew farther away all the time, she had changed

337

course several times, and Tubbs was, after all, wounded. Bolder now, following first one sheep trail and then another, she moved deeper into the Cotswolds, and when she sighted a shepherd seated on a hill watching his flock graze, she waved to him and rode up boldly.

The shepherd's dog came running to meet her and circled her warily, but the shepherd called to him in a low voice and the dog went back to his master. As Lenore rode up, she saw that the shepherd was an old man, stooped, with pale eyes used to studying far distances.

Glad of the company in his lonely vigil, he offered her a bit of stew and as she ate, gratefully, he studied her with those shrewd pale eyes.

"Where are ye bound, mistress?"

"To Twainmere," said Lenore before she thought. And suddenly she knew that was where she would go, for it was the only place that, without money, she was sure of a roof. Flora would take her in. When Snowfire was well again, she'd take him out on the road and race him at the fairs for a living, just as she'd planned. "I am a widow," she improvised, "and must return to my people."

"Twainmere," he murmured. " 'Tis a long way off."

"I know," she said. "I think I'm lost."

He smiled and pointed out directions and told her what landmarks to watch out for. She thanked him warmly for the stew and rode away, and he followed her with his pale eyes as long as she was in sight. Widowed she might be, he thought, but not for long. Such a woman as that would have another husband soon. Somehow seeing her had increased his loneliness, for once he'd had a young wife . . . once long ago. Now he recalled too vividly what it had been like to hold her in his arms, to sleep with her, to wake up with her beside him in the pink dawn and turn over and lay a sleepy arm across her breast. He sighed and got up to move his sheep to a new pasture.

Feeling easier now that she was sure of her directions, Lenore pressed on, following the sheep trails, which indeed were almost the only roads of these Cotswold Hills. She moved by easy stages because of Snowfire's leg, riding by daylight, hiding by night in sheltered copses where she was beset by nightmares that left her white and shaken in the moonlight. She prayed that there would not be a summer thunderstorm to bog down the track and make the going more difficult for Snowfire—and she was fortunate, the weather held.

Her shoulder no longer hurt her much, and her scratches were well on their way to healing, but her food had run out and she was very hungry when in the fading light of a red sunset she reached Twainmere. People were at supper, she guessed, as she rode down the deserted street of the familiar village.

The honey-colored stone of the cottages was turned deep pink by the rosy light. But the smithy was empty, the cottage behind boarded up and deserted, the garden that had been Flora's pride overgrown with weeds. Lenore dismounted and with a sinking heart peered in through a broken shutter. The dimness showed her an empty room with a rat scurrying about. Flora's cat must have left, too. Somehow she felt the cottage had been empty for a long time.

Lenore, usually so resolute, for once was daunted. Could Flora, disheartened by Jamie's death, have packed up and gone back to Scotland? If Flora had left, Twainmere might not be safe for her. Tom Prattle would be quick to denounce her, and there'd be none who'd care to take in the town flirt, come back with a babe in her arms. Doubt twinged at her. No one had seen her yet—perhaps she should leave quietly the way she had come.

She remounted, feeling a sudden rush of homesickness for a village that no longer had a place for her. She remembered then that Robert Medlow, the young vicar —one of the few men in Twainmere who had seemed immune to Lenore's wiles—had been very fond of Flora. If anyone would know Flora's whereabouts, Robert Medlow would. She wheeled her mount and headed down the deserted street, past the churchyard where Meg slept beneath a fresh-hewn stone, and dismounted at the vicarage.

It had not changed—just as nothing in Twainmere seemed to have changed. She hesitated, then carefully placed the sleeping Lorena in one of Snowfire's saddlebags—she did not want to answer questions about the baby just now, and the young vicar was sure to ask. Lorena continued to sleep peacefully. Lenore flexed her arm, which had gone nearly numb from holding Lorena for so long, and stood studying the pleasant ivy-covered building with its yew hedge and low stone wall overrun with red roses. She had been careful to tie Snowfire to the hitching post, as well as the gray mare. For these were familiar surroundings to Snowfire, and she wouldn't want him limping down to Tom Prattle's lean-to stable, expecting hay and currying and a comfortable bed of straw!

She had rapped but once on the oaken door of the vicarage before it was flung open and Flora herself stood before her in the rosy evening light. Each was as startled as the other.

"Flora!" gasped Lenore.

Flora, her blue eyes filling with tears, held out her arms and Lenore went into them with a sob. They stood there rocking and laughing and crying. Lenore hadn't realized until this moment how much she'd missed Flora; somehow gaunt Flora had taken in Lenore's heart the place of Meg who was gone, and now here she was at the vicarage and somehow she couldn't stop crying.

"There, there," said Flora, moved. Surreptitiously she wiped the tears from her eyes as if it were shameful to cry. "We thought you'd died at Worcester, Lenore. We got word you'd been seen going into the town—at least, some wild tale; we thought it must be you from the description—but none had seen you leave. We thought you might have been buried along with—with the others."

With Jamie, she meant.

Lenore stood back, smiling through her tear-blurred eyes and catching her breath. "I wanted to stay, Flora —I wanted to bury Jamie myself. But a cavalier wouldn't

340

let me—he said I'd be taken if I stayed. 'Twas he who saved me from the Ironsides, Flora; he got me through Cromwell's lines outside the city. We ran half across England together. How is it you're not at the cottage, Flora?"

"I married Robbie—the vicar," said Flora simply.

Lenore's eyes widened. The vicar, no less! "I'm glad for you," she said sincerely.

Flora sighed. "I would have married Robbie long before this," she admitted, "but for Jamie. I felt Jamie needed me, for he wouldna settle down—and you were but a young thing. But come and sit yourself down, Lenore. Robbie's out visitin' the sick and I'm waitin' supper for him. We can have us a talk. You'll be stayin', of course?"

Lenore hugged her. "Indeed I will. And just wait till you see my baby!"

"Baby!" Flora trailed her out. "And I see you've still got Snowfire!"

Lenore nodded proudly. "But he's gone lame and needs resting." She drew Lorena out of Snowfire's saddlebag. "Flora, this is my little Lorena."

She held Lorena up for Flora's inspection, and the older woman bent down and smiled at the child—then she peered closer and her eyes widened in shock.

" 'Tis Jamie's," she whispered. "That hair, those eyes . . ."

"Yes," said Lenore in a tight voice. "That hair, those eyes—that's why my cavalier left me. He said the baby wasn't his, but belonged to the Scot."

"And he was right," cried Flora in an excited voice, bending over the baby. She looked up sharply at some inflection in Lenore's voice. "This cavalier was your lover, then?"

Lenore nodded gravely. "I'll not keep it from you, Flora. I lived with him when we were on the run, and later in Oxford where I went to bear the child. I would have married him, Flora, but—I learned he already had a wife. He left me after Lorena was born."

Pity shone in Flora's eyes. She looked at Lenore, so beautiful in the rosy copper light from the dying sun.

"You are young," she murmured. " 'Tis no more than I would expect. Young blood runs wild. But ye're scratched and bruised, Lenore. Did you take a fall?"

"Yes—a fall." Lenore did not feel she could tell Flora about all the recent things that had happened to her just now; that must wait till later. "I'd nowhere to go after he left me, and I thought of you and hoped you'd take me in."

"And you were right to come here," said Flora warmly. "Come into the house. My, it's getting dark—I'll light a candle. You must be hungry, Lenore."

"Yes, but—Flora, could I take Snowfire and the gray mare back to the stable? Snowfire's exhausted, and I'd like to feed him and water him and bed him down in the straw. I've been bathing his ankle in the streams and springs every chance I got, but 'tis badly swollen still."

"Of course. Put the bairn down on my bed—ah, she's a sweet child with a fair face!"

"She may wet your bed," Lenore objected.

"Let her," said Flora crisply. " 'Tis good to have a bairn in the house—and this one Jamie's." Her eyes sparkled, and in the candlelight dusk she looked suddenly years younger. "She's my niece, you know," she added proudly.

Together they fed and bedded down Snowfire and the gray, and Lenore tended Snowfire's hurt foreleg.

"Your gray mare looks to be a valuable horse," commented Flora.

Lenore nodded. She did not explain how she came to have the mare, who was probably stolen like the amethyst ring. She could not bear to speak of the crossroads attack, which still haunted her dreams. For now she would let Flora think this gray riding horse was a gift from her lost lover.

"You can have the small room at the back," decided Flora. " 'Tis an extra room we don't need and 'twill be a great help to me to have you about again, Lenore."

It was all Lenore could do not to cry again. She gripped Flora's hand thankfully.

Robert Medlow, the vicar, was a pleasant, vacant-faced,

unassuming young man of medium build who always seemed a bit absent-minded. In a way he seemed a strange match for tall, gaunt Flora, but when Lenore saw the way they looked at each other, she knew they were in love. There was something shy and humble in the way Robert Medlow treated Flora. He greeted Lenore with courtesy and much less surprise than Flora had, saying it must have been God's will that had spared her at Worcester—and see, here was the fruit of it!—indicating Lorena.

Lenore, remembering the horror of Worcester, thought grimly that it had indeed been God's will- and Geoffrey's will, too, for had his hard fist not rendered her senseless at Barbour's Bridge, she would have stubbornly stayed and doubtless gone to her death for it, like other hapless souls.

They made her comfortable and fed her a good supper of cold mutton and cider and berry tart. Afterward Flora led her into a little room that was better than anything she had ever had except at Oxford. That night she slept dreamlessly, even able to forget the nightmares of the road.

The next day, walking with Flora in the scented old garden with its moss roses and musk roses, surrounded by hedges of clipped yew, she paused in the shade of a May-flowering beech. "I don't deserve you, Flora," she said simply.

"Ah, that's foolishness," said Flora, flushing with pleasure. "Robbie is as glad to have you as I am."

"But to take in not only myself, but the baby, too—it's very good of him, Flora." She brushed away a lazy bumblebee that wanted to light in her hair.

"Robbie's glad to have a bairn around the house," said Flora, carefully smoothing her full linen skirt. "Since there's not likely to be one of our own." She reached down, plucked a musk rose, and cupped it in her bony hand. "The bees are all at work gathering honey. Our hives should do well this year."

Lenore blinked. "Do you not plan a family of your own, Flora?" She would not be put off by talk of bees.

Flora looked away, through the beech branches toward the north. She might have been looking at Scotland, so distant was the look in her shadowed blue eyes. "That is denied me," she said in a low voice. "God's will or man's will, it is all one—I'll bear no child."

Lenore was puzzled. "I don't understand."

Flora sighed, looking down into the musk rose as if she might somehow find the answer there. "Robbie's been very good to me," she said carefully. "He'd offered for my hand before you and Jamie were handfasted, Lenore, and I'd always said no, I must look after my wild young brother. But when Jamie died, Robbie hurried over and offered for my hand again. I said no, 'twas not proper—there should be a period of mourning—but he told me roughly we must be married right away. He was right, Lenore. Marrying Robbie was all that saved me from the wrath of the village. For there were those who claimed Jamie was a traitor who'd rebelled against the Lord Protector, and they might have whipped me through the village tied to the tail of a cart. But once I married Robbie, all was forgotten, for the people here love Robbie."

"I know that, Flora, but what has all that to do with your raising a family?"

Flora turned and gave her a level look. Her voice was wistful. "I've no child of my own, nor like to have any, since Robbie comes not to my bed."

"Never?" gasped Lenore.

"Not once." Flora sighed. "Robbie is an humble man, a man of God, and——he had a strange childhood. Robbie holds me in high esteem that will not allow a sinner such as himself to touch me."

"Robbie a sinner?" Lenore stifled a laugh. "Get him drunk," she advised. "Maybe he'll forget he's a sinner and remember that he has a wife!"

"Robbie touches not spirits," declared Flora gloomily.

"Nor women?" Lenore asked hesitantly.

"Nor women," said Flora firmly. " 'Twas hard getting used to, for my first marriage was—was not like that. My Kenneth strove with me every night and thrice got

344

me with child—though each time I miscarried. I had not thought that Robbie . . ." She tossed the moss rose away. "But now I manage to turn my mind to other things." She held out her arms and took baby Lorena and rocked the child in her arms and began to croon to her.

Lenore looked pityingly at Flora, a stiff but kindly woman, so eager to give affection, yet balked at every turn. "'Tis something I'd never get used to," she told Flora frankly. "I've need of a man's arms about me." *Geoffrey's arms,* she thought sadly. *No one else's will do. Not now, not ever.* Since those arms would never hold her again, her bed would be as cold as Flora's. Her eyes flew to the baby. Lorena would get her through it. Bringing up her child would fill her days, her nights. . . .

"Robbie's a good man," said Flora absently, smiling as the baby began to laugh and coo. "Mayhap one day . . ." She shrugged. "Meanwhile it will be almost like having my own child to have Jamie's bairn in the house!"

"Do people here still feel so savage toward those who fought for the King?" Lenore asked, troubled. "It could be they'll think that I aided—

"Robbie will tell them better, and they'll believe him. 'Twas bad here at first with neighbor suspecting neighbor and treason in the air everywhere. 'Twas worse at other villages than our own. We had no hangings here."

Lenore shivered. How often she and Geoffrey had come upon gallows erected at the crossroads and looked up and seen their grim burdens swinging aloft. "Those were bad times," she murmured soberly. Even as she acknowledged how bad those times were, she realized now they had brought her the best thing in her life—her love.

"Bad times are still with us," Flora told her in a crisp voice. "These vengeful Puritans," she said in a cautious, lowered voice, "would take the starch out of everyone. Why, a laddie can scarce make eyes at a lassie without courting the stocks! But my Robbie's a godly man, and his cloth will shield us from troubles others might have. But ye'll wear no red dresses here at the vicarage, Lenore," she added sharply. "Nor red heels, either!"

Wistfully Lenore remembered those notched red heels . . . notches for would-be lovers . . . How long ago it seemed! She followed Flora into the house, pensive.

"First ye must change your hair," Flora decided. "It may have been proper in Oxford, but 'tis outlandish here. If ye want the town to accept ye, Lenore, ye must quieten down your wild looks."

Meekly Lenore arranged her hair in as severe a style as she could. It gave her dignity but only made her more striking.

Flora peered at her and frowned. "Ye're still too beautiful, Lenore. Ye'll incite envy. Your dress, now—we'll take the lace off those cuffs. It's torn anyway." Lenore winced as the delicate point lace was ripped free and tossed aside. "And we'll replace that collar with a new one that hides you better." Flora shook her head and sighed. "Anyone would think that having a baby would have made ye heavier, steadier, but ye look like a girl still!"

Lenore was proud that should be so, whatever Twainmere felt about it, but she made no comment.

"On second thought," said Flora, studying her with her head on one side, "ye still look like a flirt. I'd best cut down this gray dress of mine for you." She pulled a dress out of a chest and showed it to Lenore. "The material is old—which will show ye're not rich. And plain—which will show the old women ye've repented."

Lenore quirked an eyebrow at Flora.

"Whether ye have or not's another matter," said Flora grimly. " 'Tis the *appearance* of repentance that counts!"

"I never made a very good impression on the village, if you'll remember!" Lenore reminded her wryly.

"We'll change all that." Flora was confident.

"Will we?" Lenore gave her a troubled look.

"Yes. Ye were a flirt then, out to make all the men want ye, out to make all the other girls jealous. Now . . ."

Now I'm a woman with a child, a deserted woman. . . . Lenore finished the sentence silently. *No longer a woman to be feared, but one to be pitied.* It was a galling thought.

346

She bent her head over Lorena so that Flora would not guess what she was thinking.

Lenore settled in at the vicarage, although Twainmere's reaction was mixed. None raised the question of her possibly traitorous acts at Worcester, for she was now a member of their well-loved vicar's household. Tom Prattle glowered and muttered whenever he saw her—but that minor irritation Lenore could ignore. The lads who had been so hot to wed her had thinned out. Two had moved to distant towns, three had married village girls, one had drowned in the river while fishing. Dick Fall and Stephen Moffat, who had fought over her by St. John's bonfire Midsummer's Day before last—how long ago that seemed to Lenore!—looked startled when they saw her. Dick Fall was now betrothed to honey-haired Mollie Paxton, of whom Lenore had once been so jealous. And big Stephen had wed a girl from the next town and gone to live with her people; it was said they had a baby on the way—he was seldom in Twainmere.

Not that Lenore would have lacked for suitors, had she shown any interest in the matter. Young Bob Sonners had lost his wife to a distemper in May—she'd been cupped and bled to no avail—and he was looking for someone to share his bed and care for their three children. Cart Moffat, Stephen's older brother, whose health had long been so poorly none had expected him to live, though he'd been treated with all manner of herbs and even conserve of violets, had finally rejected all treatment—and had magically recovered from his mysterious ailment. Now, though still thin and pale, he was casting sly sheep's eyes at village maids. And old Dunster, who had made life so miserable for his milkmaids when he was in his cups, had hiccupped and said loudly after church that if no one else wanted Lenore, he'd have her—aye, and her babe, too!

But Lenore's heart was filled forever with memories of Geoffrey. The pain of his defection was deep and searing. These were good offers, by Twainmere's standards, that she was receiving, she knew, for she was dowryless, no longer a virgin, and saddled with a small baby—but good offers or not, they were not for her. She supposed she should have been grateful for them, but she was not. These offers made her feel vaguely guilty, as if her stormy heart should have been willing to settle for something less.

Michael's fate haunted her. At times it seemed that he could not have perished at the crossroads, that she would look up and see his round, smiling face, his lively red cloak. Then she would look down at Lorena and realize that had not Michael slowed down big Tubbs— and died doing it—neither she nor Lorena might be alive today. Her world seemed ringed round with guilt and heartbreak. Some nights she woke screaming from her sleep thinking of the cutthroats who had pounced upon them at the crossroads. Sometimes she woke from bright shining dreams of Geoffrey . . . and remembered he was gone and thrust her face into her pillow, soaking it with her longing tears.

Outwardly she remained calm. She walked the cobbles and the dusty paths in her plain gray dress with eyes cast down. She was like a penitent, doing penance for sins she could scarcely remember . . . for Twainmere knew naught of Geoffrey; it was wild, golden Jamie they remembered.

She did not seek company, but walked alone . . . sometimes to the churchyard to stroll among the graves. It was redolent with the sweetness of wild honeysuckle that in summer made a riotous growth over the grave-stones. Her lovely young mother she had hardly known lay buried there, her stern carpenter father who had never loved her—and Meg.

It was Meg's grave she wept over, touching the cold stone—so new among so many mossy ones—with quest-ing fingers as if to bring Meg back. Vividly she remembered the young Meg who had been so sure life would be good to her. She shivered. She wouldn't want Lorena to end up as Meg had.

It did not occur to her that she, too, might end up as badly.

On lazy summer afternoons she sat on the churchyard's low ivy-covered wall and looked at the blue and yellow wildflowers that had burst into bloom over Meg's grave, and past it she saw the simple stone that Flora had erected for Jamie, her handfast lover, even though his body lay at Worcester in some unmarked grave. And sometimes she pondered over how different her life would have been had Jamie not belatedly remembered he was a Scot and fallen beneath Worcester's south wall. . . .

That Lorena was Jamie's she did not doubt. Her coloring was too perfect a match for Jamie's. She sighed. Geoffrey had been right about that, although it still puzzled her, for by her count Lorena should belong to Geoffrey. . . .

One day she saw the black-haired girl, Lizzie, who had giggled with Jamie in the marketplace. Lizzie was trudging past the vicarage on her way to market, carrying a huge basket of fruit. And in her browned left arm was clutched a small baby just a little older than Lorena and already with a mop of hemp-white hair and blue eyes. When she saw Lenore, Lizzie came to a sudden halt, and her dark eyes flashed.

"What a pretty baby," said Lenore in an attempt at friendliness. "Can I hold him?"

"No," said Lizzie sullenly, backing away. "And it's a her, not a him." She hurried away dragging the baby and the heavy basket of fruit.

Flora came round the corner of the house.

"Have you seen Lizzie's baby?" asked Lenore.

Flora gave her a keen look. "I have. 'Tis Jamie's." Flora's voice was gruff. "I knew he was seein' her," she said. "Slippin' over to her house in the afternoons. But ye must not feel bad about it, Lenore—'twas not in Jamie's heart to be faithful to a woman. Lizzie married Silas Tilson right after—after Jamie was killed at Worcester."

"Silas Tilson? But he must be past ninety!" gasped Lenore.

"Aye. And glad our Lizzie was to get him—so she'd have a name for her brat! I think he knew about Jamie, when he offered for her. He's not like to have any children

349

of his own at his age, and now he has a young wife and a child he claims as his." She shrugged.

"Poor Lizzie . . ." murmured Lenore, for Lizzie had had a light dancing foot.

She noticed that after that day Lizzie avoided the vicarage and reached the market by some other path.

Lenore looked about her more keenly after that. After Jamie's death, there had been a rash of marriages in Twainmere, it seemed. Lighthearted Jamie on his visits to village maids had enjoyed more than honey-cakes . . .

Mollie Paxton alone had held out—and she was being married on Thursday.

When Mollie's wedding procession filed past the vicarage on a path strewn with wildflowers and rushes, Lenore stood with her baby in her arms at the low wall watching them go by. She thought Mollie looked radiant in her russet dress, with a circlet of myrtle crowning her honey-colored hair. Mollie tossed her head and gave Lenore a triumphant look as she passed, a look that said plainly she had taken Jamie from Lenore—if only for a while—and now she was taking permanent possession of another of Lenore's erstwhile suitors, Dick Fall.

Flora came up behind her. "Find a good man and wed him," she advised, seeing Lenore's wistful gaze follow the procession. "Although 'tis true I'd miss the bairn"—her voice roughened, for she now loved little Lorena almost as much as Lenore did—"but 'twould be best for ye."

Lenore, the flirt who had gaily notched her red heels—a notch for every offer, and from all the best catches in the village—gave her a shadowed look. Was that the way to forget Geoffrey, for whose arms she longed every night?

All that first week after her arrival she had had wild nightmares when she had cried out for Geoffrey. Sometimes in those black dreams she was running lost and barefoot through endless dark forests, being stalked by terrible pursuers—Swan, Tubbs, and dark faceless demons that boiled up out of a hell that seemed near and close—behind that next tree, past that clump of thorn bushes. As she fought her way through brush and vines and low-hanging branches with her breath sobbing in her throat, she would see before her a clearing and know in her heart that all would be well could she but reach it. And just as she broke through the last of the tangled foliage, Swan would leap out to bar her way, grinning hideously. At those times she screamed for Geoffrey and woke up in a cold sweat, shaking.

" 'Tis—'tis the nightmares," she'd gasp, when Flora would burst in.

"I know." Flora was a grim figure in her nightcap, but her voice was gentle. "I've had them."

Lenore remembered Flora's nightmares, how she had seen a blood-soaked countryside before the Battle of Worcester. On one of these occasions she turned a frightened face toward Flora.

"What do you see for me, Flora?" she asked. "You have The Sight. We all know it."

Flora gave her a troubled look. "I see nothing," she mumbled. "Sometimes The Sight is given me and I can foretell a thing as clearly as if it were happening before me—but for you I do not see the future."

To Lenore as well as Flora her future was impenetrable.

At first she had planned to write to Michael's mother, had even chosen the words: "Your son died bravely. . . ." But a letter could be traced, and she had to remember that Gilbert waited vengefully in Oxford and would like nothing better than to see her on the gibbet. How could she be sure Michael's moher would not be in touch with Michael's Oxford friends, who would casually pass on to Gilbert what they had heard? She waited, telling herself that Michael's mother already knew of her son's death, for he had been felled at a crossroads marker and his body would have been found by the first passing traveler. It never occurred to her that Tubbs might have hidden Michael's body.

She had not even told Flora of her terrible experience in the woods, or of Michael's death . . . for her explanations of why she had not written Michael's mother her condolences would have brought out other painful recollections of Gilbert . . . and of Geoffrey, who never ceased to haunt her dreams.

Resolutely she tried not to think of Geoffrey, filling her days with caring for baby Lorena. She launched into the housework at the vicarage with a vengeance. She'd have loved to go to market, swinging a basket over her arm, but Flora said wisely that the people of Twainmere would have to get used to her gradually again—going to church was all right, but she must not appear to flaunt herself, Flora would do the marketing. Sometimes, left alone at the vicarage, she was plunged into sadness, remembering Geoffrey, who was—God alone knew where; he'd made it to France, she supposed, back to his French wife . . . The thought made her cry, and she cursed the day she'd met him, for she doubted her sad heart would ever be her own again.

Oh, why could he not have believed the child's coloring an accident of fate, gift of some remote ancestor? Why could he not have accepted Lorena as his? She realized, of course, how much he had counted on the baby, how he had looked forward to Lorena's birth—and what a shock it must have been to see that blond hair, those blue eyes staring up at him from her small piquant face. Well, it had been a shock to Lenore, too. She had counted up the days so carefully, and she had been so sure, so sure. . . . She smiled down at baby Lorena through her tears and the child cooed back at her. She sighed. It was all over now. Her girlhood had changed into womanhood, and her womanhood into motherhood, and she would never see her lover again.

"Don't grieve so," said Flora abruptly one day as she carried in a basket of fresh sun-dried laundry.

"I—I'm not grieving," protested Lenore guiltily.

"Yes, you are. Any fool could see it. Your life isn't over, you know. I thought my life was over when my Kenneth went a-hunting in Scotland and fell and twisted his leg and froze to death and never came back to the glen. I was sure I'd go to my death a miserable, weeping woman. But then Jamie was having so much trouble with the kirk—he being young and only wanting to be a natural man and have good times—and I found myself thinking about him instead of my own troubles. You've got Lorena—you should think about her."

"Oh, I do." Lenore gave a wan nod.

"The hurt will stop," stated Flora, so firmly that it must be a fact.

The hurt did not stop, but it abated from time to time. The community, which had been aloof at first, was beginning to accept her again. Sedately Lenore now accompanied Flora to church on Sundays. A new and different Lenore, garbed in a plain gray dress with a white linen collar—and with her flaming hair bound up tightly beneath a coif. People who had frowned when they first saw her on the street began to unbend and nod to her pleasantly. Men who at first had looked at her warily, eyeing the child in her arms, began to give her long, lingering glances again. It would not be long, Flora warned her, before suitors would come banging on the vicarage door, and Lenore would be well advised to take one of them.

But this lull in Lenore's stormy existence was not to last. Before the month was out, Flora came flying into the house on a sultry day with her face a thundercloud and grabbed Lenore, who was making a pie on the kitchen table, her linen apron dusted with flour. She grasped Lenore by the shoulder and spun her around so fiercely she knocked over the flour crock.

"Why did ye not tell me ye'd killed a man?" she cried, shaking Lenore. *"Why?"*

"But I didn't!" gasped Lenore, choking on the white cloud of flour that had arisen and borne almost back to the kitchen wall by this onslaught.

Flora, too, choked on the dust that filled the kitchen. Her face encrimsoned and she was temporarily unable to speak. Lenore beat her on the back and then ran and opened the kitchen door to let out the white cloud. She tore off her linen apron and flailed the air with it.

"I was—almost to Lizzie Tilson's, bringing her a poultice for her sick child," gasped Flora, and stopped to cough. "On the other side of the hedge I heard two men questioning Old Ben, the mute. They were angry because he wouldn't answer their questions, and I was about to call through the hedge to them when I realized they were asking about *you!* Some student was found dead at the crossroads north of Oxford. He'd told a friend you were running away together, and the friend swears you left Oxford with him. His mother says he had money on him—she believes *you* killed him for it! They traced you through a shepherd who directed you to Twainmere when you left the road and got lost. They're here to arrest you, Lenore!"

Her face almost as paper-white as the flour dust that covered it, Lenore laid down the apron. "I did not kill him, Flora," she said. "And we weren't running away together. He was on his way home to Coventry and I was to Banbury to race Snowfire at the fair. We were attacked by robbers at a crossroads. They killed Michael and—and I may have killed one of them, for I plunged a dagger into his back rather than let him harm by baby."

Flora stared at her, blue eyes blazing from her floury face. "I believe you," she said shortly. "But others will not, for no robbers were reported seen about, and the student's was the only body found. They'll ask why ye did not report it, why ye fled."

Slowly the force of that sank in on Lenore. She was trapped. Everyone would believe she'd killed Michael— lured him away from Oxford and killed him for the money in his pockets! The very fact that she'd not reported his death was a black mark against her. She could hardly explain she'd not reported it because she was fleeing treason and assault charges in Oxford!

"Oh, Flora," she whispered, appalled, "what am I going to do?"

"You must run for it," said Flora grimly. "For they'll be here soon, and I'll have no way to keep them from taking you."

The two women looked at each other.

"Lorena . . ." whispered Lenore, brushing the flour from her white face.

"Ye must leave her with me. Snowfire's leg hasn't healed well enough for a long ride and—'twas a daft idea, anyway!

Whoever heard of a woman making her living racing at fairs? Lorena will stay with me—till you can come for her. . . ." She let that trail off. "I'll find a wet nurse for Lorena and take care of her as if she were my own child. Come, Lenore, ye must pack!"

But Lenore was hardly listening. She was looking instead out the kitchen door, past the bee-haunted musk roses, past the clipped yew hedge, out at the low hills of the Cotswolds. She had hoped to lose herself at the fairs when Snowfire was well enough again to race, for the hunt for "traitors" was dying down and it was unlikely assault charges would be pressed beyond the walls of Oxford. But murder! For that they would hound her the length of England—and to deliver herself from the one trap would be to fall into the other.

She dusted the flour off her hands and swallowed. Never had she meant to give Lorena up. But—what chance would Lorena have, if her mother was on the run? It would be hard enough to make it alone, impossible with a small baby. Here Lorena would be raised with all the care and trappings of a vicar's daughter, she would learn to read and write and to cipher—arts Lenore had so recently slaved over herself at Oxford and in which she was hardly proficient. Her beloved daughter would be well-dressed and housed, for Flora would see to that.

A sob escaped her.

"There's no sense crying," Flora flung over her shoulder. Already she was throwing together meat and cheese and bread and honey-cakes into a linen tablecloth which she knotted at the corners. "You'll take the gray horse," she said. "I'll tell them you rode away on Snowfire so they'll be looking for a woman on a white horse. Tuck your hair under a coif, for it's conspicuous. I'll hide Snowfire in the woods and 'find' him later. You can be sure I'll be good to him." She turned. "Where are you, Lenore?"

Lenore was in the next room bent over Lorena, hugging the child's small body to her own and crying. She pressed a last kiss on Lorena's sweet, smiling face. Her baby . . . she was leaving her baby! Lorena gurgled and lifted a tiny hand toward her, and Lenore's will nearly turned to water.

"Lorena well may die if you take her with you," Flora warned from the doorway. "A baby cannot stand the hardships we can. Here." She thrust a purse into Lenore's hand. "This will get you gone. Seek the back ways. I'll say you went west. If ye're careful," she added gruffly, "it should be enough to take you all the way to London."

Lenore shook her head and put the purse down on the bed. "I've taken too much from you already," she said wearily, "and you will need that money for Lorena's keep. I'll take nothing with me, Flora—that way they can search the house and you'll have proof you expected me back shortly."

Flora's eyes glinted with a kind of fierce admiration. "I will insist they search," she promised. " 'Twill slow them down."

"I'd best go." Lenore fled from the room back into the kitchen. Already her arms felt empty. She had need to place distance between them. For if she stayed another minute, she'd snatch Lorena up and run away with her . . . and then Lorena might end up like those other children she'd seen in a dozen towns, children who'd once had secure homes and were orphans of the war and were now small tragic beggars on the highways.

"I'll write to you," she mumbled.

"Letters can be traced," warned Flora. "The townsfolk will not take this lightly. They'll expect you to write, and some will doubtless keep a sharp eye out. I wouldna write were I you."

Lenore expelled a ragged breath. "Very well, then I will send you money. In pincushions. Expect them—for somehow I will get it. I mean to pay for Lorena's keep."

She took the food Flora thrust upon her and hurried out the back door before her decision could crumble.

Flora followed her to the stable and offered to help her saddle the gray mare, but Lenore was traveling light. "Sell the saddle and saddlebags and buy Lorena things she needs—I'll ride bareback, I've done so before. And in my room there's a linen handkerchief beneath the mattress and in it an amethyst ring. 'Twas in the saddlebag of the gray mare that I took from the robber that I stabbed after I'd lamed Snowfire trying to escape him—'tis his horse and his ring, and I've no doubt he stole both. But I do not want the crime of stealing the amethyst ring charged against me, too, so keep the ring against a time Lorena needs the money."

Flora's eyes misted over. "You take too little for yourself, Lenore."

Lenore's delicate jaw tightened. "I have made my own troubles, Flora. I will not visit them on my daughter. She deserves more good things than I can give her."

She threw her arms about Snowfire's white neck, buried her face in his silky mane, and whispered a goodbye. He nuzzled her lovingly and whinnied as she led the gray mare from the stable.

"Take care of Snowfire for me." Lenore's voice broke as tears streamed like rain from her tormented violet eyes, "I want Lorena to have him—she'll love him as I do. And— thank you for everything, Flora."

Flora gave her a rough hug. "All will be taken care of," she said huskily. "You need have no fears for what you leave behind, Lenore."

Lenore did not answer. She couldn't just then. She swung up on the gray mare's back and skirted the garden and plunged into the trees. She did not look back at the vicarage, for she could not have seen it—the world before her, green and leafy, shimmered with her tears.

Flora watched her ride away to the east with troubled eyes. She was sure she would never see Lenore again, and her heart ached for the valiant girl to whom beauty had been such a dangerous and deadly gift. At least the bairn would be safe, for she'd care for Lorena tenderly—that much she could do for Jamie and his wild young handfast bride. Sighing, she led Snowfire deep into the trees and left him tethered by a little spring where none would find him. She gave him an encouraging pat as she left—he'd have water here, and she'd come back for him tomorrow.

When she returned to the vicarage the men who had come for Lenore were waiting for her. She pretended shock at their news, asked endless questions to slow them down, insisted they search the house, and at last told them that Lenore had said she was going to take some cakes to old Mother Greer, who'd been ailing lately—which was strange, now that she came to think of it, for old Mother Greer lived to the south of town and Lenore had ridden her white horse away to the west.

The two men exchanged significant glances and left quickly, asking her to let them know if Lenore came back. Flora watched grimly as they rode away to the west on the wild-goose chase on which she'd sent them.

The vicar had come in just in time to hear her last revelation, and he frowned as they disappeared from view. "I doubt me that Mistress Lenore was on her way to see Mother Greer, Flora. They were not on friendly terms."

Flora sighed. "She'll not be back, Robbie. The bairn is ours. 'Twill be up to us to bring her up."

The hills and vales around Twainmere were thoroughly searched, but no trace of Lenore was found. When Flora reported next day that Snowfire had limped in from the west, a new furor erupted, for it was assumed Lenore had been thrown. After a while it was believed she might have fallen into Watson's Gorge, which lay to the west, and that the dangerous whirlpool just before the river disappeared into the mountain might have sucked her body down to whirl forever in dark endless depths.

It was a fate some of the village women had once wished upon Lenore.

With Jamie dead and buried and Lenore gone under such evil circumstances—for her flight was considered an admission of guilt—her reputation was any man's game. Wild were the tales they told of her at the local tavern. Half the men in the village bragged they'd bedded her. Boys so young they'd barely have reached up to her shoulder insisted they'd spent long, wild nights with her; older men winked and muttered stories to each other and guffawed.

Mollie Paxton came to believe she'd been done out of her sometime lover—Jamie the Scot—by a veritable demon, a murderess at the least and perhaps a witch to boot, who had by sorcery lured Jamie to Worcester to his

358

doom. Married now to Dick Fall and of a garrulous nature, she fanned the gossip to flame.

Around Twainmere hearths at night they talked of Lenore, enlarging, expanding the tale with each retelling. Children listened round-eyed and then stared surreptitiously at Flora as she walked by carrying baby Lorena.

Wild young Lenore Frankford with her red dancing shoes and flame-colored hair had become a village legend.

CHAPTER 23

Her departure from Twainmere marked a time of terror for Lenore. She felt hunted as a fox is hunted, and at first was afraid to break cover lest some farmer or wandering shepherd report seeing a bright-haired woman and her pursuers start off with a fresh scent. That first day she rode as far as she dared, and when the gray horse was exhausted, spent that first night hiding in a deep copse and weeping for Lorena.

The next day was uneventful, but toward evening she heard mounted men moving about and sometimes she could hear shouted orders and curses. Hastily she retreated to a grove of beech heavily laced with thorn, where she hid the night. She had no way of knowing whether the men were hunting her (indeed they were not, but sought a rogue who had escaped the gallows in Cirencester), but she dared not take chances. So as soon as it was light she kept the gray mare floundering down the rocks of a narrow winding stream and over rocky places—in case of pursuit by dogs, though she'd heard no hounds baying—until the mare gave her such a reproachful look that Lenore felt pity for her and guided her out upon a soft green hillside, doubtless soon to be used by sheep, and dismounted to let her graze the waving green grass.

She'd avoided hamlets and taken the twisting sheep trails, and by the next afternoon, when she rode deep into a forest, she was thoroughly lost. On she blundered, seeking a high place that would give her a view of the countryside where she could find her bearings—and came to an abrupt halt at the sound of clashing swords.

She might have turned and ridden away in panic, but the sound of swordplay was promptly followed by loud laughter and a ribald masculine voice crying, "Nigel, ye do be awkward today—ye're supposed to run me through! Try again."

This startling statement was too much for Lenore's curiosity. She slid off the mare's back, slipped her bridle over a dead tree branch, and tiptoed forward to peer between some low-hanging limbs into a small woodland clearing.

There, ringed about by a small ragged company, who sat or lay at their ease as they watched, two men flailed cheerfully away at each other with swords that flashed bright in the sun. As she watched in amazement, the shorter one cried, "Aha!" and plunged his sword into the chest of the taller.

With a hoarse cry the taller one fell backward, clutching his chest while the smaller fellow withdrew his sword—amazingly bloodless—and strode away. A moment later the tall one scrambled up.

"Is that better, Monty?" he asked anxiously, addressing a man whose back was to Lenore.

"Aye," was the cool reply. "And 'twill be realistic enough when you have a bladder of sheep's blood tied beneath your jerkin to soak through and confound the audience!"

"Nigel had best not strike me too hard," objected the tall fellow, "for 'tis only a part of that sword that slides into the hilt—slippery with goose grease or no!"

"I'll be careful of your timid hide!" roared short Nigel. "Was it not well done, Monty? Was it not?"

Amid general laughter Lenore relaxed and took a deep, sighing breath, remembering the play she'd attended back in Oxford. These men must be strolling players, rehearsing their lines. And like herself, actors were outside the Lord Protector's stern law, so she need not fear them.

"Well done!" she cried and began to applaud.

All heads turned alertly toward the leafy foliage that concealed her from their view.

"It seems we have an audience!" cried the man called Monty. "And an appreciative one! Come, show yourself."

Lenore stepped boldly forward into the clearing and for a moment their voices were stilled at the sight of a beautiful woman, come apparently from nowhere into their midst.

"By the Lord Harry—a maid!" muttered Monty. He came over to her, limping a little, but a courtly figure nonetheless. Tall and thin with a shock of thick white hair that waved to his shoulders, his white beard trimmed to a point, he wore a threadbare red velvet coat with a handful of dirty lace at his throat, flowing knee breeches of tattered olive silk, and a pair of boots that seemed about to depart his legs. But his stride was vigorous, his step firm, and his stance and the look he gave Lenore marked him as one of authority--and admiration. Although he must be more than twice her age, before that admiring gaze Lenore found herself wishing she were not clothed so unattractively in Flora's made-over gray dress.

He made her a handsome leg, this old-young man, his wavy hair almost sweeping the grass as he bowed low.

"Montmorency Hogue at your service, mistress."

"Lenore Frankford," said Lenore and bit her lip. She should not have given him her right name.

"How did you find us, mistress? For we thought ourselves well hidden in this glade."

"I was not seeking you," Lenore told him frankly. "I was but passing by when I heard your voices and peered through the branches in time to see that mock duel."

"Ah, don't call it a mock duel," Montmorency Hogue

chided her humorously. "For Alan and Nigel take it as seriously as any real life contest. As you could see, they're very desperate about it! We are but a company of strolling players and have not much to offer a lady, but would you share a tankard of cider with me?" He shook his head to warn away those who would have crowded around Lenore and led her a little apart from the others. There he poured a tankard of cider for her and one for himself and set back the keg.

Lenore accepted hers gratefully. She had had only water to drink since she had left Twainmere, and she was fond of cider.

Montmorency Hogue dusted off a fallen tree trunk with an elegant gesture—and a threadbare glove—and bade her sit.

"Whence came you, Mistress Frankford?" he asked with studied casualness that belied the alert look in his green eyes. "And . . . did you chance upon anybody on the way here?"

That, thought Lenore shrewdly, was what he really wanted to know. She took a sip of cider. "Last night I heard mounted men riding by shouting to one another," she admitted cautiously.

Hogue frowned.

"But I have heard no one today," she added hastily.

It was his turn to be shrewd. "These mounted men—did you ask them what they sought?"

Lenore sat a little straighter. "No. They—they seemed to be going in a different direction."

"A different direction . . . I see." He studied her and then he laughed. "I believe it possible they were seeking *you,* mistress."

"Or possibly *you,*" countered Lenore, her eyes glinting.

He gave a courtly nod. "Either one. We are wanted for giving an unlawful performance of one of Will Shakespeare's plays outside Coventry, and we've been harried ever since. I know not why a theatrical performance should be counted so great a crime!" He sighed, downed his cider, and rested the tankard on the tree trunk. "And you, mistress?"

Lenore liked this white-haired man with the young face and keen eyes and genial smile. She took a deep draught of the cider and decided to take him into her confidence. "On the road north from Oxford, robbers attacked us. My friend was killed, the robbers got clean away—and now the law seeks me, for 'tis the general belief that I killed my friend for the money in his pockets."

Montmorency Hogue drew in his breath in a long, low whistle. "Methinks, mistress, ye are in worse case than we!"

Lenore nodded. "I am not sure I can prove my innocence, so I am in flight. Could it be"—she gave him a look of entreaty—"that I could travel with your troupe?"

His heavy eyebrows elevated. "A woman? But as you can see, we are all men in our troupe. If you have seen any plays, mistress, then you must know that young boys perform the female roles."

Lenore looked about her. "I see no one here under thirty."

He laughed. "Yes, we are all growing old. 'Tis unfortunate, but there are few new recruits for a poorly paid profession that these days must be performed on the run. There were brave days for us in the old king's time—I myself have performed at Blackfriars and at the Hope—but the Lord Protector has closed the theaters. Our clothes grow tattered and hardly keep out the winter cold, we can scarce afford feed for the horses that draw our cart, and the men of our company can afford to keep neither wives nor doxies!"

Lenore flushed. "I am not a doxie," she said tartly.

"Nor did I mean to imply it," said Montmorency Hogue hastily. "But what could you do to earn your keep, mistress? Stitch a fine seam on our worn costumes? For all here must work."

"I do not stitch so fine a seam," admitted Lenore in a rueful voice. " 'Tis not one of my accomplishments. But I could do your laundry—and there must be a great deal of it, for you are so many."

He sighed. " 'Tis another service we perform for ourselves when we camp along convenient streams and rivers. Poverty makes a man master of many callings."

Lenore felt crestfallen, but she comforted herself that she had not really hoped to join them. She rose.

"I thank you for the cider," she said. "And I will be on my way."

"No, stay a moment." Montmorency Hogue was considering her thoughtfully. "Could it be you know the way to Cirencester, mistress?"

"I have been to Cirencester," admitted Lenore. "Once. To a fair. But now I am quite lost. If I could but climb to the top of a hill and perhaps see where I am—"

"No matter, I will point out the way. You see, we have been waiting for our advance man all week."

"Advance man?"

"Aye. We have a man who goes ahead of us and prepares the way. He arranges for our lodgings, he finds a place for us to hold the performance, he feels out the land to see if the authorities keep too fierce control and we should shun the place and seek another—and he makes arrangements with one or two good men in the community to let out the word in the right quarters that a theatrical performance is to be held."

Lenore gave him a look of surprise, and he said grimly, "Did ye think plays were impromptu affairs, mistress? Much careful planning do they take in advance—and now with the law stalking us, even more so. Will Summers is our advance man, and he has been gone these two weeks to Cirencester, where we are to perform *Twelfth Night* . . . we hope. Will should have been back a week ago, but we have heard naught from him. Our faces are too well known in Cirencester for any of us to go and seek him there, in case aught is amiss. But we would give you money for your food and night's lodging in Cirencester, and shelter and protection to the next town we visit after Cirencester, if you would go in and see what is keeping Will."

"It could be. that my face would be known in Cirencester also," murmured Lenore. "Yet I would do it if—do you perhaps have a costume I could wear? Those who

365

seek me will have a description of what I wear and know the color of my hair."

Montmorency Hogue rose. "That I can." He led her to a high-sided cart. "We cannot afford costumes for the male parts," he admitted frankly. "We wear our own clothes, whether we play *Julius Caesar* or *King Lear* or *Hamlet*. But for the female parts the men don dresses. We have needle and thread—you can baste one up to fit you. And I think we could find you a black wig."

He was pawing through a large wooden chest as he spoke, spilling out laces and tinsel, an orange-plumed hat and a broken fan. He straightened up holding a gown of yellow satin garnished in copper lace. It was stained at the hem, but Lenore looked at it wistfully—how beautiful it must have been when new!

He watched her finger it lovingly. "It would not be wise to wear so bright a gown to Cirencester, mistress," he chided gently, taking it from her. "This would do better." He pulled out a costume of widow's weeds complete with a heavy black veil. "This veil will hide your features well. And this wig—though it may sit a trifle askew until you have gentled it a bit—is yours as well." He handed her a tousled black wig and a coarse wooden comb. "And when ye return from Cirencester with word of Will Summers, we'll have a brown wig for ye, and ye can wear the yellow satin then."

Lenore knew that was subtle bait to ensure her return, for he could not know that she would keep her promise; with lodging-money in her pocket, she might well continue her journey in the opposite direction. She smiled her thanks, knowing no way to reassure him—but something in her steady eyes managed that very well. He found her a needle and black thread, dug into his pocket, and gave her some coins—she suspected his store of them was meager— and waved his arm at the trees. "Your dressing room!"

Lenore retired into cover of the foliage. And when a little later she paraded out before the company in her somber mourning garb—the black gown basted with big stitches so that it outlined her delightful figure—and tossed back the black curls that now fell down over her ears, there was a general round of applause.

"None would know you, mistress," approved Montmorency Hogue. "And Will Summers will be easy to remark. He will be laying over at the Ox and Bow, for he was once on friendly terms with the innkeeper's sister—before she married a man with a less chancy profession. Will is of medium height and very florid—his nose is as red as a cherry. He will be wearing an orange coat, for 'tis the only one he possesses, and he has long stringy hair the color of butter. You might pretend to be his niece seeking him. Will professes to be from Torquay and has many nieces." He grinned.

"I will find him," promised Lenore. Indeed, how could she miss him, she wondered—a man who looked like that? "Is it your wish that I should start out now?" She cast a longing look at the cookfire at the edge of the clearing where two of the company were roasting venison.

"Nay, tomorrow is soon enough, for we want no mishaps on the road. It could be that Will is taken, and the law must not be led back to us. You understand?"

Lenore nodded her black curls soberly, for his admonition had reminded her that her present assignment was not without its dangers.

That night, ringed around a campfire, the company feasted on venison, and Monty and the others told her stories of the great days when they had worked at Blackfriars Theatre, built on the ruins of an old monastery—or the Swan or the Globe or other open-air theatres. Monty bragged of knowing Will Shakespeare, dead more than thirty years, and the others chimed in. For most of these men had spent their lives on the boards; they had been boy actors or had come of acting families.

In their company for a little while she was able to tear her mind from Lorena—was she happy, was she smiling, did she—and this very humbly—did she miss her mother? Lenore knew such thoughts were useless, for the die was well cast, but they tormented her just the same.

Monty fixed her a bed in the wagon and promised kindly that she would not be disturbed. She took his meaning and gave him a rather trusting smile. She slept well, not feeling a need to stay alert lest something pounce on her in the night.

She waked once at the cry of an owl, night-hunting.

A white moon cast its frosty light upon the forest, silvering the little clearing. All were sleeping but one; hands clasped behind his back, head bowed, Montmorency Hogue walked back and forth. She had learned enough this night to know that the responsibility for this company lay on his shoulders and that times were indeed hard for them. She liked him and thought that no matter how many summers lay behind him, he would never truly grow old.

The sun and sounds of stirring around the campfire's ashes woke her the next morning. Automatically she reached out to make sure Lorena was all right—and pain struck through her that her baby would not soon lie in the crook of her arm again. By the time she could come for her, the first bloom of babyhood would be gone, and Lorena would look to Flora, perhaps, for mothering—not Lenore.

Lenore lay there in the morning sunlight with her eyes squeezed shut, willing tears not to trickle down her face. And that morning she swore a great oath to herself: she would not look back. As soon as she could, she would go back for Lorena, but she must not waste her energy in grief, she would need all the strength she had to make her way in the world so that she could have her daughter with her again. She refused to let Geoffrey enter her mind—but he was there, always, in her soul, in her broken heart.

She ate a companionable breakfast, with the company, of cold venison and cider. Before she had finished, some were already hard at work learning their lines, practicing their swordplay—or the jigs the whole company performed between acts. They looked very merry as they pranced about the green, and they gave her a rousing cheer as she mounted up.

Feeling well fed and with her horse fed and refreshed, she set out for Cirencester along the path to which they directed her—a black-haired woman well disguised in her widow's weeds. Many roads since time immemorial had led through the Wold to Cirencester: the White Way which led to Winchcombe, and the great Salt Way—and when she had lived in Twainmere, Lenore had ridden both of them. But now Lenore caught the Fosse Way, which had been built by the Romans on an ancient Celtic track, and which led from Exeter to Lincoln and passed Cirencester en route. So deserted was this stretched of blue-stone road as it wound through what Will Shakespeare had called the "high wild hills" that she passed but one village before she rode out of the leafy green woodlands, predominantly of ash and elm and beech that would flame to red and yellow come September, and saw ahead the towering perpendicular spire of Cirencester's beautiful cathedral-like church with its famous peal of twelve bells.

Though she had been there but once, to a fair with Meg, Lenore remembered Cirencester well. Lenore could not have told you that this had once been the lavish Roman city of Corinthium, wrecked by the Saxons at the end of the sixth century—but she knew where the Ox and Bow was. The ruins of the great abbey she could see—and regretted its state of disrepair—and she had once been told that the city had been taken during England's Civil War by Prince Rupert. But Cirencester's rich past was far from her thoughts as she rode in; what interested her was the tall-hatted Puritans who walked or rode by, studying the woman on the gray horse with interest. Lenore looked down, intently studying the road, for any of them, she feared, might remember having seen her at some time—in fact, there might be among them someone from Twainmere.

Deciding it was best to take a bold course, she rode directly up to the Ox and Bow—thankful, at least, that this was one place she was not known. She dismounted, strode into the common room, drank a tankard of cider, and inquired of the innkeeper about her "uncle," Will Summers, who had arrived here some two weeks past. Her own husband, she declared with a deep sigh, had recently passed away, and she was seeking her uncle, who would "know what she should do."

The innkeeper's sympathy was aroused at once. He was

more than helpful to the lissome young widow who asked his aid so prettily. Regretfully he informed her that Will Summers had indeed stopped here. He had seemed of good health, he had drunk deep of the claret, eaten generously of the leg of lamb, and more than generously of the plum pudding—and that night had complained of great pains in his stomach and chest. Though the doctor had been hastily summoned, Will had died—and since none knew where his relatives might be that they could notify them, he had been hastily buried in an unmarked grave as a pauper. Will had once said he lived in Torquay; did he still have people there?

Lenore murmured that she would let them know.

Will's clothes and the few coins on him had not fetched enough to pay for his burial, the landlord promptly explained but Will had had a watch he always carried, and the landlord had saved it in case any relatives showed up looking for Will.

Dabbing at her eyes—for she pretended to be much affected by the news of her "uncle's" death—Lenore suggested that the landlord's sister might like to have it as a keepsake; "Uncle Will" had been very fond of her.

The landlord brightened and refused to take any coin for the cider and urged on her a pasty and a joint of meat. Regretfully Lenore refused this offer. She had managed to down the cider gracefully, holding the veil so that it concealed her eyes, but she would have to throw aside her veil to eat, and this would expose her face to the curious view of the inn's patrons. She was, she choked, too upset to eat a bite, but she thanked him deeply.

As she remounted the gray mare, her mind was racing ahead.

Will Summers's death in Cirencester would indeed be a blow to Monty. With their advance man gone, the troupe would be in desperate trouble. Will had apparently had no time to make any arrangements, had died, in fact, the very night he arrived. She could turn about, of course, and ride back the way she had come and bring the disappointing news to Montmorency Hogue.

Or she could make the arrangements herself! With

mounting excitement she rode the gray mare to a public horse trough and let her drink. Why should she return with bad tidings? Why should she not make the arrangements for the performance herself? There was an old stone barn outside town where illegal cockfights were held. She and Meg had stopped by there once for a dipper of water from the farmer's well on the road to the fair. The farmer—a pleasant round-faced man in his forties—had been enchanted by the two pretty girls from Twainmere and had leaned upon his pitchfork and engaged them in conversation in the midday heat. He had even unbent so far as to bring them a tall pitcher of milk which had been cooling in his springhouse, and Meg had twitted Lenore all day about her "conquest."

That barn, which was easily reached by a good road, yet was isolated, would make an excellent theatre—far better than the barn where she had attended a play in Oxford. Its stone walls gave coolness against the muggy summer heat, and—she would do it! If the arrangements were successful and Monty approved them, he might let her take over Will's job—she would be able to earn her keep, she could even in time look forward to having Lorena with her again!

Seething with excitement, she guided the gray mare out of Cirencester on the road to Twainmere. It made her uneasy to be heading so directly for Twainmere, for anyone from Twainmere might well recognize her gray horse—even if they did not immediately identify the rider—and she was glad when, without incident, she saw over the next rise the roof of the big stone barn she remembered so well. That the farmer would recognize her, she had no fear, for her widow's weeds and black wig were a good disguise. She could tell him her late husband had frequented his cockfights and so feel him out about holding a play there. He must be well acquainted, he could circulate the word and so procure the audience!

As she approached, she slowed her pace to a demure jog, mindful that in her widow's weeds it would seem odd to dash up at a great speed. In the distance she could see the farmer's wife washing goose feathers to stuff a featherbed, and a couple of bright-eyed little girls who seemed to be leaching wood ashes for lye to make soap. She was growing anxious, for she did not wish to speak to the woman and children about this, and she could not remember the farmer's name. But just then arround the corner of the barn walked the farmer, a bit plumper than she remembered him, and she greeted him.

He came politely over to the side of the road, and she told him she was riding out "for the air" since her "good uncle" had died as well as her young husband, and the black hangings of her room made her mournful. The farmer nodded and asked her who her "good uncle" and young husband might be, would he perchance know them?

When she replied hesitantly that her young husband was from Bath and had died there, but that her uncle was named Will Summers and had been staying at the Ox and Bow, the farmer looked surprised. "Aye, I knew Will," he replied. "And I am sorry indeed to hear of his death."

"Then—then you knew how he earned his livelihood?"

"Aye—he did arrange for plays to be held."

"I—I knew you used to hold cockfights here," she ventured, hoping the little breeze that had sprung up would not blow back her veil, for he well might remember her, might have heard indeed that the law was looking for her. And if a reward had indeed been offered, she would not care to put any man to the test—he might seize her and haul her to the nearest authorities, even though some of his own doings would not bear looking into.

"Aye, I held them. Until last year. Then the authorities closed down on me and did put me in the pillory. See this eye?" She peered at a long, jagged scar that ran from his eyebrow past the corner of his eye and down his cheek. "Someone did throw a rock at me while I was in the pillory and I near lost my eye!" He went on vengefully denouncing the Puritan authorities, and Lenore felt the time was ripe.

"Would you let our players hold a performance here in your barn?" she asked him bluntly. "For now that Will Summers is dead, we have no one to take his place. I rode in for news of him."

"You are not Will's niece, then?"

"No, I never knew him. I come from Montmorency Hogue."

The farmer reached down and pulled up a grass blade, bit into it, and spat. He appeared to be thinking.

"Aye—I might," he said at last. "For you see yon feathers my wife washes? Two geese run down by coaches within a week! My barley crop ruined by blight. No cock-fights in more than a year—I'm hard put to rub two coins together! Yes, I could give ye shelter for the players, a place to perform—and I could arrange for the audience, too, for I've but to pass the word around!"

She had chosen the right man! Lenore was congratulating herself when he gave her a sudden sly look. "Of course, I'd need some money now to get me started. . . ."

She hadn't expected that. She hesitated. "Monty never expected anything like this to happen. All I have with me is lodging-money for the night. I could give you that, if you'd let me sleep in your barn and have a bite of bread and cheese for supper."

"Ye can sleep in the barn," he said shortly, "and ye can eat with us. But the money's not enough."

Desperate, Lenore promised him a share of the profits and told him they'd be ready to perform three days hence —she hoped it was true the troupe would be ready and prayed Monty would find the deal reasonable. If not, she was out the lodging-money and would have spent the night in a barn for nothing.

The farmer seemed so mollified by the share she had mentioned that she wondered fearfully whether it was too large.

"Come in and sup," he said.

Lenore bethought her that he might remember her face if she took off her veil; a careless word that she'd been seen in Cirencester and they'd be after her again, hound her to her death.

"I—I have a rash on my face and do not wish to be seen," she objected.

" 'Tis not a pox, is it?" he cried. "We want no pox here, mistress!"

Lenore sighed. "Actually 'tis bruises from a cuffing my

373

husband gave me when I wanted to join up with Monty's troupe. I am ashamed—I will have no one staring at me."

The farmer peered at her suspiciously. Muttering to himself, he went back to the farmhouse and she noticed that he brought out her food himself—his wife and daughters stayed within the farmhouse. She breathed a sigh of relief and ate hungrily the thick clotted country cream, the fresh berries, the wholesome brown bread and thick slab of cold mutton that he brought her. After eating she climbed into the loft and slept while below her the gray mare bedded down contentedly, having eaten her fill.

When morning came, she downed a hasty breakfast of barley-cakes and a big tankard of milk and departed with a bag full of apples to eat on the way. She'd slept later than she meant to, and she had to ride hard to reach the woodland glade, where the troupe waited, before sundown.

Monty strode to meet her when she rode in. She threw back her veil and slid from the gray mare's back.

"What news?" he demanded.

"Bad news, I'm afraid," said Lenore, and told him of Will Summers's death.

Monty was stunned by the news, and around him the others gathered, muttering. There was a general air of consternation.

"We'll miss Will," said Monty slowly. "We've known him for a long time."

"What will you do now?" asked Lenore.

"Will's death means we must have a new advance man," he said, running a hand through his thick white hair. "And there are none of us who do that well." His green eyes looked sad. "I would hate to disband the troupe."

"You've no need to," Lenore told him. Amethyst lights flickered in her violet eyes, and her voice held an undertone of suppressed excitement as she outlined the arrangements she had made.

An amazed smile broke over Monty's face. "I cannot believe it," he said. "We have found our new advance man —and she is a woman!" He turned to the others. "I think Will himself could not have done better. Are we not agreed that Mistress Lenore should be our new advance man?"

374

There was surprise on every face as they looked at Lenore. Then heads began to nod.

"It is agreed!" cried Monty. "And if there's enough money from the performance in Cirencester, we'll erect a stone to Will!"

There was a murmur of approval, and Lenore smiled at Monty—she approved of erecting a stone to Will, too.

So a strange new occupation opened up for Lenore. As "advance man" for a troupe of strolling players, putting on clandestine Shakespearean plays in stern Puritan England, she had need to use her wits. The varied disguises their wigs and costumes gave her helped considerably. Sometimes she rode into a town in the guise of a tavern maid, seeking employment; sometimes as a lady with a plumed hat and lace—albeit a bit mended—at throat and cuffs; sometimes—as at Cirencester—as a widow in deep mourning garb. Although her activities were known, none could really identify her.

The beauty from Twainmere had found a new profession.

And it was well she had, for with Geoffrey's loss and the stunning additional blow of having to desert Lorena—and no matter how good the home where she had left her, Lenore considered that she had indeed deserted her daughter—ice had locked around her heart. The bitterness she had felt as a girl toward men—and which had made her a shameless flirt—now hardened into a cold inner hostility. For Lenore, Geoffrey's abandonment was the first bitter blizzard in a long, cold winter of the heart.

She did not take a lover. If the troupe found that odd, they kept their silence about it because Lenore was so valuable to them. And, too, she was seldom with them, because as soon as a performance in one town was arranged, she must be off to another town to arrange the next one.

She journeyed openly into towns, always with a new story and differently garbed. Sometimes her wig was red, sometimes brown or black or even pale as honey. Her beauty quickly gained her the confidence of men, and she made arrangements for the players' performances to be held swiftly and well. As time went by, the troupe came to consider her their lucky charm.

Her share of the profits was not so much as she had hoped. Although she often wore fine clothes and even stayed at good inns, the troupe was always beset by money problems, and Lenore always remembered that she—and they—were outside the law. She must not attract too much attention lest she be too well remembered. She must not form lasting attachments . . . the rules of the road were harsh.

Still she earned enough that sometimes she could send pincushions with a few gold coins stuck inside, to Twainmere by way of travelers crossing the Wolds. It was dangerous, and she was careful never to send letters, but Flora knew whence these coins came and bought Lorena pretty clothes and bright ribbons for her hair.

Monty would gladly have taken Lenore to his bed. She knew that from the way his green eyes glinted as they followed her, from the timbered resonance of his voice when he spoke to her, from something indefinably protective in his manner—more than from anything he said. But Monty, too, was interested in keeping the services of a superb "advance man." He made occasional overtures—a gift of a pair of sheer silk stockings or beribboned garters, the offer to share a bottle of sack with him when they were in funds. Lenore talked to him companionably as an equal, but she did not share his bed.

Sometimes when she rode into camp after a long, hard, dusty ride, and heard his pleasant melodic laugh ring out, she asked herself why. Why could she not love him? She liked him, she admitted honestly to herself that he attracted her, that she might even be happy living with him, but . . . Monty's way of life was precarious and she knew she could never have Lorena with her if she became his mistress.

There was another reason, too—Geoffrey. Her love for him, so deep and real, acted as a barrier between her and other men, a high wall that she could not climb over even if she wanted to. Bitterly she reminded herself that Geoffrey was the past, which was over, but something young and stubborn in her heart would not have it so. She was being true to Geoffrey—but she would never have admitted it.

Nights when she longed for Geoffrey's arms, and to hold little Lorena to her breast again, Lenore tossed on her pillow at strange inns and fought back the urge to write to Flora, to send for her child, or even to ride boldly into Twainmere and take Lorena and Snowfire away with her. But in the sleepless gray light of dawn she always realized her folly. Her life on the road was dangerous and impermanent. She could provide no proper home, no proper friends for a growing child. Perhaps it would not always be so; she could pray and hope for a better day. A day when she would be reunited with her golden daughter; hoping that love could one day reclaim her heart . . .

BOOK
III

THE
LONDON
WENCH

PART ONE

THE KING'S DOXIE

London, England 1660—1662

CHAPTER 24

It was the last of May, and a great day for England. For on Friday just after dawn King Charles II—who had fled from Worcester in defeat nine years ago—returned in triumph to his homeland. In beautiful clear weather he landed at Dover and knelt on the beach to give thanks. His journey to London was a triumphal march. Cheering crowds lined streets hung with garlands of ribbons, and scarves and spoons, and even silver plate.

Having banqueted at noon on Tuesday with the Lord Mayor, the scarlet-robed aldermen, and numerous notables whose gold chains glimmered against the black velvet of their clothing, the young King was at last ready to enter his capital. And at half-past four the mighty procession poured over London Bridge and into the City, where costly tapestries festooned the streets and the conduits ran with claret.

In the jostling crowd along the Strand, Lenore Frankford waited for the procession to pass. Her thick, red-gold hair had been carefully combed into a shining coil at the back, while fashionable long side curls reached down to her shoulders. She was dressed in the best she owned—an amber silk gown with a low wide neckline which showed her gleaming white shoulders to great advantage. Her tight bodice hugged her round breasts and tapered to her narrow waist, and her billowing skirt was slit down the front and tucked up at both sides to reveal a full petticoat of rippling russet satin. From beneath her full skirts peeped a pair of dainty square-toed shoes with high yellow heels.

The effect was so striking that of the many admiring glances she'd received as she hurried to join the crush along the Strand, few had noticed that her dress had been cleverly mended in several places, that her petticoat was threadbare, or that her high-heeled shoes were badly worn. Who would guess that she wore one glove and carried the other because it was too badly stained to wear? For the woman in the amber silk gown would always command attention. When a tall man with a cane elbowed her with a curt, "Sorry, mistress," in an attempt to get a better position, Lenore turned and looked at him. Looking down into her lovely face, he had said softly, "Sorry, indeed!"

Lenore was used to these tributes to her beauty, for she was as slim and as lovely as the day she had ridden out of Twainmere, seven years ago. Her complexion was as sheer and fair, her glorious violet eyes had the same heart-stopping quality, and her swift, blinding smile still dazzled the viewer.

But the years had given Lenore other things—a sense of style which she had not had in Twainmere, and a certain hardness of viewpoint. She had not made her way easily, and often she'd endured hard times, but she had never once given up. Now she stood on the Strand in the full flower of her beauty, looking a woman of molten gold in the sunlight.

Nearby hawkers cried their wares—little cakes and pies and other sweetmeats. People shouted to one another and leaned out the windows from above. In the distance now came the sound of trumpets and hooves. The procession was approaching, and the crowd strained forward.

Beside Lenore, a stout little woman pulled her small

daughter back from the street. "Look where those pikemen are standing, Sallie," she told the child. "That was where Charing Cross stood until the Ironsides tore it down! Well, the new King will put it back, you'll see!"

Lenore's gaze flew to the company of six hundred pikemen who waited to parade before the new King. All London, she knew, had mourned the loss of Charing Cross, erected in 1290 by Edward I as a memorial to his dead Queen. A lovely monument to love, destroyed in the struggle between the Ironsides and the King. Just as in another way that struggle had destroyed *her,* she thought with a fine sense of detachment . . . first Jamie, then Geoffrey, and finally Lorena had been wrested from her. And now the bachelor Charles was returning to London to ascend his throne—bloodlessly, by invitation!

Shouts and applause dinned in her ears, for the procession was in sight now. Three hundred horsemen flashing drawn swords in the sun and wearing scintillating cloth-of-silver doublets led the way. They were greeted by a mighty roar. Many other companies followed, and Lenore was pushed this way and that as people shoved each other and craned to see better. Now came the trumpeters, adding to the din, and eighty red-garbed sheriff's men, the silver lacing of their cloaks aglitter. And now the City Companies rode by, with liveried footmen attending them. From the windows ladies richly gowned leaned out waving scarves, their eyes bright. For England was to have a King again, a tall, handsome King—*and* he was a bachelor!

Buffeted and pummeled by the exuberant crowd, her pretty shoes trod on painfully more than once, and with several black and blue marks where she'd been elbowed, Lenore watched the great Companies ride by almost in a blur. So much . . . so very much had happened to bring her to this day. Now, with the crowd around her going wild, her own life seemed to pass before her in review.

After her first triumph at Cirencester, she had settled into her job as if she had been born to it. Montmorency Hogue had bragged that she was the best "advance man" in England! She had bethought herself always of the safety of the troupe of strolling players who depended upon her

—indeed, one mistake on her part could bring them to ruin. Early on, she had learned to be crafty in her choice of men to deal with in strange towns; she had learned to study men across a tankard of cider, or from beside the public horse trough in the village square—and to assess them for what they were. Her beauty—impossible to disguise—had been a mixed blessing. Often she had found it necessary to fight off unwelcome advances—once or twice with the aid of a large pistol. She had done her work unstintingly, making sure the towns she chose were "safe"—if anywhere was safe for such as they. She had even managed to save a little money and had dreamed of emigrating to the Colonies and taking Lorena with her—the old dream she had shared with Geoffrey.

When in September of 1658 Oliver Cromwell had died, her heart had leaped in hopes that the King would be restored—and she would be cleared of at least one charge they could raise against her; she could no longer be called a traitor to the Puritan regime. But Cromwell's thirty-one-year-old son Richard had succeeded him, and nothing was really changed. Dancing was still forbidden, alehouses were still closed on Sundays—and constables could still forcibly enter people's houses and search them for evidence of breaking Sabbatarian laws. Celebrating Christmas was still forbidden. . . .

But not only Lenore, all of merrie England was heartily sick of grim Puritan ways. Morris dancing and May Day games—even archery and cockfighting—had never been stamped out entirely in the villages, and although there was now a death penalty of adultery, juries all over England were refusing to convict accused adulterers. Nationwide there was a rising revulsion to stern Puritan repression.

In 1659 rumors were rife. The King was living in the Spanish Netherlands, holding his impoverished court at Brussels. Tall, athletic, good-looking and cynical, at twenty-eight he was more popular with the English people absent than was Richard Cromwell present. Monty ran his fingers through his white hair and his young-old face showed pent-up excitement as he told Lenore enthusiastically that it was just a matter of time—England would turn the fierce Puritans out and there'd be plays again, and dancing, and general merriment. She'd see!

What Lenore saw was something quite different.

On a quiet Thursday she rode into Winchester, casting about for the most likely sporting inn that would furnish information of the kind she needed. And scarce had her arrangements been made before she received word that somewhere on the road Montmorency Hogue had been recognized by a magistrate who passed by in a funeral procession—and he and his entire troupe had been taken. Lenore rode back at a gallop to try to help, pretending to be a bereaved sister of Monty's. He muttered in his jail cell that she should save herself—he and the others were like to be transported, if not worse.

Lenore, who had come to feel indeed that she was Monty's sister, had taken an emotional farewell of him. But she had taken his advice and ridden for London. She had arrived there on a bitter winter day—and found the city torn by riots. Strife had broken out all over England; the country was fast sinking into anarchy.

Monty's troupe of strolling players had avoided the larger towns through fear of arrest, and Lenore was amazed at the size of London. A city of some four hundred thousand souls, it was a warren of narrow streets and winding unpaved alleys, muddy, filthy, with no proper drains and continually weeping waterspouts and roof drips which drenched the hurrying passersby long after the rain had ended. Smoke from the "sea coal" and fog from the river combined to make the air a dirty soup, and coughing and consumption were rampant. Overcrowded and noisy, rat-infested, whole families were crammed into single rooms, and the poor and the wretched overflowed damp, dark cellars.

But it was an exciting place, for careening coaches and hurrying horsemen and people afoot filled the streets and, weaving between them, sedan chairs carrying great ladies and bewigged gentlemen who took snuff.

Lenore was enthralled by it. Like any visitor from the country, she took in the sights, staring in amazement at the great hulk of St. Paul's Cathedral and the mighty Guildhall, so huge they dominated the City's other buildings. Wistfully she studied the great Banqueting Hall at Whitehall, before whose handsome windows a great scaffold had been erected and Charles I beheaded there. It seemed to her an unnecessary indignity that the King should have been forced to climb a scaffold looking into the windows where he had so often dined, but she was even more shocked to learn that the lovely Tudor palace at Greenwich had been converted by the irreverent Commonwealth into a biscuit factory. The inns of London were still jolly places—if one had money to buy food and drink —but sometimes at night Lenore dreamed of the gaiety that must have been here before the Puritans came.

Lenore, who had saved a little money but had no real vocation, had decided to take lodgings and see which way the wind blew—commonwealth or monarchy. For surely, she told herself, the issue must be decided soon—England could not hang poised on the brink forever. She settled in at the George in Southwark near London Bridge, where another lodger, a Mistress Potts, took an immediate liking to the lovely young newcomer with the dazzling smile. Mistress Potts was a fat, garrulous woman in her midfifties who spoke in stage whispers and nodded her head significantly at her own remarks. She'd been widowed in Brighton and had sold out and taken her "widow's mite" and come to London to live out her days. She had no deep convictions about king or commonwealth, and since she received letters from friends scattered all about England— people she had met while they vacationed in Bath— Lenore found her a good source of news.

The weather was so cold that December that the Thames, its flow slowed by the great piers that supported London Bridge and the houses that lined it on both sides —froze bank to bank, and a great Frost Fair was held. Stalls were set up on the ice selling food and souvenirs and fancies. Lenore bought for Mistress Potts a slip from a printer's booth bearing her name and the imprint "The Thames," which Mistress Potts—temporarily bedridden by a cold—exclaimed over and hung on the wall of her room.

By the end of January there was open talk of a Restoration. General Monk, at the head of a large force, had crossed the Tweed—word reached London that his troops had waded knee-deep through snow and icy water in Northumberland, but he had reached York and then Nottingham. Lenore chafed at the delay. If England was going to become a kingdom again, she wanted them to get on with it.

Although several men at the George showed an immediate interest in her, Lenore gave their advances her habitual cold shoulder. Coolly she returned the stares of hot-eyed men and admiring youths who stripped her with their eyes and brushed on by them, intent on her own affairs. This was Geoffrey's legacy to her . . . she still, in her heart, considered herself his wife. It would have galled her to realize that she was a one-man woman and was being faithful to him all this time, but it was so.

Mistress Potts leavened Lenore's time of waiting with gossip. She was one of those women who were certain every man she met intended to rape her. The stable boy, she whispered hoarsely to Lenore, had patted her bottom as she passed by him in the stable! Imagine! She had not told on him, for if the innkeeper knew, it well might cost the stable boy his job. Indeed, what were young men coming to?

Since Mistress Potts was nearly as broad as she was tall, and panted as she waddled about, Lenore thought it more likely that Mistress Potts's posterior had been caressed by a saddle hung from a beam or some other likely dangling implement as she lumbered by, but she forbore to say so. Mistress Potts was always so happy with her near-brushes with lascivious disaster.

"You should not go out on the public streets without a mask," she reproved Lenore. " 'Tis dangerous to do so! There are footpads about—and worse!"

Lenore sighed. Although it was true that many ladies wore masks at popular public gatherings—such as execu-

389

tions—she had always been quite happy to go about bare-faced. But when in late January Mistress Potts presented her with a face-mask like her own, Lenore took it—and accepted Mistress Potts's invitation to sup with her at the Swan in Fish Street. Since it was a fine, sunny winter day, marred only by the smoke from the sea coal pouring out of the chimneys, they walked there by a circuitous route. Along the way Mistress Potts kept nudging Lenore and loudly whispering that this fellow in the broad hat, or that one with the great beard, was attempting to attract their notice—and wasn't Lenore glad she'd worn her mask for this public outing "as proper ladies do"? Lenore was glad for quite another reason: Mistress Potts's stage whispers of imagined advances was attracting amused attention. With her face red above and below the mask—which left most of her forehead and her lower face below the eyes exposed—Lenore quickly interrupted to point out buildings of no possible interest, children playing with wooden swords—anything to distract Mistress Potts from her favorite subject.

At Cheapside Mistress Potts was distracted by something else, for there the rioting apprentices had set up a gibbet. She paused to exclaim over it, but Lenore seized her arm and forcibly hurried her on.

"But 'twas interesting!" Mistress Potts kept wailing. And later over their feast of marrowbones and loin of veal at the Swan, her round face grew avid, and she whispered loudly, "Think you there will be a hanging in Cheapside?"

Lenore gave her a quelling look. She had seen enough of gibbets, of bodies dangling at the crossroads, when she had ridden with Geoffrey after the King's defeat at Worcester.

"Oh, well!" said Mistress Potts in a huff. "If you don't *care* to know what's going on!" But a moment later her interest had shifted. "See that gentleman in the purple coat with gold buttons over there?" she hissed. "He is making eyes at me!"

"Is he?" murmured Lenore absently.

"Indeed he is! Well—I suppose he has given up, since I have not condescended to notice him," she said, as the gentleman rose and left. "Do try the tart, my dear—and these prawns and cheese are delicious!"

But memories were eating at Lenore. Memories of a dark sardonic face and arms that had held her close, memories of long languorous nights spent on the lonely wilds of Dartmoor, and an interval at Oxford when she had thought nothing could separate them, nothing mar or damage their love for each other. Her heart wept, and she shook her head at the great tart and hardly touched the prawns and cheese.

"I've been meaning to tell you," confided Mistress Potts. "You know that man in the blue coat who sits in the common room at the George every night smoking a pipe?"

Lenore, roused from her reverie, gave her a puzzled look.

"The man with the sharp-pointed nose and the very strange boots," elaborated Mistress Potts. "I think he comes to the George to watch you, Lenore."

"I think he comes there because he has nowhere else to go," said Lenore flatly. "He seems lonely and speaks to no one."

"But that's the worst kind! Mark me, he'll bear watching. I've seen him turn his head and look at you when you weren't looking!"

"Mistress Potts," said Lenore whimsically—for she refused to call her friend by her first name out of deference to her age—"you do me too much credit. Not all the men I meet are interested in me—some have very satisfactory wives or mistresses at home!"

Mistress Potts bridled. "Those that won't heed timely warnings may end up badly!" she said in a tart voice.

Lenore sighed. She had already ended up badly, by her way of thinking: deserted by her lover, out of touch with her child because charges of being a Royalist and a murderess hung over her head . . . she really did not fear the man in the blue coat, or anyone, for that matter.

Mistress Potts's concern for Lenore's threatened virtue became so obsessive that Lenore was almost relieved when, on the last day of January, the tense city's—and Mistress Potts's—attention was diverted by a public hanging at Tyburn.

The culprit was a woman who had disposed of her un-
wanted child by placing it in a large covered pot and taking
it to a nearby bakehouse to be baked. When the horrified
baker discovered the child, there was a public outcry.
Mistress Potts had talked of little else for days. Her *child!*
Imagine doing that to her little baby!

When Lenore heard about it, she felt physically ill and
promptly turned down Mistress Potts's eager suggestion
that they watch the convicted murderess "dance" at
the end of a rope at Tyburn. But shy Mistress Potts
outwitted Lenore, and asked Lenore to accompany her on
an errand to High Holborn, where they stood with a large
goggling crowd watching the hanging cart go by. Lenore
stared at the dazed, terrified woman and clenched her hands
and thought of Lorena. Thank God Lorena was safe with
Flora, who would love her and keep her—both because
Lorena was Jamie's and because Flora was Flora. And because Lorena was *hers.*

" 'Tis not too late to reach Tyburn and see her swing if
we hire a chair!" cried Mistress Potts, fired by the sight of
the condemned woman standing in the cart. "And there'll be
seats for ladies for hire at Tyburn, I'm sure—though the
lucky ones will watch from their coaches!"

"Perhaps she is not guilty," said Lenore coldly.

"Nonsense! Who else would place her child in a pot?"

"Her enemies," Lenore said soberly. The searing thought
had come to her that people believed *her* a murderess, too!
Perhaps this poor woman . . . she could not bear to look
at the cart any more and turned away abruptly. "I do not
feel well," she told Mistress Potts. "You go on to Tyburn—
I think I will go back to the George."

By the first of February the City seemed calm again—
until suddenly the next day the unpaid soldiery quartered
near Whitehall blazed into mutiny and stormed Somerset
House. There they mounted seven guns and threatened to
blow up Parliament. Joined by a mob of seven hundred
angry apprentices, they marched through Cheapside until
dispersed by cavalry, with some forty jailed.

On the third of February General Monk's troops, five

thousand strong, marched down Gray's Inn Road into London.

Mistress Potts said admiringly that a general who would march his men three hundred miles through snow and ice water could handle anything—even London.

Her assessment seemed true. Amid a wave of mutinies which seemed to break out spontaneously everywhere, General Monk calmly took possession of the Tower of London. He ordered the handsome city gates and portcullises destroyed and took up headquarters at the Three Tuns in Guildhall Yard. When he decreed that the present Rump Parliament should not sit later than May 6, the City went wild—for this meant the young King far away in Brussels would soon be restored to his throne. Bonfires lit the streets, all the bells were rung, and amid the clangor and smoke everyone choked and slapped one another on the back and drank the King's health. Amid a wave of public whippings and executions, General Monk moved into Whitehall, and Tuesday, February 28, was celebrated as a day of public thanksgiving.

Mistress Potts was jubilant. From a seesawing middle-of-the-roader she had become overnight an ardent Royalist. Wasn't it wonderful? she beamed. The King would be on his rightful throne again, he'd be coming home—all the way from Brussels!

Lenore gave her a somber look. That meant Geoffrey would be coming home, too, for she had no doubt he was with the King in Brussels. She knew she should bestir herself to find employment but a strange lethargy possessed her, a feeling of waiting. . . .

March was a month of heavy rains, and on March 20 the swollen Thames overflowed its banks. Lenore fought her way home to the George against a strong east wind. They were rowing boats down King Street, she noted. She came in wet and shivering, to find Mistress Potts leaning back in the common room, filling the whole of a chair with her girth and toasting her square-toed shoes at the hearth. She waved a letter at Lenore and told her in an excited whisper that the soldiers in Dunkirk were drinking the King's health openly in the streets!

Glumly, Lenore tossed off her wet cloak and warmed herself by the fire. She hoped the King would come soon, for her money was running low. When she had arrived in London, she had had nearly enough for passage money for herself and Lorena, but now she would have to find a way to earn more. Somehow she had expected this change from commonwealth to monarchy to come overnight—with Cromwell dead, the King would immediately be restored to his throne. But the political machinations had dragged on for a long time.

It was some comfort that elections were at last being held and amnesty discussed. The two official newspapers had hastily changed their names; then there were rumors of a riot in York. But just when things finally seemed to be settling down, Lambert—who everyone felt was capable of raising a revolt—escaped from the Tower. Lenore had it from Mistress Potts that a lady had smuggled a silk ladder into Lambert's cell and he had made it down the wall into a waiting barge—while the girl, who'd received a hundred pounds for her efforts, had crawled into the prisoner's bed attired in his nightcap—and so they had found her in the morning! Mistress Potts tittered at this, but Lenore wondered uneasily what would happen to the audacious girl, who was now in custody.

The City was tense now. Chains had been set up, and three regiments stood guard. By Good Friday it was learned that Lambert had been cornered in a house in Westminster and escaped in a coach wearing a woman's dress and a mask. But on Easter Sunday he and the troops who had risen with him were defeated, and Lambert was once again a prisoner.

Lenore's interest quickened when late in April there was an attempt to reopen London's closed theatres—but this move was quickly stopped by the Council of State as being premature. Lenore, thinking sadly of Monty and his dedicated troupe of players, agreed with Mistress Potts that it was too bad—and joined her in watching Lambert brought by in a coach with two of his officers on his way again to the Tower. Lenore shivered as she watched them pass; it was sad to be a prisoner.

The new Parliament assembled, and on May 1 England was again declared a monarchy. That night was bright as day, for London was lit by bonfires end to end. Maypoles (which had been forbidden under Puritan rule) were set up everywhere—even the King's flag was hoisted atop a maypole at Deal, where the fleet lay at anchor, and the castle guns fired a lusty salute.

Not till May 4 at Breda did the young King hear the news. He was champing at the bit when the following Tuesday he was again proclaimed at Whitehall. Amid much pageantry, with the sheriffs in scarlet and the Lord Mayor in crimson velvet gown and hood, a joyful procession wended through the streets to the Old Exchange. Everywhere was the King proclaimed. The fourth time was in Cheapside, where Lenore and Mistress Potts stood in a great crush of people. All the bells in the city began to ring, and the shouting around them grew so loud that they could not even hear Bow bells rung. Mistress Potts lost her heel and limped home with Lenore as the proclamation was read at the Old Exchange. They reached the George as the guns from the Tower fired a salute. That night was lit with bonfires and no one could sleep for the merry clanging of bells.

It has happened, thought Lenore. *It has really happened. The King will set sail at last. And . . . Geoffrey will accompany him.* Her violet eyes grew dark at the thought, and an involuntary shiver went through her. *Geoffrey would be coming home . . . she would see him again. She knew it.*

It seemed almost anticlimactic when Mistress Potts received a letter saying her stepsister had died in Oxford and left her a fustian blanket and a down bolster. She read the letter aloud dramatically, standing in the common room of the George.

"Will you go to Oxford to the funeral?" asked Lenore soberly.

Mistress Potts looked up and shook her head. "Nay, we've not seen each other for years—but the fustian blanket and bolster were my mother's, and we made a pact that she could use them whilst she lived, but I was to have them on her death. Besides, I wouldn't want to miss the King's return to London—oh!" She sounded disappointed. "I missed this part! It says here that when the King was proclaimed at Oxford on Thursday, the conduit ran claret for *hours!* The Mayor gave away hundreds of bottles of wine, and barrels of beer were set up in the streets—and a hundred dozen loaves were given to the poor!"

Lenore thought sardonically that Mistress Potts was wishing her stepsister had died last week so she could have attended both the funeral and the festivities in Oxford at the same time. Oxford . . . she had tried to keep that town of honey-colored spires and wrenching memories from her thoughts.

Channel gales postponed the King's embarkation, but at last on May 22 the sun burst through, and at four o'clock the following day the fleet set sail and anchored at Dover two days later at dawn. The young King went down on his knees on the beach and while the shore guns fired in salute, he thanked God for bringing him safely home again.

And then began the triumphant march to London—from Dover Castle to Canterbury, from Rochester to St. George's Fields, where the Lord Mayor of London waited, and on across London Bridge through cheering, tapestry-hung streets, toward Whitehall.

Lenore, standing in her threadbare mended finery in the crush of the Strand, watched them pass and thought of Worcester, of those who had gone and those who would return.

The kettledrum and five trumpets were passing now, the noise deafening. And now the Lifeguards, and more trumpets. Lenore had eluded Mistress Potts, who had intended to view the procession near London Bridge. If she should see Geoffrey ride by, she thought she might burst into tears and . . . that would require explanations.

Now the City Marshal, the City Waits, and all the City officers were filing by, splendidly garbed, now the red-robed sheriffs and the aldermen—complete with liveried footmen, heralds, maces. Now the Lord Mayor with sword upraised—and with him General Monk and the Duke of Buckingham.

Lenore took a deep, ragged breath and felt her heart must

stop. Geoffrey should be somewhere among the group about the King. She stood on tiptoe and clawed her way forward to get a better view, for the crowd had gone wild, waving scarves and cheering and screaming. That sudden outburst had to mean the King had come into view.

Ah, now she could see him. It was the King, flanked by the Duke of York and the Duke of Gloucester. The King, his trim, athletic figure clothed in a dark suit of cloth, his hat waving with scarlet plumes. Lenore studied him somberly as he passed. She had seen him once before, charging across the field at Worcester, his black curls flying, a flash of diamonds at his chest. Frantically her eyes searched among the King's close friends, riding by. That tall man in the wide-brimmed hat, could that be Geoffrey? The light was shining in her eyes. No—he was blond. Perhaps the man in rich blue velvet riding between a cavalier in scarlet and one in gold-emboidered satin, she could not see him—ah, there he was looking around; it was a handsome face, but it was not Geoffrey's.

One by one she watched them ride by, until there were no more to see. For seven long hours she had stood on her high heels in the Strand watching the procession. Now at last she settled back from tiptoe to stand flat upon the sidewalk. Many cavaliers had returned with the King but—Geoffrey was not among them.

She turned away with an ache in her throat, not waiting to see the six hundred men of the City Companies ride by with their footmen. She had seen enough.

He must be dead, then, she thought sadly. For if he were alive, Geoffrey would have returned to London with the King. Perhaps he had never made it to France after all. . . .

Through tapestry-hung streets, past people giddy with joy and staggering from wine, a sad Lenore made her way back to the George. She found Mistress Potts waiting for her.

"Where've ye been?" she demanded of Lenore. "I've been afraid ye'd miss the party!"

"Party?"

"All London will have a party this night!" declared Mistress Potts. " 'Twill be a sight to see!"

And London did have a party. It went on for three days and three nights. Mistress Potts urged a mask on Lenore and they went out into the streets together, trailing by innumerable bonfires, seeing innumerable effigies of Cromwell burned. Everywhere, there were barrels of beer and wine, wine, wine—one foreign envoy kept a fountain of wine spurting before his very door.

Numbed, Lenore allowed herself to be dragged through these revels by energetic Mistress Potts. But when the festivities dragged to an end—mainly through the exhaustion of the participants—she sat in her lonely room with her head in her hands and at last admitted to herself how much she had been counting on seeing Geoffrey again, that it was the real reason she had lingered in London all this time.

Mistress Potts did not know the reason for Lenore's despondency, but she tried to cheer her. She brought daily bulletins of the athletic young King's doings. On Sunday he had played his favorite game—tennis; now he had taken up river bathing and every evening went with the Duke of York as far as Battersea or Barn Elms to swim.

When she learned that on a Saturday the King had touched six hundred people for "the Evil," Mistress Potts hurried to the Banqueting House on Monday to be touched. She returned with a white ribbon bearing an angel in gold which the King himself had placed around her neck. There'd been two hundred and fifty people there, and she urged Lenore to procure a ticket from the Royal Surgeon in Covent Garden—though, she added regretfully, there'd been such a crush that 'twould only be done on Fridays now.

Lenore was roused to hysterical laughter. As if a King's touch could excise the evil which had so long beset her! But she listened to the gossip that garrulous Mistress Potts had brought back from the Banqueting House—that not only the King but his brothers were hot in pursuit of beautiful Barbara Villiers—and she a married woman, wed to Roger Palmer! Mistress Potts was thrilled. Lenore said dryly that royalty was seldom *not* in hot pursuit, and Mistress Potts tittered inordinately.

But Mistress Potts's talk of the King's touch alleviating

evil had set Lenore thinking. It was said that all those who had helped the King during the days of his defeat and exile were hastening to London to claim rewards—and that he was giving them rewards with a lavish hand. Of course, she had never really *done* anything for the King, but . . . was she not known as the Angel of Worcester? And had she not suffered for it?

She took a walk to think about that, and as she passed the Queen's Head Inn she was hard put to avoid a limping man who stumbled on the cobbles and nearly plummeted into her. Instinctively she put out a hand to help him and as he regained his footing and turned to thank her, she realized that she was looking into the face of Montmorency Hogue, the head of the company of strolling players for whom for so long she had been the "advance man."

"Monty!" she gasped, and hugged him.

Monty Hogue, who was older and thinner than she remembered him, his face lined and weathered, was almost knocked off balance again by this onslaught.

"Mistress Lenore!" he cried. "I'd ne'er thought to see your face again!"

"Nor I yours, Monty! Word had it you'd been transported, that all the troupe had been. How come you to London?"

" 'Tis a long story," he said, and she saw that his cheeks were sunken and sallow; whatever his experiences, they had aged him. "We might have been let off with a light sentence, but I've a sharp tongue in my head, and I flayed the magistrate with it. We were transported right enough. The rest were sent to Barbados, but I was shipped to Virginia, where I was indentured to an elderly planter. He'd a mind for frivolity, and at supper I would entertain his guests with recitations. He was so pleased with me that when he decided to return to England he brought me with him. He died of bad food on the journey, but when his will was read, he had freed me of my indenture and left me fifty pounds to boot!"

"Then you're staying in London, Monty?"

"Nay, I was even now on my way to take a stage westward. I'm for Stratford, where I hope to assemble a troupe of strolling players again. And you, mistress, how do you fare?"

Ah, how she wished he would ask her to go with him. "I fare well enough, Monty," she said soberly. And then, with hesitation she asked, "Will you be needing an advance man, Monty?"

He gave her a look of sympathy, but he shook his head emphatically. "Nay, Mistress Lenore, that I will not. England is changing for the better, now that the King is restored to his throne. There'll be no need of advance men making clandestine arrangements to hold a play. We'll wander about the country with our cart and hold our plays in any likely place. 'Twill be like the old days when the old King reigned!"

She felt rebuffed. And yet—why should Monty go to the expense of using an advance man if he did not need one? "I wish you well, Monty." She smiled at him.

"I know that." He wrung her hand, his own thin and bony. It somehow hurt her heart to see how old he had become. Transportation had changed him, it had erased the youth from that buoyant young-old face, and now—like a dry leaf—he was blowing to the west. If she had thought he would rally her as he had once done, his twinkling eyes and merry manner urging her to his bed, she was mistaken. Wryly she asked herself if she had hoped to be asked to go along as his mistress, mending the costumes for the troupe—and perchance mending her own heart as well.

But . . . Monty was a part of her past, the only part she still dared cling to. "Will there not be plays in London, Monty?" she asked wistfully. "Could you not stay here?"

He shook his head. His voice was bitter. "The Puritans have ruined the theatre in London—at least for now. There's no good place to hold a play! They pulled down the Globe, and sent soldiery to wreck the Salisbury Court and the Fortune and the Cockpit—and five years ago they even pulled down the Blackfriars, saying they needed the space for tenements!" He gave a short laugh that was more like a bark. "No, I'd like to take you with me, Mistress Lenore, but acting is a man's profession in England—though if you could get to the Continent, women play the female roles there."

"I'd not thought to become an actress," Lenore told him ruefully. "Nor have I the funds to reach the Continent if I had!"

Monty took out a large gold watch. "My patron left this to me, as well," he said. "And it tells me that I must hurry if I'm to catch my stage. Good health to you, Mistress Lenore."

"Good health, Monty."

He limped rapidly away, and Lenore stood looking after him a little sadly.

The encounter had taught her one thing: a road which she had thought still open to her—not with Monty's disbanded troupe, but with some other troupe of strolling players—was now closed. She felt caught in a vise of despair that would never release her.

CHAPTER 25

The next day she applied for a job in a baker's shop— and got it. It paid little, but offered lodgings above the shop and meals with the baker's family. She was able to give up her room at the George, which she could no longer afford.

But Mistress Potts did not desert her. She huffed and puffed from the George down to the hot, low-ceilinged room where Lenore, a big white apron almost enveloping her dress, her arms sometimes white with flour, sold heavenly smelling loaves of bread.

Mistress Potts deplored Lenore's leaving the George, and her visits were always sprightly. Did Lenore know there'd been so many duels in London the King had had to proclaim against dueling? Lenore dusted off her floury arms on her white apron and said with amusement that she hadn't known it—very few duels had been fought over her of late.

Mistress Potts missed the irony of that and rushed on. Did she know Mister Milton's books had been declared treasonable—and Mister Goodwin's, too? They were both in hiding! And had she heard of the capture of the cleric Hugh Peters? He'd hidden in a certain Mistress Peach's bed —and she with a child born just two days before! The searching officers hadn't wanted to search the woman's bed, of course—and Peters had got clean away! But the next day, she added regretfully, they'd caught him, and now he was in the Tower. Had Lenore any news, or was she so buried under this mountain of loaves she never heard anything?

Lenore smiled and received payment for a big loaf of bread. She turned to Mistress Potts. "I did hear that peace had been proclaimed with Spain."

"Peace? Oh, yes, peace." Mistress Potts made a gesture shrugging off war and peace as trivialities. "But did you hear the Duke of Gloucester died? Of the smallpox, they do say! Well"—as Lenore was once again busy selling loaves—"I suppose I must go if I'm to be home before dark. The traffic in London is terrible these days—hackney coaches everywhere, they'll run right over a body! You must come and see me when you've a day off, Lenore."

"I will." Lenore smiled and watched her go.

That fall London buzzed, for the men responsible for beheading the new King's father were rounded up and tried —most of them were executed at Charing Cross. Mistress Potts hurried over to tell her that Anne Hyde had given birth to the Duke of York's baby! And in Parliament a great debate took place on a bill that would prevent married women from leaving their husbands. A Mister Walpole stood up and said that if the bill were passed all the women in England would surely leave!

Lenore felt downcast. With all the wild revelry of Restoration London about her, she was in as bad case as ever—worse even, for she was busy at her job from morn to dark and eked out a bare living. Though no one could charge her now with being a Royalist, she could still be brought to trial for murder, and she was no closer than ever to sending for her daughter.

She, who had always been so buoyant, now found herself pensive as she worked, ignoring the bright-eyed overtures of the elderly gentleman from across the street who bought enough bread for a household of eight, though he lived alone. He bought it a loaf at a time, lingering over his purchase. The jaunty married man from the next block she ignored, too, for since Lenore had come to the bakery, he had taken over his wife's duty of buying bread and never failed to try to rally the bright-haired woman who sold him the fresh loaves. The only man she talked to much was the soldier who had lost a leg at Worcester—no matter he'd been fighting on Cromwell's side, Lenore felt a kinship with him, for he'd been but a green boy dragged into the battle—and when he left to join his relatives in Nottingham she missed him.

In November Mistress Potts showed her a new book she had purchased called *The Horn Exalted: Or, Room for Cuckolds*. Mistress Potts tittered that it was very bad indeed—she had promised to send it to all her friends. London was uneasy now; even the carpenter who'd built the old King's scaffold had been arrested, and Oliver Cromwell's body had been disinterred from Westminster Abbey, where he'd been buried with such ceremony, and he'd been hanged in his coffin at Tyburn and reburied beneath the gallows.

The weather, in tune with the times, was wild; the Thames had overflowed its banks again, and Mistress Potts complained she had had to be rowed in a boat through the streets of Westminster when she went to visit a friend. A plot against the King was suspected, and forty men were imprisoned, and the Commons was rewarding many of those who had aided King Charles in his escape from Worcester (several had received a thousand pounds).

Anne Hyde, now Duchess of York, was holding court at Worcester Court, but Mistress Potts whispered the King's mother still refused to accept her! Lenore wondered how she felt about the King's mistress, Barbara Palmer.

On Christmas Eve the King's sister died of the same disease that had killed her brother—just when all believed her out of danger. But not even a royal death could stop the merriment of Christmas celebrations in England—so long forbidden by law. And although it looked to Lenore as if she was going to have floury arms and handle fresh-baked loaves for a long time, that Christmas was a bright spot for her.

That winter of 1660–1661 was a snowy one, and Lenore, now that the baker's wife had had another child and needed quarters for a wet nurse, was forced to give up her lodgings above the shop—although the baker granted her a small increase in wages to compensate. She moved into cheap, tiny lodgings with a grim view of the walls of Bridewell Prison—a workhouse and prison for women. Sad, pale-faced women entered those gates—and sometimes left in carts for burial. Every day it was a grim reminder to Lenore of where she could sink if her past was uncovered, and a reminder that she must take care not to entangle Lorena in her life— even though she never ceased to yearn to hold her child in her arms again—lest those grim walls enclose them both . . . and then Lorena could be torn from her to spend her young days in an orphanage, many of which were only slightly less harsh than Bridewell Prison.

But spring came at last. At Whitehall new earls and barons were being created right and left for the forthcoming coronation. And on St. George's Day in April, King Charles strode through Palace Yard over cloth of blue to the throne in Westminster Abbey and was crowned with St. Edward's crown by the archbishop. Salvoes from the Tower guns proclaimed him throughout London.

From the bakeshop where she was preparing hugh crocks of dough for the next baking, Lenore looked up as those guns sounded. Her face was flushed, and she looked tired. Crowds had come to London for the coronation, business was booming, and the baker and his wife had left her with only a small boy to help her and gone to stand outside the Abbey and view the notables. They came back talking excitedly of all they had seen, "so many fine gentlemen in great plumed hats riding prancing steeds," but Lenore turned away sadly and finished her backbreaking work. Out of all of Charles II's train, there was only one fine gentleman she had hoped to see—and she had waited for him in vain for seven hours at Charing Cross.

"The King will marry that Portuguese Princess—you'll see!" The baker's wife wagged her head at her husband and critically sampled a roll. "Not that she's a beauty or will bear him children!" Her voice was contemptuous. "But for the dowry!"

Hardly listening to the baker's mumbled answer, Lenore stumbled as she finished carrying the last of the great crocks of dough.

"Here, let me take that." The baker stepped forward. "Ye must be tired."

"A little," admitted Lenore, wearily brushing back a lock of damp red-gold hair. "I've been at it for sixteen hours!"

Too tired to go home, she fell asleep at once on the pallet the baker's wife graciously provided on the floor of the bakeshop. And dreamed of Portugal and princesses and of Geoffrey, who was never coming home.

The baker's wife proved right, for in June a wedding treaty was signed with Portugal—King Charles would marry the Infanta, Catherine of Braganza. Vast sums were said to have changed hands.

Lenore had lost her job at the bakery, for the baker's wife had angrily accused her of seducing the baker when she had found the two of them crouched by the oven. That they had only been picking up pieces of a broken crock made no difference—she had flared up and discharged Lenore. Lenore might have argued the point and got the baker to keep her, but she knew it was only a matter of time till the sturdy baker did indeed bear her to the earthen floor, for he'd been harder to handle of late, slipping up behind her for a sly pinch or a quick bear hug. The baker's wife had near caught him at that more than once—indeed, it was a sudden ill-timed pinch that had made Lenore drop the crock of dough!

But honest jobs were hard to come by, even for a beauty like Lenore. She worked briefly at several jobs, and for a short, terrible time was even reduced to being a laundress at Moorfields, scrubbing all day and spreading out the clothes to dry on the ground! If only she could have unlocked her heart to one of the many men who wanted to care for her, but Lenore was like a widow in permanent mourning. She wanted only one man—the one she'd never again have.

From this work the pretty laundress rebelled and in the fall found a situation as housekeeper in the home of a widowed mercer. The elderly widower was enchanted with Lenore and twice proposed marriage. She might even have considered it, for it would have meant she could have Lorena with her, and in a prosperous household where she would be well brought up—but the mercer's two elderly sisters were forever stabbing questions at Lenore about her background which made her fear the past would be all raked up again if she sent for Lorena. She managed to hold the mercer off, for—except that London had a heavy smog compounded of fog and sea coal smoke which coated the furnishings with grime—the job was an easy one, and she liked his younger children. But at Christmas his two elder daughters came home from school, were briefed by their aunts, and promptly schemed to be rid of Lenore, for they feared she might become their stepmother and—as the aunts had whispered—when their father died, turn them out.

Lenore, feeling herself secure in the mercer's regard, ignored their enmity in the rush of preparations for the holidays. On Christmas Day, Lenore—who felt the mercer's family would be happier celebrating Christmas alone—accepted an invitation to share Christmas dinner with Mistress Potts, whose health had been poorly of late. As she left, wrapping her warm brown shawl around the russet linsey-woolsey dress she had managed to procure with her earnings, the mercer's eldest daughter slid up to her in the hallway.

"Where did you say you came from, mistress?" she asked Lenore in her high-pitched treble.

Looking into that sly face, framed on both side by dangling corkscrew curls that flapped about like a spaniel's ears, Lenore came instantly alert. "I said I came from Winchester," she said lightly. "Where I worked for the Wynants on Candle Street just off the High."

"That is strange," said the girl, cocking her head so that her curls wagged and eyeing Lenore with bright inquisitive eyes. "For I asked Gwen Custer, who lives in Winchester, and *she* never heard of the Wynants."

"Perhaps," sighed Lenore, "they did not move in the

same circles. Or perhaps they have moved away. *I* never heard of Gwen Custer."

The mercer's daughter looked confused, and Lenore walked briskly out of the house before she could be asked any more questions. But the incident had sobered her. It had reminded her that—favored servant though she might be here, she was still a wanted woman, with a murder charge hanging over her head. Her past could still catch up to her.

She hardly heard the sleigh bells that rang in the cold snow-washed air as she headed for the Hart and dinner with Mistress Potts. Around her children munched sugarplums and hot roasted chestnuts and played at snow forts and threw snowballs—other people's children. Was she never to have her own beside her?

To be free of the charges against her, she knew she would need a royal pardon—for she did not feel she could trust the courts. She had fled—and that would be counted against her. She might well end up on the gibbet. Lenore was determined she should have that royal pardon.

Thrice she had attempted to gain an audience with the king—though she was not sure exactly what she would have to tell him. Thrice she had been turned away from Whitehall—indeed, there had been several snickers when the good-looking baker's girl had told them she was the Angel of Worcester.

"Claims to be a phantom!" someone had said in a hollow, sepulchral tone as she left, red-faced, the last time. And someone else said, "A fine, juicy piece she looks to me, and no phantom! Someone should bed her down and she'd forget to pretend she's an Angel and be content with earthly delights!"

Grimly, Lenore had decided she would see the King in spite of his minions. Although she tried at Hyde Park—and was nearly knocked off her feet by a prancing horse and then by some footracers for her pains, and though she haunted Whitehall for a while, she did not see the King.

When she reached the Hart, she found Mistress Potts waiting—and ready to chide Lenore for not wearing her face-mask through the streets. Lenore warmed herself at the hearth of the common room, smiling at Mistress Potts's running summary of London gossip, and then sat down to share with her a hearty supper of roast stuffed goose and plum pudding. Afterward she hurried home to the mercer's through falling snow, listening to the merry sound of bells and Christmas carols from jolly groups of carolers.

But for all the merriment and idle gossip and drinking of toasts, Lenore had learned something useful from Mistress Potts.

"You're trying to see His Majesty in the wrong places," shrewd Mistress Potts had chided her, for she knew of Lenore's futile attempts to get into Whitehall. "The play's the thing! The King's always there at one theatre or the other—and usually with his mistress, Barbara Villiers!"

"Barbara Palmer," corrected Lenore dryly. "She's married, even though she may not be working very hard at it."

Mistress Potts ignored that. "Rumor has it the King's going to make her husband an earl!" she declared vivaciously, and immediately launched into a long-winded tale of how the gentleman in the blue coat—did Lenore remember him, the one who smoked the clay pipe by the fire?—had tried to seduce her to his lodgings, doubtless for immoral purposes, but she had fended him off!

Lenore smiled politely—Mistress Potts must indeed have recovered her health to be so exercised about her virtue! But her mind was racing ahead. At a play . . . of course! Why hadn't she thought of it? She'd heard, of course, that the new King had given Royal Patents to Thomas Killigrew and William Davenant, both of whom had been playwrights in the old King's time, in the hope of getting London's theatres started again. These two companies were known respectively as the King's and the Duke's; the King's Company was performing at the old Red Bull while building their great new Theatre Royal near Drury Lane; the Duke's Company performed in the Salisbury Court Theatre while they remodeled Lisle's Tennis Court in Lincoln's Inn Fields. If she merely waited outside the theatre, she would be able to see the King as he entered—and somehow manage to speak to him.

All the way home that night she planned how she would

go about it, and the mercer's daughters were surprised to see how preoccupied she was, hardly responding to their best-directed barbs.

On the next day that a play was to be given, Lenore dressed in the amber silk gown in which she had watched the King's procession enter London. It was shabbier than ever, but the fit was just as snug, and if one did not look too close, the effect was dazzling. Studying her reflection remorselessly in the mirror, Lenore decided the neckline should be lower—this was, after all, a King noted for his appreciation of womanflesh. Frowning, she managed to lower the neckline a bit so that it showed an even more extravagant sweep of milky neck and shoulder and the pearly tops of her round breasts. The mercer had objected to her taking the afternoon off, for he had declared his gout was most painful today. He sat stiffly in a high-backed Spanish chair with his gouty leg propped up on velvet cushions, flanked by his two elder daughters, clad in rustling taffety. Both girls—so glad to be rid of Lenore on Christmas Day—now glared their disapproval of this "desertion" of their father in his hour of need.

But Lenore was used to these bouts with gout. She was aware that the mercer was already bored with his children home-for-the-holidays and was merely being pettish about her leaving.

"I am sorry," she said with decision, "but I must not be late for my appointment." She did not say with whom, but she stopped and studied the mercer, who might be suffering more than she thought. "On my way home, would you like me to ask the barber-surgeon to call?"

"No need," replied her employer testily, adjusting his leg with a groan. "I'll probably have lost the leg afore that!"

Lenore gave him a look of mild amusement. He'd been irritable when she went anywhere of late; it occurred to her that his sisters might be inventing tales about where she went—and with whom. No matter, that could not be helped —she must be at the theatre well before the opening hour.

"Anyone could tell she has a lover, Father," she heard one of the mercer's daughters whisper as she left.

Lenore paused, wondering if she should take the time to

410

refute that, decided against it, and hurried out into a strong biting wind. She wrapped her heavy shawl around her and hoped she would not break her neck on her high wooden pattens on the icy streets. Her breath frosted the air as she made her way to the Red Bull in St. John's Street where the newly organized King's Company was giving a play. There she waited, standing in the cold outside the theatre.

When the King's coach arrived, Lenore tensed. Courtiers and great ladies brushed by her, carelessly shunting her aside. But when the King—tall and wearing his preferred black, with a sable-lined cloak—stepped from his coach, Lenore stepped forward, too. As he approached the entrance, she darted swiftly between the courtiers to reach him, tripped over a dress sword worn by a courtier in silver-embroidered velvets, and sprawled at the surprised monarch's feet.

"Here, wench! What are you doing?" Rough hands assisted her to her feet.

"Your Majesty," panted Lenore, her shawl at her feet, her bright hair tumbled from her fall, and one shoulder of her dress pulled down even further by the jerk to her feet one of the courtiers had given her. "I have been trying for months to gain an audience with you!"

The King paused and his cynical dark gaze studied that impudently bare white shoulder, the sheer lovely skin of her pulsing throat, the large pleading violet eyes under their fringe of dark lashes, the saucy figure and general look of dishabille. "Such diligence should be rewarded," he murmured flippantly, and turned to the courtier in silver-embroidered velvets over whose sword Lenore had tripped. "Tomorrow at two. See to it, Ramsay."

Lenore curtsied deeply and managed to retrieve her shawl. Beside the King a richly gowned woman gave Lenore an irritable look and then swept on beside His Majesty. The courtier, Ramsay, remained. "Your name, girl," he demanded curtly.

"Lenore Frankford."

"Be at Whitehall tomorrow at one o'clock. You will be admitted."

"But the King said two," pointed out Lenore.

Ramsay gave her an angry look. His great periwig

411

trembled with disdain. "Do you think His Majesty will wait for you? 'Tis you must wait for him! One o'clock, I say—and mind you be not late!" he finished testily and hurried on in an attempt to catch up with the King's party.

"*I'll* not keep ye waiting, pretty wench!" cried a drunken voice, and Lenore turned to see a beaming young apprentice, reeling from too much beer and carrying a shilling for a cheap seat. "Ye can sit on my knee and watch the play!"

She laughed and shook her head. Jubilant, with her shawl clutched around her against the cold, she hurried back to the mercer's through a lightly falling snow. He looked up sourly as she entered. "And what tale will we have now?" he demanded in a vinegary voice.

Lenore was too happy to be upset by his heckling tone —or by his daughters, giving her malicious looks from their chairs beside him.

"I am to have an audience with the King," she announced. "At Whitehall. Tomorrow at two."

The mercer's jaw dropped. One of his daughters dropped her embroidery, and the other stuck her finger with her needle and cried out sharply.

Lenore would have turned to go, but the mercer's stern voice called her back. "I have been too lenient with you, mistress," he declared, and Lenore thought bitterly that his daughters must have rehearsed him in this speech. "And these wild tales must cease."

"But it is true," she explained patiently. "I do indeed have an audience with the King."

One of the taffety-clad girls laughed contemptuously. "Audience with the King, indeed! More like a stroll in the park with some likely apprentice with a strong back and a soft head!" she scoffed.

Lenore swung about to give her a crushing response, but the old man was trying to struggle up. His eyes were flashing with rage and suspicion. " 'Tis easy to see ye're deceiving me, taking advantage of my good nature!" he rasped. "So now 'tis an audience with the King, is it? I think not, mistress. And I think that ye will be at your duties tomorrow at two—yes and after, at your duties till well after sundown!"

412

Lenore sighed. She had really liked the old man and was saddened that his daughters had managed to place this wedge between them.

"Then I will be leaving you tomorrow," she said soberly. "For the King I must see."

His face suffused with color and he fell back into his chair looking so disconsolate that she felt real pity for him.

"Please try to understand," she cried, moving forward. But one of his daughters blocked her way.

"You have said enough to upset my father," shouted the young girl, her face almost as empurpled as his. "Have the goodness to pack your things and get out!"

Lenore turned to the mercer for a stay of execution, but saw his jawline harden. He refused to look at her.

"Is it your desire that I leave at once, or in the morning?" she asked coldly.

"In the morning will be sufficient time," he said in a strangled voice, and Lenore stalked up the stairs to pack her few belongings.

No one saw her leave the next day. The door of the mercer's study, where he sat by a warm fire at this time of day, was firmly closed. Lenore guessed his daughters had closed it, and doubtless were patrolling it, as well, to keep their father from weakening and asking her to stay. But . . . even if he did, it would be but for a short time, for they would soon be leaving school and coming home for good, and then life would become impossible for the pretty housekeeper.

Lenore went to the George and left her few possessions with Mistress Potts, who clucked over Lenore's being dismissed. But Mistress Potts's eyes grew round when Lenore told her she was to have an audience at Whitehall, and she insisted on taking Lenore there in a hackney coach.

"After all, ye cannot arrive there looking winded or blue with cold!" she cried as they bounced and skidded over the icy cobbles.

"I looked blue with cold yesterday when I tripped and tumbled to his feet," Lenore said ruefully.

"Ah, but you'll not trip today! Today you'll be graceful

413

as a gazelle," Mistress Potts said romantically, snuggling into her fur muff.

Lenore laughed, but she was becoming edgy as they approached Whitehall. The royal palace had never looked so imposing to Lenore as it looked this day.

"Driver, we will wait," ordered Mistress Potts, leaning back in the coach with a languid wave of her muff as if she were herself royalty.

Very nervous now, Lenore alighted and gave her name to the first lackey who looked her way. He was a liveried footman with a fresh country face and merry eyes, who escorted her into a large handsome room alive with bustling courtiers. There she was handed from one bewigged and satin-clad personage to another, always in an ascending scale of importance. Some of these fine gentlemen regarded her thoughtfully, some were merely contemptuous, and one kept her waiting for a long time, then took snuff and looked down his nose at her in an insulting fashion. Lenore was sure they thought her a new doxie brought in for the King's entertainment and—from her threadbare garb—wondered at his low tastes. Though her color rose at this condescending treatment, she kept her head high. At last she was ushered into a small private antechamber and the door closed discreetly behind her. Obviously the King would see her . . . alone.

She saw that the room was devoid of furniture, though the walls and ceiling were sumptuously decorated. Lenore stared at them, twisting her gloved hands together—Mistress Potts had lent her a pair of hers and they did not fit. Her gaze wandered across the polished floor to the several pairs of double doors—all shut—which led she knew not where. There were two tall windows, both heavily draped, and impulsively she stepped behind those drapes and looked out into sumptuous gardens glittering wtih ice. It was cold here but her blood racing in her veins kept her feverishly warm.

She heard a small sound as the door opened, and turned to see through a slit in the heavy damask drapes that the King had entered the room. She had a good view of him from where she stood. He was of an athletic build and exceptionally tall—a height accentuated by the rather narrow effect of his rich black velvet clothing, and he seemed quite oblivious of the cold. A single gold chain accented by a huge ruby hung around his neck and his whole stance was that of a man born to command—and enjoying it.

Surprised at seeing no one in the room, his swarthy face swung round irritably—and Lenore stepped forth from the damask curtains and made him a deep curtsy with a rustle of amber silk.

He stepped forward gracefully and took her hand. "You may rise, mistress," he said imperturbably and Lenore looked up into a pair of smiling dark eyes above a wide sensuous mouth. "What do they call you?"

"Lenore Frankford, Your Majesty."

He gave her a keen look that took in the too-daring cut of her gown, the ripe beautiful figure beneath it. "And why d'ye seek this audience with me?"

Lenore lifted her head. "Your Majesty," she said, taking a deep breath, "although you are doubtless unaware of it, I too had a small part in your return to your rightful throne."

King Charles regarded her cynically. He was used to false claims and over-inflated "services" rendered in the past in his cause. But . . . this wench was very pretty. "And how is that?" he murmured, studying her rapidly rising and falling breasts.

Lenore hesitated, fearful of appearing ridiculous. "Men called me for a while the Angel of Worcester," she blurted.

As she had feared, a smile curved that wide sensuous mouth, and his dark eyes glinted with amusement. "The naked wench on the white horse who rode with a flaming sword toward the town? And I had thought it all lies! But now you're telling me *you* were this Godiva?"

Lenore flushed. "There was no flaming sword, and I was certainly fully clothed. But I did ride my white horse into Worcester on the day of the battle. 'Twas to find my handfast husband who had ridden out of the Cotswolds with his claymore in hand to enlist in your cause."

The lively interest in that dark face continued. She could almost feel those cynical dark eyes stripping the clothes from her body, feel a lazy royal hand pushing down

her chemise to caress her naked back, her naked breasts.
. . . "And did you find him?"

She nodded.

"What was his name? I trust he seeks some reward from me?"

"He seeks no reward," Lenore replied shortly. "And find him I did—his body lay cold and dead by Barbour's Bridge after the battle."

King Charles had seen many men die—in his cause and others', but a wench was a wench. He took a step closer. "But surely you seek something?" he challenged.

Lenore drew a long, ragged breath. This tall, dark man who leaned so close was dangerously attractive. "I was falsely accused of murdering a student named Michael Maltby whom I knew in Oxford. He was giving me his protection upon the road north to Banbury in the summer of 1652 when robbers attacked us, killed him, and—and fled." No need to mention that she might have killed one! "His mother refused to believe I did not kill Michael for the money in his pockets and brought charges against me. I—I am a fugitive, Sire."

He reached out and carelessly toyed with a shining red-gold curl that fell silkily down beside her ear. Involuntarily, as his hand brushed her neck, she flinched. "And are these all the charges against you?" he asked gravely.

"There—there is also a charge of asault against the person of one Gilbert Marnock in Oxford in that same month and year," she said hurriedly.

Was that laughter she saw glimmering behind those dark worldly eyes in the dark face that bent over her own? His voice was sober enough. "And how did you assault this Gilbert Marnock?"

"With a hot poker. I marked his face because—because he had raped me and then tried to blackmail me into becoming his doxie!"

His dark brows lifted, but he nodded thoughtfully. "A just punishment surely. Have you any more crimes against you?"

She thought he looked fascinated and mumbled, "No, Sire," with her face crimson.

His dark face came closer, closer.

"Ye'll have my pardon," he murmured thickly. "No matter who ye've killed!"

For a feverish moment their eyes met, locked. His brown eyes had lost their cynicism, they were fierce, intense, brown liquid pools, too deep, too dark—a woman could drown there. Lenore was trembling. And yet . . . his lips brushed hers and involuntarily she turned her head away, she did not know why.

He stepped back, chilled of his ardor.

"As the Angel of Worcester, I may owe ye a debt," he said dryly. "for your name was a rallying point for the people . . . they believed in you, as a legend, something to hold onto when hope was gone. So for both these offenses, I will give ye a royal pardon, Mistress Lenore. Through that door on your way out, stop and tell that huge booted man at the desk about it. 'Twill be done, I promise you."

Lenore's face was flushed, for she was still shaken. She had been sorely tempted there for a moment. "Thank you, Your Majesty." She made him a deep curtsy that bared her décolletage for his interested gaze and turned to go.

His sharp eyes, watching her retreat, noted the hole in her stocking as her skirts swung round. His rich voice arrested her; it sounded speculative. "Could it be that ye seek employment, Mistress Lenore?"

She turned, saw the direction of his gaze at her ankles, and winced. He had seen that hole in her stocking! She lifted her dainty chin and gave him back a challenging look. "Employment—yes, Sire."

A ghost of a smile trembled on his cynical mouth at her slight emphasis on the word "employment." Lenore's color deepened. Tempted or not, she would not be a doxie, she thought rebelliously—no, not even a royal one! Her heart was hers for the giving, but it was neither for sale nor for rent!

"I've a thought where ye might find employment that would please ye. Ye have a certain flair. Have ye thought of the theatre?"

"I—I thought men played all the women's roles."

"No longer. Now, as on the Continent, we shall have

417

beauty in the theatre. Half the singing and dancing students of London have already been recruited!" he said jokingly. "The theatre will soon be bursting with young ladies of . . . virtue that will perhaps not equal your own." His voice was whimsical. "Your face is fair. I could well imagine you in a breeches part—if ye've the legs for it. Could one see your legs, Mistress Lenore?"

At this impudent royal request, Lenore, as if hypnotized, lifted her skirts just above her pretty knees.

"Turn around," he said, bemused.

A breeches part—and not in some barn or forest glade, but here in the London theatre! She would be part of the theatre again! Enthusiasm made her whirl about too fast so that her amber skirts and russet satin petticoat whipped up about her lissome hips and her lovely long legs were appealingly bared to the royal view.

"Do that again," he said, stepping toward her, his dark eyes becoming intense again.

Lenore stared at him, her breath coming fast, her violet gaze beneath her sweeping dark lashes defiant, wild. If she raised her skirts for him again, she knew what would happen. A long arm would snake out and grasp her. He would lead her swiftly through one of those tall double doors to a handsomely appointed chamber dominated by a great soft canopied bed, perhaps with the royal arms emblazoned in gold. There he would seize her and crush her naked body in his arms and discover all her secrets. She would move luxuriantly beneath him, moaning as she responded to his masculinity and . . . and she would become a royal mistress. She would compete with all the other women he slept with casually—and with his premiere mistress, the beauteous Barbara Villiers. She had heard as she moved through the crowd in that large room outside today that the King had made Barbara's husband, Roger Palmer, Earl of Castlemaine —just to send him off to Ireland so he could have his wife. 'Twas said the lovely willful Barbara held the King in the palm of her hand, that he feared to cross her, that she held him in thrall. But . . . something silky and devious in her mind murmured as she basked in that hard, hot royal stare . . . *she could take the King away from Barbara—if she tried.*

She felt mesmerized by his gaze—a rabbit paralyzed before the owl. Their eyes locked and held, and an unspoken challenge passed between them. So intent were they that they heard nothing, saw nothing but each other.

"I said . . . do that again, Mistress Lenore." He smiled lazily but she could feel the tension building up in him—just as it was building up in her.

He was a King . . . he had commanded her. Yet when his lips were brushing her own, she had turned away. Why? Why had she done that? For a man who had left her? For a man who was dead? A wild revulsion of feeling came over her. This was the life she wanted! She would make up to him for her coldness—the life of a King's mistress must indeed be eventful and wonderful!

She gave him her flashing magical smile and swirled her skirts alluringly again—and ended with a shriek as a whip flicked over her legs, and a voice at once husky and exciting and vividly angry cried, "Strumpet! Out! Out!"

Lenore whirled to see a beautiful woman attired in a green satin riding habit and a hat atremble with green plumes advancing upon her, whip upraised for another slash. With the quick grace of the athlete he was, the King leaped forward and clenched a bronzed hand down upon the dainty wrist that bore the whip. The woman's beautiful eyes flashed, and she tried angrily to twist away from him, to strike with her other hand at the royal countenance.

Lenore stood rooted as they grappled there.

No one had to tell her who this wild beauty was. She was looking at the celebrated Barbara Villiers—Lady Castlemaine.

The King's eyes were alight as he subdued his enraged lady, whose breasts heaved with effort and fury. She writhed in his arms, and now the deep intensity of his gaze, all his absorbed concentration was focused—as she had meant it to be—upon his fiery mistress, Lady Castlemaine. He wrested the whip from her and let her go free. In the struggle her plumed hat had fallen off and skittered across the polished floor, and now she swung away from him with a billow of green satin skirts and ruffled silk petticoats, paused with her dainty boots planted wide apart, and considered Lenore vengefully. Up and down two pairs of bold feminine eyes raked each other, while the King watched in amused silence.

"Who is this wench?" Barbara demanded icily.

King Charles gave her a wary look. Lady Castlemaine was a spirited mistress and not given to taking second place —not even to royalty.

"She is the Angel of Worcester, my dear," he said wryly.

Barbara looked startled. Then she shrugged. "She looks like a serving wench," she observed, her sweet voice dripping insult. "Faith, they get homelier every day!"

Lenore paled with anger, and her fists clenched. This richly garbed woman might call herself "Lady Castlemaine" because the King had bestowed an earldom upon her husband to get him gone from their sight, but in what other way were they different? Both of them—mistresses!

"Your ladyship would do well to hold her tongue," Lenore advised her with an insolent smile. "For a trollop on her way up meets the same faces on her way down."

The King laughed hugely, but Barbara's beautiful face whitened in fury. Her gloved hands were clenched at her sides, and Lenore guessed they itched for the whip. "Get you gone, wench!" she cried hoarsely. "From my sight!"

"As His Majesty commands," said Lenore in a brittle voice, making no move to go. "*He* will decide which of us leaves this room."

Barbara made a swooping dive for the whip, which the King had pitched aside, but he caught her easily. She trembled with fury in his grasp. "Are you going to let this street girl insult me?" she panted.

The King shrugged. Everyone knew how he felt about his dashing mistress—he would give her anything. Suddenly, before Barbara knew what he was about, he stripped a ruby ring from her finger and flung it to Lenore over Barbara's shriek of anger. "Take this to Killigrew of the King's Company—you'll find him at Gibbons's Tennis Court in Vere Street; they've moved from the Red Bull since yesterday. Killigrew will recognize the ring. Tell him I said you were to be given a breeches part, Mistress Lenore."

Lenore caught the ring in midair, this small token of a King's passing favor, and as their eyes met, a small smile crossed her face. Kings were like other men, she realized suddenly. Afraid of their wives, afraid of their mistresses. Whoever wrested Charles from the dashing Barbara would fight a hard battle.

"I thank Your Majesty." Her legs still burning from the whiplash, Lenore swept into her lowest curtsy, her bright hair almost touching the floor.

When she rose they were walking away from her, the King a tall elegant figure in black velvet with his vast black periwig of shining curls—and swaggering a bit; Lady Castlemaine with her haughty head in the air, her green satin skirts billowing. That was the last Lenore saw of them—the sight of their backs as they moved through the tall double doors and into a long handsome corridor, a pair of thoroughbreds indeed.

After they had gone she stared down at the ruby ring he had tossed to her. Just one of many, doubtless, that he had bestowed on his favorite, Lady Castlemaine. She looked after that tall figure thoughtfully, just disappearing down the corridor. If she had followed through and not wavered, she might have had him in spite of vivacious Barbara—for she had seen the quick interest burn in his dark eyes. If she had made her move at the right time . . . but she had thrown away her chance. Deliberately.

Why? Why? Why? She passed a weary hand over her face. Had Geoffrey so marked her that she would never find happiness in any other arms but his? Or . . . was it her stupid, stiff-necked pride that insisted she must *want* her mate, indeed must choose him? Was she unable to give herself for mere ambition?

Perhaps that was so. . . . If it was, she told herself, she had come to a sad pass indeed, for romance as she had known it with Geoffrey was not apt to come to her in lascivious Restoration London, which men now called the wickedest city in the world.

CHAPTER 25

The King had promised Lenore a royal pardon, and though she was slow in getting it, it came at last. Her job in the theatre came much quicker. She had left Whitehall and hastened over to Vere Street to speak to Thomas Killigrew, holder of one of the two Royal Patents given by the King in the theatre monopoly. She had found him very busy, almost inundated by young ladies who filled his outer chamber and overflowed into the hall. He was a bit testy with her. When she explained she was from the King, he muttered, "Another one!" And when she added that the King wished her placed in a "breeches part," he exclaimed that half the young ladies in the other room were from the King or the Duke of York or some other highly placed personage—all of whom wanted some special favor! Lenore who had thought them all candidates for acting careers from schools of singing and dancing, opened her violet eyes wider.

She explained—in a burst of honesty with this harassed gentleman—about the royal pardon she was to receive.

Killigrew stared at her, his brows drawn together.

"Pardon? Bah! You do not need a royal pardon to be an actress in London, mistress!"

Lenore gave him a startled look.

"There is a theatrical monopoly here now," he told her. "Two companies patented by the King—mine and William Davenant's. 'Tis but a revival of the old days. But no player in either company can be arrested or sued without the Lord Chamberlain's permission. Think you this will be given?" He gave a short laugh. "All apprentice players must work their first three months without compensation. Agreed, mistress?"

Lenore bit her lip. How would she live those three months?

"I see you are puzzled. Perchance you are not so well off as some of the young ladies outside?" Lenore had indeed noted many rich garments adorning the chattering females in the adjoining chamber. Killigrew sighed. "There are many gallants available to a winsome smile—such a smile as I see you have. And . . . you said you were sent by the King." A significant pause.

Color stained Lenore's cheeks. "I am not his doxie!" she flared. " 'Tis because he felt I had aided his cause at Worcester that he sends me to you!"

A skeptical glance greeted this. She was too beautiful to be believed. A face such as hers? Kings would vie for her, Killigrew thought with a wry smile. He doubted his new apprentice player would starve before she could reach the boards.

"Should you become disorderly or join others in riotous behavior," he warned her sternly, "a King's Messenger will arrest you. You could be whipped or imprisoned in the Gatehouse at Whitehall. Remember that you are here on sufferance and can be discharged at will. *Then* you would need a royal pardon for any crimes you may have committed!" He gave her a fierce look to emphasize his words.

Lenore nodded. She got up to leave with a rustle of amber silk skirts, but at the door she turned, suddenly curious. "Why did you decide to hire actresses? I thought young boys usually played the female parts."

423

Killigrew gave her a sharp look. "There were no trained young boys available for the work. Acting suffered a decline during the King's exile and as you'll observe, most of our actors are in their thirties and forties. Also the King and his court enjoyed the actresses of France and Italy." Lenore noted that he did not say "enjoyed their performances" but "enjoyed the actresses." She frowned. Killigrew saw her rebellious expression and added waspishly, "These young women onstage have proved a difficult lot to handle. To control them we now swear them in as royal 'comedians.' You also must be sworn in, mistress!"

Lenore nodded again, made her escape into the next room, and forced her way through a tittering crowd of young women. She gave them a harder look this time, seeing among them many obvious prostitues as well as arch ripe young things schooled in music and the dance.

Someone touched her arm. "Please, is he—is he very fearsome?" whispered an angelic-looking young girl with rich brown hair and large blue eyes.

Lenore paused and turned to look at the speaker. Barely fifteen, if she was a judge, with skin like Devon cream, and a dress that marked her as fresh from the country. "He'll eat you for supper," she grinned. And then, because the girl's lips trembled she added more kindly, "Killigrew is a busy man. He's brusque—at least, he was brusque with me, but he might be more gentle with you."

The girl swallowed; she looked about to turn and run.

"Have you acted on stage before?" asked Lenore. She knew what the answer would be, but it seemed a safe subject.

"Nay." The girl shook her brown curls vigorously. "But I daresay nobody else here has, either—I heard one say so."

"But all do wish to act . . ." murmured Lenore humorously, turning to survey the glittering group of females who milled about chattering glibly to each other.

"Oh, I am sure they do," agreed that eager young voice. "But I think all were sent here by various nobles, to hear them talk—all but myself."

"And what brought you here?" asked Lenore, whose

heart was light, in spite of the obstacles she faced. She had found employment that would support her—after the first three months were lived through. She was going to be a London actress!

The girl's answer surprised her. "Oh, I do not not really wish to act," she quavered. "On the stage—before so many people!"

"Then why"— Lenore looked with amazement into those wide, innocent blue eyes—"would you apply for a position as an apprentice player?" she wondered.

The girl clasped her hands; she might almost have been praying. " 'Tis because I do so wish for a noble protector," she breathed. "I came to London thinking to better myself, but in the butcher shop where I work, all the men have greasy hands. But the theatre will be filled with great cavaliers and—and one of them might fancy me!"

Indeed they might, thought Lenore, eyeing that dainty waist, that silken skin, that ingenuous expression. *More than one might fancy this pastry from the country! So the girl wished for a noble protector. . . .*

"What is your name?" asked Lenore.

"Emma. Emma Lyddle."

Lenore's witching smile played over young Emma. "When you speak to Thomas Killigrew," she counseled, "hold up your head. Your eyes are good, so stare at him directly. And" —she reached out a hand and gave the girl's bodice a tug—"see if you cannot pull your neckline down a little lower. Tell him you are seventeen. He'll not believe you, but 'twill ease his conscience nonetheless. Tell him—tell him you have watched performances given illegally in barns near your native village and that your great ambition is to excel in comedy. Blink your eyelashes—so—as you say it." Here Lenore batted her lashes fetchingly and gave Emma a demure look upward through their thick, dark fringe.

Emma tried it. The effect was heartrending.

"Yes, that's the way," Lenore encouraged her, "I think Thomas Killigrew will be enchanted!"

"I saw you go into his private chamber," breathed Emma. "But you spent such a short time with him—how did you learn so much about what he would like?" Her childish face was very appealing.

Lenore burst into laughter. "I was born a flirt—for me the part needs no rehearsing!" She was still laughing as she left and Emma Lyddle's breathless voice followed her. "Oh, thank you, mistress . . ."

"Frankford," called Lenore lightly over her shoulder as she breezed out. "Lenore Frankford." She was not afraid to use her own name again, and the sound of it was good to her ears. So many last names she had used, but now she was come into her own again—as soon as she received the King's pardon!

Mistress Potts, who had missed Lenore's company whilst she worked long hours at the bakeshop, and later while she was immersed in the mercer's affairs, insisted she move in with her for the months of her apprenticeship. Gratefully, Lenore accepted this kindly offer and moved back into the George, where men who had formerly regarded her as a circumspect young woman now made bawdy remarks within her hearing—for word had got out through Mistress Potts's ill-timed loud whispers that Lenore was now an apprentice actress. Had she been an apprentice strumpet, she could not have received more undesirable attention.

Lenore was able to ignore it, for she found her work in the theatre hard but exciting. It would be some time before she actually appeared in a play, but sometimes when an actress fell ill or for other reasons failed to appear at rehearsal, she was allowed to rehearse the part as an "understudy." These rehearsals were noisy affairs, and sometimes the players had to shout their lines to be heard above the noise of singers learning new songs, dancers stamping and whirling about, men practicing fight scenes —either fisticuffs or dueling. Under these crowded conditions, wherever they could find room, the tirewomen patched and mended and altered the costumes—which were mostly cast-off finery from the Court.

Lenore was first put in the charge of a raffish young actor named Blakelock, who wore tremendous unkempt wigs, and had melting eyes. He considered himself a divine gift to women and assumed outrageous postures that they might better admire him. Lenore detested Blakelock on sight, and when, in teaching her stage business, he casually ran a hand up under her skirts and gave her bare bottom a playful pinch, she turned and struck him such a blow as caused him to lose his balance and pitch backward upon the boards, to the delight of several older actors who had witnessed the incident.

Lenore left him there, lifted her head, turned on her heel, and went over to watch some players practicing a jig. Behind her she could hear Blakelock swearing testily that he'd have no part in teaching "that awkward piece" how to move about gracefully onstage! Lenore turned back angrily and was about to confront Blakelock again when Ralph Ainsley, a long-faced Shakespearean actor in his mid-forties, seized her arm.

"Mistress, we owe ye a debt," he declared merrily, still chuckling over Blakelock's discomfiture. " 'Tis good to see Blakelock cuffed by so dainty a hand!"

"Yes," sighed Lenore, "but now I have lost my teacher."

"*I* will be your teacher," he declared gallantly. "I was reading parts before Blakelock was born! Come, mistress, we will see if you can make a graceful entrance!"

Lenore liked Ainsley. Perhaps because of his deep-sunk eyes and melancholy face, he was mainly used in tragedies, where he played victims or villains with equal aplomb. But beneath his long face was a lively wit, and he spent long hours instructing his new protégée in swooning, gamboling, and good stage manners.

"Ye need no instruction in making '*doux yeux*,' " he observed. Lenore turned, puzzled, and asked, "Do what?"

"Languishing eyes," he grinned. "The last aspiring actress put in my charge had to be taught to coquet, to flourish a fan gracefully—even how to walk across a stage without lumbering. You, mistress"—he swept her a graceful bow—"are already beyond my teaching in these things."

"But I am not a very good actress," Lenore gravely acknowledged.

"Perhaps not," he shrugged. "But in a 'breeches part,' none are likely to notice your acting—they will be too busy admiring your silken legs! Tell me, hast found a protector yet?"

"I am not looking for a protector."

"Be of good heart," he said lightly. "You'll find one yet."

Lenore laughed ruefully, for Ainsley had but expressed the general feeling that actresses were promiscuous creatures, they were all looking for wealthy admirers. Occasionally one was so fortunate as to make a good marriage —most of them, Lenore suspected, would wind up in brothels such as "Mother" Moseley's or "Lady" Bennett's. Both were famous madams, and "Lady" Bennett had noticed Lenore when she visited the rehearsal one morning and had even asked her if she would care for an evening of well-paid frivolity. Lenore had politely declined this offer, and several of the young rakehell actors listening in delight nearby broke into chuckles.

"Mistress Chastity will have none of you, 'Lady' Bennett," sighed one of them—and Lenore recognized the voice as Blakelock's. "Mistress Chastity seeks to clasp a King to her bosom!"

"Mistress Chastity? Indeed, is that what they call you?" "Lady" Bennett turned an astonished face under her plumed hat to Lenore. "But you surely cannot be the one Blakelock calls The Iron Virgin?" Her laughter pealed.

Lenore glowered at Blakelock, who had so christened her in retribution for her well-timed blow. He grinned back at her and swaggered away. "Lady" Bennett, still laughing, followed him, and Lenore swept away angrily.

But the name stuck. Lenore had become "Mistress Chastity," the Iron Virgin of the London stage.

Not long after that, during a pause in one of the endless rehearsals, Lenore saw Emma Lyddle again. She had almost forgotten her encounter with starry-eyed young Emma, assuming since she had not seen her at the theatre that Killigrew must have turned her down. On this particular morning, during the rehearsal of an energetic scene in which she struggled with the villain, one of Lenore's

428

garters had burst and she had hurried up to the tiring-room to see if one of the tirewomen could mend it quickly. There in the large room, its walls hung with green baize, she saw a short young woman standing before one of the big looking glasses the room afforded. She was pulling a voluminous dress of blue taffety over her head, and as Lenore approached, passing almost all the twenty chairs and stools provided for the use of the female comedians, she saw that the flushed young woman who had just struggled into a costume several sizes too big for her was Emma.

"Mistress Frankford!" cried Emma rapturously. "They have accepted me at last!"

Lenore stood and smiled at her. "I am glad to hear it. Is this your first day?"

Emma nodded blissfully. "But my costume," she added with a sad shake of her head, "is far too large."

"Indeed you're right." Lenore seized a handful of blue taffety that billowed around Emma's slender young waist. "We must have the tirewoman stitch it up to fit you."

"I was afraid to ask," admitted Emma in her soft voice. "They all seemed so busy and they turned their heads as I approached. Yet—I was told I must appear in it in half an hour!"

Irritably Lenore looked about for a tirewoman—they all seemed to have disappeared.

"They ignore the newcomers," she told Emma grimly, "for the regular players do reward them well."

Emma's eyes widened. "I—I did not know," she faltered. "And I'm afraid I—I have no money."

"You should not need money. 'Tis their job to see your clothes do not fall off of you onstage!" Lenore marched to the green baize hanging that separated the men's dressing room from the women's. "Tirewoman!" she called in a voice that carried. "In here, quickly!"

A woman's head poked through the curtains. "I am busy," she whined.

Lenore sighed. "This will not take long," she said, "but at least the waist must be tucked in and the hem basted up. As you can see, poor Emma will trip if she tries to walk across the stage in a dress so long."

The tirewoman came through the green baize curtains reluctantly. She was carrying with her a voluminous dress of mulberry satin. "But I'm already promised to shorten the hems on this costume for Mistress Gwyn!" she cried, aggrieved.

"And who is Mistress Gwyn?"

"A new apprentice player—like this one." The tirewoman bobbed her head at Emma. "I'm told they were both sent over by Master Killigrew this morning."

Lenore sighed. Actresses came and went in this place as if blown by on a strong wind—and most of them were prostitutes who'd walk out on the arm of any likely patron and return to the theatre when their patrons grew tired of them or—and more frequently—when their patrons' money ran out! She thought young Emma deserved her chance.

The tirewoman came forward muttering, thumped herself down upon a stool, and made to continue her work on the mulberry satin.

"Mistress Gwyn must wait," insisted Lenore, "for Emma here is supposed to wear this blue dress onstage in half an hour."

"Mistress Gwyn does not choose to wait!" rang out an imperious new voice that had in it the tang of the London streets. Lenore turned to face a shapely chestnut-haired girl in a red dress who flounced into the room. She judged the girl to be even younger than Emma, though the hazel eyes that challenged her were infinitely worldlier.

Lenore sighed. "Are you then to appear in this costume onstage?" She indicated the mulberry satin lying on the tirewoman's lap.

"Certainly—tomorrow!" snapped the girl in the red dress.

"Then it can certainly wait," said Lenore, and snatched the mulberry satin from the tirewoman's lap and thrust it upon the newcomer. "For Emma must appear immediately —and she cannot do so attired in a dress big enough for all of us!"

The chestnut-haired girl made a threatening gesture

toward Lenore but was distracted by Emma's eager voice.
" 'Tis too large because it belonged to a Duchess!"

The new girl looked down at the mulberry satin. "Belonged to—?"

"You heard her," said Lenore. "A Duchess. Some of them are fat. This one obviously was!"

"We're fortunate the gentry do give cast-off clothes to the theatre for the players," chuckled the tirewoman, already at work with her swift needle on the bodice of the blue dress.

"Cast-off!" said the chestnut-haired girl with an affronted look at the mulberry satin she now held in her arms. "And is this gown cast-off, too, pray?"

"They all are," said Lenore more kindly. Obviously this girl was unused to the ways of the theatre. "Else we'd have no alternative but to wear our own clothes onstage!"

The girl cast the mulberry satin gown from her angrily. "Well, *I* will not wear cast-offs!" she cried with a curse. "I mean to wear beautiful clothes—all made for *me!*"

The tirewoman was chuckling as the angry girl flung away. Lenore watched her go—good face, good figure, and fiery—good theatre. "What did you say her name was?" she asked.

"Nell Gwyn," said the tirewoman, looking up and biting off the thread with her teeth. "And she came to Killigrew well recommended," she added with a laugh. "By three Baronets and an Earl!"

"*Three* Baronets!" Emma sighed in envy.

"And an Earl," Lenore added crisply. "Don't forget him."

"She's a saucy one, is Mistress Nell," said the tirewoman. "Her mother kept a bawdyhouse in Covent Garden, and Nell was brought up there. Her sister Rose is one of the orange girls. But I think me Mistress Nell may surpass them both!"

Lenore cast a speculative eye after the saucy street wench just flouncing out through the green baize curtains. She was inclined to agree with the tirewoman. Young Mistress Gwyn might make her theatrical debut in new clothes after all!

But the next day she was told Nell Gwyn had demanded new clothing from Thomas Killigrew and had been dismissed even before she could begin her new career—everyone was chuckling over it. Lenore looked down wryly at the shabby creation she was wearing—of much-mended watered taffety. Not that it mattered, she was only wearing it at a rehearsal. For young women were almost fighting to get their chance in the theatre, and Lenore had not yet had a chance to act onstage.

Emma had. She had appeared briefly as a water nymph—once again in a dress too large—and just as she made her entrance the entire dress fell down over one shoulder, showing a great deal of pink and white skin. The audience had roared with laughter, but the incident had served Emma well, for a young Baronet had noticed her and asked her to a coffee house after the performance.

Emma had been so excited that Lenore had felt it necessary to see that she had sufficient coins in her purse to take a hackney coach home in case of need, and that she had not put her right shoe on her left foot or vice versa.

"It is my chance!" cried Emma, enraptured. "A Baronet! And so handsome! Oh, Lenore, do you think—do you think he will like me?"

Lenore surveyed that round, innocent face, the silky young skin, the big sparkling blue eyes turned so appealingly upward. How different was Emma from Mistress Gwyn! "There's little doubt he will like you," she said dryly. "The important thing is to be sure *you* like *him*."

"But how could I not? Have you not seen him? So tall and commanding—and such gorgeous clothes!" She touched Lenore's arm impulsively. "Oh, Lenore, won't you come with me? I am sure he must know other Baronets!"

Lenore shook her head. "Don't you know they call me the Iron Virgin?" she quipped. "It is because I do not frequent coffee houses with strange Baronets!"

Emma looked mystified. She took a last look in the mirror, was jostled away from it by another actress, one Lenore recognized as a notorious prostitute, and hurried away. Lenore smiled as she watched her go, and the prostitute, whose name was Floss, turned and gave Lenore a curious look.

"You're a fool—you know that," Floss said bluntly. "You could have a Duke with your looks. Is it true you're saving yourself for the King?"

Lenore laughed and shook her head, but her smile had turned rueful by the time she reached the room she still shared with Mistress Potts at the George. Perhaps she *was* a fool not to go to coffee houses with the glittering gentlemen who frequented the theatre. Perhaps silly young Emma had the right idea—to go out and find herself a man.

"You work too hard," said Mistress Potts, observing Lenore's strained expression.

"No," sighed Lenore. "I think too much. 'Tis a bad habit that I must somehow learn to break."

The next day Emma left the theatre for good. She came by at rehearsal time to tell Lenore breathlessly that she had found at last "a noble protector"—her Baronet! And the next week to twirl about displaying the new pink silk dress he had bought for her—it had been stitched up by a seamstress who had at one time worked for *the Queen!* Emma was breathless. She did not return to the theatre again. Once Lenore saw her riding down Drury Lane in a coach; she was handsomely dressed in rose sarsenet and waved gaily.

Then grimmer news reached her. Emma's Baronet had passed her along—to the notorious Lord Wilsingame. Lenore frowned at the news. One of the more vicious young peers who had come to London to seek the new King's favor, Wilsingame had rented a handsome house perched in the mid-section of London Bridge and had gathered around him wild young men of like kidney. There he gave roistering parties and there he was said to have installed his mad sister, whose screams rent the night. It was said she had several times attacked her serving-women, for often their screams were blended with hers. Lenore thought grimly of Emma, so young, so childlike, with her wide, believing blue eyes . . . Emma, who had yearned not for honest marriage but for "a noble protector."

She determined to learn how Emma fared. Twice she made her way onto the narrow dangerous coachway that threaded between the tall houses that rose up on both sides of the bridge itself. The buildings overhung the street and leaned out precipitately over the River Thames, and several times Lenore walked through short dark tunnels on the bridge where the buildings met above her head. There were shops here, too, on London Bridge, and twice Lenore fell back hurriedly from the narrow street into an open shop doorway to dodge onrushing horses, for a coach going by filled the street—the bridge was so crowded with houses it was not wide enough for two coaches to pass!

This narrow press of houses and shops spanning the Thames seemed to her somehow menacing—to Emma, so full of young dreams. It was with foreboding that she banged the great boar's head knocker of Lord Wilsingame's tall, narrow house. A surly manservant stuck out his head and told her that Emma was not at home.

Lenore came back a week later and was told by the same servant that Emma had departed London for the country. *Used by Wilsingame and thrown away,* thought Lenore bitterly. She regretted that she had not seen Emma before she left, but she hoped poor foolish Emma had gone back to the pleasant country town from which she had come and would find herself there some stout country lad and forget her brief unfortunate venture in sinful London. She thought back to her friend Lally, who had been used, discarded, and she too had disappeared without a goodbye.

It was spring before Lenore got her first part in a play—and then because both the leading man and leading lady were sick (having drunk too deeply of the royal malmsey the night before), the play was cancelled and another put in its place. It was scheduled again—and once more postponed because Killigrew had promised Lady Castlemaine that its first performance would be played before the King, and the King had gone to Sandwich to join Catherine of

Braganza, the Portuguese Infanta. Twice did he marry his Portuguese Princess—once by Roman Catholic rites, and once by the English service—and great wealth did she bring with her: Bombay and Tangier, and two million cruzados. But in London the players tittered when they learned that Lady Castlemaine had been appointed one of the young Queen's ladies in waiting!

Since being sworn in as a royal player, Lenore had glimpsed the King only in the middle distance, from backstage, on those occasions when he attended a play. She'd seen his dark, saturnine countenance often split into a wolfish smile at some particularly broad remark onstage. Nor had it escaped her that there were always bewigged, besatined, and beauteous ladies about him—and most often next to him she glimpsed beautiful imperious Lady Castlemaine, to whom all deferred. Lenore found herself rather sorry for the young Queen, pitted against such a determined beauty.

Although it had been promised speedily, Lenore's royal pardon had not yet come through and she debated trying to gain another audience with the King, but reluctantly put the thought from her. If she saw him again at close quarters, dark, aggressive, virile . . . she might well become one of that perfumed, handsomely dressed group of doxies, patrician and otherwise, who swarmed about him. It was something she wished to avoid. Not because of conscience or fear that such an alliance might endanger her reputation—indeed in lascivious London being bedded by the King would only enhance her reputation! But because something strong and deep within her rebelled at the thought.

She had been Geoffrey's mistress without a qualm, but . . . she had loved Geoffrey. She did not love the King, she only found him physically attractive. If she became his mistress, she would be no better than that high-born strumpet, Lady Castlemaine!

But the slowness of her royal pardon bothered her, and when the play that had been deferred was finally rescheduled for private showing at Whitehall before King and Court, she determined to find a way to speak to the King again about her pardon.

Playing Whitehall was very popular with the players, who were poorly paid and almost always in debt. Low in the social scale (for the players were listed even below the royal rat-killers) they often sneaked their handsome stage costumes out of the theatre's tiring rooms and wore them about the City. Though the actors wore swords, considering that the mark of a gentleman, they were never accepted as equals by the gentry. Lenore, as an actress, felt this less than the men, for a pretty woman could command her own respect. But she knew that at the King's private theatre at Whitehall, the players supped well and drank deep of sack and claret and beer. This was to be an important performance, and there would be understudies for all the parts, for the show must indeed go on.

Lenore was as excited as the rest by the prospect of opening in a new play at Whitehall—perhaps more so, for this royal performance would mark her debut on the boards. Her part, though small, was a good one—that of a girl who disguised herself as a boy to spy on her unfaithful lover, and Ainsley had said that if she succeeded in this part (which meant, she knew, if the King was pleased with her performance), it could mean advancement for her. She had two costumes for the role: a full-skirted peach satin in which she would appear in the last act, and an olive-green doublet and tight trunk hose and peaked hat for her masquerade as a man in the second act.

Opening night came at last. The players were all assembled in a chattering fluid group at Whitehall, and backstage Lenore repeated her lines to herself over and over— she must not forget them, this was her chance to impress the King and perhaps gain another audience to press for her royal pardon!

Through the curtains, from backstage, she watched the play proceed, the actors warmed with malmsey and delivering their lines in ringing tones, the actresses bowing so low their bare breasts almost slipped from their low-cut bodices, their skin creamy and golden in the light of the huge chandeliers with their hundreds of candles.

Past the players she could see King Charles in a huge black periwig, his glossy black curls spilling over onto the froth of Alençon lace at his throat, frosty against his purple velvets. He was leaning back at his ease, knees crossed nonchalantly. Beside him, a sultry beauty in mauve satin, lounged Lady Castlemaine, waving a delicate ivory fan. Around them were grouped the courtiers, wearing black patches on their faces and taking snuff from enamelled boxes, and the ladies-in-waiting, dressed elegantly in the French fashion which Charles admired. But nowhere was the young Queen to be seen. Lenore had heard backstage that the Queen had pleaded a "headache" and gone to her chambers—it was rumored that she and Lady Castlemaine were waging a pitched battle for the King and that Lady Castlemaine was winning.

Lenore gave the reckless beauty beside the King a sardonic look; it was her opinion that Lady Castlemaine would stop at nothing to hold her place on the royal lap. She smiled dangerously to herself, a smile that boded ill for the lady in mauve satin. That hot look in the King's eyes when he had looked at her that day when he had promised her a royal pardon could be summoned up again! Perhaps the young Queen could not take him from Lady Castlemaine, but the self-assured flirt from Twainmere had no doubt that *she* could do it if she put her mind to it!

And perhaps she would have a try for him, after all! It was something she would decide as she played her part before him tonight.

"Are you ready?" hissed Blakelock. "Hurry, you'll miss your cue!" He gave her a solid push that propelled her through the curtains and onto the stage.

Lenore, who'd hardly been following the dialogue as she toyed with dreams of becoming a royal courtesan, realized belatedly that her cue had indeed been given. She rushed onstage, propelled by Blakelock's push, wearing the long tight stockings and bright smile her part required—a smile she flashed directly at the King.

But Lenore got no chance to play her "breeches part" that night at Whitehall, for as she rushed onstage her foot slipped on a greasy spot on the floor and she fell headlong,

437

almost knocking over the leading man and sliding half across the stage. Everybody laughed at such clumsiness, and Lenore's face was red as she tried to spring up—only to sink wincing to the floor again, for her painful ankle would not support her weight. The play was held up as Ainsley and several others hurried out to help her offstage.

Biting her lips to keep from crying out as she limped away on Ainsley's arm, Lenore met the mocking gaze of Lady Castlemaine above her lazily wielded ivory fan. Behind the fan she thought Lady Castlemaine might be laughing. The King looked thoughtfully at the greasy spot at the edge of the stage where Lenore had slipped, and his dark gaze narrowed as he turned to consider his beautiful, amused mistress; then he shrugged. He was after all accustomed to having women fight over him.

Backstage Ainsley eased Lenore onto a bench and lifted her ankle, red and beginning to swell, onto a red silken cushion which somebody had placed on a low marble-topped stool. He gave her a sympathetic look and handed her a glass of malmsey which Lenore took with shaking fingers. Lenore knew that her understudy—some new girl who had rehearsed the part this morning while Lenore was undergoing last-minute fittings of her costume —would be already dressed and waiting somewhere in the company. She looked around, wondering who her understudy was. In a moment she would come forward and the play would continue. She took a sip of the malmsey. "How did that slick spot get on the floor, Ainsley?" she groaned. "I didn't even see it!"

Ainsley shrugged. "Perhaps 'twas drippings from the great chargers that were carried across it for the King and Court to sup on dainties before the play began. You should have looked where you were going, Mistress Lenore." His voice was blunt.

Lenore gave him an angry look. She had, she was sure, studied every inch of the floor she was to walk over. But that was during the first act. Something must have been spilled on it since then, while she was daydreaming. Who had made his entrance from that particular spot during the second act? None but Blakelock, for a brief appearance—

and 'twas Blakelock who had given her that sudden push which had sent her plunging onto the stage. She studied the malmsey and thought about Blakelock. True, she had struck him for impudently reaching up under her skirts to pinch her bare bottom—and he had fallen from the blow and others had laughed, but . . . she could not think he would be so vengeful as to spoil her entrance for that.

Who had most enjoyed her discomfiture? Lady Castlemaine, surely, laughing behind her fan. And Lady Castlemaine could well have known the action of the play, for it was one of her protégés who had written this one—which was why it had been so long postponed; she wanted the King to be among the first to view it and give it the stamp of royal approval.

Hot with fury, Lenore decided it must have been Lady Castlemaine who had caused that spot to be oiled so that she would fall and make a ridiculous entrance.

After a brief pause, the play was now about to resume, and Lenore saw her understudy hurry forward. She could not see who it was, for people kept stepping between, but it must be her understudy, for the girl was wearing trunk hose. Lenore swallowed her malmsey at a gulp and promised herself that she would indeed play for the King's favor when next she appeared—if only to infuriate Lady Castlemaine!

But she was not to have that chance. For the young actress who hurried forward to replace Lenore in her "breeches part" was small and shapely and chestnut-haired—and back in Killigrew's company once again. As she swept past Lenore, her hazel eyes sparkled with malice and her lips, as she threw the curtains aside to make her dramatic entrance, were curved in a winsome, secret smile. She cast a quick covert look at the oily spot on which Lenore had so ignominiously slipped—and just before she disappeared onstage she gave a laughing nod to Blakelock, who stared innocently at the ceiling. Lenore seethed as she stared at the ripple of curtains through which her understudy had gone.

On the other side of those curtains, they were staring at her, too. For she wore a splendid costume of cream and gold satin, did Lenore's replacement, with creamy silk trunk hose to outline her pretty legs. The costume was rumored to have been provided at great expense by the elderly Earl of Wytton—as was the gold chain around her slender neck. She wore her luxuriant chestnut hair in ringlets, and she swept onto the London stage with flashing eyes and made it her own. The King noticed her, too, and he straightened a bit from his lounging position. Beside him Lady Castlemaine moved restively. The King's cynical eyes darkened and grew fixed as they stared at the cream and gold "youth" who moved with such a graceful feminine walk up and down the stage. For the moment, he had lost all interest in Lenore, who had been ignominiously carted away—and even in the dark beauty, Lady Castlemaine, who sulked beside him.

The fiery young actress's name was Nell Gwyn.

An instant success, Nell was promptly invited to sup with the King—to the indignation of Lady Castlemaine, who was reputed to have smashed her wineglass and later to have attacked her hairdresser in rage. She was right to be angry, for before the evening was over, everyone knew that a new royal mistress would enjoy the delights of Whitehall.

By the time Lenore's ankle was healed enough so that she could walk gracefully again, London was baking in the summer heat. The King left for the country to escape it, taking with him the Queen, the Court—and Lady Castlemaine. Nell he had left behind, and she was sulking. Theatregoing customers fell off so badly the theatres closed down for the summer. It was a bad time for the players, for they were supposed to work forty weeks out of the year, with Sundays off, and they received no "sharing dividends" when the theatres were closed.

But Lenore received her royal pardon that summer and came home to the George shining-eyed. Not just immune from arrest while she worked as a royal player, she was a free woman at last! No longer wanted anywhere for any crime!

Now at last she broke her long silence. She sat down and wrote a long letter to Lorena.

PART TWO

THE ORANGE GIRL

CHAPTER 26

September found Lenore a regular member of Killigrew's
company, taking part in the onstage dances and masques
that were held between acts and playing occasional small
parts. The glittering gentlemen who frequented the theatre
were quick to notice her blazing beauty onstage, and
Lenore was besieged by offers to parties and little suppers
in private rooms. Although her heart was still frozen in
her chest where men were concerned, some of the teasing
ways of the Twainmere flirt had returned, and one day,
with a light laugh, she began notching her heels again—
each time for an offer, whether it seemed honorable or no.

In time she might have slipped into the ways of the
other actresses, some of whom were married but nearly
all of whom had a succession of lovers. Many were little
better than prostitutes—some indeed were famous prostitutes and were hooted at by a ribald audience whenever
they played virtuous parts onstage. Or she might have
married one of the lesser gentry who thronged the play-

houses and eagerly sought the company of young and pretty actresses.

But Lenore had made enemies—and they were her undoing.

One of her enemies was Nell Gwyn, who was by now a favored mistress of the King and never forgot that it was Lenore who had snatched her costume from the tirewoman in favor of Emma. Although Lenore was certain Nell had caused her downfall at Whitehall, there was no way to tax her with it, and Nell eyed her vengefully, perhaps sensing in Lenore a rival who could sweep both her and Lady Castlemaine out of the way.

Another of Lenore's enemies was Lord Wilsingame of evil reputation, into whose home young Emma Lyddle had disappeared without a trace. Lord Wilsingame was relentless in his pursuit of actresses and a steady patron of both those famous madams "Mother" Moseley and "Lady" Bennett—from whom he bought kidnapped virgins, young girls fresh from the country who had come to London seeking domestic employment.

Wilsingame was on hand when Lenore made her debut in a small part—on a night when the King was elsewhere. Lenore was to note that somehow whenever she played any part the King was engaged elsewhere, and she wondered if this was Nell's doing—for Nell and Killigrew had become very close. But Wilsingame, like the other jaded London rakes lounging in the pit, straightened up and leaned forward to watch the startling beauty of this new adornment to the London stage. When Lenore had finished her first speaking part, he sent a messenger to her backstage to inform her peremptorily that my Lord Wilsingame's coach would be waiting for her outside.

In the madhouse of the tiring room, where the messenger had found her, Lenore—who had unpleasant memories of being turned away from Wilsingame's house on London Bridge when she went there in quest of Emma—raised her high-arched brows and concentrated her calm attention on Lord Wilsingame's sallow-faced young messenger, whom she rightly guessed to be his groom.

"Tell my Lord Wilsingame I am otherwise engaged," she said in a clear, carrying voice.

Wilsingame was well known among theatregoers. At the sound of his name some of the buzzing of voices stopped and several backstage visitors turned curiously to look at Lenore.

"And tell my Lord Wilsingame," added Lenore with deliberate emphasis, "that I will also be engaged tomorrow—and the day after that." Calmly she turned back to considering her reflection in the mirror, and several dandies who'd been urging two young actresses to accompany them to a coffee house and had stopped to listen began to laugh.

"That should set Wilsingame back on his heels!" cried one, and Lenore gave him a cool smile and hurried out to brush by Wilsingame's coach and climb into a hackney cab.

"The Spur," she told the driver in a ringing tone, glancing back to see Wilsingame's gaze follow her in astonishment as he listened to the report of his sallow-faced messenger. Lenore smiled to herself all the way to the Spur—for she had changed lodgings when Mistress Potts had begun to sleep late and had objected to Lenore's rising early for rehearsals at the theatre in Vere Street.

The next night the same play was repeated, and Lord Wilsingame, his appetite for this insolent flame-haired beauty whetted by her refusal to notice him, sent backstage by his sallow-faced messenger a large nosegay and a pretty pair of glass earrings—and another summons to his coach.

This time in the tiring room there was a group of dandies clustered about Lenore, urging her to a party to be held at Dunster House. She was laughingly turning them down when the nosegay and the earrings were thrust toward her and the sallow-faced groom bleated out Lord Wilsingame's invitation. Nearby a dandy in rosy silk nudged another clad in russet velvet. From the corner of her eye Lenore could see them watching her with interest, and coldly she remembered Emma Lyddle, who had been passed on by her Baronet to Lord Wilsingame—and disappeared from London.

445

With a bright, fixed smile she presented the nosegay to a passing tiring-woman, who curtsied in astonishment. Around her the company tittered.

"Take this bauble back to Lord Wilsingame and tell him I have seen better." Lenore's tone was disdainful as she tossed the earrings back to the startled messenger with a light, contemptuous laugh. Around her the party of young dandies roared with merriment.

In his coach outside, Lord Wilsingame, benumbed with shock, studied his returned gift with glazed eyes.

Beside him one of his friends nudged another, heavy with gold lace. They exchanged droll looks, and a third, de Quincy, drawled, "She is playing with you, Wilsingame —like a cat with a mouse. Soon she will take you at a bite and be done with you!"

Wilsingame grew red with mortification.

"Come now, admit ye're outmatched!" coaxed de Quincy with a sadistic grin.

Wilsingame's discomfiture deepened. "I vow I will bed the wench!" he grated. "And no later than the morrow! Like other wenches, she has a price—and I'll meet it, for I mean to have her!"

His words could be heard by several others in the crush of coaches surrounding the theatre entrance, and by the next day word was all over London that Lord Wilsingame was in the market to buy Mistress Chastity's favors— indeed he had vowed to bed that Iron Virgin this very day!

Not surprisingly, a large and interested audience was on hand to watch Wilsingame's messenger—his face no longer sallow but flushed with importance—march up to Lenore in the tiring room after the play.

Lenore saw him coming out of the corner of her eye, but did not pause in rearranging her hair before the mirror.

"Mistress Frankford!" he cried.

"Yes?" murmured Lenore in a bored voice, concentrating all her attention on a recalcitrant curl that defied her comb.

"Mistress Frankford." His voice rose pompously, for he was well aware that he had an audience. "My Lord Wilsingame has instructed me to give you this."

He held out a handsome blue-enamelled box. Heads craned to see it.

Lenore sighed and laid down her comb. She turned and gave the boy a disinterested look but made no move to touch the box he tendered.

"Tell my Lord Wilsingame enamelled boxes do not interest me—I have several at home." It was a lie, but it had the ring of truth. In the tiring room, one could have heard a pin drop. Not even the spurs of the gentry jingled, for everyone was hanging breathlessly on her words.

"But mistress!" The boy's voice cracked in his excitement. "Please to look what's inside! My Lord Wilsingame said to tell you 'twould match your eyes."

Lenore raised her eyebrows and opened the box. She pulled out an amethyst necklace, each stone vivid and deep violet and ringed about with diamonds. A fabulous gift—scarce an actress in the theatre he could not have commanded for such a price! A collective sigh went over the assembly as Lenore let the diamonds and amethysts trickle like water through her fingers.

So Wilsingame thought he could buy her . . . and after his treatment of poor Emma! Lenore's expression hardened. Ah, he had played into her hands tonight! Bent on making him suffer, she held up the glittering necklace for all to see. The diamonds sparkled alluringly in the wavering candlelight, and the amethysts seemed to smoulder with a fire of their own. In the hush, everyone waited expectantly for her to capitulate before this handsome gift.

"Take this pretty trinket back to my Lord Wilsingame," she said negligently, dropping it back into the blue-enamelled box and shutting it with a snap. "For I doubt not he goes with the gift. Tell him I'll be no man's doxie— but if 'twere a role I chose, I'd be a *royal* doxie—not his!"

The story was so good it was repeated to the King, who was reported to have laughed over it uproariously.

Lenore did not admit to herself that by her cavalier treatment of Lord Wilsingame she was not only striking a blow for poor Emma, she was revenging herself on all men who would use a woman and leave her—she was making

Wilsingame pay for all the heartaches she had suffered when Geoffrey left her.

In selecting Wilsingame for her vengeance, she had made a dangerous choice. Made ridiculous at Whitehall—where he was inordinately jealous of his reputation, for he would have gone to any lengths to seek favor with the King—Wilsingame abruptly stopped his pursuit of Lenore . . . but he did not forget. Lenore knew that from the way he watched her from the pit, his cold, hard gaze insolently studying her breasts and hips and then flicking contemptuously over her face—hard as a slap.

Lenore only shrugged. What cared she how Wilsingame felt about her? She was one of the royal players and, as such, subject to discipline only by the Lord Chamberlain!

In any event, she had decided on a new path. She had written Lorena several long letters (much inflating her position in the theatre) and had scrupulously enclosed what little money she had been able to save. Come next summer she meant to go to Twainmere and claim her daughter, to bring Lorena back to London with her—yes, and to dress her well and educate her! She would need money to do that, and she meant to get it.

The road to Whitehall still lay open to her—she had but to reach out at the right moment and seize it!

She made that decision one night when her petticoat had been torn on one of the stage props and she realized she must buy a new one—for the actresses had to furnish their own petticoats as well as shoes and stockings, scarves and gloves. The price of a new petticoat would keep her on half rations for a week! Lenore glowered down on it—and called for a tirewoman. As she swept onto the stage in her mended petticoat and a handsome green satin gown trimmed in silver lace from the Great Wardrobe (a cast-off of Lady Castlemaine's, the tirewoman had whispered) Lenore had reached an internal boiling point. What future was there for her in the theatre? She would never make enough on her meager "sharing dividends" to have Lorena with her! Ah, but she could mend her fortunes! She would do it as Nell Gwyn had—by taking a royal lover!

Having made that decision, Lenore lifted her head and

delivered her lines in such ringing tones that there was a small round of applause from the appreciative audience.

Lenore turned to acknowledge that applause with a smile—and froze in fury.

She was looking into the face of Gilbert Marnock.

For a moment her senses swam and she was submerged in memories. She was back again in her lodgings off Magpie Lane on a bitter cold winter night. She had waked to find herself bound by Gilbert's clutching arms, weighted down by his lean body. She could feel his hands impudently pawing her breasts and his hot breath searing her skin as she wrestled with him in her bed in Oxford.

From backstage Ainsley saw her shiver and reel on her feet. He wondered if she was coming down with some distemper, and would they all catch it? But she quickly recovered herself and went on with her lines.

"What ailed ye there as ye turned to the audience, mistress?" he asked her curiously as she stepped offstage. "For a space there, I thought ye would fall!"

"I remembered something," said Lenore grimly. "Something I'd prefer to forget." Her face was so pale and set that Ainsley, though curious, forbore to question her further.

That night Lenore wore a large black wig and a vizard mask when she went home from the theatre. She had no desire to encounter Gilbert again, and she had the uneasy feeling he might seek her out.

She was right. He sought her out at rehearsal the very next morning.

Lenore could not know with what care Gilbert had dressed for his planned confrontation. For two hours before, his hairdresser had been combing and pomading his caramel curls, which were more luxuriant than any wig and cascaded over his rose satin shoulders. He had cursed his barber, and he struck his valet when he discovered a spot on his satin knee breeches. Accepting the cuff with servility, the man—who wore Gilbert's livery—hastily brought Gilbert another suit, this one of violet taffety, and helped his cursing master into it.

Gilbert could afford these luxuries of temper. His parents had recently died, and he had come into a considerable inheritance. With more money than he had ever had before in his life, Gilbert had promptly hied him to London, that hub of iniquity for which his dissolute soul had hungered for years. He had arrived but last week, had busied himself with setting up a gentleman's establishment and hiring servants and ordering new clothes. This was the first time he had attended the theatre, and he had come in hopes of seeing the King so that he could later brag he was an intimate and back up what he said with a knowledgeable description of the monarch. But in that he had been disappointed, for the King had favored the cockfights instead of the play on that particular night.

It had been a mind-searing shock to Gilbert to see Lenore Frankford, seemingly more beautiful than ever and with a poise that even he did not remember, swish out upon the stage wearing Lady Castlemaine's cast-off green satin ballgown.

He had sat thunderstruck as she met his gaze and went rigid with shock. For a moment he had thought she would faint and had leaned forward tensely, but she had recovered herself and the play had gone on.

How wonderful she had looked with her flame-bright hair glowing beneath the myriad candles. Like a graceful flower she had swayed and turned as if blown about by the wind, while Gilbert's hard caramel eyes, hot with memory, had roved over her supple body. Her breasts were just as he remembered them, her waist as narrow. She still had that flaunting walk that drew men's eyes, that challenging smile. He remembered vividly what it had been like to hold her in his arms, to possess her. His heart thudded in his chest with his hot rememberings. He turned his head sharply as two seats away Lord Wilsingame leaned forward and muttered, "Damned vicious beauty! If I had my way, I'd have—" Gilbert did not hear what Lord Wilsingame would have done if he'd had his way, but he saw the vein standing out in Wilsingame's forehead, the way his jaw worked; he could *guess* what Wilsingame would have done if he'd had his way! Gilbert knew Wilsingame but slightly, having met him at a gaming hall the night before, but he admired him enormously as a self-proclaimed court favorite—new to London, Gilbert had no way of knowing that Wilsingame was but one of a small army of hangers-on, eagerly finding any means to seek the King's favor.

About him in the pit, Gilbert could see London's wild young rakes lounging about on bulrush-covered benches; their eyes were filled with naked desire as they viewed the beautiful woman in green satin onstage, and more than one licked his lips. Gilbert turned thoughtfully to look at Lenore again. So she had made it to London, this woman he had meant to bend and humble—and enjoy . . . and now she was flaunting herself on the London stage!

She had escaped him, but not before she had marked him. His brows drew together in a malicious line. He would enjoy her yet, by God!

After the performance, he had shouldered his way through the milling crowd into the tiring rooms, but was told Lenore had already left. On the street outside he had searched for her, but she was nowhere to be found. He had felt a brief sense of panic—had she escaped him again?

But common sense had asserted itself. Lenore was a royal player; as such she was shackled to the London stage—as much a part of the theatre as the curtains or the green baize-covered floor. At the theatre he would find her, for like the other players she must rehearse!

Now with his hot blood somewhat cooled but with his hands still tingling at the memory of her flesh beneath his kneading fingers, he strolled through the crowd seething about during morning rehearsal at the Red Bull in Vere Street where Killigrew's company gave their performances. He was an elegant figure, faultlessly garbed in violet taffety (his clothing was the reason Lord Wilsingame had noticed him, believing him fresh from the country and wealthy enough that he could borrow money from him if he ran short of cash) and he tapped a tall beribboned cane as he walked. Onstage a new play was being rehearsed, but as Lenore would not appear until the second act, she was sitting on a low stool across the room, studying her lines. She looked up to see Gilbert brush by an aspiring singer, wailing earnestly off-key, saw him wend his way past an eager young girl clad in doublet and trunk hose wavering along with a book on her head. Gilbert almost collided with her, and she dodged to avoid him, dropping the book with a groan. Ainsley, who was coaching her, gave Gilbert an irritable look and retrieved the book; he set it back upon the girl's head and urged her to walk gracefully, *gracefully,* make her hips *sway!*

Lenore sat, hypnotized, watching Gilbert approach with all the self-assurance of a Duke or a Prince. Every inch a fop, she thought contemptuously—lord, how she hated him! And to think that in Oxford for a time she had actually considered him attractive! Then Gilbert had passed Ainsley and stood before her, his handsome, scarred face lit by a smile of triumph.

Lenore rose warily, noting the cane in Gilbert's hand. Gilbert saw the look on her face and waved his gloved hand with a lazy gesture that billowed his delicate point lace cuffs. "There is no need for alarm, Lenore."

"I know there is not—for I'm a royal player now, and under the King's protection!" But she moved a step away from him.

Ainsley noticed her backing away and turned from his young protégé with the book on her head. Frowning slightly, strolled toward them.

"Send yon graybeard away," said Gilbert in a low voice, indicating the approaching Ainsley. "I am not here to exact vengeance."

"No, nor will you! For I've a royal pardon!"

"Send him away," said Gilbert, his eyes threatening. "For we've much to talk about, you and I."

"We've naught to say to one another! Ainsley—"

With deliberate grace, Gilbert stepped between them with his back to Ainsley. He leaned upon his beribboned cane, hovering above her as if to overwhelm her with his masculinity. "Can it be ye've forgotten the night ye spent in my arms?" Gilbert's brows lifted mockingly. "But ye were hot for me then!"

Lenore paled and her hands balled into fists. "You raped me! And I marked your face for it—as you deserved!"

Gilbert shrugged. "I am magnanimous. I choose to forget that." Gilbert turned and waved Ainsley away with a disdainful flourish of lace cuffs. "You may go, sir. This is a private conversation." He turned back to Lenore as Ainsley hesitated, frowning. This would not be the first dandy Ainsley and others had had to eject from rehearsals; he placed his hand upon his sword.

"I will even allow you to make amends," Gilbert was saying expansively. "*In bed,* where amends should be made." He paused and smiled; Lenore did not like the look of that smile. She remembered it only too well. "If you do not come," he added softly; there was a threat behind the words, "you will have cause to regret it, I promise you."

Cause to regret it indeed! The blood flowed back to Lenore's pale cheeks in a hot surge. She drew herself up to her full height and looked at Gilbert with scorn. "Powerful you might have been in Oxford, Gilbert, playing both sides and able to blackmail poor women who feared for their lovers! But here even good Master Ainsley yonder"— she nodded toward Ainsley, who had now drawn his sword from its scabbard and was testing the edge with his fingers for sharpness while he studied Gilbert—"can mock you! As can I! For we're the King's players and sworn in, and not subject to arrest by any but the Lord Chamberlain himself!"

Gilbert gave her a lazy look from those caramel eyes. The face that had once been blindingly handsome now had a long weal down one cheek where she had burned him, and another mark, a deep pit in the other cheek. She could not know he had acquired that second scar when Geoffrey had hurled him from the window of his lodgings in Oxford.

"Did ye know I am paying my addresses to the Lord Chamberlain's daughter?" he drawled. It was untrue, but it was a thrust calculated to inspire terror.

Lenore's face grew a shade paler. She leaned forward.

"I care not if you are courting a princess of the blood!" she blazed. "If you so much as lay a finger upon me, Gilbert, I swear I will bring the matter before the King himself! And *then* we will hear again your explanation of why you did not fight for him at Worcester!"

If Gilbert was discomfited by this counter-thrust, he did not show it. None of his aplomb left him. "But I am your best friend, Lenore," he sneered in a voice that carried clearly to Ainsley. "Am I not always kind to my cast-off doxies?"

For a moment the world went red before Lenore, and she struck out savagely at his face, but Gilbert had been expecting the blow and dodged easily.

Ainsley, who had leaped forward at Lenore's sudden assault on this faultlessly garbed gentleman with the scarred face, was halted by Gilbert's words. Cast-off doxie? Who was he to come between a man and his doxie, cast-off or otherwise? He pressed the point of his sword into the floor and leaned upon the hilt.

"You have a nasty temper, Lenore," chided Gilbert. "Already you have been seen to assault me—by yon rough fellow there." He indicated Ainsley with a jerk of his head and swept Lenore a handsome bow. His voice rose mockingly. "I'll bid you good day, mistress. And I do regret that you cannot share my bed tonight, but I find myself otherwise engaged. Perhaps another time?" He turned arrogantly on his heel and was gone, weaving swiftly among groups of players toward the theatre entrance.

Lenore swung on Ainsley, who was looking after Gilbert, round-eyed. His expression said plainly: what, Mistress Chastity pleading to bed a cavalier? She must be his cast-off doxie indeed! "You saw that, Ainsley," cried Lenore. "He is a liar and worse. If he harms me, you must be my witness!"

"I saw no intent to harm you," Ainsley said dryly, sheathing his sword. "Indeed, I saw you strike out at him. But what provoked you, I could not say, for he had a smile on his face the whole time."

Lenore gave Ainsley a bitter look. Like so many others, he had lately fallen under the spell of Nell Gwyn, and Nell

Gwyn was certainly not one of *her* friends. But . . . in honesty, what had there been to see? Gilbert had been clever and had made her appear in the wrong. He had always been clever.

Shaken with bitter memories, she turned away; the second act had begun, and soon she must march on stage and speak her lines.

Gilbert left the theatre with a deep frown etched on his scarred face. He nodded his caramel curls absently to a passing lady in scarlet silk he thought he recognized—and then turned and gave her a swift, ingratiating smile, for he had recognized the King's new doxie, Nell Gwyn. A pretty piece, he thought, with her riotous chestnut hair and saucy face. But not so beautiful as Lenore with her deep expressive violet eyes and challenging smile. Lenore, who made him go hot and cold, who made his blood race in his veins. His jaw tightened. He would bring Lenore to heel. And punish her. Exquisitely.

But first he would humble her.

Deep in thought, Gilbert strolled along the Thames, with the salt breeze blowing stiff in his face. He paused, leaned on his beribboned cane, and watched the white-sailed merchantmen bringing "sea coal" from Newcastle, wine from Bordeaux and Cadiz, spices and rich carpets from the Levant, and salt from Scotland. About him roared and jingled a great city, filled with gaming houses and brothels, palaces and corruption. He filled his lungs with the lusty air of London—ah, this was home to him! Lucky Wilsingame, to have been able to reside here almost since the Restoration of the King! The night before last over a game of dice, Lord Wilsingame had regaled him with tales of the wild parties he held at his house on London Bridge. He had bandied names about, of famous bawds and courtesans, and behind his hand he had even muttered spicy tidbits about nights spent with Nell Gwyn.

Nell Gwyn! Suddenly Gilbert struck his thigh and laughed aloud, for the perfect way to humble Lenore had come to him.

So loud was his laughter that several seabirds perched nearby took wing and flew away, calling raucously. His mirth and the jaunty swinging of his cane as he left attracted the attention of several dirty little urchins from the docks who, seeing such a jolly gentleman, ran up and begged him for a penny. Contemptuously Gilbert struck at them with his cane, and they retreated, muttering. From a distance one picked up a rock and hurled it at the fine gentleman in violet taffety just turning the corner away from them.

Gilbert might have given chase, but he had a more urgent mission, one which set his blood to singing. He was headed for a tavern Wilsingame had warned him away from as being frequented by scenekeepers and lackeys from the theatre—especially did he wish to meet those who worked in the Great Wardrobe. There was malice in Gilbert's face as he swung through the tavern door and looked about him, for he had no doubt his plan would work.

Mistress Lenore, he promised himself grimly, would soon be removed from the King's protection, and would be impelled into *his*.

CHAPTER 27

Though the King had recently been patronizing cockfights and bear-baiting, confining his playgoing almost exclusively to Davenant's company of players, who held their performances in the remodeled Lisle's Tennis Courts in Lincoln's Inn Fields—and naturally the Court trailed him—Lenore's own star had been rising of late and she had once again landed a "breeches part" in a new play. The play had been written by Killigrew himself, and it was whispered that the King was sure to attend, for Nell Gwyn was in it.

Up to now, vivacious Nell had been able to keep Lenore out of plays in which she appeared, but she had had a falling out with Killigrew over her dialogue—she wanted it lengthened—so this time Killigrew had ignored her demands and cast Lenore in the "breeches part." The part was indeed a juicy one, and Lenore's eyes had widened in surprise and delight at the glamorous costume the woman had been stitching her into. She turned about before the mirror in the tiring room studying it. It was almost as showy as the costume Nell had worn at Whitehall, of white and yellow satin, with amber silk trunk hose that clung to her lovely legs.

This morning was the dress rehearsal for the new play, and Lenore, finally free of the tirewoman, hurried forward on cue. Onstage she could see Nell Gwyn (who must have dressed for her part at home, because Lenore had not seen her in the tiring room), dressed as a shepherdess and waving a tall beribboned shepherd crook. Looking the saucy wench she was in her blue and white gown with its huge full skirt and bodice cut so low her round breasts seemed about to bounce out, Nell shook her chestnut curls and simpered roguishly in the direction of the royal box which Charles would occupy during the performance.

Everyone knew she was sleeping with the King.

Lady Castlemaine was absent from the city for a short time, and in her absence Nell was enjoying Whitehall—everyone wondered what would happen when spirited Lady Castlemaine returned.

Personally, Lenore hoped Lady Castlemaine turned Nell out. She strode onstage and spoke her opening line. "Ho there, varlet! What do you with yon maid?"

Nell, who had been absent from all the rehearsals, sending word insolently to Killigrew that she "already knew her lines," obviously had not known Lenore was to have a part in the play, for she turned sharply as she heard Lenore's voice and her hazel gaze swept over her would-be rival.

Nell did not like what she saw. Lenore was a sumptuous figure in tight amber silk trunk hose that clung like her own skin and displayed her lovely legs clear to the hips. The white and yellow satin jerkin did little to conceal Lenore's beautifully shaped outthrust bust, and her yellow satin sleeves were slashed and graceful. She wore shoes with high yellow heels (she had starved for a week to buy them) that gave her the advantage of height over the shorter Nell, and she had chosen to wear her own hair instead of a wig; it cascaded down around her slender shoulders in riotous red-gold splendor.

She was too beautiful, Nell saw that at once—such a

458

woman would surely arrest the gaze of the King. Nell, who hoped to supplant Lady Castlemaine and become first woman in King Charles's heart, was not pleased. She had been stumbling over her lines, for all she'd said she knew them. Now she abandoned her dialogue altogether and advanced on Lenore.

"Take off that costume and return it to the Great Wardrobe," she cried angrily. " 'Twas given by the Earl of Marford and promised to me for the play we do next week."

Lenore stopped where she was, rested her hands on her satin hips, and gave her rival a scornful look. "I'll not," she said. "Next week you may wear it and welcome, but for this performance the tirewoman gave it to me. She's been spending all morning altering it to fit me."

"Off, I say!" cried Nell, who'd not been getting much sleep, what with having such an amorous and athletic lover as King Charles. Her nerves were on edge, and her strident voice showed it.

"No!" Ignoring Nell's interruption, Lenore turned to continue her part. She waved a graceful slashed-sleeved arm. "Unhand the maiden—"

But she never finished her lines. With the fury of the street girl she was, hot-tempered Nell was upon her. She plummeted into Lenore from behind, ripping at Lenore's satin doublet, grasping Lenore's long hair and jerking her head backward. Lenore, who was taller than Nell and had a longer reach, stumbled forward gasping at the suddenness of this unexpected assault from the rear but recovered nicely, spinning around and striking Nell away from her. Nell struck out at Lenore with her shepherd's crook as she reeled backward into Blakelock's arms, propelled by the force of Lenore's blow. She was spitting curses and street language, and from all about the company ran to watch as Nell struck Blakelock's restraining arm away from her, knocked over a turkey-work chair and some tin candlesticks, and came at Lenore once again.

Lenore was ready for her this time. As Nell plunged at her, she sidestepped, but reached out to grasp a handful of delicate frilly bodice. She gave it a jerk, ripping away a long ruffle. Nell shrieked with fury as she saw her bodice was torn and suddenly darted under Lenore's guard, seized her around the waist, and by the very momentum of her charge, knocked Lenore off her feet. They went down together in a flailing heap of yellow silk legs and voluminous pale blue shepherdess skirts. Around them the tirewomen screamed, the actresses cried at them to desist and shouted for Killigrew, and the actors laughed and offered bets as to which would win—for though Lenore was taller, Nell was sturdy, and opinion was that they were evenly matched.

Lenore gasped as Nell's sharp nails raked her face, barely missing her eyes. In anger, she wound her fingers tightly in Nell's chestnut ringlets and gave her head a sharp bang on the green baize floor. Nell screeched and kicked Lenore's shins with her square-toed blue shoes. Lenore countered by stamping on Nell's instep with a punishing yellow heel. Nell bellowed and bit at Lenore. Over and over they rolled on the green baize floor as Lenore tried to avoid the other girl's sharp teeth.

Panting, Lenore had her rival pinned down when Killigrew arrived on the scene. He strode through the company, scattering players and tirewomen to right and left, and pulled the contestants apart amid scattered applause and raucous cries of "Encore! Encore!"

"Since the ladies are willing, perhaps we should incorporate that scene in tonight's play!" cried one jolly voice.

Killigrew, who was holding the two women apart, gave the speaker a scathing look. He ignored Lenore's scratched face and torn costume. "Are ye hurt, Mistress Gwyn?" he asked anxiously, standing Nell on her feet. Lenore, struggling to her feet without assistance, thought wryly that that bleat of worry was for the King's favorite—Killigrew dared not let Nell come to harm in his theatre.

Trembling with rage, Nell dashed his arm away. "I'm all right, but my costume is ruined!" She fairly spat the words at Killigrew, reaching up to smooth back her tousled hair—indeed a tuft of that hair, departed from the scalp, was still clutched in Lenore's fingers. Nell looked down in fury at her shepherdesss gown, sadly dirty and torn. "That wench attacked me!" she shouted at Killigrew.

"I did not!" cried Lenore, incensed. " 'Twas *she* attacked me, for she wants my costume!"

"The costume was promised to me for next week's play, and I do not want her appearing in it before I do—'twas given to the company by the Earl of Marford that I might wear it!"

Killigrew looked pained. "I promise she will wear it only for this performance, Mistress Gwyn. There's no time to find her a new costume now. The tirewoman—"

"Devil take the tirewoman!" panted Nell, her face flushed. "She's not to wear it at all! Do you hear me?"

Killigrew bit his lip. Everyone could see that he was warring within himself. The possibility of feeling the King's displeasure if the current royal favorite was not appeased was very real. He straightened. He had made his decision. Although his face was pale, it was expressionless as he turned to Lenore. "Take off the costume, Mistress Frankford. The tirewoman will find you something else."

Lenore gave him a mutinous look. She opened her mouth and checked herself. Killigrew's decision in these matters was, after all, final.

"Ye can get your revenge this afternoon in the play, Mistress Lenore!" called a raffish voice after her. "When ye stab her in the second act!"

Nell sniffed and whirled away, trailing ripped ruffles, and Lenore stalked off to return her torn costume to the Great Wardrobe and to seek a new one.

The one they found for her was not nearly so nice, nor was there time to make it fit properly. But Lenore knew bitterly that there was no alternative, she would have to wear it.

That afternoon they played to a packed house. The King was in attendance, Lenore was told excitedly by a passing actress. As the First Music struck up, Lenore, who was dressing in the women's part of the baize-hung tiring room, looked down contemptuously at the dull gray trunk hose and cheap red doublet they had found for her. Gone were the handsome slashed sleeves. Only the shoes with their high yellow heels remained, for they were her own, but

461

they looked strange with those dull gray trunk hose. Lenore suspected them of deliberately seeking for her a shabby costume in order to pacify jealous Nell and dabbed angrily at her scratched face.

She rose for a last inspection of herself in the mirror—and that mirror told her that the red doublet clashed with her hair, that the gray trunk hose were too loose and sagged, making her legs appear awkward. She gave the stool on which she'd been sitting a kick that sent it skidding to the far end of the room, and several other actresses who were dressing in the room turned to stare at her. From the far end of the room came a burst of laughter, and Lenore shot an angry look in that direction. There Nell Gwyn was holding court, fluttered over by actresses and tirewomen, who knew she was sleeping with the King and hoped to gain her favor.

Nell's costume was a wonder, Lenore noted bitterly. A most unlikely shepherdess's costume, made of silver gauze and trimmed in tinsel, but beautiful nonetheless. All eyes would be on her indeed!

Lenore was so angry she hoped she would be able to remember her lines. At least there was one part she was not likely to forget. In the second act—and unrehearsed, for this morning's dress rehearsal had broken down after Lenore's fight with Nell, Nell having refused to go on with the rehearsal in a torn costume and Killigrew throwing up his hands and stalking out—Lenore was supposed to give Nell a stab in the chest with a stage dagger. Lenore had used these stage daggers before—the blade would disappear into the hilt at the thrust, but the blow would burst a tiny pouch of sheep's blood which Nell would wear concealed between her breasts. With a realistic red stain spreading on her bodice, Nell would fall gracefully to the green baize floor—and die dramatically onstage.

Lenore looked down angrily at her ugly costume. She would give Mistress Nell such a blow as would burst the laces of her shepherdess's bodice!

Still furious, she waited by the curtain for her cue and strode onstage. In the blazing candlelight, Nell, in her tinseled silver gauze, looked lustrous.

"Ho there, varlet!" cried Lenore in a ringing voice to Blakelock, who had hold of Nell's white arm. "What do you with yon maid?"

" 'Tis naught to you," cried Blakelock sulkily, with an exaggerated stage gesture.

Out of the corner of her eye Lenore could see King Charles smiling sardonically from the audience, his gaze all for the lustrous Nell Gwyn, one white hand clutched to her bosom.

"Unhand the maiden and give her up to me!" cried Lenore furiously, drawing the knife and brandishing it.

Blakelock pretended to cower and ran away offstage. Nell rushed forward.

"My savior!" she cried.

"Nay," said Lenore grimly, as the plot called for her to do. "Not your savior, but your rival. 'Tis you who have seduced my lover!" She raised the knife.

"No, no!" cried Nell, with well-simulated panic. She turned gracefully to run, and Lenore grasped her by the wrist, spun her back and struck straight and true with the fake dagger—and with such force that Nell screamed and staggered backward, landing on the green baize with a thump instead of collapsing gracefully. The little pouch of sheep's blood hidden between her breasts broke under the assault as planned and stained her bodice red, but Nell did not spread her arms out fetchingly and "die." Instead she struggled up, her face contorted with pain. "She has killed me!" she shrieked hoarsely. " *'Twas a real dagger!"*

Pandemonium reigned in the audience as King Charles leaped to his feet, cavaliers vaulted onstage, actresses and actors came running from everywhere. Killigrew himself rushed onstage in the hubbub and tore from Lenore's paralyzed hand the dagger she had used on Nell.

" 'Tis a stage dagger," he said with relief, pressing the blade with some force back into the hilt, and Lenore fell back against Ainsley in relief. Her hands were shaking. She had meant to strike Nell—but certainly not to kill her!

"She has cut me!" cried Nell, giving her bodice an angry rip that exposed the white flesh between her breasts. There indeed was a small cut where the malfunctioning dagger

463

had penetrated through the bodice and pouch and gouged a quarter-inch into her white bosom. "She did it deliberately!" Her voice rose hysterically. "Dismiss her! I demand she be dismissed!"

Across the heads bent over Nell's prostrate body, Killigrew gave his frowning royal master a worried look. He took the knife and plunged it into the top of a trestle table onstage. The blade retracted. He tried again. It stuck.

"The knife may have been tampered with," he muttered.

"But I am not to blame for that!" cried Lenore. "I but took the knife the scenekeeper gave me!"

"She attacked me this morning and tore my costume!" shrilled Nell, aggrieved. "How do you know she did not substitute another knife with a rusty blade that would stick?"

King Charles's frown deepened.

Killigrew swallowed. Abruptly he seized Lenore and dragged her, protesting, from the stage. Nell, recumbent and watching, suddenly waved a graceful hand and insisted bravely that she would go on with the performance even though the pain was—here she batted her lashes and pressed a hand dramatically to her bared breast—"almost too much to bear."

Lenore thought Nell's whole performance over what was scarcely more than a scratch too much to bear. She could hear the cheers and applause that greeted this popular suggestion and looked back to see Nell being helped to her feet by half the gentlemen from the pit. She wondered if Nell could not have stabbed herself with a hatpin to draw attention to herself, but Killigrew brushed this suggestion aside as he dragged her along.

"I saw ye fighting with her this morning," he said grimly. "This is a theatre—not an arena. God's breath! The two of ye could get me hanged!"

" 'Twas not I who started the fight this morning—" began Lenore, but Killigrew thrust her from him.

"I care not who started it!" he bellowed. "Get ye gone! Ye are dismissed!"

Lenore stared back at him, her eyes wide and accusing. Then she turned on her heel and stalked back to the tiring room to change into her street clothes. She knew there was no use arguing with Killigrew.

Nell had won.

Gilbert was standing by the door as Lenore, dressed in her own clothes and carrying a tapestry square that contained her belongings, emerged upon Vere Street into a thick, soupy fog. She started as his scarred face loomed up before her and would have brushed past him, but he stepped forward like a disembodied ghost and barred her way.

"I hear ye have been dismissed, Lenore."

Lenore paused in mid-stride. How could he have known so soon? Word could not be about yet.

"So it was you. . . ." she said bitterly.

His triumphant smile told her everything. Somehow Gilbert had arranged for the daggers to be switched—the wonder was that she had not killed Nell with that malfunctioning dagger! For a moment Lenore stood there indecisively. She wanted to run back and tell Killigrew that she had deliberately been given the wrong knife. But she knew it would make no difference, had seen it on Killigrew's set face as he dragged her offstage. Killigrew was looking to his own job, his own future; he had placated Nell by dismissing her, he would not take her back now—perhaps she could try later.

In the meantime there was Gilbert to be dealt with. Gilbert, who bent close to her. Shrouded in fog, they seemed to be alone in the world, and his voice held a strange wistful caress. "Ye can still turn to me, Lenore—*I* would protect you."

"Protect me? *Protect* me?" she cried on such a note of wild derision that she could see him wince. Her eyes narrowed. Gilbert had arranged her downfall, but she still had the power to make him suffer. "What did you do to Lally, Gilbert?" she shot at him. "That she left you so suddenly?"

"Lally?" Caught off guard, Gilbert gaped at her, his handsome scarred face made almost ridiculous by surprise.

"Was it the same thing that made 'Mother' Moseley bar you from her brothel?"

465

Gilbert paled.

Lenore laughed scornfully. "Did you think I would not know? But we players hear everything backstage! We know who sleeps with the King—and who does not. And who is thrown downstairs at 'Mother' Moseley's for . . . why did she have you thrown downstairs, Gilbert? Because of what you did to her best girl, Gertrude?"

"Gertrude is a whore," panted Gilbert. "What could it matter what I did to her?"

"Gossip has it poor Gertrude—now that she's up and about again—has promised to ease a dagger between your ribs if you return. Do you always wear out your welcome, Gilbert? Was it so in Oxford? What tale would Lally tell me, Gilbert, if I were to see her again?"

"We quarreled," he grated. "Nothing more."

"I've no doubt you quarreled," said Lenore relentlessly. "I could see plain evidence of the arguments she lost on her bruised face!"

" 'Twas impossible not to quarrel with her!" he burst out. "She'd no thought of anyone but Ned!"

It was probably true, but Lenore, smarting from her unfair dismissal, was hardly in a charitable mood with the man who had caused it. "One cannot blame Lally for preferring a better man," she sighed.

Gilbert seized her arm vengefully. "You will end up at 'Mother' Moseley's yourself before long," he hissed, "where you'll be glad enough of my favors—or anyone else's who has the price! Geoffrey knew you for what you were!"

At that mention of Geoffrey, Lenore's face paled. "What did you say?" she asked menacingly.

"I say he knew you for a whore!" shouted Gilbert, driven too far. "Why do you think he did not bring you to Oxford sooner?"

He saw the effect Geoffrey's name had on her, and a terrible light flashed in his eyes. He would give this insolent wench something to think about! "Did you not know Geoffrey's wife had died in France before your lying in? He learnt it on one of his journeys. Geoffrey could have wed you—but he would not."

Agony burst over her.

466

"It is a lie!" she cried fiercely.

"Not so," he gloated, enjoying her disarray. "All in Oxford knew of it—all but you."

Was *that* what they had been whispering that day she had gone with Gilbert and Lally to a play in a barn near Oxford? Those voices in the audience behind her that had been so suddenly hushed as she was recognized?

"It isn't true," she whispered.

He laughed scornfully. "Believe what you will. Geoffrey told me he would never wed you. Know you not why he was absent so often? He was seeking a rich bride to buy him a pardon!" He watched in triumph the shattering effect these lies had on her and smiled in demonic satisfaction as her face broke up.

"Geoffrey knew you for a whore," he taunted, raking the raw wound. "He had promised me that when he tired of you, *I* might have you." His sneering face loomed toward her eerily in the fog. "What think you of that, Mistress Chastity?"

For answer she brought up her knee and struck him in the groin. Gilbert gave a sharp barking cry and went down into the mist. At her feet he rolled on the cobbles, doubled up in agony, clawing at the hem of her skirt.

Ashen-faced, Lenore stared down at his writhing body, shrouded by the thick white fog. Her mind reeled. *Considered her a whore . . . seeking a rich bride . . . his wife already dead in France . . .* Gilbert was Geoffrey's cousin; he would have known if Letiche had died . . . and it was reasonable that he would tell her now to make her suffer. And she was suffering.

Oh God, she had thought Geoffrey had left her because of the child, but if he had been lying to her all along, if he had really meant to turn her over to Gilbert when he tired of her . . . ! She stared down at Gilbert's recumbent form without seeing him. She was seeing instead a bright vista of hell wavering at her through the fog, and the awfulness of that picture blurred her sight.

She stepped over the body of the satin-clad dandy who writhed and moaned on the cobbles and stumbled away into the fog. Somehow she made it home to the Spur.

Twice in the soupy fog she crashed into passersby, receiving a curse for her awkwardness. And once she blundered into a lamppost. She would not have cared if she had tumbled into the Thames and the dark waters had closed over her head. For she moved through a darkness of the soul that was absolute.

And when she climbed the wooden stairs to her room and barred the door, she fell upon the bed with great sobs wracking her body. Geoffrey had never loved her, never . . . she had been a toy, a plaything to be used and thrown away.

Rocking in an agony of the spirit, she faced it all that night in the darkness of her small room. The white moon rose and waned and still she lay there, filled with grief and pain. The next day she did not go back to the theatre to try to get her job back. She did not go out; she did not eat or sleep. It was a full week before she could command herself to go back to the theatre. She wandered in listlessly and asked to speak to Killigrew.

He kept her waiting, but at last he saw her. The waiting was no hardship to Lenore; she did not care how long she sat there. Killigrew was startled at the sight of her. She was thinner, pale, her hair unkempt, her dark-fringed violet eyes great gashes in a lovely face grown suddenly ethereal. She told him she had been ill, and he believed it —she looked ill enough now.

But—he would not consent to take her back. He was firm about that. She had been dismissed by the Lord Chamberlain.

He was relieved at the way she took it—apathetically. She did not seem to care. He wondered uneasily what had happened to this blazing beauty whose fire had put all the other actresses in the shade. Had his dismissal . . . ? No, surely not; he put the thought aside. Still he felt guilty, for in his secret heart he had considered Lenore the most beautiful of all the young women who had trod the boards in his theatre, and he would have cast her in leading roles long before this had it not been for the enmity of Nell Gwyn.

Killigrew coughed. She could, he suggested, work as an

orange girl. Lenore, who cared little what she did or where she went, agreed at once.

"Orange Moll will show ye the way," he told her.

Lenore nodded without interest. Orange Moll, she knew, was the fruitwoman and queen of the orange girls.

Soon Lenore had joined the buxom, brawling, good-looking group of young women who hawked their wares in the pit. She made only a fair living selling oranges, for she did not choose to respond in kind to the bawdy remarks the young bucks made to orange girls, and her swift bright smile flashed but seldom.

"Thinks she's above us, she does," said Orange Moll, aggrieved. "I wouldn't of taken her on except for Killigrew—he asked me."

The other girls agreed with Moll. They bawled their wares and shook their hips and flirted their skirts and wore their bodices cut so low they almost exposed breasts as big as juicy oranges. They jeered at Lenore for having been nicknamed "Mistress Chastity," and one or two tried to trip her in the crush.

Lenore did her best to ignore them. She was fallen low, but she hoped as best she could to preserve her dignity. Men looked at her with open curiosity as she struggled by them through the crowded pit, calling out her wares. But enough of them bought her oranges that she could live—though she had to move from the Spur into cheaper lodgings—and a bare existence was all she cared for in this period of despondency.

But as the days passed and she began to eat again, her beauty was restored, and she was soon the wistful target of all eyes as she swayed gracefully through the crowd in the steaming pit, selling China oranges for sixpence apiece. Around her the other orange girls bawled their wares so loudly they obliterated the sounds of the First Music, but Lenore kept her voice low. It was her beauty that made patrons call her over to them. They wanted to fill their eyes with her, and so they bought her oranges.

In time she might have become an actress again, but . . . at an evening performance she looked up and saw Gilbert again.

469

It was a hot night, a special performance, crowded with luminaries. Onstage between acts, the company was performing a lively jig. Lenore had been threading her way carefully through the boisterous crowd in the pit, trying to avoid a noisy quarrel that had broken out between some wild young bucks just in from the West Country and a group of London apprentices that threatened to break into a full-scale riot. Insults and curses flew about, the dancers stomped, the music pounded, and the orange girls tried to bawl their wares above the din.

Lenore's attention had been completely absorbed by the brawling that had erupted, and it was a shock to find herself looking directly into Gilbert Marnock's face.

She stepped back warily, treading on a booted toe and muttering an apology, scarce heard in the uproar. Gilbert did not speak, but naked hatred leaped out at her from his hard caramel eyes. All the lust with which he had always studied her seemed erased, all remnants of humanity had disappeared from his gaze, and Lenore was shaken by the sheer evil of his glare.

She turned away, having to clamber over a protruding satin knee, slapped away some impudent pinching fingers, and struggled between two fat gentlemen, almost wedged together at the ends of two bulrush-covered benches. She was tired, she could feel perspiriation dripping down her back causing her thin worn dress to stick to her, and the noise was giving her a headache. Last night fighting had broken out in the pit and erupted onto the stage when three half-drunk cavaliers had leaped onto the green baize, pushed aside the actors, and elected to fight it out with swords in full view of the audience. She hoped nothing like that would happen tonight. Some distance away one of the apprentices had leaped to his feet and was calling "To me!" Someone else pulled him down. If only she could sell her oranges and go home . . . She struggled on, ignoring Gilbert's smouldering glares, selling her oranges where she might, evading as best she could the surreptitious pinches and pats of the young bloods who thought orange girls easy prey.

Lenore would have done well to keep an eye on Gilbert.

But she was intent on keeping her ankles from being cut by the big spurs on the gentlemen's boots—they were so fashionable they were even worn in drawing rooms—and on avoiding the vicinity of the bristling apprentices.

So she did not see Gilbert get up and push his way through to the little clot of disreputable cavaliers who were the constant companions of Lord Wilsingame, did not see them part to admit Gilbert, did not see Gilbert bend over his lordship and engage him in conversation. At what he said, Lord Wilsingame's hard face registered first shock, then anger. He turned and spoke to the heavyset gallant who sat next to him, whose name was Bonnifly, and Bonnifly lurched to his feet and stared openly at Lenore's back until those behind him shouted at him to sit down. A place was hastily made for Gilbert beside Lord Wilsingame, by the simple expedient of pushing an elderly gentleman not of their party, who sat at the end of the bench, off onto the floor. He landed with a yelp, but Bonnifly gave him such a threatening look that he rose and fled through the crowd.

Lenore would have done well to note all of these things, for the group around Lord Wilsingame were drinking heavily this night, and Lord Wilsingame had been publicly humiliated by Lenore. She could not know that Gilbert, with his hypnotic voice and insinuating manner, was fanning Lord Wilsingame's erotic interest in Lenore to flame by describing strange, wild delights he'd enjoyed whilst sharing her bed in Oxford. She would have screamed in fury had she heard Gilbert recount the things he had done to her and the wanton passion she had displayed.

"Can it be true?" wondered Wilsingame. "Our Mistress Chastity a whore?"

" 'Tis true, I swear it," said Gilbert glibly. "In Oxford all knew of her exploits. In truth," he added on a lewd note, "in Oxford all knew *her!*"

Wilsingame frowned. "Then why so coy with us in London? Answer me that!"

Gilbert shrugged and took a pinch of snuff from an enamelled box. "Oxford is far from London. Here she could set herself up as a virgin—perhaps to entrap a King. As Nell has done."

Wilsingame drummed his fingers on his hard satin-cased thighs. "Then Mistress Lenore should be taught a lesson, it seems to me!"

"I doubt you can buy her," warned Gilbert. "She likes to keep up the fiction that she is a virgin."

"Buy her? I do not intend to try," said Wilsingame brutally. "It strikes me that I have been too nice with our Iron Virgin!"

These were the words Gilbert wanted to hear. He turned with a snicker to mutter some bestiality about Lenore into Wilsingame's ear. Wilsingame looked astonished. He smote his knee with his fist. "She'll do that for me, too!" he cried. "Aye, and for all of us!"

Gilbert sat back, well satisfied. "I doubt me there's a trick you could mention that Mistress Lenore does not know," he drawled. "Of amorous delights, she's a mistress! Though she'd never admit it. . . ."

"A taste of the whip will spur her memory," said Wilsingame heavily.

"Mistress Chastity has always bested you, Wilsingame," laughed the dissolute de Quincy, turning around from the seat just in front. "Take care that she does not best you this time!"

"That she will not!" Wilsingame rumbled an oath. "She will be taught a lesson this very night. No, not tonight." He looked irritable. "Tonight I must bide at home to waylay one who will be crossing London Bridge on the King's business."

Gilbert pricked up his ears. He had been learning London ways, and he now knew that hangers-on like Wilsingame waylaid passing notables whenever possible and urged hospitality upon them—in hopes of gaining a useful friend at Court. "But why not tonight?" he said craftily. "Provide your guest with ripe entertainment—Mistress Lenore herself!"

Wilsingame brightened. "Why not?" he muttered. "My manservant can watch for him as he crosses the Bridge and bring him in—no need for me to do it. We'll serve her up like a bird on a platter!"

472

"Ah, she'll not disappoint you," sighed Gilbert. "Though it may at first take some persuasion to urge her on."

"Come with us, Marnock," urged Wilsingame. "We'll have sport together."

Gilbert laughed, but dodged that neatly. "I'd like that, Wilsingame—but alas, I've a ripe wench of my own who waits for me at my lodgings. She'll grow restive if I'm late. But having heard you once fancied Mistress Lenore and that she had palmed herself off on you as a virgin, I thought 'twas only just you be apprised of her true nature. A veritable strumpet! In bed she is devastating!"

Wilsingame's heavy-lidded eyes widened enough to emit a lusty sparkle. "She will be put through all of her paces tonight," he growled. "You can rest assured of it! And I count it a favor that you have brought me this agreeable piece of news, Marnock. My door is always open to you." Graciously he offered Gilbert his gold snuffbox.

"Your lordship is too gracious." Delicately Gilbert took a pinch of snuff and sneezed. "Ah, a good blend!" He looked up to see that the jig was ending and the third act was about to begin. "Well, I've seen this play so often I think I'll take myself off before I start reciting the lines along with the players! Good health, gentlemen!"

Wilsingame's friends nodded affably and Gilbert got up and pushed his way over a tangle of booted feet, past a number of skirts and petticoats which he disarranged in struggling through, and made his way quickly down the long passage and out of the theatre.

He wanted to be well away from what was about to happen—in case Lenore should ever in future command the interest of the King, for he'd heard about her interview at Whitehall. Then, no matter what she said, no blame could be placed on him—'twould only be the hysterical accusation of a spiteful woman; he, Gilbert, would neatly escape the royal wrath.

The orange girl, he told himself with vicious emphasis as he rode home in a hackney coach, would not be so crisp and arrogant after tonight!

473

CHAPTER 28

Lenore, quite oblivious to these schemes, struggled through the unruly crowd, handing out an occasional orange, trying to make change—and knew a moment of gratitude when she looked back and saw Gilbert Marnock leaving the theatre. Then someone trod painfully on her foot and she groaned and forgot him.

But her progress through the pit was being surveyed grimly by Lord Wilsingame, who had lost all interest in the third act of the play—even though onstage a masked devil with a forked stick had just disappeared through a trapdoor in the floor and above the stage a tinseled angel was being flown about movable "clouds," maneuvered on ropes. Wilsingame drummed his fingers on his satin knee and stared at the lovely orange girl with such a combination of lust and vengefulness as would have chilled her blood had she but seen it—but her attention was elsewhere, on the apprentices who had settled down for the moment but might grow restive again.

Finally, having set his mind upon the object to be

gained, Wilsingame gave thought to how to go about it. He bethought him that this was a play with a loud thunderstorm near the end—and very loud thunder indeed would be produced by the scenekeepers backstage as they rolled great cannon balls over sticks and pounded wooden mustard bowls, whilst others flashed pans of gunpowder and musicians pounded out a rumble on big bass drums. A noisy ending for a noisy play. It occurred to him that the timing of the thunder would suit him perfectly. He leaned over and muttered a few words to the evil cronies with whom he surrounded himself. They laughed as at some great jest, and two of them heaved themselves to their feet amid cries of, "Sit down! Sit!" and wormed their way through the audience and out of the theatre.

Pleased with himself, Wilsingame sat back and watched the play proceed. He waited till it was near its end, and then when Lenore came weaving through the crush with her oranges, he leaned forward and snapped his fingers.

"Here—orange girl! To me!"

Lenore turned at the cry of "orange girl" and frowned slightly when she saw who the speaker was. Wilsingame smiled ingratiatingly.

"Mistress," he drawled in a bored tone, "I would buy all your oranges if you would but deliver them to my coach outside."

"Quiet!" someone yelled from behind. "And move aside, orange girl—you are obstructing my view of the players!"

Lenore moved aside a step, but she hesitated. Lord Wilsingame's unsavory reputation had grown even blacker of late. It was common gossip at the theatre that he bought virgins and that he gathered together groups of his friends and held mass deflowerings. Although wags at the theatre insisted most of the wenches were not virgins at all, but fakes palmed off on him by the knowing madams, most of those who were, ended up as prostitutes in their plush establishments, and it was rumored that two of the unfortunate wenches, ill-used, had died and their bodies had been tossed into the Thames from Wilsingame's upper windows. Lenore had no reason to doubt these bizarre stories, and gave silent thanks that young Emma had got away from him. But as she sold her oranges she had always been careful to give the unsavory Wilsingame a wide berth. She hated the very look of the man: those heavy-lidded dark eyes always seemed to crawl over her body like reptiles, chilling her very skin.

Tonight she saw that he sat among his friends—men whose company he was seldom without and who were known to her by reputation. Her uneasy gaze roved over them: de Quincy the swordsman, a dissolute brawler but reputed to be the best blade in London; tall and lean, he had turned to watch, and his narrow green eyes were licking over her body. Flemmons, with a cold reptilian look—a graceful dandy who'd been barred from half the bawdy-houses of London for his manhandling of their bawds; he frowned darkly at her because in better days Mistress Chastity had snubbed him. And Alverdice, a wealthy young lout newly in from York and eager to plumb the depths of depravity, who now considered her eagerly, as if she were an orange herself, ripe for peeling. And perhaps the worst of the lot—Bonnifly, a heavyset monster of a man with reaching fingers whose painful pinches Lenore had endured more than once as she tried to edge by the group who surrounded Wilsingame. Bonnifly was said to have smashed a young actress's jaw because she resisted his advances, and had been barred from Court. His surly face turned to watch the hesitant orange girl. She thought there'd been two others with Wilsingame, but they seemed to have gone.

Soberly Lenore considered the arrogant Wilsingame. He hated her, she knew, for having held him up to public ridicule. Still . . . that was some time ago and he'd undoubtedly debauched a number of virgins since then—and she had fallen low; he might consider that she had been punished enough for flaunting him. She did not regret humiliating him. She'd do it again, if she had to.

An angry bellow came from one of the apprentices. He turned and soundly cuffed the man behind him, yelling that he'd been struck from behind. Someone pulled him off his bench, and a moment later they were rolling among

476

boots and spurs on the floor, locked in combat. There was a rising clamor between the West Countrymen and the apprentices. Lenore knew it was only a matter of time before large-scale fighting erupted—and the last time that had happened, all her oranges had got knocked to the floor and trampled to pulp.

Wilsingame yawned and deliberately took a pinch of snuff. "Well?" he asked testily, snapping his gold snuffbox shut. "Do I buy your oranges, mistress? Or do I procure them from another?"

Lenore disliked the idea of going outside at Wilsingame's behest. But the play had not yet ended, and it was doubtful either Wilsingame or his cronies would leave early—they never did. She was tempted . . . all her oranges. Let the apprentices and the West Countrymen fight it out in the pit! Having sold all her oranges, she could go home to her cheap lodgings in Southwark well ahead of the crowd and she could get some sleep—if sleep she could, for her lonely, restless nights were even more tormenting than her days.

"Give the oranges to my coachman." Wilsingame thumped the money into her hand as if it were a fact accomplished and turned back to give his rapt attention to the play.

That gesture of dismissal decided Lenore. Of course she would deliver them to his coach. No need to fear. Wilsingame and his cronies obviously were going to stay in the theatre. No doubt he was entertaining some doxie tonight and wished to favor her with high-priced oranges which she could bite into on the way to some other feast.

Lenore threaded her way out of the audience, where the noise of the combatants was fast drowning out the best efforts of the shouting players, and went swiftly through the long passageway that led out into Vere Street. She knew Wilsingame's coach by sight—all knew it because it was flaming red with much gilding and the green and gold Wilsingame arms emblazoned on the side. Ah, there it was now, just coming up to the door to wait for Wilsingame, who would be coming out as soon as the play ended—if he could make it through the brawlers. She hurried toward it and reached up toward the coachman with the oranges.

As he reached down to take them, the door of the coach burst open, and two men jumped out. Lenore recognized them as Taggart and Lymond, the two missing members of the coterie that surrounded Wilsingame.

She screamed and turned to run, dropping her oranges. The oranges rolled over the cobbles as greyhound-lean Lymond, leaping forward, caught Lenore's shoulder in a punishing grip and spun her around. She would have lost her footing but that burly Taggart caught her other arm and together they dragged her back to the coach.

Lenore's screams might have attracted attention, but just as she opened her mouth the very building behind her began to boom with artificial thunder. As they dragged her to the coach, the warring apprentices and West Countrymen spilled out into the street exchanging blows and shouting curses—and Lymond and Taggart appeared to be rescuing a hysterical lady from the mob. They fairly threw Lenore into the coach, and Lymond promptly sat on her legs, pinning her down effectively while heavyset Taggart held onto her flailing arms.

Wilsingame had timed the attack exactly right.

Lenore was not going to give up without a struggle. Even though pinned down, she sank her teeth into Lymond's lean arm. He let out an angry oath as she bit him, grasped her arms from Taggart, and jerked them behind her so that she writhed in agony and a dark veil of pain descended over her eyes. When her vision cleared, she realized that she was twisted into a half-sitting position on the floor of the coach and surrounded on all sides by booted legs—and shiny spurs. She swung her head around. She stared upward and knew terror. Fearsome Bonnifly had joined Taggart and Lymond, and the heavy-lidded eyes above those loose cruel lips that smiled down at her belonged to Wilsingame himself.

"If you scream again, Mistress Lenore," Wilsingame said in a voice so polite he might have been asking her to share a glass of malmsey with him, "Bonnifly here will cuff you hard enough that you'll lose your senses—and that would be a pity, for there's another coachful of gentlemen following close behind us, all of them as interested in your charms as we are!"

At that chilling statement, the bold courage that had never failed her came back to Lenore. Haughtily she lifted her head. "Lord Wilsingame," she said defiantly, "if you do me harm, the King shall hear of it!"

"Ah, but you are not in the King's favor—'tis Nell who sleeps in his bed," pointed out Wilsingame calmly. "Besides, who said we meant to harm you? We mean to *enjoy* you. Surely the King himself would approve of that!"

Lenore returned that relentless stare with an insolence she did not feel. She had heard too many stories of Wilsingame's sport with women not to believe some of them were true.

"Where are you taking me?" she demanded.

"Home—where else?"

Stonily, Lenore turned her face away from him and inspected the large spurs on Lymond's boots. She would not let them see the terror she felt.

In silence the coach jogged along toward Wilsingame's house perched in the middle of London Bridge. Lenore tried to scream once when she saw a pair of sturdy gentlemen edging by the coach as they entered onto the Bridge, and Bonnifly clapped a rough hand over her mouth, seizing her around her slender waist and laying rude hands upon her breasts. She tried to wriggle away from him and kicked out, managing only to tear her stocking on Lymond's spurs. Bonnifly raised a threatening hamlike fist, but Wilsingame lifted his hand.

"Enough, Bonnifly, enough," he said mildly. "Remember I've a gentleman coming by this evening that I wish to impress—'twould not do to mark the wench."

Bonnifly subsided, grumbling, and Lenore was left trembling on the floor of the coach as they passed through first one and then another short tunnel where the houses that lined the bridge met overhead.

She made one last attempt to break free as she alighted from the coach, to fling herself down to the cobbles and take off running down the narrow way. But even as she took flight she was snatched up in a mighty bear hug that drove the breath from her lungs, and Bonnifly carried her lightly through the oaken door that opened discreetly to admit them. She had a brief glimpse of the impassive face of the manservant who had told her Emma had left London and gone to the country.

Behind her she could hear the clatter of feet from a second coach that alighted before the house, and the occupants hurried in to cluster around her. Several of them she did not even recognize. God, there were so many of them —nine or ten all told! Two were very drunk, swaying on their feet, and one lurched toward her and peered down into her face.

"I know this wench," he muttered fuzzily.

"So will we all soon," snickered Bonnifly.

Lenore gave him back a defiant look, but she offered no resistance as Bonnifly carried her up the stairs with Wilsingame close behind. The manservant unlocked a door at the head of the stairs, and Lenore was thrust inside; the door slammed and locked behind her.

She had a swift impression of a candlelit square bedroom painted with fat rosy cupids in the French manner and dominated by a large canopied bed. The canopy parted suddenly, and a face peered out, to be swiftly followed by a thin female body. Across an expanse of worn carpet Lenore saw a fragile blond girl in a low-cut pink satin dress trimmed in black lace. The girl was emaciated, and her eyes appeared sunken and suffering in her white face that brightened suddenly in recognition.

"Emma!" gasped Lenore. "Oh, Emma, what has he done to you?"

Emma ran forward with a cry and impulsively threw her arms about Lenore. She seemed to collapse like a broken doll. "It's been terrible!" she sobbed. "You wouldn't believe—" Sobs choked her voice.

Lenore pushed her away and studied that pretty tear-stained face. "They told me you'd left London, Emma."

Emma shook her head, sobbing.

"*What* has he done to you?" Lenore demanded sternly. "And what happened to your Baronet?"

"At first—at first he was kind," Emma faltered. "And I even thought I loved him. But then one night he drove me here and—and left me. Lord Wilsingame said I was payment for a gambling debt!"

"But you're so thin! Doesn't he feed you?"

" 'Tis my own fault I'm thin," sighed Emma. "I thought —I thought that if I did not eat, maybe I would die the sooner."

Lenore looked at her sad little friend, appalled. "Surely it cannot be that bad!"

" 'Tis worse," Emma said simply. She looked down in misery. " 'Tis not only *him,*" she whispered. " 'Tis his friends. They hold big parties sometimes two or three nights a week, and young virgins are brought here to be 'broken in,' they say! Some are no more than thirteen— one was only twelve! Lord Wilsingame and his friends frighten them into submission by . . . by doing terrible things to me, Lenore. In . . . in public where all can watch!" Her eyes filled again with tears.

"Don't talk about it," said Lenore harshly, moving to the window. "Is there no way out of this place?"

"None. All the doors are locked—and that great footman, Bales, guards the halls. Once when I tried to run, he near broke my arm—and then he had his way with me on the stairs while Lord Wilsingame watched. He—he laughed, Lenore, and said Bales could have either me or his wages but not both—and Bales took me!" She shivered. "How did you come here, Lenore?"

"His friends abducted me from the front of the theatre."

Emma gaped at her; then hope sprang up in her eyes. "Then they will come looking for you!" she cried. "We will be saved!"

"Don't count on it," said Lenore grimly. Orange Moll hated her for being "above herself." Killigrew and the rest would assume she'd found a "protector" and gone off with him. She doubted she'd even be missed!

481

Emma's face fell. "You are right," she sighed. "I thought somebody might come looking for me—but nobody did."

"I came looking for you," said Lenore, "but I was told you'd left the City."

"Would that I could! Lord Wilsingame has circulated a story that he has a mad sister locked up in here and that her screams rend the night, and that sometimes they are joined by the screams of serving-women she attacks. But there is no mad sister. Mine are the screams they hear—mine and the poor virgins' who are dragged in here for deflowering and for . . . for terrible games that are played downstairs."

Lenore did not ask what games those were. "Have you no weapon?" she asked sharply.

Emma went over and lifted a corner of the carpet that stretched under the edge of the bed. She pulled out a small kitchen knife. "Elsie, who brings my food, forgot this one day, and I kept it and hid it. I meant to plunge it into Lord Wilsingame's chest the next time he tormented me—but I had not the courage. Then I thought as they dragged me back from the games downstairs and flung me into my room—for I could not walk, so badly had they treated me—that I would plunge it into my own breast and be free of them. But I had not the courage for that, either." She stood looking down at the knife in forlorn fascination. "Perhaps one day I will find the strength to use it," she sighed.

"Give me the knife." Lenore reached out and took it from Emma's limp fingers. " 'Tis not much against so many, and I doubt we can do much damage with it, but it might serve for surprise so that we can dart past that large footman."

"Bales? He always stays in the hall outside. 'Tis only Elsie comes into this room. 'Tis long since Lord Wilsingame visited me here—he prefers to make me come downstairs so that he may make sport of me with his friends."

Lenore tried the casement. To her surprise, it was not locked. She opened it and peered out. This building overhung the river, and she found herself looking down into the black waters of the Thames.

"There is no need to keep the window locked," mourned Emma, "for there is only the river below. Sometimes I have thought of hurling myself out and ending this wicked life I am condemned to—for I do not swim. But I have always so feared the water. My sister died by drowning."

"You're not going to drown," said Lenore energetically. "Nor submit to that evil pack again, either! Here, help me drag this—heavy—cupboard against the door," she panted, setting her shoulder to the work. Emma heaved her pitifully slight weight against it. It moved protestingly over the floor. "And now this—great—chest!" Panting, Lenore stood back and surveyed her handiwork. "Where does that other door lead?"

"Only into a small dressing room. But—they'll break down the door, Lenore."

"We'll gain time by making it harder for them to get in. Have you any possessions? Tie them into a bundle—quickly." She moved again to the window. "And I'll need that necklace you're wearing—unless you've money?" She reached out for it.

"I've no money," said Emma, bewildered. "And I think—I think the stones are glass."

"No matter," said Lenore. "They'll look real enough in the moonlight! Hurry!" Behind her she could hear Emma open a chest. She glanced back to see her bundling her clothing into a sheet which she tied at the top.

They could hear feet ascending the stair, and a key turned in the lock—but Lenore had seen what she wanted on the river below: a rowboat with a single oarsman had just slipped from under the bridge. She leaned out and called down to him. "This necklace if you'll take us downriver to safety!"

He looked up, startled, his face pale in the moonlight. Lenore dangled the brilliants temptingly. They had an expensive glitter. Behind her now there was a thundering on the door and Wilsingame's voice cried, "They've blocked the door somehow—Bales!"

From below the boatman bobbed his head. "Aye,

mistress, I'll take you where you want to go. Toss down the necklace!"

" 'Twill be on this lady's neck!" said Lenore, clasping it quickly around Emma's neck—the girl had just stuck out her head. "You must fish her out of the river for it! And here are her possessions!" She tossed down the bundle of clothes, and the boatman caught it and rowed rapidly back to position as the current swept him away.

Behind her Lenore heard Wilsingame say, "They've pushed something against the door, Bales. Bend your back, man!"

"Jump, Emma!" she cried. "I'll be right behind you!"

Emma clambered onto the windowsill and looked down fearfully. "I cannot do it," she cried hysterically. "I cannot jump into the water!"

"You must!" Feverishly Lenore sought to free the girl's clutching hands from the sill. "Emma, jump!"

Behind her she heard the great chest move, and the heavy cupboard toppled over with a crash that shook the house. At the sound of that crash, Emma's hands suddenly were loosed in fright, and Lenore gave her a strong push. With a shriek Emma went plummeting into the water and the boatman reached out and grasped her by the arm to pull her into the boat just as Lenore leaped to the windowsill poised to jump.

But it was a jump she was never to make. Even as she would have spun off into space, a pair of strong hands clutched her around the waist, and she was jerked backward into the room.

"Row!" she screamed to the boatman. "Bring help!"

Even as she spoke, she knew how futile that appeal was. Poor exhausted Emma would be lucky if she got away herself, would be lucky if the boatman actually delivered her to some place of safety downstream. But— even if he did not, her fate would be no worse.

"The wench Emma has escaped!" cried Bales, keeping his grip on Lenore's waist as he leaned out the window. "Milord, she is being rowed away in a boat!"

Wilsingame's cold voice cut in contemptuously. "No matter, Bales. I was about to get rid of her anyway—

she'd no spirit left in her. I want a woman, not a wooden doll! We've a better wench here, Bales."

"But milord, suppose she tells—"

"She'll tell no one anything, Bales. She'll fear to! She'll hide in fright that I may get her back!" He chuckled, and Lenore realized the chilling truth of that—Emma would probably fear to speak up in any event.

Wilsingame turned to Lenore. "Behave yourself, mistress. If you please my important guest from Kent, so that he speaks well of me to the King, I may reward you by letting you drive about London with me in my coach. Release her, Bales."

As Bales's fingers loosened their grip on her waist, Lenore tore free and clawed at the window, but the casement was inexorably pulled shut against her best efforts and a heavy body pushed her aside. Big Bonnifly had come into the room and was leaning against the window grinning at her. He reached out and gave her a shove, and she found herself standing unsteadily on her two feet, facing Wilsingame.

"I will not entertain your guests—or yourself!" she panted. "I warn you, Wilsingame, that if you force me, I will give you no pleasure!"

Wilsingame's hand lashed out, and Lenore reeled back as he gave her cheek a stinging slap. "On the contrary," he sneered, his expression turning as bleak as his eyes. "You will give me great pleasure, orange girl—aye, and my guests, too! We will sport with you as long as it pleases us, and when we've done with you, 'Mother' Moseley can have you—with my compliments!" He took a threatening step forward.

Lenore would have prudently backed away, but from behind her Bonnifly's big hand pressed against the small of her back and propelled her forward. Before Lenore was aware what he was about, Wilsingame had grasped the front of her bodice. He gave it a violent jerk that split the fabric to the waist and—combined with her forward momentum from Bonnifly's shove—tumbled her to the floor at his feet.

Lenore scrambled back away from his boots, aware

that her white flesh showed in a cleavage that now reached to her waist. Desperately she clutched the material around her with one hand and managed to regain her feet.

Boots planted, Wilsingame towered above her. She thought hopelessly that she had never seen a more ruthless face.

"See that she puts this on," he said in a colorless voice, jerking his head toward a black silk gown trimmed in creamy lace that was tossed over a chair. "Where've ye been?" Lenore saw that he was speaking to a frightened-looking gray-haired serving-woman who was just staggering into the room burdened down by a large metal tub partially filled with water.

"Bales said ye'd brought in a woman, milord," she faltered, almost groveling before Wilsingame as she set the tub down and straightened up with difficulty. "And I've been heating a bath for her. I thought you'd want—"

"Very well." He cut her words off contemptuously, and she scurried away for towels and soap. "Nail the window shut, Bales," he ordered his burly manservant, and Bales hurried away for hammer and nails. "Bonnifly, you might guard this door to see that our pretty bird does not fly away before we've clipped her wings. You'll doubtless enjoy watching her in her bath."

Bonnifly grinned, moved to the doorway, and lounged against the jamb. Lenore edged toward the window, meaning to jerk it open and hurl herself out and take her chances on swimming to safety, but Wilsingame guessed her intention and seized her wrist.

"Not so fast, mistress!"

"I feel faint," she complained, noting that the kitchen knife Emma had meant to use on herself had been dropped below the sill as she tried to urge Emma through the window.

But Bonnifly's keen eye had spotted it, too. "Ho!" he cried from the doorway. "The wench seeks a claw to scratch us with!" He sauntered over and picked up the knife, tossed it in the air, and caught it by the hilt. " 'Tis a kitchen knife, Wilsingame. Your serving-woman should be careful not to leave sharp things lying about."

Lenore felt her heart sag to her worn slippers. That kitchen knife had been her last hope.

Glowering, Wilsingame waited until the serving-woman came back, carrying linen towels and soap. Bonnifly handed her the knife, and she blanched.

"How do you explain this, Elsie?" Wilsingame asked gently.

Elsie shrank back. "I—I do not know how it came to be here, sir!" she stuttered.

"Another example of your carelessness," barked Wilsingame, giving Elsie an angry shove that sent her skittering across the room, dropping her towels and soap. "One more such blunder and I'll dismiss you!"

"Please, milord!" Elsie fell to weeping. "I've seven children at home, and my husband's hurt and can't work!"

She went about picking up the scattered towels and soap and was still weeping as Bales hurried by, hammered the window shut with stout nails, and left.

"See that Mistress Lenore is well prepared, Elsie," Wilsingame told the old serving-woman sternly, at last letting go of Lenore's arm. She rubbed it against her hip, for it was almost numb from his harsh grip. "She must look very fetching, for I've a guest riding in from Kent tonight."

"A guest?" laughed Bonnifly. "That's hardly the word for it! Does he know he's coming here?"

"Bales will waylay him outside as he crosses the Bridge, unless he misses him in the darkness. You may soon laugh on the other side of your mouth, Bonnifly, for this man has the King's confidence. If we woo him well, he may gain for us a Royal Patent to trading rights in the Indies. 'Tis my plan that our orange girl here will give him such entertainment this night as he's not enjoyed before!" He laughed discordantly, on a note of mounting excitement, and Lenore cringed inwardly. " 'Tis only a pity we've no time to teach her special tricks, for I doubt me she's the expert Marnock claims her to be."

Marnock! Lenore gasped.

"A novice is better, anyway," stated Bonnifly.

"You may be right. She looks to be a hot wench, and

from what Marnock said, she was a whore in Oxford—before becoming a virgin on the London stage!"

"He lied!" gasped Lenore, clutching her torn bodice around her. "Gilbert Marnock raped me in Oxford! I was never his willingly!"

"Ah, so you admit you've lain with him?" Wilsingame's short, unpleasant laugh chilled her. "Yet you returned my gifts as if you were some mewling virgin newly come to town! Well, tonight we shall play games with the Iron Virgin! Tell me now, Mistress Chastity, how many men have you known?"

"Three!" flashed Lenore. "And *you* shall not be my fourth!"

Wilsingame's contemptuous laugh seemed to linger in the air as he brushed past Bonnifly and clattered down the stairs.

"Your bath, mistress," whined Elsie, who had dried her eyes on her apron. "We don't want it to get cold, you might catch a distemper!"

"I will not bathe while this man watches!" stormed Lenore, backing away, clutching her torn bodice with both hands.

"Please, mistress," coaxed the old serving-woman, trying to take hold of her hand. "His lordship will dismiss me if you refuse to bathe!"

"Then jump out this window after me when I smash this small chair through the panes," muttered Lenore in a voice too low for Bonnifly to hear. She took her right hand from her bodice and rested it casually on the back of a small straight chair. One spring and she could be at the window smashing with the chair. No matter if she was cut by broken glass, if she could but leap through . . . !

The old serving-woman shook her gray head sadly. "You heard me say I've seven small ones at home, for my sister just died leaving me her brood, and there's few will hire one so old as me—I must find work where I can. For years I did work for 'Mother' Moseley, making up the featherbeds for her young ladies to tumble in—but she dismissed me because I was no longer young and spry enough. 'Tis lucky I am to find any work at all."

"Then trip Bonnifly as I smash the window, and I'll find work for you myself—at better pay," muttered Lenore.

Elsie looked tempted, but she hesitated. "I am afraid, mistress."

From the doorway Bonnifly guessed her intention and leered at Lenore. "That chair will not break through the window, mistress, but if ye try it, I promise I'll have ye first—on yon big bed—before the rest of them have ye downstairs! 'Twill be my reward for preventing your escape."

Lenore removed her hand carefully from the back of the small chair. Bonnifly was probably right, the little chair was too frail to break the stoutly nailed casement before Bonnifly would be upon her. He was a big hulking man, and she had no desire to push him too far, for she had no doubt at all that he would make good his threat and not be pulled off of her, not even by Wilsingame, until he had achieved his purpose. No, she'd best take her chances downstairs. Perhaps, she thought forlornly, she could find a way to slip past them, make it out the front door onto the Bridge, and throw herself on the mercy of some passerby—if there were any crossing the Bridge at this time of night.

"Please take your bath and put the pretty dress on, mistress," pleaded old Elsie. " 'Twill not aid your cause to wear a torn dress!"

No, that it would not. "I will wear the dress," agreed Lenore with spirit. "Since your master has seen fit to destroy mine! But I will don it behind the hangings of yon bed. And I will bathe only if *you*"— she glared at the serving-woman—"will hold those hangings betwixt this man's evil gaze and the tub!"

"Mistress, mistress—"

"If you do not do it," said Lenore in as brutal a tone as she could muster, "I will take these sharp fingernails of mine—see them?" She held them up. "And I will tear at my face and neck and breasts until I am all scratched and bleeding. And I will tangle and rend my hair so that I will look like a woman who has slept in the gutter for a week, instead of the 'juicy morsel' my Lord Wilsingame expects!"

So white and determined was her face that the serving-woman fell back in alarm. "I'd best do as she says, Mister Bonnifly," she muttered. "Else she might do herself some injury and then Lord Wilsingame would blame us that we let her mar her beauty!"

In the doorway, Bonnifly shrugged. His nasty gaze said he would be viewing her naked body soon enough.

Looking resigned at this duty, Elsie the serving-woman held out the heavy bed-draperies as a shield behind which Lenore disrobed, pinned up her long hair, and stepped into the warm water. It felt good, and she sank down into a sitting position with her knees drawn up before her because of the shortness of the metal tub. She saw that she had been provided with expensive scented soap ("Soap like 'Mother' Moseley's girls use," bragged Elsie proudly) and she lathered it soberly down her white arms and across her breasts.

She bathed slowly, moodily, remembering another bath —one taken on a day of sun and wind in the raw wilds of Dartmoor. She had stood naked on a rock in the sunshine in a clear swift-running mountain brook, and Geoffrey, his gray eyes alight and laughing, had dipped water from the stream with his hat and poured it over her bare shoulders until her white body glistened and her round breasts pinked with the coldness of it and her pink nipples hardened under his provocative touch. He had bathed her with loving hands and dried her tenderly with his shirt. He had kissed her bare back and her gleaming shoulders, and his lips had roved exploringly over her breasts and stomach. And then his arms had tightened and he had taken her to him and there beside the gurgling brook they had lain together in the soft grass, their arms and limbs intimately entwined as he led her on to passion and fulfilled all her dreams of womanhood.

Tears misted her violet eyes. Love to her was a sacred thing, worth fighting for, worth dying for. All these years she had endured hardship and humiliation when she could easily have become somebody's kept doxie, making men pay dearly for her favors. She had done that because she felt her body was her own and should be freely given —not bartered or sold. Nor would she easily brook the taking of her by force.

She thought of Emma, who had been so young and so pretty and so full of foolish dreams when first she'd seen her in Killigrew's outer chamber—now Emma was broken and spiritless. Poor Emma, who had been used for cruel sport and tortured to frighten the young virgins Wilsingame "bought" from "Mother" Moseley into submission.

Well, *she* would not be used so! The hurtful memories of her beautiful days with Geoffrey—those days that had opened the floodgates of her heart and then when he had gone become an ice jam locked around that heart—came back to taunt her. She would not see Geoffrey again; he was dead or he'd have returned with the King—and perhaps he'd never loved her. No need to live for him.

And Flora had written that young Lorena was "lovelier than even you could have dreamed" and that all the best catches in the village were but waiting for her to grow up. A sad smile crossed Lenore's face. That lovely young daughter she had not seen since she was a baby . . . At first they'd been kept apart because she feared to endanger her child, feared she might end up in prison or a harsh orphanage, her young life ruined. And then when she received her royal pardon, she'd written lying letters of her new affluence, her success—lies she'd meant to make come true—and her stupid pride had kept her from going back to Twainmere to visit her, for Lorena would see at once that her mother was but one step from the almshouse.

No, she need not live for her daughter. . . .

Sitting pensively in the soapy water, she brooded—and suddenly Bonnifly's big hand jerked away the bed-hangings from Elsie's grasp and he laughed down at her.

With an angry shriek, Lenore brought up both her hands filled with soapy water and dashed it into Bonnifly's grinning face. The soapy water struck him in the eyes and he fell back, rubbing at them, unable to see.

"Lor, mistress," muttered the shocked serving-woman. "Ye'd best mend your manners, or they'll do terrible things to ye downstairs! They'll brook no interference with their sport. One poor girl fought them and kept fighting, and they did hurt her so bad she later died!" She stopped abruptly, as if fearful she had said too much. "I do but warn you," she muttered. "Even poor little Emma, who was afraid to deny them anything—"

"I am not Emma," cut in Lenore curtly.

She rose and suffered Elsie to pour a pitcher of warm water over her body to rinse off the soap. Her head was lifted now, her chin held high, for she had made up her mind. An arrogant naked figure, lovely as a water sprite and gleaming in the candlelight, she stepped from the bath and toweled herself dry with clean linen cloths. Then she climbed into the dainty black silk chemise trimmed in lace that Elsie had brought, sat down on the bed and smoothed on her long lovely legs a pair of sheer black silk stockings, and fastened them with the garters of silver tinsel that lay at hand.

Never in the theatre had she worn underthings or stockings so fine—and perhaps it was fitting that she should, for this, her last performance.

She looked up with an odd little smile. "Dress me well, Elsie," she said grimly, "for I would look my best this night."

Elsie gave her a frightened, uncertain look from her watery eyes. Could it be that this beauty's mind had come unhinged from fright? Here she was about to become the single victim of a mass sport—mauled by a pack from whose rough caresses she would emerge as the others had, trembling and screaming with fear and pain—and she wanted to *look her best* for the ordeal?

Lenore stood up. The black chemise was cut artfully low so that the tops of her white breasts gleamed. She no longer cared that Bonnifly, the soap cleared from his eyes, was staring at her hungrily. Let him rest his covetous gaze on what he would never possess!

492

CHAPTER 29

"And now to comb out your long hair," crooned the serving-woman. "I used to comb hair for 'Mother' Moseley's young ladies—ah, but you've prettier hair than any of them!"

Lenore, sitting bolt upright on the small chair she had intended to use to smash the window, suffered the old woman to comb her hair down around her shoulders.

"We could pile it up but—they would only pull out the pins and it would be worse tangled," advised the serving-woman. "First you will walk down the stairs—slowly, like a bride, mistress. Milord likes that. Bonnifly will walk with you, and you mustn't hang back, even if you're frightened. They're harder on them that's scared."

"No one will have to drag me!"

"If you don't walk down proper, I'll plant my boot on your round bottom and send you down amongst them sprawling," warned Bonnifly in a surly voice. He felt he'd been robbed of his fine private showing and angrily eyed the cooling bath water.

"When you get downstairs," continued Elsie, "Bonnifly will lead you into the drawing room, and there you'll take off your clothes—slowly like. The gentlemen like to lounge about on the benches and watch."

Lenore's throat felt dry. She kept her gaze steady and serene in the mirror, while her heart pounded. "And then?"

"They may make you dance a bit—first." Elsie was reluctant to upset the beautiful doll she had been ordered to gown.

"We'll tell you what to do!" snickered Bonnifly. "For me you'll—"

"I could fix your hair real cunning like," Elsie quickly interposed, with a frown at Bonnifly. "I could put little satin flowers in it. There's some in the chest there. Oh, I was a real ladies' hairdresser at 'Mother' Moseley's—let me show you."

"I've no doubt you're an expert, Elsie," said Lenore with a composure she did not feel. "But we will not seek for fashion tonight, since it seems I'm to wear this gown so briefly—we will seek instead for beauty. We will dispense with the flowers. Think you, is this dress cut low enough?" She held it up for critical inspection—it was artfully cut, she saw, and frothing with creamy lace at the top. "I would have it reveal my bosom, which is very white, don't you think?"

Elsie choked and looked frightened. " 'Tis indeed white as milk," she agreed. " 'Twill inflame them," she added timidly.

Lenore peered into the mirror. "I will pinch my cheeks to give them a high color, but my hair—no, my hair is my best feature. I will wear it combed down about my shoulders so that it will swing like a great shining shawl as I walk. Elsie, these shoes I'm wearing won't do, don't you have something better?"

"I—I might have," gasped Elsie. She padded out and brought back a pair of dainty black satin slippers with high red satin heels.

"Ah, that's better," purred Lenore, who now stood up

in the black silk chemise trimmed with a froth of black lace that barely concealed her nipples.

Awed, Elsie helped her slip into the clinging black gown trimmed at the bosom with creamy lace. It fitted Lenore's round breasts and clung to her narrow waist like her own skin and then flared out into a huge billowing skirt. The cream-colored lace frothed around her bare shoulders and hid part of her plunging bosom.

"I like not that lace," murmured Lenore, frowning as she turned about before the dressing mirror. It was so large she wondered if Wilsingame had got it from some theatre. No matter, it was the last looking-glass in which she would ever see her reflection. "Bring scissors that I may trim it away."

"Trim it away?" Elsie gaped at her. Of all the frightened women who had been dragged into this house, none had ever asked to cut their necklines lower.

Lenore nodded. "And a fan—I will need a fan, Elsie. Lord Wilsingame will wish me to appear as a great court lady, not as an abandoned wench from the streets. Am I to go bare-handed like a serving maid? Are there no black gloves?"

Elsie ran out and returned with scissors, a lovely fan of carved ivory and black ostrich plumes with a dainty mirror in its base, and a pair of black silk gloves. She watched in fascination as Lenore promptly cut away the offending froth of lace so that the daring dress now possessed not only a plunging neckline but a regal dignity.

Lenore studied her reflection grimly. All black . . . save for her white shoulders and the pearly tops of her breasts gleaming pale and her high red heels, she might almost be in mourning. And in a way she was. Mourning for her lost love, her lost lovely life that had somehow slipped through her clever fingers.

She set down the scissors and before Elsie could pick them up again she distracted her by saying, "My hair—it has become tangled again as I turned about, and I want it to fall as truly as running water. Comb it out again while I struggle into these gloves. And be quick about it, for I think I heard the front door open."

495

Downstairs there was indeed some commotion. A door slammed and they could hear a hubbub of voices downstairs, and over them all Wilsingame's booming, "Ah, but ye must stay—at least for a while. We've an entertainment planned, and 'tis about to start!"

Lenore controlled a shiver. An entertainment! *Herself!* She picked up the black silk gloves, fragile and delicate —and recoiled from their smooth touch. To whom had they belonged, and was their owner dead? Or cast out upon the streets or into some brothel to make her way? She straightened up, getting control of herself again, and eased the tight gloves over her fingers.

For a long moment she stared into the mirror. A vivid beautiful reflection, violet eyes alight, stared back at her. She could hardly believe she was doing this!

"You do be beautiful," sighed Elsie, laying down the comb and stepping back with a wistful look to view her handiwork.

"Yes, I want Lord Wilsingame to admire me," said Lenore in a level tone. "This effect should please him, don't you think?" She picked up the mirrored ostrich feather fan—and with it the scissors—and wafted it gently, careful to conceal the scissors from their gaze.

Elsie stood as if hypnotized, spellbound before this magnificent creation. She nodded her head in dumb approval. "I do think he don't deserve such," she muttered huskily. " 'Mother' Moseley would pay a packet to get hold of you!"

"But 'Mother' Moseley shall not have me, Elsie!"

Elsie's eyes widened. So that was this beautiful wench's game! She meant to *win* Wilsingame! She gazed at Lenore in admiration. None had so far done it, but . . . none had looked like Lenore!

From the doorway, Bonnifly, too, watched her—with avid soap-reddened eyes. She must keep his heavy hands from her—somehow. She turned arrogantly to Elsie. "I do not wish to have Bonnifly jerk me downstairs as if I were some kitchen wench squalling at her fate," she said in a cold voice. "Go and tell Lord Wilsingame that I wish to make a grand entrance. Tell him I wish to trail down the stairs all alone—without Bonnifly to mar the picture. Go and tell him how I look, Elsie. Make him grant me this request."

Elsie bobbed her head and scuttled away. She'd give odds she was looking at her new mistress here! And when she whispered to Lord Wilsingame that the saucy wench upstairs wanted only to *please* him ... !

Lenore waited, wafting her fan and turning about to keep Bonnifly's eyes occupied, to keep him from thinking about where the scissors might now repose. Downstairs there was a shuffle of boots and a clank of spurs. She could hear Wilsingame call, "Bring her down, Bonnifly."

Bonnifly surged forward to seize her, and Lenore stepped back to elude him. "You heard me say I wanted to go down alone!"

"What ye want don't matter!" grated Bonnifly, grabbing her by her left arm. In her right reposed the plumed and mirrored fan—and concealed in it the precious scissors. She had studied them well as she trimmed away the creamy lace—one plunge into her breast should be enough!

Bonnifly had dragged her protesting to the door when Elsie came running back. "The master says ye're to let her come down the stairs alone, Mister Bonnifly. If she's bent on bein' tractable, he don't want her upset again. He says you're to stand well back—he don't want the scene destroyed. He wants to impress his guest!"

Bonnifly let Lenore's arm go with a curse and lounged sulkily back in the doorway, and Lenore came out on the landing. A long flight of stairs yawned at her satin-shod feet. She drew a ragged breath. Life, which she had been so willing to throw away a moment ago, seemed suddenly sweet and dear to her.

But ... in the wide hallway below, clustered at the foot of the stairs leering upward, was a knot of men. In the forefront she saw faces she recognized, those who had been with Lord Wilsingame at the theatre: the lean de Quincy, lounging against the newel post as if to be in position to seize her first; reptilian Flemmons with his elegant yellow wig and his elegant rose satin ruffles;

young Alverdice, his heavy face flushed from wine, swaying on his feet, mouthing newly learned obscenities; Lymond, Taggart, they were all here. Indeed the nine or ten seemed to have swelled to beyond a dozen. Mingled among those she knew were some she did not recognize by name, but at least four of them she had seen about the theatre; they were a vicious lot, known for their shocking exploits. Several faces she could not see behind the great plumed hats and enormous curled periwigs, but there were many, *so many!* It seemed to her anguished view that Lord Wilsingame had invited all of London to witness her shame—and partake in it.

"Ye must start down now," hissed Elsie, crouched behind her lest she spoil the effect. "Remember, walk right past them into the big room at your left. 'Tis there they'll have their sport with ye."

Lenore swallowed. Life was not that dear! She did not reply to Elsie but gripped the mirrored plumed fan—and the concealed scissors—the tighter. Her delicate jaw had a grim line. The elegantly dressed gentlemen below would be disappointed if they hoped to have sport with her tonight!

With a regal gesture she lifted her head and tossed back her lovely hair so that it rippled about her back and shoulders like shimmering silk. She made a startling picture in the clinging, low-cut black silk gown, with her large grave violet eyes shadowed by long thick lashes, her brows dark wings against her white forehead, her slightly parted mouth seeming to promise so much. A pulse beat in her slender throat, and the candlelight gleamed on her white shoulders and arms, dramatic against the black silk gloves. The eyes below feasted on that throat and on the pearly tops of her round, beautifully molded breasts—almost fully exposed against the rich clinging black silk of her seductive gown—that rose and fell with her rapid breathing.

Lenore no longer hesitated, for she knew what she must do. Somewhere down the Thames, poor destroyed Emma quaked—she had gone through all this, and it had broken her. Now was her own moment of trial—and it would not find her wanting. Long ago Geoffrey had called her brave. Tonight she would prove it. She would take her own life before she would let this evil pack have her for a plaything.

Some fierce female instinct deep within her made her determined to flaunt before them the beauty that would never be theirs. To make them hunger and burn for what they would never enjoy. To snatch the cup just as they were about to drain it.

With a provocative, swaying walk she moved on her black satin slippers lightly down the stairs. Below her, rapt and avid, the pack waited.

"Gentlemen, our evening's entertainment approaches," observed Lord Wilsingame. "Is Mistress Lenore not a delicate repast to whet the most jaded palate?"

Midway down the stairs Lenore paused and gave Wilsingame a mocking smile. From the landing above, Bonnifly frowned. Was the wench going to balk at this point and have to be dragged downstairs, after all? Others had tried to flee back upstairs when they saw how many awaited them below!

Resting a hand gracefully on the railing, Lenore wafted her plumed fan with an airy gesture. She posed there so that her elegant shoulders and plunging neckline showed to best advantage. So arrogant was her stance that she might have been a princess about to greet her subjects. Below her rose a collective sigh.

Cold and hard, her voice rang out. "You will have to kill me, Wilsingame. For I will not submit to you while I live!"

"Kill you?" From below Wilsingame laughed unpleasantly. "We but wish you to provide us with an evening's entertainment such as Marnock says was your custom in Oxford."

Her flung challenge had been answered. Lenore dropped the ostrich fan, which swung from a ribbon around her wrist, and the scissors flashed in the candlelight as she raised them high. "Then throw another dead woman into the Thames!"

"No!" shouted a voice from below.

But Bonnifly had crept soft-footed down the stairs behind her. Even as she brought the scissors down he arrested their flashing flight with a wild leap and pinned her to the balustrade with his heavy body. The scissors were torn from her grasp and clattered down the stairs into the hallway below.

"There'll be no gainsaying us, mistress," growled Bonnifly. " 'Tis not," he mocked, pulling her down the stairs with him, "as if ye had a champion!"

"*I* am her champion!" cried a ringing voice, and Lenore twisted about in Bonnifly's grasp. Her eyes were staring in her head at the sound of that voice. Before her paralyzed gaze a dark head reared up topped by a wide plumed hat above a great black periwig, and a tall, lean, russet-clad body swept impetuously past Wilsingame and up the stairs. Swiftly drawn, a naked blade flashed in his sinewy hand, and Lenore stood rigid as the point of that cruelly sharp blade was suddenly pressed against Bonnifly's throat.

"Release her!" roared a voice calculated to strike terror into the bravest. Hastily, before the menace of that dark, saturnine face so near his own, and the blade that already had drawn a drop of blood from his pulsing throat, Bonnifly dropped Lenore's arm and stepped back, almost tripping over his own feet in his haste.

"Geoffrey!" whispered Lenore, and sagged against him even as his long left arm reached out to catch her.

From the hallway below, Lord Wilsingame let out a bleat of dismay. "Wyndham—man, are ye mad? 'Tis but an orange girl from the theatre! We intended her no harm!"

Grimly, back to the wall, Geoffrey came down the stairs supporting Lenore with one arm. "Not only will ye do her no harm this night or any other—we will have your apologies to the lady, as well!"

Lord Wilsingame's face suffused with color. He appeared to be choking. "Ye have my apologies, Mistress Lenore," he said in a stifled voice, and then burst out, "but *why,* Wyndham?"

"This woman is mine," said Geoffrey tersely, sweeping by him.

"By what right?" From the shuffling group, de Quincy's cold voice rang out.

Geoffrey turned on him a face so threatening that Wilsingame and the others fell back a step. "She is mine by right of possession," he said coolly, making steadily for the door.

They had almost reached the door when de Quincy's sword flashed from its scabbard and he leaped forward. "I challenge that right!"

"Gentlemen, gentlemen!" Wilsingame was dismayed. "Let us not quarrel! Wyndham is our honored guest. All can be resolved! You may have the wench first, Wyndham —all can be appeased."

"Nay, *I* will have her first!" cried de Quincy insultingly, making his blade sing in an arc through the air.

"You will not have her at all!" Geoffrey roared, pushing Lenore behind him. Her heart was beating so hard she thought it would fly out from her chest. *Geoffrey!* her soul sang.

"De Quincy, remember Wyndham is a court favorite!" pleaded Wilsingame in a tragic voice.

"De Quincy is the best blade in London." Flemmons's laugh jarred. "He will kill you, Wyndham—court favorite or no!"

"And if he does not," chimed in Bonnifly heavily from the stairs, his gaze passing Geoffrey to rest on Lenore's white bosom, "the rest of us will bring you down."

"There are too many of them, Geoffrey," Lenore whispered. "If you kill de Quincy, they will be on you in a pack."

He turned his head, keeping his wary eyes trained on de Quincy. His voice, barely a whisper, reached only her ears. "Flash your fan mirror in his eyes when I lead him back to the door."

The mirror in her plumed fan! She had forgotten that. Tense, she watched Geoffrey step forward, presenting his naked blade to de Quincy. De Quincy's blade snaked forward to meet it. Blade slid along blade; for a moment

501

their faces were close, they were smiling grimly into each other's eyes—then both sprang back.

But for a moment Lenore had seen surprise in de Quincy's face—he had thought his sudden thrust would bring Geoffrey down, she realized. Now they circled each other, making sudden thrusts and parries, both wary antagonists, for each knew the other's reputation with a sword.

There was rapt attention on the faces of the men, and Lenore shrank back toward the door, surreptitiously testing the mirrored fan, which she held tensely in her black-gloved hand, to see exactly where it threw the light from the crystal chandelier overhead. Ah . . . there it was, a circle of light on that bust of Plato. Now she flashed the light on the eye—there, she had it, a flick of her fingers could control its beam.

The swordsmen were evenly matched, and as they lunged and withdrew, the company fell back to give them room lest they be pinked in passing. Scant attention was paid to Lenore, although from the back of the hall the footman Bales kept an eye on her lest she try to escape. But Lenore knew they would bring her down within moments—and Geoffrey, too, for all the swords would be unsheathed then and they would hack him to pieces. Stiffly she stood there, giving them no cause to think her in flight.

The swordsmen were too evenly matched. Their blades clashed, they sprang back—feints, parries, lunges. Once de Quincy stumbled over a footstool, cursed, and recovered as Geoffrey's blade brushed his hair; once Geoffrey slipped on a corner of the carpet and righted himself in time to let de Quincy's singing blade sweep harmlessly by. Geoffrey, ever attacking, had pressed de Quincy back and back, almost to where the footman stood. Now he seemed to weaken, and de Quincy, pressing his advantage against an apparently tiring opponent, was leaping forward in renewed attack, pressing Geoffrey back and back toward the front door whence he'd come.

"A bit rusty, Wyndham?" taunted de Quincy with sinister emphasis.

"I may be, but my blade is not," panted Geoffrey. He was imperturbable, but to all present he gave plain evidence of tiring.

De Quincy chuckled; he was a cool executioner. "I will have you the next time," he boasted. "I will split you like a chicken just as we reach the wench!"

Geoffrey's back was to Lenore, who was pressed against the wall. Slashing, striking, de Quincy pressed his opponent. Geoffrey parried, but his blade seemed a trifle lower. De Quincy's cold eyes gleamed. Soon he would finish this!

Borne back, Geoffrey had almost reached the door. Oh, God, she must time this exactly right! She could do it but once, for de Quincy would cry out and someone would leap forward and wrest the mirrored fan from her grasp. Geoffrey had fallen back—de Quincy was about to lunge forward for the kill!

With a tiny twist of her wrist she flashed the shining light directly into de Quincy's triumphant eyes.

Instinctively he jerked his head to the right. A slight movement, but it deflected his aim at the moment of making his thrust. A matter of delicate timing, and at the crucial moment the light had blinded him.

Geoffrey took full advantage of it.

Suddenly not tired in the least, he brought up his sword and swept de Quincy's blade from his hand. As it clattered across the floor and de Quincy—who had disemboweled so many men—stood before him rigidly, waiting to be impaled, Geoffrey suddenly grasped his tall opponent and flung him with all his force at the others who had crowded forward to watch the finish—and to kill the victor.

As de Quincy's flung body bore them backward in a tangled heap of satin knees and elbows, boots and spurs, Geoffrey whirled—but Lenore already had the door open and was running through it. Geoffrey went through it like a shadow and slammed it behind him.

Outside a stable boy—the same sallow-faced messenger Wilsingame had sent to Lenore—was holding Geoffrey's horse, for Geoffrey had agreed to come in "for but a moment" at Wilsingame's urging.

Snatching the reins from the amazed stable boy, who

retreated before that naked blade, Geoffrey landed in the saddle in one smooth leap, swept Lenore up before him and tossed a golden coin to the stable boy. "That's for tripping the first man to clear the door!" he called—and they had swept past the gaping boy and were thundering down the narrow track through the maze of tunnels between the houses that bestrode London Bridge.

Clinging to him, Lenore could not believe it. Geoffrey! This moment had been dreamed of, prayed for. . . . For a wild moment she could almost believe she felt the pain of the scissors biting deep into her breast—and that she had died and gone to heaven.

For it was sheer heaven to cling to Geoffrey as she had in the days of their wanderings when they were perpetually on the run, to sway with the strong horse galloping beneath them, to feel the wind in her face and blowing her long silky hair—and pressed tightly against her breasts Geoffrey's broad back, pressed tight against her inner thighs Geoffrey's lean thighs, reminding her, reminding her . . . of long, wild nights with the cry of the loon and a feeling of Eden before the Fall and fierce primeval delights.

Behind them now there was a muffled howl as men spilled cursing out of Wilsingame's house and shouted for the stable boy to bring their horses—but Geoffrey and Lenore now had a long lead. Though they were traveling double, none would catch them now before they reached Southwark and the safety of an inn.

Lenore floated back to earth as Geoffrey galloped into the courtyard of the Tabard Inn in Borough High Street and dismounted. He swung her down from the big black horse, holding her a little longer than was necessary while she thrilled against his hard body.

A bright-eyed stable boy with a shock of tow hair hurried up, and Geoffrey tossed the boy a coin. "Mount up and ride my horse through the streets until you lose the rabble who follow me here—be about it, man!"

The stable boy blinked down at the gold coin in his hand. He did not hesitate. In a bound he had leaped astride Geoffrey's horse and a moment later had cleared the courtyard, clattering fast away. Geoffrey drew Lenore back under the shadow of a pillar as Lord Wilsingame and his disappointed guests straggled by, their hooves thundering on the cobbles, their voices raised in an assortment of complaints and curses.

"The boy knows how to ride—they'll not catch him," said Geoffrey with satisfaction. "Nor will they know where we went. By tomorrow, when they've had time to think about it, they'll become frightened—we'll have no more trouble with them." He turned a stern visage to Lenore in the deserted courtyard. The moonlight gleamed down on his great periwig and plumed hat, caressed his broad shoulders, and shadowed his eyes. "Where is Michael," he growled, "that he would allow this to happen?"

"Michael?" Lenore was staggered. "Michael is dead, Geoffrey!"

"You are a widow, then?"

"A *widow?* Michael was killed by robbers before we reached Banbury—I fled, for 'twas claimed I murdered him!"

Geoffrey's head lifted abruptly, and in the moonlight she saw that his dark face had gone blank with astonishment. "But I searched for you on the road to Banbury, at Coventry—everywhere. When I could not find you, I believed you fled with Michael to America."

She just stared at him. He had *searched* for her?

And then the ice jam about her cold heart melted and she felt warm again, free again, in love again. *Geoffrey had not deserted her—he had searched for her!* Her happy heart sang the words like a refrain, it was she who had deserted him—not the other way around! Gilbert had lied, Gilbert had lied!

"And all this time"— her soft voice caught—"you did not forget me?"

"Lenore," he said huskily, "your face has haunted me. Though I thought you had fled me, you were always there destroying my delight in other women."

Ah, so he had not gone back to Letiche . . . Her heart leaped. "So it has been for me, Geoffrey," she whispered. *"Always."*

He took her face in his hands and looked deep into her eyes. "Lenore, I was wrong in Oxford, wrong about the child—I came back to tell you so, but found you gone. Gone with Michael, they said. Come inside, Lenore—Wilsingame's crowd may ride back this way." He opened the inn door and as she went through it, a bell above the door tinkled. They found themselves in a spacious, empty room filled with rugged tables and chairs and benches, and facing a large stone hearth where banked coals glowed. Geoffrey turned to her again. "When my search proved vain, I came back to Oxford to wring the truth from whoever knew it—and was jailed by the Ironsides. But forget you—never!"

She gave him a soft look and touched gentle fingers to his lips. Time enough for explanations tomorrow; but for now . . . she had him back! Back after the years of pain and loneliness. Back in her arms; for he was always in her heart. "Hush, Geoffrey—the innkeeper is approaching."

"Your pleasure, sir?" Rubbing sleepy eyes, the fat innkeeper bustled forward.

Geoffrey looked fondly down at Lenore. "A room for the night."

"Aye, sir. What name?"

Lenore spoke up. "Daunt. We are the Daunts of Williamsburg—in the American Colonies."

Something flamed up in Geoffrey's eyes, and she lifted her head proudly and looked back at him, a splendrous woman in the candlelight with her white shoulders gleaming, her half-bared bosom seductive against the low-cut black silk. Her violet eyes were lustrous and slanted at him provocatively through dark lashes, their flickering light promising reckless delights. She smiled up at him, that swift, blinding smile that was like summer sunshine breaking through the clouds, and in that smile was a sweet promise of what was to come. Of what had always been there . . . just for him.

From the street came two rollicking male voices singing a raucous drinking song off-key, and from the stableyard came the giggles of a kitchen maid meeting one of the grooms in a dark corner—giggles and a sharp slap and

506

an aggrieved feminine voice crying, "You promised you wouldn't!"

Lenore smiled to herself. This was wild, unbridled London—the London of Frost Fairs and theatre brawls and maypoles and wild court parties. But it was also a great and busy port, and tomorrow they could begin their plans to make an old dream come true, they would embark on a tall white ship and sail to the American Colonies. They would become indeed the Daunts of Williamsburg, and Lorena, her lovely daughter, would be with them!

In the Colonies, with all their mistakes behind them, they could start a new life, better than the old. They could forget the past and become at last the people they were born to be . . . ah, she would make Geoffrey such a good wife!

But for tonight—and this was a part of the promise her reckless violet eyes foretold—tonight as Geoffrey's lean body sank into his warm bath, she would—very slowly—remove her black silk gloves, one by one, easing them down her lovely arms. With a tantalizing smile she would unfasten the hooks of her black silk bodice, plunging its daring neckline even lower, until—with a twist that would make her breasts bounce—she would drop the heavy silk dress to the floor and step out of it.

And while he watched she would ease out of her elegant black chemise, letting the lace rasp delicately down her smooth white skin until the black silk whispered to the floor at her feet and she stood before him clad only in her red-heeled black satin shoes and sheer black hose.

As he leaped from the tub and eagerly toweled dry—with his glowing eyes never leaving her!—she would kick off her high-heeled shoes, plant a foot upon the footboard of the great fourposter and with great concentration remove her silver-tinseled garters, slide the sheer black silk stockings down her elegant legs and toss them like smoke rings toward the cold hearth.

That hearth would be the only cold thing in their room tonight!

Tomorrow was time enough to talk of sailing, of a new

life—but tonight was for twining naked arms and limbs, for soft murmurings and ardent caresses, for seeking the wild, free heights of love's stormy passions. Tomorrow they could plan to sail to the American Colonies, but tonight—tonight was for lovers!

There is more to the unforgettable love story of Geoffrey and Lenore. And young Lorena grows into a beauty surpassed, perhaps, only by her glorious mother.

Watch for HER SHINING SPLENDOR, the dazzling sequel to THIS TOWERING PASSION. Coming soon from Warner Books.

If you like romance, you'll love Valerie Sherwood!

Millions of readers have thrilled to the magic
of Valerie Sherwood's bestselling historical romances.
Brimming with adventure and passion,
each Sherwood novel is a page-turner you won't
be able to put down until you've read
the last delicious page!

THIS LOVING TORMENT (82-649, $2.25)
Born in poverty in the aftermath of the
Great London Fire, Charity Woodstock
grew up to set the men of three continents ablaze
with passion!

THESE GOLDEN PLEASURES (82-416, $2.25)
From the stately mansions of the east
to the freezing hell of the Klondike, beautiful
Roxanne Rossiter went after what she wanted—
and got it all!

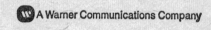

THE BEST OF THE BESTSELLERS
FROM WARNER BOOKS!